Carol Smith, formerly a leading London literary agent, now concentrates full-time on her writing career. She is the author of the highly successful *Darkening Echoes*, *Kensington Court*, *Family Reunion*, *Unfinished Business*, *Grandmother's Footsteps* and *Hidden Agenda*, all published by Time Warner Books. For more information about Carol Smith's books visit her website at *www.carolsmith.com*.

Praise for Carol Smith

Hidden Agenda
'Both a thriller – I was hooked by the very first page – and a gripping story about the power of female friendships – a winning combination!' Marika Cobbold

'A gripping and beautifully constructed story' Lizy Buchan

'Carol Smith has done it again, an unput-down-able thriller with a twist . . . Smith holds the reader in her grasp from start to finish, and gives us compelling psychological insights on the way' Julia Neuberger

Grandmother's Footsteps
'*Grandmother's Footsteps* . . . will keep you entertained, reading and guessing all the way to the end' *Crime Time*

'With its teasing insights into the mind of a serial killer, *Grandmother's Footsteps* keeps you guessing until the end' *Sainsbury's Magazine*

Unfinished Business
'If a pacy thriller is your thing, *Unfinished Business* will suit you to perfection . . . an addictive read' *Sunday Express*

'A thriller which certainly keeps you turning those pages . . . gripping right to the end' *Daily Mail*

Family Reunion
'A gripping read' *Family Circle*

'Full of action, twists and surprises, this intricate suspense story offers a fascinating new take on the nature of family ties' *Good Housekeeping*

Also by Carol Smith

CAROL SMITH

Vanishing Point

Gift from Mark
14/9
2005

TIME WARNER
BOOKS

TIME WARNER BOOKS

First published in Great Britain in August 2005 by Time Warner Books
This paperback edition published in September 2005
by Time Warner Books

A CIP catalogue record for this book
is available from the British Library.

ISBN 0 7515 3746 2

Typeset in Berkeley by Palimpsest Book Production Limited,
Polmont, Stirlingshire
Printed and bound in Great Britain by
Clays Ltd, St Ives plc

Time Warner Books
An imprint of
Time Warner Book Group UK
Brettenham House
Lancaster Place
London WC2E 7EN

www.twbg.co.uk

Acknowledgements

My thanks, as always, to my publishers, Time Warner, for doing their usual immaculate job. Especially to Joanne Dickinson, my editor, Sarah Rustin and the rest of the team including, of course, the Sales and Marketing people. Also to my agent, Jonathan Lloyd at Curtis Brown.

Prologue

A leaden sky and relentless rain; Belgium in February could not have looked more bleak. Frankie, slumped in her chilly carriage, stared out across the railway tracks and resolved in her heart that, if she moved on, it would be to a warmer climate. Her chilblains throbbed and her muscles ached; her throat felt decidedly scratchy. Normally she would have used the truck but, at least till they fixed the fanbelt, she was going to have to do without it on these monthly expeditions.

The train was halted outside the station, awaiting a signal change. If it didn't move soon, she might well perish with cold. With a grinding lurch it shuddered into life as another one, with mud-splashed sides, moved sluggishly past on the opposite track, the cause of the delay. Frankie mechanically zipped up her jacket and wound her scarf tightly round her throat as she watched the empty carriages racketing by. The sooner they got into Antwerp, the better. By now her teeth were rattling in her head so she thought she might treat herself to a cup of tea. She could do with a little time to herself, away from the others, for quiet reflection. She had recently heard that her mother had died and, although they had been estranged for years, unwelcome memories had come flooding back that she'd tried all these years to suppress.

Which was when she saw it, the face in the window, moving slowly past, just feet away; an image etched into her brain for the past thirty years. The unmistakable face of her lover: the vivid blue eyes and black curly hair that haunted her nightmares as well as her waking thoughts. The face of a man she had loved and lost, which had irrevocably blighted her life.

The face of a man she knew to be dead for she had killed him herself.

Part One

1

It was one month earlier. The start of the year; early
January and biting cold. Cabbages, turnips, carrots,
beets: traditional Flemish fare, with celeriac thrown
in as a special treat. Frankie was in charge of the
vegetable garden. She planted them, hoed them and
yanked weeds out between them, then bodily
wrenched them from the soil and sluiced them down
at the standpipe in the courtyard. At this time of year
it was not pleasant work; her hands were raw and
chapped, with swollen knuckles. Her chilblains ached
so she couldn't sleep and now she was fairly sure she
was getting arthritis. The only thing going for this
arduous lifestyle was that, all things considered, it beat
prison.

It was Magda who had coaxed her into making this
decision, Magda to whom she also owed her life. When
her sentence was up and they let her go, Frankie,
facing a total abyss, had seriously considered ending
it all. She was tired of having to keep battling on, had
died when he did, at least in spirit. But the older
woman, doing her job, had kept her under close

5

supervision and, by not letting her out of her sight, had stopped her harming herself. Later, when they talked about it and Frankie revealed the depths of her despair, it was Magda who'd urged her to take herself in hand and not waste the precious gift of life on something that should, by now, be over and done with.

'You learnt your lesson and you paid the price. Now is the time for a fresh start.'

Frankie couldn't really argue; what Magda said was true. She was twenty-four and had nobody else, except the mother who had betrayed her and this brusque, compassionate Polish woman on whom she had learnt to depend. So when Magda had first mooted her plan – worn out by the prison service herself, she felt in need of a total change – Frankie had gone along with it. Together they'd moved to Lier, outside Antwerp, where they now shared a cramped but picturesque cottage. Not just a cottage but part of the Beguinage, an exclusive commune that was mainly a spiritual retreat.

When Frankie thought back to her privileged child-hood, it still amazed her that life could have altered so much. The prosperous Wirral, where she had been raised, had in no way prepared her for hardship like this. Her family home had a tennis court; she had even owned her own pony. Her life had been rosy and much indulged, until she had done the Terrible Thing after which she'd become a social leper, entirely ostracised. Why, Chad had asked her, that first time they met, had she risked so much to make a rebellious statement? She had been through it all, many times before, and never come up with a plausible answer, but his eyes were amused (she'd say even admiring) and the smile he flashed had entirely melted her heart. Because . . . she had started to say, then faltered. It was to be several weeks till she told him the truth.

The walk from the station had soaked her right through but she was now well inured to constant discomfort. Her boots were leaking, her woollen mitts sodden; all she wanted to do was rip off her clothes and soak herself in a steaming tub. With piping-hot chocolate, whipped cream on the side, and someone to towel her dry. No chance of that; her smile was fixed as she raised the latch of the barn and pushed open the door.

Of the seventeen inmates, eleven were fixtures and most of them present this wintry afternoon. The barn, still with its original beams, was vast and draughty and smelt of lingering smoke. There were hurricane lanterns placed here and there, to cope with the rapidly vanishing light, and a cluster of beeswax candles in the hearth, not yet lit.

'You're back!' said Magda, looking up with a smile. 'Can it be that time already?' Her bobbins clacked as her skilful fingers worked at the intricate lace. Sister Mary broke off her reading while Sister Agnes was working in clay. An audiotape of pan pipes enhanced the feeling of harmony. A group of women working with their hands, united in a close sisterhood. Suddenly Frankie felt safe.

They asked, as they always did, about the market, and this time she could report complete success. She felt like a child before her elders as she proudly related what she had achieved. 'The onions were a particular hit. I could have sold many times more if I'd had them with me.'

'So learn,' said Magda, regrouping her pins. 'And next time you'll know to take more. Perhaps when the truck is back on the road. Would anyone care for tea?'

Later, once they had laid aside their work, they all moved closer to the hearth while Berthe scrabbled around in search of matches. They took it in turns to prepare the evening meal and two of their number were already in the kitchen, chopping carrots and jointing rabbits for the stew. Berthe found the matches and lit a taper.

'Excuse me,' said Frankie, suddenly chilled. 'I must go and change my clothes or I'll catch pneumonia.'

Despite all the therapy she had been through, the sound of a striking match still made her feel faint.

2

Cristina Calvão was in a lousy mood but that was nothing unusual. Yvette, her surly recalcitrant maid, had been late coming up with her café-au-lait and it had not been as hot as she liked, while the croissants were rubbery and stale. In addition, Cristina had chipped a nail and her favourite manicurist was fully booked, or so the lying receptionist would have her believe. It was all too tiresome; she slammed down the cup, spraying coffee all over the starched linen sheets. It was nearly noon. She would soon have to dress and go to meet Claude at Le Crillon for lunch to try to talk him round about the wedding. Cristina had lived in Paris twelve years, since she'd tired of the glitz of Brazilian nightlife and hooked up with an older man wealthy enough to support her. One of the things she liked best about Claude was that he was Catholic and indissolubly married. She had never intended to tie herself down and place all her eggs in the same restrictive basket – until she encountered Rocco Pereira and flipped. Which had been, she was obliged to admit, the story of her life.

He was a racing driver of international fame, sexy, Latin and twelve years younger than herself, which made an exciting change from Claude's ageing flesh. They had met in Rio at Carnaval and soon were hitting the tabloid headlines as well as all the hot celebrity nightspots. In Brazil, that was; word had not yet reached Paris which was why it was so essential she now look her best. She slithered out of her satin pyjamas, dropping them carelessly on the floor, and scrutinised her naked body, which only served to sour her mood even more. In recent years, since she quit the catwalk, her panther-like beauty had sagged and blurred. She no longer enjoyed making love with the lights on, another reason she clung to Claude who was, despite his numerous faults, a gentleman to the core.

How he would feel about this latest liaison, Cristina could not predict. Furthermore, she could not care less, had fallen in with his wishes all these years and now felt she'd earned the right to take a stand. It suited his lifestyle to keep her on the side, devoting his Mondays to Thursdays to her, then motoring home to his château at weekends to play the uxorious husband. He knew she occasionally saw other men; he was not unrealistic. But to hear that she contemplated marrying again might very well be the final straw and would require an element of finesse. Fortunately Cristina was expert at this, had spent her adult years negotiating. What Rocco would think was another matter. She would cross that bridge when she had to. She had not survived all these years on her beauty alone.

With a final scowl at her thickening waist, she flung open the doors of her spacious closets and tossed great armfuls of clothes all over the bed. For today's performance she must look just right, neither provocative nor too showy but understated and winningly demure.

'Yvette!' she screeched down the stairway to the maid. 'Come up here at once and get me dressed.'

Her outfit of choice had to be discarded; the seam beneath one arm was ripped and had gone unnoticed till now. Of course she laid all the blame on Yvette, though she herself had thrown it aside the instant she heard the stitches snap and knew she had put on weight.

'I can fix it, madame,' said Yvette but there hadn't been time. Claude would already be at the table and he hated her to be late. So she settled instead for an understated two-piece, cut on the bias for a slinkier movement, which stopped right on the knee to display her legs. She twirled and frowned, then removed her briefs; visible panty line would destroy the effect. Jewellery was the next requisite, tasteful and not overdone. She yanked out drawers and riffled through boxes, strewing their contents all over the dresser for Yvette to tidy away when she had gone. Diamonds, Claude said, were vulgar at lunchtime and pearls not Cristina's thing. With her bronzed and sultry exotic looks, she needed some sparkle to set herself off. She compromised with a Tiffany choker and the lucky earrings she'd had from Cal to celebrate their first six months together.

11

As she hooked the wires through her delicate lobes and watched the effect against her tawny streaked hair, she thought back to that time long ago and tears sprang into her eyes.

'Madame, is there something wrong?' asked Yvette, as she skilfully teased Cristina's mane, brushing and lacquering it into a tousled birds' nest. The raucous diktats had suddenly ceased; what the maid observed in the glass was wistful and sad.

'No,' snapped Cristina, herself again, shaking her head to improve the effect and applying another shimmering coat of lipstick. 'Dépêche-toi and get me a cab toot-sweet.' Mustn't risk keeping him waiting.

They laughed at her, the household staff, sick of her posturing and fancy airs; they considered her third world trash. The way she ordered them all around as though they were of a lesser class and had no feelings nor standards of their own. They only stayed on because of Claude, who always treated them courteously and wasn't averse to putting his hand in his pocket. Not so Cristina, with her chronic meanness, who siphoned money off the elderly fool but hated to part with any of it herself. Yvette gazed sourly at the wreckage of the bedroom – the coffee-stained sheets that would have to be changed, the couture clothing abandoned on the floor, and she hadn't even yet dared to check the bathroom. She vowed, as she regularly did, to leave forthwith. This pig of a woman was not worthy of her care; she would sooner sweep the floors or empty the bins.

Yvette, however, had burdens of her own: an ailing mother, a sickly child, a husband with a taste for too much Pernod. She lacked the security to throw in the job and it did have occasional bonuses. Clothing Cristina had grown tired of or too big for, soiled or torn but redeemable by a patient seamstress who valued the cut and the cloth. A bottle of perfume she no longer liked or a handbag now last year's fashion; even, once, a pair of uncomfortable shoes. Though usually shrewish, Cristina had moments when something unexpectedly cheered her and the sulks and petulance fleetingly changed to laughter. Only then did she show her true beauty, the mixed blood siren who had lived all her life on her wits.

And now she declared herself in love. Yvette decided to stick around, at least until she saw how the future panned out. The Brazilian lover, Madame's latest craze, should provide, at least, a little diversion. He was all Cristina could talk of these days. Yvette was curious to know how Monsieur would react.

Cristina slumped limply into the cab, fighting to hold back her tears. Lunch with Claude had not been a success; things were not going well for her today. To start with, he had been furious she was late, equated unpunctuality with bad manners. He had a meeting at three with his bank so could only manage two courses. His admiration was losing its lustre; there had been a time when, in his eyes, Cristina could do nothing wrong. Then they never met for lunch without his producing some elegant love-gift: a piece of

13

exquisite jewellery, a sumptuous chinchilla scarf. He would fuss and fawn all over her, insist on arranging the bauble round her neck, which gave him a chance to caress her caramel skin. Those days, however, had slipped away. Now, whenever he looked at her, his eyes lacked approbation. He was growing bored; she recognised the signs. Soon, if she wasn't careful, he might even dump her.

Since Claude was testy and short of time, she hadn't dared bring up the subject of Rocco. She would simply have to wait and play it by ear. As the house was nominally hers, not his, and he wasn't there for three days every week, it was up to her how she spent her time and whom she entertained. The night that Rocco had mentioned marriage she had been too giddy for rational thought. All she'd seen were the stars and the phosphorescent waves, with a jaunty background of salsa music and Rocco toasting her with champagne while also surreptitiously fingering her crotch.

Put like that, it did seem crude. Cristina's misery deepened. The truth was she hadn't felt this strongly for a man since Cal Barnard, who had broken her heart by dropping out of her life and disappearing.

The gardener, Serge, was trimming the topiary when Cristina's cab pulled up outside. He watched her from the top of his ladder as she tossed a handful of euros to the driver, then stalked straight past him without so much as a nod. Not a good lunch; he could see that from her snarl and privately smiled to know that she didn't always win. M. Daumier was a good employer; Serge had worked for him for fifteen years which was longer than that trollop had been installed here. And he intended to outlast her too, had seen the discontent in the master's eyes. That luscious body might be seductive but she lacked the grace of a true Parisian, besides being rude and coarse. It was hard to see now what had attracted Monsieur, apart from the obvious factor of raunchy sex.

Cristina slammed the heavy front door and Serge smiled with satisfaction. From his vantage point he could see into her bedroom, enjoyed the way that she flounced inside then threw her Hermès purse across the room. She bounced around on each four-inch heel as she tried to unbuckle her sandals, then ripped off her little couturier outfit, angrily scrunched it into a ball and hurled it against the wall. Serge laid down his shears and lit a cigarette while he studied her voluptuous naked body, for she rarely wore anything underneath her clothes. Soon, he sensed, he would get what he was after; she was clearly very much out of sorts and that, as any true Frenchman knew, was because she was not getting laid.

Though they said in the kitchen there was someone new, someone she seriously hoped to marry. Serge stubbed out his cigarette and resumed his desultory clipping. She had pulled the shutters to, presumably for her afternoon nap, so the show was over for another day and he could get back to his work.

No, there weren't any messages, said Yvette when she came up later to run Cristina's bath and lay out her clothes for the opera. Wagner tonight; she hated the music which made her positively gag with boredom but the opera house was an absolute must for any upwardly mobile socialite whose principal purpose in life was to be seen. Claude, still grumpy and unrelenting, had set off early for his country estate, leaving Cristina with an extra ticket for the second row of the stalls. She had rung round her coterie of hangers-on, mainly men of the gay persuasion, who were usually all too keen to help squander Claude's money. She rarely had difficulty finding a date; she was still well known and scrubbed up well, but tonight, for whatever reason, she had no takers. So she ended up doing that most mortifying thing, falling back on the company of a female friend, the Countess de Bourgrave, a good-time girl currently in the throes of her fifth divorce.

Which certainly didn't improve Cristina's mood, especially since she had no idea where in the world Rocco could possibly be. Throughout the evening she tried his number but his mobile appeared to be permanently off. She could only hope it meant he was on his way.

3

Cabbage soup was all very well but, after all these dreary months, definitely starting to pall. The Belgians cooked it with caraway and dumplings which, combined with the coarse black bread, made Frankie feel like a peasant herself, bloggy and overstuffed. Not that there was much wrong in that; she certainly wouldn't dare say so in the commune. She stood at the window, watching the weather, an incessant downpour that streaked the panes. Soup tonight, oxtail stew tomorrow; their diet was basic as well as relentlessly dull. She made a note to lay down more potatoes. After the harsh winter they'd had, supplies were perilously low. At least, with all the hard work she did, there was little chance of her gaining weight. She still had the lean, rangy figure of her youth with narrow hips, a flat stomach and enviable legs. Not that anyone noticed or even cared. Sometimes she felt as much a prisoner here as she had in jail.

Magda, quietly stitching by the stove, was used to these flashes of malaise. She could tell from the tension in Frankie's shoulders that her jaw would be set and her eyes hazed over with grief. There was nothing, Magda had learnt, she could do except wait for the storm clouds to pass. Frankie's outlook still remained bleak, her heart and mind consumed by a hollow ache.

'Well, you're the boss,' tried Magda brightly. 'So why not go wild and come up with something new? If you plant it we'll have to eat it, so go ahead and surprise us. Artichokes, perhaps, or aubergines. Allow yourself some artistic licence. That, after all, is why we're here. To work but also to create.'

'As long as you don't ask for Brussels sprouts.' Slowly Frankie turned her head, her expression softening into a foxy grin. When she smiled, which she did all too seldom, she was still a striking woman, good for her age. 'It's okay, you don't have to humour me. I just wish this beastly rain would slack off a bit.'

Communal living was all very well, and the other women were nice enough, but there were times when Frankie felt she needed privacy to stop her losing her mind. Magda, all too aware of this, humoured her by discreetly withdrawing whenever she thought she should. Most meals and meetings were held in the barn; they only came back here to sleep or relax on the rare occasions they were not actually working. Since Frankie spent most of her time outdoors, she'd developed an all-year-round weathered look which tempered the sallowness of her skin and gave her a glow that became her. She kept her straight dark hair cut short and never ever used makeup, yet when fleeting laughter lit her face, a hint of her vanished beauty could still be seen.

Magda, older, was solid and square-built, an inheritance from her ancestry, and her once fair hair had turned to iron grey. They rubbed along companionably enough, careful of each other's space and needs. After twenty-three years of sharing together, there was little about each other they didn't know. And before that had been the prison years. It was still a source of pride to Magda that she'd managed to gain the tortured young woman's trust.

'Do you know what I'd really like?' said Frankie, still with a hint of a smile. 'Pheasant, casseroled in red wine with bacon, mushrooms and shallots.' She smacked her lips. 'With just a soupçon of brandy in the sauce.'

'Wow!' said Magda, pausing mid-stitch. 'When in the world did you ever eat like that?' Frankie had been locked up since her middle teens.

'In my childhood,' said Frankie airily. 'There is still a lot you don't know about my life.'

The colonel, Frankie's stepfather, had been an excellent shot. And there had been a time, when the marriage was new, when he treated her as he might have done the son he had never had. Which included taking her out to follow the guns.

'Be careful,' her mother had warned, alarmed, aware of her daughter's capriciousness; but Humphrey had waved her protest aside in his customary autocratic manner. Women and animals: he lumped them together, though then, in the aftermath of new lust, he treated the little filly with more care. She was a sprightly child, good-looking too. It fed his vanity having her around. That was where the pony came in; anything Frankie wanted she could have. Skinny and agile, a natural athlete, she had entered woman-hood unenlightened. For the first two years they were the best of pals, the gawky child and the overbearing man. But as she grew, she got prettier too and soon had more on her hands than she'd bargained for.

'Dirty old bastard,' she would later say. 'Whatever he got, believe me, he richly deserved.'

None of this had she shared with Magda; her lips concerning the original crime remained sealed. At the hearing she had been stoically defiant, which was how she had come, at just fifteen, to find herself locked up. There was no support from the colonel now; as far as he was concerned she could rot in hell. A damaged child, Magda's colleagues had assessed. Even after what happened next, they never found out quite how much.

Most evenings, after they'd had their meal, everyone reconvened in the barn and gathered around the hearth. Some of them sewed by candlelight; the rest preferred to relax. They all worked hard at their various chores and this was the time they liked the best, when the spirit of the community came to the fore. Frankie, who had worked eight hours straight, stretched out on a beanbag and nodded off. Occasionally somebody told a story in the fine trad-ition of oral folklore or else they broke into groups to catch up on the chat. Tonight they felt in a party mood, so Sister Breeda brought out her fiddle and soon had them dancing Irish jigs and clapping along to the tune. Even Frankie opened her eyes and propped herself up to watch. She had laboured so long in the biting cold that her fingers were swollen and starting to throb but the hearty soup had done its job; she felt calm and soporific.

Inspired by the dancing, they wanted to sing, so Sylvia, with the seraphic voice, took her place next to Sister Breeda to lead them all in a folk song. Frankie watched the firelight flickering, which brought back memories she'd sooner forget. She liked it here: it was womblike and safe, away from the terrors of everyday life. The lack of male company didn't bother her at all; within the closeness of the sisterhood, she had finally found a kind of peace.

But then Sylvia swung into 'Blow the Wind Southerly' and, all of a sudden, it became too much. The melancholy sadness of the beautiful song struck a chord in Frankie's heart and she stumbled to her feet and out of the barn. She ran the few yards through the driving rain then up the stairs of the cottage she shared and threw herself down on her narrow bed in anguish. Whenever she thought she was coming to terms with the past, the whole thing persisted in flooding back. After all this time, she could still not erase the memories of that terrible day when her life had effectively ended.

4

The woman alone in the Danieli bar was stylishly dressed but looked lonely and sad. She was fiddling with the stem of her glass; the waiter crossed and politely inquired if she'd like another bellini. She looked up, startled and ill at ease, checked the time – it was 7.15 – then shyly told him she would. English; he had guessed that from the quality of her clothes but the fluency of her Italian surprised him.

'You are staying here, signora?' he asked, picking up her glass.

'I am,' she said. 'I arrived today.' Then, giving him a tentative smile, she ducked quickly back into her book.

Fine eyes, he thought as he walked away. A woman like that should not have to drink alone.

Cassandra Buchanan, here on impulse, could still not quite believe what she had done. The first time she'd been here was on her first honeymoon, an unbelievable thirty-eight years ago. She wondered now where the time had gone and wished she could relive those happier days. As a bride of eighteen she had loved the Danieli, awed by the dignified splendour of its rooms. She smiled to remember how gauche she had been, but Edwin could not have been a better guide for a wide-eyed teenager, just out of school, who had never before left Cornwall. They had walked every inch of the magical city and he'd introduced her to its finer sights, telling her just enough not to lose her interest. It was he who had sown the seeds in her of a lifelong passion for things Venetian. She had studied its art and absorbed its culture; strange, therefore, that she hadn't been back for so long.

The fleeting smile faded, replaced by a frown. She was here to escape the shocking events that had blown apart the calm of her family life. When Charles had lobbed his grenade at her, she had not remotely seen it coming. She had truly believed that her second marriage was even more successful than the first. Her feelings for Edwin had been dutiful and fond and had not prepared her for the turbulent ride of twenty-two years with the highly unorthodox Charles. True, some of the passion had lately faded, for no one could maintain such a high-octane love. But to have it suddenly fall to ashes was still almost more than she could believe. For the advent of Charles in her life had been a genuine *coup de foudre*.

She was up from the country, a recent widow, overwhelmed by the bustle of the London streets to which she was so unaccustomed. Cornwall had always been her home; she had never felt any particular urge to stray. She had been content, as a dutiful wife, to remain at home and raise her girls with her husband always at her side, running his sprawling estate. Darby and Joan, he had fondly described them, reflecting the humdrum nature of their lives. All Cassie did was run the house, walk the dogs and weed the garden and, twice a week, take coffee with her mother. Old before her time, she had realised, when the heart attack had suddenly carried him off. She had studied her face and regretted the crows' feet, stroked the skin of her crêping neck and wondered if she would ever know happiness again. Thirty-three and already bereft, with two adolescent daughters just reaching the difficult stage. Cassie had been desolate, resigned to the fact that her life was over before it had properly begun.

How wrong she had been; again, that smile as her mind went back to the giddy events that morning at the Basil Street Hotel. If it happened once, why not again? She did not believe in conceding defeat. She drained her glass and caught the waiter's eye, which had never really left her. Three bellinis might be one too many but she was no longer a country mouse nor answerable to anyone any more.

What with their uneventful life and Edwin's slowly declining health, Cassie had rather neglected her household chores. With two lively children, two cats and three dogs, and Edwin clumping around in his boots, she had started just to sluice down floors and turn a blind eye to the animals' ruining the furniture. It had never been smart but was certainly comfortable; most nights, year round, they lit a big fire, a focal point around which the family clustered. Instead of watching television, they talked and read books or did a huge jigsaw together. Country living might be remote, but it provided a solid base from which they taught the children the true fundamentals of life.

The day that followed Edwin's funeral was bleak and Cassie, for the first time ever, found herself with very little to do. The mourners had left, the girls were back at school; everyone had agreed that was for the best. Cassie, alone in the great rambling house with only cats and dogs to talk to, found that time weighed heavily on her hands. The estate, overseen by a competent manager, more or less ran itself these days and, now that she had no meals to prepare, she didn't know what to do. So she looked around, took stock of the place and saw how rundown it had become. For fifteen years it had been her home, since she first moved in as an ingénue bride, and now she was a widow.

The curtains needed cleaning, if not replacing, and the rugs and armchairs were strewn with hairs and mysterious stains that did not bear too close inspection. Fuelled by manic energy, brought on by grief, she made lists of everything that needed to be done; then she and the cleaner did what they could, which wasn't nearly enough. So Cassie did something she had never done before: went up to London on her own.

The Hawksmoor family, for generations, had always stayed at the Basil Street Hotel, which was close to Harrods where Edwin had an account. The fabrics department was warm and soporific and did wonders for Cassie's shattered nerves. She reminded herself that she wasn't short of cash and the poor old house was long overdue for a facelift. With the help of a sympathetic sales assistant, she chose heavy brocade for the downstairs rooms and flowery prints for both the girls' bedrooms to replace the nursery fabrics. Then she threw in a whole pile of cushions as well until she was laden down.

'Would Madam like it delivered?' asked the salesman, checking delivery days for Tintagel.

'No, no,' said Cassie, suddenly inspired and eager to get down to work. 'I am staying nearby, just round the corner, and should be able to carry it there myself.'

A dark-haired young man in a well-cut suit had been listening quietly and looking on. He now stepped forward and offered her his help. Taking him for another sales assistant, Cassie admitted she might, after all, need a hand. 'Just as far as the door,' she said. 'After that, I am sure I can manage.'

'I can do better than that,' he said, grabbing her parcels and leading the way. 'I am, as it happens, just cooling my heels till it's time for lunch at my club.'

Overriding Cassie's protests, he insisted on walking her to the hotel and explained on the way that he had just returned from abroad. He was, he told her when she asked, in pictures.

'Pictures?' said Cassie, for a moment confused. He certainly had the looks and charm.

'Works of art,' said Charles Buchanan. 'I dabble a bit on the side.'

*　　*　　*

26

After the third bellini, she strolled past the Doge's Palace and on into St Mark's Square. The night was balmy; the square was packed so she settled down with a glass of wine to listen to the music outside Florian's. Later she'd look for a quiet trattoria. She was not yet ready to face the fancy hotel dining room. Venice, for all its crowds, was benign. Even without a male protector, she felt quite safe in the streets. She needed to spend some time on her own, which was partly why she had come here. So much had happened in the past few months, she had to be able to think things through without interference or comment from her children.

From this point on, she was on her own; they no longer really needed her and the last thing they would want was a clinging mother. Rose and Daisy had lives of their own and Aidan would soon be gone too. It was time to start thinking for herself, to do, for a change, what she wanted to instead of always putting the family first.

She found a restaurant on the corner of a square that was just what she'd had in mind, neither too lively nor too smart, with muted lights and tables outside, round the corner from the Accademia Bridge. Over a plate of excellent pasta, Cassie found herself starting to relax. It was spring, it was Venice; she had plenty of money and no one waiting up for her at home. The night was young, she would enjoy herself. Then figure out what to do with the rest of her life.

5

Meeting Chad was like a ray of sunshine penetrating the murk of Frankie's existence. For months she had been in such a state of disgrace that no one, not even her docile mother, had anything to say to her. First the police, then the social workers, had turned it into a major event, yet no one appeared to have even considered what might make a normally biddable child act the way she had. These days, it could no longer happen. The system had gradually grown in compassion and insight.

For months she had lingered in a halfway house while they debated what to do with her and, when she eventually ended up in Middlesbrough, the very first of the inmates she met was Chad. It was in the refectory the day she arrived, to which she was brusquely led by a member of staff.

'Help yourself,' the warder said, handing her a tray. 'You may sit wherever you like.'

With her meagre supper – there was very little left – and a glass of milk to wash it down, Frankie chose a corner table where she could mope in peace. At the far end of the almost empty room – her arrival had been delayed by traffic – a group of boisterous lads were crowded around their obvious leader. Frankie clammed up in her usual way. Though tall for her age and not easily scared, she was not yet prepared for a head-on confrontation. She was quite confused enough as it was, not to mention mentally bruised.

It took him all of fifteen minutes and then she shrank from the sound of approaching feet.

'Hi,' he said, looming over her. 'I'm Chad. Who are you? Come and join us.'

Mumbling something he couldn't quite catch, Frankie shook her head. Then, when he didn't go away, she raised it defiantly to meet his gaze full on. He was not the thug she had taken him for, though she wouldn't have wanted to meet the others late at night. He was even taller than she was herself, with cropped black curls, an inviting smile and eyes of a startling blue.

'Come along,' he said, reaching for her hand. 'You'll have to learn to put up with us. Nowhere else you can go to. We don't bite.' Then he swooped and carried her tray away so that Frankie, unwilling to be seen to lose face, had no alternative but to follow him. This wasn't the moment to make a stand; she had never felt more alone. They listened wordlessly to his introductions, then slid apart to allow her space to sit. That, she was later to realise, was a piece of incredible luck. For Chad, indisputably, was leader of the pack and where he went, the others compliantly followed. By offering Frankie his hand in friendship, he had also established his rights.

It was true that, when she gradually got to know them, they were not as bad as she had thought, mainly under-privileged kids who had ended up in remand for petty crimes. Chad and Frankie stood out because of their height, their striking looks and the fact that they both had educated accents. The other girls there were a paltry crew, habitual shoplifters, a baby-snatcher, teenagers caught on the game. They resented Frankie but dared not show it. A single glance from her scornful eyes was enough to make them cringe and slink away. Likewise the boys who were nowhere near her equal, though some made lewd remarks until Chad intervened. The two of them were an impressive pair, matched in almost every way although Chad, at seven-teen, was two years older.

They both had a sense of humour, too. The first time he managed to make her laugh lifted a weight from Frankie's soul. Their shared perception of the other inmates and anarchic attitudes to the screws turned them into the Bonnie and Clyde of their set. Why was she in there, he wanted to know, and when, at last, she reluctantly told him, he roared with approving laughter. To set fire to anything took guts and daring; to have burnt down her family home earned his full respect.

'Are you a pyromaniac?' he inquired. 'Or was it simply a chilly night?' And grinned when he saw her finally starting to thaw.

An arsonist, they had called her in court. There was nothing sick about her act; she had done it quite deliberately, in cold blood. For which she was going to have to pay: no wriggling out on the grounds of juvenile psychosis. She should have known better, had had all the benefits; it was up to the court to decide. Her mother couldn't face attending the session but the colonel was there, at his most self-righteous. The sole consolation Frankie had was that he had lost, along with everything else, his prized collection of guns.

The spark between them was instantaneous; it seemed to Chad that the natural next step should be sex. Frankie, however, seemed oddly unsure, which puzzled him. It made no sense that a girl with her sort of fire should be such a prude.

'What is it?' he asked as he felt her recoil. 'You know you are safe with me.' But she still continued to hold him at arm's length. Even the thought of physical contact made her feel positively sick, which wasn't something she cared to explain.

Chad, however, was not easily deterred; at seventeen, he was almost a man, with more than his share of sexual conquests behind him. With patient handling and much finesse, he slowly won her over and gained her trust. And when they lay in each other's arms and Frankie asked if he loved her, he said he did.

6

Bath, all year round, was a tourist trap. By the early spring, it was heaving. An excellent thing for the catering trade if only it weren't such back-breaking work. But Jenny had nobody else she could blame, had signed the lease with wide-open eyes. As she told her friends, the realisation of a long-time dream. Already into her thirties with a baby on the way, if she didn't do it now, she never would.

'But you've no experience of running a pub.' Or any business, come to that; since leaving school she had earned her living exclusively with her pen.

'I can learn.' It surely couldn't be that hard. Over the years she had done much research by writing reviews of new restaurants, hence the dream.

'Propping up bars is hardly the same as working long shifts in a seven-day week while remaining polite and amenable to the punters.' Plus heaving crates and changing barrels and throwing out drunks at closing time, the strenuous stuff that really required a man. Which, at that time, was not something she had. In her working life she had always done well; she was just not so hot on relationships.

All her friends were suddenly experts though she sensed a hint of envy there too, that she had the courage to risk such a gamble while they remained stuck in their soulless jobs. With pension plans and equity, though mortgaged up to the hilt. What few realised was that she had had no choice. When she told Douglas she was pregnant, things had fallen apart so fast she could scarcely believe what had happened. Six years it had been and he'd sworn that one day he would leave; his wife was going through the menopause and he dared not walk out on her now. Jenny, aware that she really shouldn't, put up with it and accepted his evasions. It suited her lifestyle, she kidded herself, not to have to cook and clean or tie herself down to just one man while she was still young and sexy. That, at least, was the line she took; the truth, late at night, was quite different. The clock was ticking, she wanted a child. With every year that Douglas stalled, that dream grew steadily fainter.

'Leave him,' her closest friends all urged, but Jenny always came up with excuses. They were genuine soulmates and she had no doubt that he really loved her, but a man with so many pressures upon him could not simply follow his heart and get out. One of the things she admired him for was his loyalty to his wife. Her friends despaired; she was feisty and bright and hugely attractive to men. She had played the field for years, could do so again if only she would wake up and see what a cul-de-sac she was in. She had come-hither eyes and a cheeky grin and was still an enviable size eight. They made introductions, found her blind dates, yet Jenny continued impervious. Until her pregnancy was confirmed and she joyfully broke the news to her lover. And he sacked her.

The brewery weren't too keen at first on a single woman as licensee, but Jenny exerted her charm to win them over. These days, she reasonably pointed out, it was no longer p.c. to exclude anyone at all because of their race or sex or marital status. She was fit and strong and self-supporting, owned her own home and had always been in paid work. And that income, she hoped, would continue to flow since she'd had her own column in a glossy magazine as well as being a restaurant assessor for Zagat. She suspected that last bit had proved the clincher, that or her irresistible charm or the fear of trouble from the powers that be if she played the political card. Whatever it was, they reluctantly gave way so she set about finding more freelance work and daringly put her South London house on the market. From Brixton to Bath, she'd be daft not to do it. A change of scene as well as a change of profession.

'You are totally crazy,' said her friends. 'What if it doesn't work? Talk about throwing the baby out with the bathwater.'

But for Jenny there could be no going back. The man she had loved so deeply for so long had now become public enemy number one.

* * *

That wasn't precisely how he'd put it, of course.

'Me or the baby,' were his actual words but his eyes had turned red with hostility and she sensed from the way he was clenching his fists that he felt a strong urge to hit her. Despite the years she had dragged her feet, Jenny could make fast decisions. Without a word, she spun on her heel, went back to her office to clear her desk and was out of there that same afternoon, without even pausing to hand in her resignation.

'What,' they all asked, 'are you going to do?' Jobs like hers were not easy to find and her lifestyle would be hard to recreate. But that was no longer a priority with Jenny; the house provided some sort of security, plus she had many contacts. Until she worked something out, she would just go freelance. She had lived on her wits since she left South Wales and achieved a lot in a tough profession. Whatever happened, it wasn't likely she would starve. The object of prime importance now was to save this precious embryo from extinction.

So since she urgently needed to leave town, she got in her car and went to ground in her friend Vanessa's beautiful house outside Bath.

She had never wholly understood how Vanessa could leave a well-paid job and withdraw to the country in order to do up a ruin. They had worked together for many years, side by side on the same magazine, and become the closest of friends. Vanessa, who was arty and an expert on design, had worked her way through a series of men, collecting children and pets along the way. None of them ever meant much to her – the men, that was, not the children or the pets – but when she first saw the house she had fallen in love.

'It's the real thing. I have to have it,' she said when she brought in the agent's brochure for Jenny to check out. She'd been down in the West Country visiting friends, taken an accidental wrong turning and come upon it by chance. It stood alone on the top of a hill, and despite its obvious decrepitude something about it spoke to her and that was all it took. For too many years she'd been something of a gypsy, moving camp when her love-life dictated, never putting down permanent roots. The kids were okay but needed a base. She was weary of constantly living in temporary digs.

The brochure was certainly optimistic; in truth, the house was virtually a ruin. When Jenny drove down there to take a look and saw it first in a thunderstorm, it didn't even have a roof but was sealed by a flapping tarpaulin. They sat, huddled together in her car, while lightning dramatically split the sky and the house just stood there and glowered at them in contempt. It had lasted for three hundred years, it proclaimed, and was not going to crumble now.

Jenny could see that Vanessa was right. With her specialist knowledge and artistic flair, the house cried out for the kind of love she could give it. They ran through the rain and stood shivering in the porch. The studded front door was heavily padlocked; all the windows were firmly closed though some of the panes had been smashed.

'Vandals,' said Vanessa. 'It's been empty too long. I must raise the cash before more damage is done.'

The property developer was reluctant to sell and kept her hanging around for months. It had taken all the money she could raise – her post office savings that were meant for her children, her life insurance and her jade collection, plus loans from a few trusted friends. As well as her car. Jenny helped out with a piece about the house which landed Vanessa a real stroke of luck: a publisher offered her a fat commission for a detailed history of the place, which had both literary and artistic connections.

'You are going to have to work hard,' said Jenny, not envying her friend a bit except that her heart was set upon it and dreams were meant to be fulfilled. After three failed marriages and as many children, the house represented a stability Vanessa had never known. No man she'd ever met in her roller-coaster love-life – and, unlike Jenny, she married them all – had provided the visceral tug she got just from looking at its solid walls and sensing the cosmic vibrations of earlier owners.

'Don't you find it thrilling,' she said, when the property man ceased prevaricating and the deal was allowed to go through, 'that in this room Dr Johnson held court? I wonder if his spirit is still around.'

'It's a friendly feeling,' said Jenny, and it was. Nothing spooky in this generous house; it was simply waiting to be brought back to life by someone able to give it the love it deserved.

For the months it took to repair the roof, Vanessa's

ménage moved into the gatehouse which later, when the work was done, she hoped to be able to let. Jenny, who popped down several times, began to see the house's potential. As the reconstruction got under way, its original splendour was gradually revealed.

'I may even come to live here myself,' she said, only half joking.

Now that things had radically changed, she had nowhere else to go and Vanessa's current partner was working abroad and would be gone for several weeks. It worked out well; Jenny had her laptop and several commissioned articles to write and, from her room in the tiny gatehouse, could oversee the builders at work, while supplying them with occasional cups of tea. As spring arrived and foliage burgeoned, the countryside slowly revealed itself and Jenny, whose life had been totally urban, began to understand Vanessa's compulsion. And then she found the Coot and Hern, and everything slotted into place.

'The coot and *what*?'

'Tennyson,' said Jenny. God, what a load of philistines they were. It was by a brook. With a waterwheel. Grey stone walls with weeping willows, steep stairways and rooms to let. It would need a bit of work but so what? If Vanessa could make a go of it, so could she. She was five months pregnant and needed a job. The pub might prove the answer to her prayers.

7

Unlike Frankie, whose family had proved her ultimate undoing, Chad had nothing at all to say about his. He had been a foundling, the first she had known, left in the porch of a Yorkshire church without so much as a note pinned to his shawl. He only knew it had been midsummer and that his crying had alerted the gardener's boy.

'The church was St Chad's and the boy's name Barnaby. Voilà! A ready-made identity. The vicar announced my existence from the pulpit, and went on doing so for several weeks, but no one ever came forward to claim me. Why doesn't that surprise me?'

His eyes, of that startling electric blue, crinkled at the corners when he smiled. His teeth were good and his hair was coal-black. Frankie wondered how any mother could have turned her back on such a ravishing baby. She guessed he might be of Irish stock; 'black' Irish was what they called them. He certainly possessed the necessary blarney.

*　　*　　*

Once over the shock of being locked up, she adapted, more or less, to the rigid regime. It was not quite a prison but she wasn't free to leave; since the fire, there had been a frozen silence from home. The colonel had washed his hands of her and forbidden her mother to be in touch, despite the fact that Frankie was still her only child. Frankie had realised long ago how frail a reed her mother must be; how else could she have married that terrible man? But it wasn't till now that she'd understood the full measure of his control. If her real father were still around, things would never have come to this. But, then, her mother would not have married the colonel.

'She'll come round,' Chad assured her. 'And if she doesn't, she's rubbish.'

Frankie grinned. He was always like that: eternally optimistic. The fact that they were both on the wrong side of the law appeared not to faze him at all. But he'd been in trouble most of his life and was not ashamed to discuss it. They spent all the time they could together, though mainly supervised. His band of heavies slunk away whenever Frankie appeared. Now she'd discovered the joys of sex, she couldn't get enough of it and much of their time was spent finding ways to be alone together.

'You have the cheek of the devil,' she said, watching him use his formidable charm to get whatever he wanted from authority. The eyes, the smile, the dazzling looks worked wonders even here, on this bunch of dull screws. Something that she thought had died in her when she struck that fatal match reignited.

She had fallen completely under his spell. There was nothing she wouldn't have done for him. And yet he had casually murdered someone. It simply didn't add up.

'He was just a playground thug,' he said. 'No one of any note. One day he pushed things a little too far and – bingo!' The dazzling smile didn't flicker as he drew his finger across his throat. 'These things happen,' he said casually. 'Just one of life's little accidents.'

Before that they'd sent him to public school, the well-heeled family who had taken him in and fostered him for a while, which explained his polish and lofty air. He acted like a democratic lord of the manor, and took it for granted that everybody liked him.

'So what went wrong?'

'Expelled,' he said, with his little boy air of false contrition. 'They caught me smoking and kicked me out.'

'Smoking?' she said. It did sound harsh even for somewhere like Repton.

'Hashish. They said I was a bad example.' He laughed. 'I was only fifteen.'

So they'd sent him back to Barnardo's in disgrace and totally washed their hands of him. The Tewson-Finches, Miles and Yolande; even their names made him smile. Having been through something similar herself, Frankie totally empathised. Families who gave up on you were not worthy of the name. A parent's duty was to back you up, to love you unconditionally.

'So they simply threw you out?' she asked.

'Yup,' said Chad, who had then gone on to murder a boy in cold blood.

'Will we always be together?' she asked as they lay entwined. It was cramped behind the water tank but at least they had some space to themselves and no one knew where they were.

'Always,' he promised. She was such a child. Though tall for her age and as brave as a boy, in fact she was barely fifteen, whereas Chad, almost eighteen by now, would soon be able to vote. With his heavy beard, he'd been shaving for years and might easily have passed for twenty-two.

'When you leave here, will you take me with you?' By now she knew he was all she wanted in life.

'I will,' he said. 'You can count on that. And once we're free, who knows, we may even get married.'

8

Pippa stood ankle-deep in rubble, trying to heat the babies' milk in an improvised bottle-warmer on the stove because the power was off. All around her was builders' rubbish and a strong smell of turps pervaded the air. From somewhere in another room she could hear the distant sound of mewling. The twins were on the verge of waking; hostilities would shortly be resumed.

'Once you've stopped messing around with that milk,' said Ernie sternly from the top of his ladder, 'you might boil some water for our tea.'

'Right you are, boss,' said Pippa placidly, grinning as she tested the milk by dabbing it on the inside of her wrist. The way these workmen pushed her around, no one would guess who was paying their bills. But she loved being there in the thick of things, despite the inconvenience. Normally she would have done it herself – she'd been apprenticed to a decorating firm – but Charles had put his foot down and that was that.

'I won't have you risking it up that ladder,' he'd

said and, perhaps for the first time ever, Pippa had actually done as he'd said.

Things had happened at a dizzying pace since she had found she was pregnant. To start with, she had been petrified by the thought of how he was likely to react, feared she had scuppered their illicit relationship with this unforeseen complication. She must have been careless; it ought not have happened. She cursed herself for the slip. But when the test had proved positive and, furthermore, shown that it was twins, she'd had no other option but to tell him. It could not have been a less opportune time; her career was very much in the ascendant. But nor had she wanted to face an abortion alone. Charles, when she finally spilled the beans, at first said very little. Had gone, grim-faced, to the country to think it over.

Which meant they were almost certainly doomed; she could have kicked herself. Her mother had always said she was too impulsive. Well, this time she had majorly screwed up. Pippa, facing the future alone, at twenty-seven had huge decisions to make. If it came to it, as she knew it would, even without his support she would keep the babies. She had never been drawn to motherhood; was still too young, she felt, to settle down. But faced, as she was, with a fait accompli, she had no other choice. Charles had Cassie and their solid marriage which was, she knew, unassailable. And there were the kids to consider. Cassie's daughters were not his own but he'd supported them through their teenage years and loved them as much as he did his son Aidan. Something Pippa had always envied was his close and happy family life. She was sure he would have no love to spare for her own unwanted twins.

But now was not the time for self-pity. She needed to start making plans.

The first priority was to move. The five-floor walk-up off the Fulham Road was all very well for a fit twenty-something who rode a bike and went to the gym, but out of the question for a mum with a double buggy. So while Charles was in Cornwall she settled down at the kitchen table to draw up one of her lists. She had always been very well organised, part of the secret of her success. She ran her business almost single-handed and lived only two blocks from the shop, which meant she was nearly always there.

She'd first met Charles five years before when, a bubbly twenty-two, she was temping in Liberty's fabric department while looking around for something in design. He'd been after a chintz of a certain colour for Iranian clients in Wilton Place and had been impressed by Pippa's knowledge and the trouble she'd taken to find him just the right thing. The mutual attraction had been instantaneous. In less than a week he had got her into bed.

'Be careful you don't end up as his nurse,' her mother had warned her when she knew. 'Twenty years is too large a gap. You still have most of your life ahead while he must be almost my age.' Gorgeous with it, she had to concede but only to herself.

Endorsing a daughter's adultery was something no mother should ever do. She had played around herself, so knew the score.

The shop, which had started as Charles's idea, into which he had sunk substantial funds, had taken off with surprising speed so that now she had a mail order business too. Even apart from financially, Charles had been a tremendous support by introducing her to his clients and throwing business her way. Another good reason for Pippa to love him; she never could resist a successful man.

But now she would have to manage alone and she steeled herself to the fact. Her mother was right: he was much too old. Whatever his energies in the sack, as a future father he was a less good bet. By the time the babies turned eighteen, he would already be drawing his pension, leaving Pippa to support them all. It wouldn't be fair to any of them. She would have to face up to life as a single parent.

But Charles, as he did so often, surprised her by turning up late on the Monday night, arms overflowing with full-blown roses and a diamond brooch in a velvet box which, although too formal for her, was a generous gift.

'Twins!' he said, embracing her hard. 'If I really luck out, they'll be girls.'

Dearest Charles. As she fed the twins, Pippa was practically purring. It's a well-known fact that married lovers never ever leave their wives, but at the end of the following week, before he departed for Cornwall again, he held her close and told her his decision.

'I am going to ask Cassie for a divorce. We ought to get married as soon as we can. We don't want them born on the wrong side of the blanket.' Till now the M-word had never been mentioned and Pippa had not expected it. But he, so much older, was taking charge and wasn't going to let anything stand in his way. It was all part of the compelling charm which had landed her where she was now: in this beautiful house he had bought her in Barnes, which was in the process of being fully restored. The Pont Street flat he would keep for business and the use of the kids when they came into town. And he seemed to be genuinely chuffed by the fact that they'd soon have two more half-siblings.

If Charles had surprised her, Cassie did too by meekly refusing to stand in their way.

'Go,' she had said, 'if you feel you must.' And had taken the dogs for a walk.

Pippa was really consumed by guilt at the thought of what she was doing to Cassie, but Charles assured her it had just been a matter of time.

'She's got plenty to fill her days,' he said. 'And she loves Tintagel more than me. Now that she's got her grandchildren, she'll be fine.'

He displayed no feelings either way at walking out after twenty-one years and Pippa, despite her relief, was secretly shocked. She had only really met Cassie once, and had been very much taken by the older woman's dignity and calm. But now was no time for regrets. The die was cast; there could be no looking back.

9

It seemed to Frankie, the closer they got, that beneath the banter Chad minded not having real roots. He occasionally made a joke of it, the way he had entered the world unannounced, but sometimes she caught him unawares with a wistful look on his face. At least she knew where she had come from, despite the way it had later turned out. Her childhood, when her dad was alive, had been full of happy memories, which was also true of the early days on the Wirral. She still hadn't talked much about it to Chad but he was an expert at picking things up. He held her tight when she cried in her sleep or woke in sudden terror. These days they slept outside the main complex, in a hostel in a neighbouring street, where they managed to share a bed most of the time. The female warden, bewitched by Chad, obligingly looked the other way and, provided they behaved themselves, they could more or less do as they liked.

'I won't let anyone harm you, babe,' he said when Frankie clung on to him. Whatever it was apparently went very deep.

He liked to listen to her childhood stories of riding her pony and following the guns; the countryside was what she missed most of all. The breeze, the sunshine, the scent of damp earth, the freedom to ride all day on her own and only come home when the pony was tired; the memories lit up her face. Confined within this grim institution was no way to be spending their teenage years.

'He stole my childhood, that thieving bastard.' It was why she'd set fire to his house.

Things would have been far worse if it hadn't been for Chad. He had brought new life and hope into Frankie's life. Her parents had given up on her but Chad had taken their place. He was more than a lover, he was her protector too; even the warders respected that and it gave her a whole new confidence, along with a dawning beauty. He liked to ask about the fire and how she had managed to carry it off.

'Did it burn down completely?' he wanted to know.

'Enough,' she said. 'They knocked down the rest because it was no longer safe.' A Grade Two listed manor house set in extensive grounds, it had gone up like a tinderbox when she lit it.

'It must have been spectacular.'

'It was.' She had stood there, transfixed by the blaze, overwhelmed by a sudden manic excitement. And not until the fire was well under way had she thought to wonder if anyone could be inside. Her mother and the colonel were safely in London but there might have been others she'd overlooked. She simply hadn't thought. Which had gone very much against her at the hearing.

'Servants, you mean?' He was curious. His interest in her earlier life was intense.

'Well, hardly that. We weren't that rich. A cleaning woman, the guy who cut the grass and fed the colonel's dogs. A number of people had easy access – it wasn't exactly Fort Knox.'

'So how did they figure out it was you?'

'Apart from the fact I hated him? I stuck around, like a fool, until they caught me.'

The blaze had been totally wonderful; to this day she couldn't forget it. November the Fifth, though without the seasonal drizzle. That summer had been unusually dry; the timber was highly combustible. Especially when assisted by the paraffin Frankie had used.

'But how did you know how to do it?' he asked, not sure he'd have had the guts himself. His admiration for her grew with every extra detail.

'Intuition,' said Frankie modestly. 'I figured it out for myself. Different people have different talents. Someone worked out how to split the atom. Someone else developed lateral thinking. I just know how to set a really great fire.'

She knew it was love, had never felt this way. The only boys she had known had been kids and she'd never even been on a proper date. She worshipped Chad, was obsessed with him and clung to his every word. She dreamed of the day they would one day be

51

free to spend their lives together. His future, however, was bleaker than hers since he was in on a murder charge whereas she, all going well, would soon be out. Arson was serious but she was underage. Despite her stepfather's obdurate stand, the social workers were busy on her behalf.

'He's the one who should be inside,' said Chad, who only knew part of the truth. 'Wait till I get out and I'll fix the bastard.'

'He isn't worth it,' said Frankie wisely. 'And you're in enough trouble as it is.'

10

There hadn't been a word from Rocco; Cristina was growing frantic. By the time she got home from the opera that night, there still wasn't any news. And Claude was only gone for three nights. Unless she acted extremely fast, it could be that she'd find herself back on the streets.

Even in her middle twenties, she was still at the top of her catwalk fame, despite the fact, it was popularly rumoured, that her cocaine habit was spiralling out of control. At nineteen she'd been at her most spectacular, featured on lists of the world's most beautiful women, and had made a couple of 'art-house' movies, though under another name. It was at that age she had first met Cal, in Ipanema at the height of the season, with her credit card tucked into her minuscule bikini and her door key round her neck on a leather thong. The bare necessities of a pampered life; it was instant lust, he had told her later. They halted only yards apart, these two exotic strangers, locking eyes, before falling recklessly into each other's arms.

Brazil in the seventies was decadent and lavish, its

beaches strewn with naked flesh, its nightspots with the rich and famous, its casinos overflowing. Cristina's picture, sixty feet high, dominated hoardings all over Rio so that Cal encountered her aggrandised image virtually everywhere he looked. It meant no privacy but what did she care; adulation had become her very lifeblood. Nor could she get enough of him; he was new in the city, in his early twenties, with a natural beauty almost as striking as hers. Together they made a dynamic pair and were quickly the toast of the town. Within days he had moved into her apartment, with its penthouse terrace and ocean views, and shortly after that he mentioned love.

Since they both had money (she was very rich) they devoted most of their waking hours to prodigal spending and having fun, except when she had to work, which wasn't often at that time of year. The heat was far too great, she complained, to stand around for hours just changing her clothes. Her sponsors, who loved her, put up with it. Her sultry beauty was in such demand that if she frowned, as she often did, instant alarm bells rang and someone would be dispatched to calm her down. On the few occasions when she did a show, Cal would sit loyally in the front row, enjoying the prestige of escorting her as well as the way he knew he too was turning heads.

'Have you ever thought of modelling yourself?' The question was frequently asked. But Cal was far too fly for that. He liked the clothes and the lifestyle they paid for but considered the fashion world a tad too sleazy. Also he was basically idle, preferring to stay out late at night and sleep through most of the morning, rising at noon to mix his first drink and carry one back to Cristina in her boudoir. They were mirror images of each other: their looks, their vanity, their basic avarice. It was only a matter of time before she started dropping hints about commitment.

From the start, she encountered an odd resistance, though Cal declared he adored her. And the sex was out of this world, so what was his problem? There were few red-blooded men in the world who would not have killed to have taken his place. Cristina, accustomed to having her own way, stamped her foot and sulked. She thought he was playing hard to get so tested him by being unfaithful. She brazenly checked out an old flame who took her for the weekend to Copacabana.

That was nearly the end of them. Cal immediately packed his bags and left without leaving a contact number. It reduced her to an emotional wreck; unused to being treated like that, she expected to do whatever she damn well pleased. Five weeks later, when she'd lost seven pounds, been to a shrink, developed a drinking problem and sent out spies all over the city, desperate to find out where he was, he strolled back in with a friendly grin and asked if she would consent to be his wife.

In later years she often looked back on the man who had rocked her life then disappeared as mysteriously as he had arrived. But long before it came to that, most of her money had been spent and her adoration had changed to bitter resentment. He always remained quite a shadowy figure; she had never even been clear about his country of birth. His accent was resolutely cut-glass and he claimed connections in Hollywood, though his knowledge of London, too, seemed pretty extensive. She never found out where his money came from; he was twenty-two when they met. But he looked and dressed and acted the part of a playboy born to a life of ease, who was never socially out of his depth and always had the readies in his pocket.

'I'm a traveller of the world,' he said, when asked how he had lived before Rio, and seemed to have no profession at all apart from being a great lay. Once they were married, he moved back in and extended his personal space by one room to accommodate his rapidly growing wardrobe. They continued to party most of the time and it was he who first introduced her to coke, to the fierce disapproval of the corporate sponsors who indulged her every other whim. It would damage her beauty and reputation but at least, as Cristina pointed out, it also kept her satisfyingly thin.

Waiting in a bar for her friends, she thought back to those headier times when the world still lay at her feet. She was twenty-four now, and the drug had started its pervasive damage; these days she couldn't get out of bed without it. She spat her chewing gum into an ashtray and scrabbled in her purse for a cigarette. The others were already forty minutes late; she had started drinking without them.

Izabel, Alicia and Marie-Hélène were party girls with a vengeance. The first two, by their own reckoning, were 'starlets'; Marie-Hélène, who was far more astute, was an international adventuress. Cristina was into her second Bacardi by the time the trio burst through the door, screaming their heads off and tossing their hair, causing enough disruption to silence the bar.

'You're late,' snapped Cristina, not well pleased, furious at being excluded. It was clear all three were at least one party ahead.

'We ran into Raoul,' said Alicia, smirking, 'and he took us up to his pad for a couple of joints.'

'In any case,' said Marie-Hélène, expertly glancing around the room, 'it's not yet eleven. The night is young. The party won't liven up until after two.'

This was how they lived in Rio, hitting the high spots every night. There were times Cristina would have liked to sleep instead but she was far too imperious to say so. She and her acolytes were ever on display, strutting their stuff in the fanciest joints. She constantly craved an audience and wouldn't go hunting on her own, although the instant she made a hit she expected the others to get lost.

But this riotous living was taking its toll, on both her looks and her career. No longer rich, she could barely scrape by with the fewer catwalk bookings she was getting and the hugely inflated expenses she had to shell out. Living the high life was all very well when you were still the most celebrated beauty in town and someone else would always pick up the tab. Since she stopped being half of a beautiful couple, her notoriety had taken a dip while her unreliable reputation had decimated her income. In addition, her expensive habit was relentlessly bleeding her dry.

Now, however, was not the time for taking stock of her life. Her cohorts were restless and ready to go, so Cristina slipped off to the powder-room and returned with brighter eyes and her humour restored. She wore a shimmering satin shift, daringly slashed to the base of her spine, and as she undulated through the crowd there wasn't an eye in the place that wasn't on her.

The noise was so great as they entered the club that all they could do was gesticulate and edge their way through the heaving masses to the bar. There were flashing lights, enough to bring on a migraine, and the heat was so intense bodies glistened with sweat. The Beautiful People were out in force and, when they saw Cristina enter, they parted to allow the four of them through. Hands reached out and kisses were blown. In the popularity stakes she was still hot.

'Let's get out of here,' she said. In this light she couldn't be seen to her best advantage.

The next club was right on the waterfront, with windows flung wide and a welcome breeze that cooled and caressed her skin. Here she spotted a number of faces that, in her shifting world, she thought of as friends. When Cal was around it had all been different. He would grab her hand and lead her through and make them the focal point of any group. She missed his reassuring smile and the hand-squeeze that confirmed he was there for her. When he disappeared, she had thought she might die though by then she was hurling plates and creating scenes. She knew now that she had been too hasty. The years since Cal disappeared had been really tough.

But people embraced her and the music turned her on. In seconds Cristina was out on the floor, salsa-ing on her own to much applause. With her caramel skin and abundance of hair and a body that moved like liquid silk, she achieved the attention she always yearned for and was happy, at least for the moment. Marie-Hélène was off in a corner, schmoozing with a former beau, while the starlets had settled themselves at the bar and were competing for what they could pull. Neither could ever face going home alone; it would mean losing too much face.

Exhausted, Cristina took a breather and went to freshen up. She brushed her hair, which fell halfway down her back, and spritzed the sheen of perspiration from her face. Her feet were aching so she kicked off her sandals and massaged her throbbing toes with expensive cream. Soon she'd be ready to return to the fray, but there was one more thing she needed to do. Checking that she wasn't observed, she removed the small white sachet from her purse. In a matter of seconds her eyes were brighter and her glossy lips parted with elation.

The girls had gone but she didn't care. She was perfectly happy dancing alone with the eyes of the room upon her. She danced all night, till she almost dropped and her famous boobs were hanging right out of her dress. And just when they thought she was finally spent, she would pop back into the powder-room and revitalise herself with the magic white powder. She never knew who went home with her; by then the room had started to spin and she had virtually blanked out. She smelt his cologne and endured his groping and registered only the click of the door when he left.

She awoke next morning in crumpled sheets with a head that thundered so painfully she dared not even attempt to open her eyes. She dragged a pillow over her face to protect them from the morning glare, then sank back into oblivion for two more hours. When she woke again, it was almost noon and she'd missed her early call. The Prada people would not be bothering her again. So what? There were plenty more fashion houses. Right now all she cared about was ridding herself of this blinding pain in her head. She woke again at four with a raging thirst and an urgent need to empty her bladder but, when she attempted to get out of bed, the room swung round and she lost her balance, crashed to the floor and knocked herself out on the edge of the bedside table.

Two hours later she finally came to, sprawled in a pool of urine and blood. A gash on her temple hurt like hell, and her designer shift was all rumpled up, revealing to anyone entering the room everything she had got. She prayed the maid had not been in, looked nervously round for her morning tray but, to her relief, could see no evidence of intrusion. She raised herself, which made her throw up, then sank back into a dreamless sleep. It was almost midnight before she woke again.

Cristina staggered into the bathroom and threw up again all over the floor, then crawled on her hands and knees into the kitchen. She was now so parched she could barely swallow and desperate for a drink. Coffee wouldn't do it and she had no milk so she pulled the top off the vodka bottle and glugged down a mouthful which made her vomit again. She groped her way to the bathroom mirror, avoiding the mess on the floor, and groaned when she managed to open her eyes and saw the ravages of the night. A face all bloated with drink and drugs, with a bruise the size of a ping-pong ball and a smear of dried blood on her cheek. A whole day wasted and she'd had no food. It appeared that no one had called to find out how she was.

With the utmost effort, she rinsed her face, then tied back her matted hair. She had to get out of this stinking place and eat something fast before she fainted again. Wearing her trench coat but nothing else except for a pair of feathered mules, she ventured into the elevator, hoping not to be seen.

The porter on duty was the young, handsome one who had several times seen her the worse for wear.

'Good evening,' he said, jumping swiftly to attention, and she sensed from the way that he looked at her that he knew what her trench coat concealed. Any other time she might have been tempted; she liked his insolent stare and the cut of his pants. The way she felt now, though, it was out of the question. If she didn't get out of there fast she would throw up again.

There had, she dimly remembered now, been another wife before they met, though Cal had never been willing to talk about it. It seemed scarcely possible – he was still such a boy – but would make sense of his reluctance to tie himself down without a struggle. And it might explain where he'd got his money. Though he'd been through hers with alacrity, he had seemed to have no shortage of it when they met. He'd been staying in one of the grand hotels when he'd picked her up on the beach, and his luggage, when he moved it in, had been of the very best quality, as had his clothes.

She had loved to lie and watch him dress, preening and posing in front of the glass, patting his freshly shaven chin, as sexually confident as she was herself. No wonder they'd been such a social hit; society had adored them for their blatant narcissism. She sighed for those days which were careless and free, when the only thing on the agenda was making love. The money she'd made, plus his own private income, left them free to do as they liked. The first thing he'd bought was a red Ferrari in which they had cruised the crowded streets, hailing friends and stopping at intervals to drink. She could see him still, with his joie de vivre and eyes alight with mischief. Cal Barnard, still the love of her life, the mystery man who had had no past and now, it seemed, no future.

When he disappeared it had been without trace; she came home one day and he had gone. He had taken his luggage and all his possessions, leaving her nothing but an empty fridge and a cellophane packet containing her poison of choice. Beside it lay a single red rose and a note that just said: 'Je regrette.'

11

It would take a lot of working out. It was crucial that he anticipate possible hitches. Since the moment he had been apprehended, Chad had been planning the perfect escape and now, since knowing Frankie, favoured fire. If she had done it, so could he. She'd have got clean away if she hadn't hung around. The trick was to do it, then get the hell out without wasting any precious time or involving another person. Chad believed in travelling light; at heart he was still a loner.

He grilled her over and over again until he had every detail by heart. He knew she hadn't yet cottoned on, which made things easier for him. The basic combustibles were relatively simple; there was paraffin stored in the gardener's shed, matches in the kitchen. Frankie's device of making a long wick had been a stroke of genius, had meant she'd been able to light the fire without much risk to herself.

Chad's idea was to set fire to the hostel when none of the other residents were there, then slip away in the ensuing furore. His biggest problem was finding a way to be alone on the premises, something expressly forbidden by the governing board. The hostel was simply a dormitory, an annexe of the main reform school though situated outside the locked iron gates. Only a handful of inmates at one time were allowed the privilege of sleeping there, a sign from above that they were now worthy of trust. Frankie and the others were bona fide; only Chad had wheedled himself in through charm.

Meals were served in the main building, where they also spent the rest of the day. They were not allowed to return to the hostel unless it was an emergency. Which, he now reasoned, should include being suddenly taken ill. If he used his lethal charm again on the highly susceptible female warden, he was confident she would turn a blind eye and allow him to stay in bed. Though he must be careful not to overplay it and end up in the sickbay. Everything seemed to fit into place. There were just a couple more things he had to do.

Frankie was woken in the early hours by a sudden icy blast. The window was open and someone was climbing in. Before she could even make a sound, a hand was clamped firmly over her mouth as Chad threw himself headlong across her bed. He wore thick gloves that smelt of petrol and was clad from head to toe in black like a member of the SAS.

'What on earth are you doing?' she asked, once she had shaken him off. He would persist in taking these crazy risks. If anyone else had happened to see him, all privileges would have been removed and, before he knew it, he'd be back behind locked doors. Yet she had to admire his style; nothing seemed to scare him.

'Move over,' he said, wriggling out of his clothes and sliding in beside her. His face was cold but his pulse was fast. He was also in a state of sexual arousal.

'What have you been up to?' she asked later, when he lay exhausted in her arms.

'Never you mind,' he said. 'It's none of your business.'

In the end, however, he had to tell her because he needed her help. He was only going to get one shot and wanted her as a decoy.

'But you have to do exactly as I say,' he insisted before he told her. 'It's essential that everything goes according to plan.'

Frankie, at first, was apprehensive and keen not to get involved. She was scared his actions might jeopardise both their futures. But when he explained what she already knew, that he could not endure one more day in the place, and she heard the anguish in his voice, she saw his point of view. Soon she'd be walking out of there with the rest of her life before her while he would remain locked up, perhaps for years.

'The truth is,' he said, with his lips on her throat, 'I cannot live without you. And will kill myself if they let you go and I am left here to rot.'

12

Next morning the weather was brilliantly sunny so Cassie took a boat to the Lido and treated herself to lunch at the Hotel des Bains. The only other people there were a party of grey-suited businessmen who stayed at the far end of the terrace and kept right out of her way. It was early spring so the swarming crowds had not yet made an appearance. She sat and sipped a glass of champagne and remembered the scenes from *Death in Venice*, filmed on this same stretch of beach. Poor Dirk Bogarde, brought down by love. The way she was feeling now, she empathised.

Cassandra Elwes had been a war baby, conceived on her father's final leave and born in May, just a few days after the war in Europe ended. Her older brothers were already at Eton when her mother brought the new baby home and Cassie became their beloved play-thing, petted and cherished and always indulged, including being allowed to tag along. Cornwall, even in those days of strict rationing, lived off the fat of the land, so she was well provided for and, due to the gap between the siblings, more than able to hold her own in company of all ages. She grew up tall and naturally graceful, with solemn eyes that always seemed to be searching for the truth, and wore her thick brown hair in a single plait. Edwin Hawksmoor, who had known her from her childhood, watched her growth with a deepening affection and, as soon as she turned eighteen, astonished her father by asking for her hand. Her parents initially were taken aback; Cassie was only just out of school and still, in their eyes at least, very much a child. But Cassie herself was immensely flattered at being taken so seriously by a man on whom she'd had a crush since adolescence. So, because she invariably got her way, within the year she became his bride and moved a few miles along the coast to become mistress of his manor.

Despite the fact that he was more than twice her age, Edwin had tutored Cassie well, widening her interests and encouraging her to study so that, by the time they were man and wife, they had more in common of a cerebral nature than most new couples closer to each other in age. Having older brothers helped, of course, and she had grown up with a bright and inquiring mind. Edwin's first fiancée had perished in the Blitz; rumour had it he'd been mourning her ever since. But thrown, as he was, into almost daily contact with this pretty and impressionable child, he had found it all too easy to love again. The knowledge he'd garnered in his solitary years he now had the utmost joy in sharing with her. Their bond was founded on a master/pupil basis that gradually grew into deep and lasting love. She looked up to and respected him as a man she could revere and trust.

At the time of their marriage her father was Lord Lieutenant of Cornwall, with extensive land that bordered on Edwin's estate. Thus Cassie had little uprooting to do, and most mornings she would walk the dogs along the rambling coastal path and drop into her mother's kitchen for coffee and a chat. And when the babies, Rose and Daisy, arrived her extended family was complete, with doting grandparents on the scene to help raise the little girls.

It was a tranquil existence and Cassie loved it, content as she was to cook and potter, play the piano by candlelight or read in front of a blazing fire, her husband dozing at her side. Edwin had ten thousand acres to farm and, although he employed a capable manager, was out in all weathers from dawn till dusk, a strenuous life for a man his age who had never really been strong. Sometimes his sister, Sybil, would visit from her busy studio in St Ives where she worked, year round, as a brilliant, innovative sculptor. Three years older even than Edwin, she was inclined to be critical of the young bride. The only things she cared for were her art and the Hawksmoor land, handed down through many generations.

She still kept rooms at the rear of the house, with a view of the sea at the end of the lawn, which no one ever entered without permission. She usually came between sculptural projects, when she needed time to relax and recharge before starting something new. She was quite celebrated in her field and could choose the commissions she wanted. Her work, like her, was simplistic and stark, recognisable to the masses so that visitors flocked to her studio all year round. While she was staying with Edwin and Cassie she would work energetically in the garden, or spend long hours in the library browsing through Edwin's collection of art books.

The girls were slightly in awe of her; her speech was forthright and her manner gruff and she had very little patience with small children. But as they grew older, she softened towards them and started teaching them both to draw, displaying a kindness she usually chose to hide.

'Would Sybil ever have liked to marry?' She'd been twenty-three at the outbreak of war and had worked in a munitions factory, risking her life every night.

'No,' said Edwin. 'I am pretty sure not. All she has ever really cared about is art and her independence.'

Cassie, intimidated, secretly hoped that some of her sister-in-law's formidable talent might, in due course, be handed down to the children.

The idyll, alas, was not destined to last. When the heart attack carried Edwin off, Cassie found herself widowed at thirty-three. What had once been a haven of peaceful content became just a shuddering hulk of a house, especially when the weather at sea was bad. She would huddle with the dogs in front of the fire, listening to the booming breakers, and agonise as to how she could manage alone. Ten thousand acres was a lot to oversee, but she knew she could depend on

William Tremayne. The farm manager was a man in his forties, weather-beaten and taciturn, who had lived on the Hawksmoor estate for most of his life. His job continued without interruption; he came to the house to offer condolences but seemed to take it for granted that nothing would change. Cassie could also have turned to Sybil, but she wasn't keen to. The ingenuous child who had married so young, and always looked up to her husband for guidance, was now an adult with daughters of her own. It was up to her what she made of her life.

Talk about funeral meats furnishing the marriage feast; that rapturous morning in the Knightsbridge hotel changed for ever Cassie's perception of life. When the nice young man had come to her aid by carrying her parcels back for her, nothing had prepared her for what happened next. While she was nervously wondering whether to tip him, he tossed her packages on to the bed and kissed her.

'Sorry,' he said. 'I shouldn't have done that. I just couldn't help myself.' Then he gave her a dazzling smile and did it again.

Cassie, offended to her core, stared at him, rigid with indignation, uncertain whether to scream or faint or call for assistance from the desk. 'I have recently lost my husband,' she said, then spoiled the impact of the reprimand by bursting into tears. At which he put his arms round her and patted her comfortingly on the back, offering his handkerchief to mop her eyes. His own eyes were blue and filled

71

with compassion; she saw he meant no disrespect. And though he was clearly much younger than her, she felt instinctively that she could trust him.

Before she knew it, they were on the bed and he had taken his jacket off and, once again, was smothering her with kisses. And Cassie, after her first rebuff, found herself entering into things and behaving, she later thought, like a shameless hussy.

The deep affection she had felt for Edwin had always been more on a spiritual plane, whereas Charles was keen to make love to her all the time. Edwin had been a father figure to whom she had always looked up; he had handled her like porcelain, and she, in her innocence, had not known what she was missing. Charles Buchanan was a total contrast; lusty, sensual and twenty-three. If he'd had his way, they'd have stayed in bed all day, but Cassie was older and more restrained. With other pressing matters to worry about.

'You're insane,' she said when he told her how he felt. 'I am far too old and you hardly know me.'

'I know enough,' he said, kissing her palm, 'to want to devote my life to you and try to make you happy.'

At first she didn't mention the children, just that her husband had been much older and that she had loved him very deeply and had not yet recovered from the shock. But Charles had been there when she paid her bill and knew approximately where she lived. And that she was renovating her house so soon after Edwin's death. Embarrassed, she went on to the defensive. Her husband had been ailing for years. She was doing it mainly in memory of him.

'I'd love to come and see it some day.' The house she so clearly loved. But now would not be appropriate. She had lingered in London too long as it was, and dared not imagine what the village would say should she return with a handsome young man in tow.

'I must go home first thing,' she said.

'May I help you with your luggage?'

His eyes were bright as he stroked her cheek and Cassie felt a great wave of passion engulf her in a way she'd not known before.

'Wait,' she told him, after some thought. 'First there are things that have to be taken care of.'

'Remember my profession,' he said, holding her close against his heart. 'If your home comes first, which I understand, allow me to offer my services.'

Put like that, she found it hard to resist. In addition to pictures, he now explained, he also dabbled a bit in interior design. Cassie laughed at his self-assurance. 'Wait,' she told him again, 'until I call you.'

On the journey home her thoughts were spinning. She could scarcely credit what she had done. She studied her face in the carriage window, searching for signs of debauchery. She had acted quite out of character, behaved like a pathetic fool. Hindu widows committed suttee, while she had fooled around with a total stranger, much younger than herself. There was nobody she could possibly tell; no one who wouldn't condemn her. Because her marriage had been so close, she had felt no need of female friends. Now, for the first time ever, she realised their lack. The girls were too young to understand, which would not only apply to Charles. Both of them had always worshipped their father.

She sent Charles a telegram, asking him to wait and promising to be in touch when she felt it was time. She dared not risk public disapprobation by taking up with another man quite so soon. But she couldn't forget his expressive eyes, which started to haunt her dreams, nor the way she'd felt when he held her close and covered her face with kisses.

Charles was able to curb his impatience and when the reunion did finally take place, it all went very well. The girls both took to him on sight, put aside any rebellious thoughts, and treated him like an elder brother which, indeed, he could almost have been. He was tall and lithe, in T-shirt and jeans, and he vaulted out of his open car and greeted them with an infectious grin, his eyes concealed by dark glasses. Cassie made the introductions and Charles shook hands with them each in turn, then swept her into a passionate hug that instantly killed off any pretence that he was nothing more than a casual friend. Rose and Daisy exchanged a look but entered into the spirit of things when they saw the effect this dashing young man was having on their mother. They had not seen her so skittish in years. Being in love became her. All of a sudden she looked her age, which was young.

'It's going to be all right,' she said, after the girls had gone to their rooms.

'Naturally,' said Charles. It was what he'd expected.

It went so well that, in just a few months, he persuaded Cassie to marry him. And when she mentioned it to the girls, she was thrilled by their positive reaction. Because he treated them both as equals, they were more than a little in love with him themselves. He brought new vitality into their lives; after a father who was ailing and withdrawn, this vigorous newcomer in his early twenties was like a breath of fresh air. Cassie found herself relaxing. She still had to face the neighbours, of course, but Charles pointed out that it was none of their business. All her life she'd put others first; now, at last, she had come into her own. She'd been given a second chance of a happy marriage.

The wedding was to be small and low-key but first she had to tell the rest of the family. She was apprehensive about her brothers but more so about Edwin's sister. Sybil could scarcely believe her eyes the day she first caught sight of Charles, seated astride one of Edwin's hunters, in conversation with her nieces. For a while she sat in her car and watched, at first suspicious of the scene, then remembering that her brother's children had not, until now, had very much fun in their lives. Surprising herself, she got out of the car and walked across to greet him, knowing at almost first glance that she would like to sculpt him.

She did, however, question his motives in marrying a widow ten years older than himself, already encumbered with children. The estate was a considerable prize, not least because she'd never have children herself. Charles, however, responded to her queries with answers that were both frank and sincere. He would do his best to make Cassie happy, had simply taken one look and fallen in love. The difference in age, as the years went by, would cease to matter at all, certainly as far as he was concerned.

Cassie's brothers were similarly suspicious. If anything went against Charles, it was mainly his looks. He had the air of a young adventurer, but his charm and manners could not be faulted and there wasn't the slightest doubt that Cassie was smitten. After all she'd been through, she deserved a break. Their inquiries about his earlier life he answered with absolute candour. He'd been raised in India, sent home to public school, then furthered his education with overseas travel.

'And what exactly is your line of business?' Richard Elwes wanted to know.

'Fine art,' said Charles. 'I act for private clients, locating paintings to specific needs to fill a gap in a collection.'

'Sounds fascinating.' Richard was quite impressed. Charles had the air of a man on an upward curve.

But Edwin's lawyer was less sanguine and produced a list of questions that needed answers. The Hawksmoor inheritance was worth a lot; it was up to him to secure the children's future. 'You're sure he's not after your money?' he said, but Cassie refused to discuss it. She could take care of herself and wouldn't let anyone stand in her way when it came to following her heart.

They were married quietly in the village church and the few who attended all agreed that they'd rarely seen a more radiant bride.

And yet, after twenty-two tranquil years, without warning things had fallen apart. Charles was in love with somebody else and had once again rushed into marriage. Cassie was still in a total daze and had not properly taken it in. The love she'd depended upon for so long belonged now to somebody else. She had met the new wife on several occasions and always rather liked her. She was blonde, vivacious, a product of her age, with the confidence of the archetypal Sloane, able to cope with anything, quite unfazed. Cassie, of course, had been unaware of the true relationship between her and Charles until he'd broken the news that Pippa was pregnant. By which time, of course, it had been too late. She had done the only decent thing and offered him a divorce.

Feeling suddenly rather fragile, Cassie returned to the trattoria and was touched to be greeted like a familiar friend. She had fluent Italian and plenty of money; was no longer just an abandoned wife but a single woman of independent means. She was thoroughly through with domestic life and now had an urge to spread her wings. For one more night she would savour just being in Venice. Tomorrow she would embark on a brand new life.

13

Frankie was simply to do as he told her, act as decoy and stay right out of the way. Chad had decided the best time to move would be while they were all at their evening meal, in order to escape under cover of darkness. Frankie's job was to make quite sure that none of their housemates returned before time, until after the fire was lit and well under way.

'How do you suggest I do that?'

'Use your brain. Start an argument or even a Scrabble game. You are first rate at causing diversions. Up to you.'

'And you promise you won't leave without me?'

'I do.' He gave her his ID photograph as a pledge.

Frankie was touched. The gesture was not at all like him; he normally didn't hold with sentiment. She fitted it into her grandmother's locket, the one piece of jewellery she possessed, and hung it round her neck. 'I will never take it off,' she vowed. 'Whatever happens, I'll always have something of yours.'

In case they should miss each other in the chaos that was bound to follow the conflagration, she suggested they fix a meeting place where neither of them would be known. The railway station was far too obvious; besides, Chad was planning to hitch.

'Why not outside the church?' said Frankie. It seemed an apt way for him to depart, mirroring his entry into the world.

'Great idea.' He kissed her hard. Tomorrow was the chosen day. There was no guarantee that they'd meet again, though he didn't tell her that.

Setting a fire was a tricky business. Correct preparation was the crucial part.

'Don't use paraffin,' Frankie warned. Hers had been a malicious statement but this one had to appear to be accidental.

'Why not?' asked Chad, only partly listening since he already had it safely stowed.

'Too dangerous,' she said. 'It ignites too fast. Weren't you ever a Boy Scout?'

'You have to be kidding.' She seemed to forget that he'd been in Barnardo's and later at public school.

'Well, I was a Guide and we learnt these things.' And careful planning and building were essential. She'd provided him with a ball of rough twine which they'd soaked in candle wax, then allowed to dry. That was the secret of Frankie's success. She had stretched her wick right across the lawn and hidden in the bushes while she struck the match.

'You are sure it will work?'

'It did for me.'

But he'd keep the paraffin handy just in case.

'Do you still love me?'

'Of course,' he said. Then checked his watch; it would soon be time to put into action the first part of the plan.

The warder, predictably, was sympathetic when Chad, in a barely audible croak, told her that his throat was really bad. She peered in his mouth, which looked normal to her, but since he was not one to make a fuss, she agreed he could miss his classes that day, provided he stayed in bed.

'I will catch up on my studies,' he promised. 'I just don't want to go spreading germs around.'

Once he was sure she was out of the house and the others had gone up the road for breakfast, Chad quickly put the final touches in place. Both their rucksacks were in the gardener's shed, beneath a tangle of tennis nets, stowed away for the winter. The ball of twine, matches and a bundle of kindling were hidden in the basement. He carried them stealthily up to his room and, after a moment's contemplation, went back for the paraffin too. Despite Frankie's warning it was, he decided, always better to be on the safe side and the weather was not looking good. He studied the sky, which was bruised and angry, and hoped they weren't in for a sudden shower. But since there was nothing he could do about that, instead he checked inside every room to ensure that no one had stayed behind unnoticed. After that, there remained just one more detail before he could relax.

*   *   *

Frankie's part in the plan went off smoothly. She got the whole group telling spooky stories, a ploy which invariably worked. As, one by one, they rose to the challenge, she kept an eye on the dimming light and, as soon as darkness began to set in, announced that she was worn out and needed her bed. Her group strolled back to the gates together and the guard on duty let them out. A gentle rain was just starting to fall; Frankie worried about the fire. All that was left for her to do was raise the alarm when she saw the first flames and then fade away, unobserved.

But suddenly, from beyond the trees, they heard the sound of a muffled roar.

'Fire!' someone screamed and everyone pointed as a finger of flame erupted into the sky.

He's used the paraffin, thought Frankie dully. After she'd told him not to, the fool. How could he imagine he would get away with that?

As Chad had predicted, pandemonium reigned and Frankie's companions rushed around wildly, watching the billowing smoke engulfing their home. The rain seemed not to be making much difference; the house had gone up like a bomb. Despite her anxiety, she was proud of what he'd done. There was no need now to summon help. Within minutes the police and fire brigade had arrived.

'Everyone please stand back,' they ordered and Frankie realised the moment had come. She had no trouble slipping away for everyone's eyes were on the blaze and she had to force herself not to stay and watch. But this was the turning point of her life. A bright new future lay ahead.

Five hours she waited on the steps of the church, drenched to the skin and increasingly worried, but when, by two a.m., he hadn't come, she finally gave up hope. Since she had no money and nowhere to go, she had no option but to turn herself in.

14

They were right when they said it wouldn't be easy, especially now her pregnancy was so advanced. The worst thing about it was the very long hours. To start with, there were no overnight guests but that would change when word got around that the pub was open again. And then she'd be faced with the problem of breakfast, for paying customers had to be fed and she couldn't expect the part-time staff to help. Because of the recent upheaval in her life, she had lost the habit of cooking. Now was the time for her to start polishing her skills.

Jenny couldn't remember how or when she learnt to cook. It was certainly nothing her mother ever taught her. She grew up in Neath in a terraced house that overlooked the railway line. Her father, until they laid him off, had worked as cashier for the Metal Box while her mother, in order to supplement his income, had done regular shifts at the Co-op. Meals were basic and overcooked; tasteless roasts with soggy veg were what she mainly remembered. Jenny herself had done well at school, got five Os and left at sixteen to become a trainee reporter on the *Western Mail*.

'There's nice,' her aunties had all agreed. 'Who knows, one day we may see your name in the paper.'

And it hadn't been long before they did. From the *Western Mail*, covering weddings and flower shows, she had shot straight up the journalism ladder, moving to Reading and then to Wapping by the age of twenty-one. From the *Hardware Trade Journal,* where she worked for a year, she took a great leap to *Good Housekeeping*, learnt all she could about magazine publishing and landed a much-prized job with Condé Nast. Which was where she encountered Douglas Fairweather who, albeit inadvertently, would be responsible for altering the course of her life.

She moved around and did many jobs until she was given her own column. In addition to writing about food for the glossies, she had a practical cookery slot, and that was when she realised she urgently needed to learn the nuts and bolts. She'd lived alone since leaving home and had grown accustomed to knocking up meals, which she liked to do in the odd hours she wasn't working. Much of the time she ate out, of course, vetting new restaurants all over the south and giving them marks out of ten. Often Douglas was her dining companion. It was how things had really got going between them and provided excellent cover for their alliance.

He was forty-two and her overall boss, publisher of the magazine division, and she'd found his greying good looks an immediate turn-on. To begin with they had very little contact but he, it turned out, had an eye for the girls and Jenny, at twenty-seven, overflowed with pizzazz. She was small and trim with alert brown eyes framed by a silky fringe of dark brown hair. Like a little Welsh mountain pony, he said, and it fitted. They began by having working lunches, sometimes in the company canteen; later – when he wished to be more discreet – in chic and fashionable restaurants. That was how she got the restaurant slot; not only did it fit into his plans but he respected her knowing assessment of food as well as her slick turn of phrase.

Which was all very nice but she wasn't an expert and it soon became clear that, to do the job well, she needed the sort of basic knowledge other food writers had.

'What I'd really like,' she sometimes said, 'is to train full-time as a master chef' – if that would not mean the end of the job and be thus self-defeating.

But it underlined her interest in food so that, rather than taking time off to do courses, she ordered a load of cookery books and began to experiment at home. By then she had bought the Brixton house and the first thing she did before even moving in was have a brand new kitchen installed with all the professional implements she could afford. She cooked for her friends and, occasionally, Douglas, and found the whole process immensely relaxing as well as rather fun. No more overcooked Sunday lunches; since that was the one day she didn't work, she made it a feature of her social life. Eight for lunch became a regular fixture and her friends learnt to cancel existing plans in order to sample and wonder at Jenny's feasts.

'I don't understand how you don't put on weight,' people often remarked.

'It's the quality not the quantity that counts.' So that, even when she was eating alone or came home late and exhausted from work, she would always bother to cook from scratch and ensure that she ate well.

Which was how she now came to be living in Bath, alone, five months pregnant and without a job, with an overdraft and an outsize mortgage, gazing around a dark panelled room that reeked of smoke and stale beer.

It was good old Vanessa who had rushed to her aid, first by helping her out in the bar, then by finding a part-time cook who would also give a hand with the clearing up.

'I had never imagined it would be such a grind.' Not even press nights and last-minute schedules had prepared Jenny for this.

'It won't be so bad once you've had the baby.' Vanessa was expert at such things. And Joyce, the cook, was a practical soul who could be relied on to turn up on time and deal with any random chores that might unexpectedly need doing. They only served the most basic pub food, ploughman's lunches, Scotch eggs and crisps, sandwiches freshly made by Joyce every morning. The pub had a regular clientele, plus a dribble of drinkers who came and went, curious to see the new management and wonder if she was going to make it work. The previous landlords had been a married couple who had taken early retirement in their fifties and moved to Tenerife. Jenny never even got to meet them; the place had been closed for a couple of months.

'Just as well,' said practical Vanessa. It might have dampened Jenny's spirits to be told the true reasons they had quit. And she needed as much buoying up as she could get, faced with the daunting task that lay ahead.

There were six double guest rooms and a couple of singles up the twisting oak-panelled stairs, and the fourteenth-century beams were so low that taller people had to duck their heads. Jenny had her own separate quarters in a private section above the kitchen, without any access from the public rooms. Here she had a fair-sized bedroom, with a smaller one for the baby; a bathroom and a cosy sitting room. Her rooms overlooked the tiny yard where the drayman unloaded the barrels. It was noisy at times but that couldn't be helped. The better rooms, with the picturesque views, had to be reserved for paying guests.

Outside, the garden was spectacular. She would need some help with that too. The lawn stretched smoothly down to the brook where the waterwheel at present stood motionless, though Jenny already had plans to have it repaired. She would have to make certain the baby was safe. All sorts of bad things could happen to a child living in close proximity to water. There was no way the brook could be fenced off; it was part of the charm of the place. And the waterbirds that had made it their home were an equal part of the pub's attraction, in fact had given it its name.

With the season already under way, she had several advance bookings, though luckily no one was due for a couple of weeks. At the end of each day, when she trudged up the stairs, her legs ached and her back was bad from standing so long while carrying the extra weight. At this time of day she felt most lonely, homesick for London and her friends. She would lie and listen to the rushing stream and feel the baby moving inside her and wonder, for the hundredth time, if she had done the right thing.

Toby was born on the first of May, a tiny sprite with thistledown hair and a smile that, even though she knew it was wind, broke her heart. Vanessa, who'd acted as her birthing partner, was there to see him emerge.

'Hey, little fellow,' she said tenderly. Then: 'When are you planning to let your parents know?'

'Don't,' said Jenny, wincing at the thought. Having to face them, especially her dad, was something she hadn't the strength to contemplate now. They had never even known about Douglas. The fact of their daughter with a married man would have been too shameful; they would not have been able to hold up their heads again.

'So how are you going to explain a baby?'

'I have no idea. Don't ask.'

She was, however, now thirty-two, well able to make her own decisions. And sooner or later she would have to face up to them both. As it was, she had scarcely dared mention the pub. Women who even set foot in a bar were, in South Wales, considered loose.

'They'll be thrilled,' said Vanessa, who hadn't met them.

'Once they are over the shock.' Imagine what all the aunties would say when they heard she had been a dirty girl and gone with a man out of wedlock. Well, that was another problem to be shelved until she felt up to it. For the moment all Jenny wanted to do was cuddle her baby and shout for joy at having achieved her most cherished dream on her own.

She was back on her feet much sooner than she'd thought and working behind the bar. Toby became the focus of attention. She would place his pram in a shady spot so that he didn't get too much sun, where the outside drinkers could coo around him and check that he was all right. It was a friendly place, the Coot and Hern. Now that her face had begun to fit, the regulars soon came back.

And when she finally grasped the nettle and invited her parents for the weekend, things went off better than she had ever dared hope. At first, of course, they were taken aback, her father openly outraged. But once they had seen the setup she had created and held their first grandchild in their arms, their indignation was mollified. These were, after all, her mother conceded, far more permissive times. And London was a far cry from the valleys. At least she had now had the sense to get out and settle in elegant Bath.

Vanessa invited them over for tea and Jenny's father was stupefied when he saw the size and splendour of her house. How had she achieved it, he wanted to know. Was there, perhaps, a rich husband in the offing? A working man with basic values, he still couldn't grasp that women could manage on their own.

'He isn't my husband,' said Vanessa gaily. 'And most definitely not rich.' Nor even the father of any of the children, though she didn't intend to go into that. Couldn't have old man Matthias believing his daughter was mixing with such disreputable folk. It was clear enough from the things he said that he still hadn't quite come to terms with her owning a pub.

Vanessa offered them all more tea but a beer was more to his taste.

'*Dew*,' he said in bewilderment. 'I don't know what things are coming to these days. All this fornication. It just isn't right.'

As the months rolled by and the baby grew, Jenny got used to her brand new life. It was stressful, though in a different way from having to meet a regular deadline or keep coming up with bright ideas to help raise the circulation. She didn't miss Douglas, was still far too cross, but occasionally yearned for a man's warm body pressed against hers in the night. There was plenty of scope for flirtation here; she was young and attractive with a sparky manner and the bar was invariably packed with attentive men.

She had two male students doing shift-work at the

bar, plus Joyce in the kitchen preparing the food, and Vanessa often lent a hand when she could get away. At night Jenny went to bed worn out yet feeling at peace with herself. It was hard work, but she had anticipated that, and what she was throwing her energies into represented her financial future and her son's. It was far too soon to be dreaming of commitment but she half kept an eye out, as the customers flowed in, for that extra special someone she still hoped to meet.

When he did arrive, she almost missed him. She was down in the cellar, changing barrels, and only popped back for a second to tell the barman she was going upstairs for a shower. The stranger was standing alone at the bar, gazing around with appreciation, and when she entered he turned and smiled and something inside Jenny knew. He was tall with dark hair lightly touched with grey and the kindest, bluest eyes that drew her straight in.

'Nice place you've got here,' he said with approval. 'Mind if I look round?'

Jenny, aware of her scruffy appearance, told him to make himself at home. In the meantime the barman would fetch him a drink. He picked a spider's web out of her hair and wiped a smudge from her nose.

'A working landlady. I like that,' he said. Then casually strolled through the open door and out into the garden.

Instead of just showering and changing her shirt, she slapped on makeup and brushed her hair, then sprayed herself liberally with fragrance. Downstairs she found him back in the bar, chatting chummily with the barman and teaching him to mix a dry martini.

'The merest hint of vermouth,' he was saying. 'With a twist of lime, if you have one.'

'Transformed,' he said when Jenny appeared, looking her up and down with approval. 'Have you the time to join me in a drink?'

It was almost seven and the end of a long day. He had been on the road since mid-afternoon and needed a break and a couple of drinks before he headed on. She led him to a corner table and the barman carried their drinks across. It was Thursday night, which was usually quiet. Even Toby, for once, was already asleep.

He asked her questions about the pub and said he occasionally came this way. In future, he promised to make it a regular pit-stop.

'Have you thought of serving proper meals?' he asked. 'In a place like this, on the outskirts of Bath, there's no way you wouldn't clean up.'

Jenny explained she was new to the game, was taking things cautiously, stage by stage. At present her hands were full with the carriage trade. The stranger appeared to be thinking hard; she was not even sure he was listening.

'You would need to hire a first-rate chef, the main ingredient of that sort of venture. But you have the premises and, certainly, the location.'

Jenny's heart was beating faster; she had never been one to resist a challenge and the man's engrossed attention flattered her. She liked his style and the way he looked, as well as his obvious expertise. After a while she had to get on; it was her turn to take her place at the bar and he, having seen the time, said he must be off.

'I'll be back again very soon,' he said. 'Meanwhile, think about my suggestion. I really think you could have a money-spinner here.'

'Do you have a card?' She liked the idea and was fired with a new ambition. After all the restaurants she had written up, there was little about the business she didn't know, at least in theory.

'Sorry,' he said, patting his pockets. 'I don't seem to have any on me today. But the name, for future reference, is Clive Barclay.'

She woke very early and lay there, content, thinking about the attractive stranger. Something about him, not just his looks, had touched her profoundly. Then Toby stirred and began to wail so she dragged herself wearily out of bed and went to sort him out. Another gruelling day. But her heart was light as she set about her chores and she couldn't stop thinking about the man, with his easy charm and warm, expressive eyes.

As she changed the barrels and drained the pipes, then swept the ashes from the empty grate, she found herself giving serious thought to his suggestion. It did make sense though would mean more work and, almost certainly, huge financial investment. She knew enough from her magazine days not to underestimate the potential pitfalls. First she would need a much larger kitchen, updated to meet the stringent regulations imposed by the EU. Luckily, she had the space and could glass in part of the terrace at the side so that diners could sit overlooking the brook, next to the waterwheel. Once she got the latter working again, it would make a truly magical spot; there surely wouldn't be any shortage of patrons. But where she would find the finance, she had no idea. She was stretched, as it was, with existing costs and not yet breaking even. Unless she took over the cooking herself and brought in someone to supervise the bar.

Clive had certainly got her thinking and she started thumbing through catering magazines, seeking tips as to how to make things work. The city of Bath was awash with fine restaurants, all of them doing a roaring trade yet few with the picturesque setting that she could provide. She longed to talk it over with him, found herself constantly watching the door, wondering how often he made the journey from London. He also started appearing in her dreams; she simply couldn't get him out of her mind. The days and then the weeks went by and still there was no sign of him. Jenny started to curse herself for having been taken in.

'Men, they're all the same,' she said. 'I can't believe I was such a fool as to take him at his word.'

And then one day, perhaps three weeks later, she looked up from pulling a pint and there he was. Politely waiting to catch her eye with the same incandescent smile.

'Hi!' she said, more friendly than she should be,

ducking behind the barman to serve him herself. She mixed him a very dry martini and was pleased when he said it was perfect.

'You certainly know your stuff,' he said. 'Where did you learn to mix cocktails?'

'Well, not where I grew up,' she said. 'You can take my word for that.'

He asked if she'd given any thought to what he'd said and she told him she'd like to discuss it further, if he had the time and could stick around for a while. She was pleased when he said he would stay overnight. He'd been driving all day and was ready for a break now. Jenny was thrilled but tried hard not to show it. He was too attractive not to be married and nothing would ever induce her to go there again.

At closing time they took their drinks upstairs to Jenny's cosy sitting room and talked long after the rest of the staff had gone home. His take on what she could do with the place was well informed and reasonable. And would not necessarily need a prohibitive investment.

'What exactly is it you do?' she asked, not wishing to sound intrusive.

'I travel for a wallpaper firm. Very upmarket. Osborne and Cole. I'm sure you know them by name.'

She didn't; design was not her thing. The finishing touches to the visitors' rooms were Vanessa's. Her own expertise lay strictly in the kitchen, though she planned to learn more about bankrolling. Clive promised to rough out a business plan for discussion next time they met.

Toby woke a couple of times and called out to Mummy for a comforting hug. Clive insisted on holding him too and stroked his hair until he nodded off.

'Do you have children of your own?' asked Jenny, mightily impressed yet also apprehensive of his answer.

'Sadly not,' he said with a shrug. 'I guess I just haven't met the right woman yet.'

The second he left, Jenny called Vanessa. He'd be coming back, he hoped, in a couple of weeks.

'I can't believe he's not married,' she shrieked. 'And he's really great with Toby.'

'Watch out,' said Vanessa, pleased for her friend yet wary where men were concerned. 'You still know hardly anything about him.'

'Enough,' said Jenny with confidence. He really seemed committed to helping her out. 'I just can't quite believe that it's true. After all the shit I've been through, at last I appear to have met a decent man.'

15

Frankie was hauled before the beak and severely reprimanded. They wanted to know her involvement in the fire. They asked why she'd tried to run away and, even more to the point, what had happened to Chad. Since she didn't know the answer to that, she felt it best to stay silent. She couldn't believe he had gone without her after all the promises he had made; how he'd vowed that he would kill himself if obliged to remain there on his own.

The fire brigade, aided by the rain, had finally managed to douse the flames and would soon be able to pick through the embers and establish the cause of the fire. A band of gypsy travellers had been reported in the neighbourhood. The thinking was that they'd started the fire in order to do some petty looting. Whatever the facts, they had now moved on and seemed to be no longer germane to the current investigation.

Frankie remained the one under pressure; they wouldn't leave her alone. Or believe that Chad could have got away without her being involved. Everyone knew how close they had been, they were hardly ever apart.

'You will do yourself no favours,' said the beak, 'if you cover up for your boyfriend. Your record is good. In the normal way we would shortly be discharging you. But,' she added with eyes of flint, 'if it should transpire that you helped him escape, it will go against you in court.'

Frankie, however, remained silent. There wasn't anything she could say that could possibly make any difference at this stage.

In the course of the investigation, the grounds were searched and both their rucksacks found. Still underneath the tennis nets; Frankie was suddenly alarmed. Again she was summoned before the beak and bombarded with further questions. A lot less confident, she still said nothing, praying only that he was safe. He must have had to make a quick exit and would return later to fetch her.

At lunchtime, though, there was a commotion outside as a fleet of squad cars arrived. Everyone crowded to the windows to watch as a bunch of stony-faced policemen emerged and banged on the main door. They were ushered inside and the door was closed. Frankie's heart was beating fast. The good thing was there had been no sign of Chad.

It didn't take long for the rumour to spread. A body had been found among the ashes, too charred for instant identification. They would have to wait for the inquest. When they summoned Frankie and confirmed it was true, her heart stopped dead and she fainted. And when she'd recovered enough to talk and they plied her more kindly with cups of tea, she faced the policemen defiantly and confessed.

'I did it,' she said. 'I set the fire. He must have somehow got trapped inside. It is all my fault. Arrest me, please. I am guilty of his murder.'

If Chad were dead, there was nothing to live for. She might as well carry the can.

16

The best thing about Pippa's shop was its handy location. A stone's throw away from Brompton Cross, within walking distance of Peter Jones and only twenty minutes by car from Barnes. Each morning, when he wasn't away, they would load the baby-seats into the car and Charles would drop them all off at the shop on his way through to Walton Street. The days when he was away on business, Pippa would use her own car. Considering the vast upheaval in her life, she had taken to marriage unexpectedly well, enjoying the cosseting she received from her husband. There were things to be said for an older man. He lacked the unthinking boorishness of some of her own generation.

They had made it to the altar just in time; two weeks later the twins, Jack and Tom, had arrived. Identical boys, with their father's looks, they were miniature versions of Charles's first son, Aidan. Aidan, now twenty-one and at Oxford, was already acting the doting half-brother and would drop in to see them when he came into town, staying at his father's

Knightsbridge flat. Cassie had allowed Charles to keep the flat; she no longer had any interest, she said, in making excursions to London. Since the divorce, she had been in Venice which made the situation easier all round.

Pippa found it decidedly odd having a stepson only six years younger than herself, as tall and strikingly handsome as his dad.

'You ought to have gone for the younger model,' her mother had caustically pointed out. He would probably prove, in the long run, a sounder investment. But the opulence of Pippa's new lifestyle could not be denied. She no longer worked because she had to but simply because she refused to give up. The shop was hers and doing well, though Charles now acted as co-director and kept an eye on the financial side of things. Their allied professions worked neatly in tandem. He, the distinguished interior designer, used her shop as one of his main suppliers.

The mail order business, which was his idea too, was also up and running and Pippa had hired a couple of part-time helpers. Every morning, when she got to work, she would carry in the babies, still in their car-seats, and plonk them into the playpen she kept in the back. They were so sweet-natured they were very little trouble and hardly made any noise at all unless they were hungry or wet. If she had to go out, she would leave them with her mother who, handily, lived in Richmond, within easy reach. They were so much alike, she colour-coded their clothes as even she, at times, couldn't tell them apart.

The shop was a cornucopia of silks, brocades and other fine fabrics where customers came to browse and fulfil their dreams. Pippa was grateful to her mother for making her do an apprenticeship after she had finished at the Courtauld. She had learnt to paint and grout and tile as well as do basic carpentry but her leaning had always been more towards fabrics, a relic from the days when she'd made her own clothes.

At night she would drive the babies home or wait for Charles to pick them up and take them back to the house in Barnes, now a veritable showplace. As well as Pont Street, which he kept for entertaining, Charles would sometimes bring clients to the house. They had knocked down walls and done major reconstruction work and the handsome turn-of-the-century villa had properly come into its own. She had sold the flat in Elm Park Gardens and reinvested the money in the shop. In their separate fields they were both doing well and Charles's lifestyle, since leaving Cassie, had not visibly altered very much.

The difference was he no longer went to Cornwall, though he still spent much of his time away, visiting his clients.

'If I'd had a twin, she could have been called Aïda.' Aidan was lounging in a basketwork chair, watching the babies being bathed.

'Lucky for her, then, that you didn't.' Pippa, crouched beside the tub, was carefully sponging their hair. She had no idea where the twin gene had come from; there were none she knew of in her own family tree and Charles had always been vague about his background. There was no denying Aidan's provenance, though; he was unmistakably a chip off the old block. They were like a set of Russian dolls, a big one and two identical miniatures. The apple, as the saying goes, never falls far from the tree.

Aidan was almost the age Charles had been when he swept Cassandra off her feet. Occasionally Pippa secretly regretted that she hadn't known him then. Aidan's springy curls were coal-black while his father's hair was now frosted with grey. But their eyes remained identical, cornflower blue, intense and unnervingly bright. And they shared the same dazzling smile and larkish sense of fun. She bet he set hearts fluttering back in Oxford.

'What do you plan to do when you come down? Have you made any decisions?' Aidan was bright and a competent student though he never appeared to do much work. He seemed to spend most of his time away from the college.

'Travel,' he said. 'For at least a year. I intend to do some serious living before I have to join the daily grind.'

'Do you still have your mind set on becoming a lawyer?' A barrister might be just his thing; he would certainly look very dashing in wig and gown.

'Whatever enables me to get rich quick.' Again, that bewitching smile. 'Preferably with the least amount of effort. Only a mug works hard these days. There are easier ways of making a lot of money.' He rose and stretched then kissed the boys and said he should make a move. He was going into Soho to meet a friend.

'Male or female?'

'What do you think?' He winked and was gone, leaving Pippa feeling frumpy and, for some obscure reason, slightly put out.

Charles hardly ever mentioned Cassie though Pippa was always angling to know more about her. She was fascinated by the older woman, had always admired her looks and style and still felt guilty at having destroyed her marriage. The irony was, it had not been intended; she had entered into an adulterous fling, never expecting it to be anything more. She'd been young and pretty and utterly thoughtless, snared by Charles's roving eye, and had gone along with it just for a bit of fun. That and the fact that she fancied him rotten and liked the kudos that knowing him brought to her own sky-rocketing career.

She was just starting out when they'd first met and he'd swept her off her feet with his glamour and charm. She'd given him a lot of her time because she found him irresistible and didn't want him to leave. The next night he had taken her out to dinner.

'You know,' he'd said as they'd dined at Aubergine, 'you should think about making a speciality of providing rare and unusual fabrics to rich and discerning clients.'

Pippa had stared at him in surprise; she was only temping at Liberty's while she looked for something permanent that really turned her on.

'You mean like the Designer's Guild?' She was passionate about the King's Road shop and always popped in when passing. Fabrics, paint and fantastic wallpaper; how clever he was to know so precisely where her true interests lay.

'Something like that.' He grinned at her expression, seeing he'd scored a direct hit. 'Only maybe restrict it to fabrics alone. Sometimes the boutique approach works better.'

'I don't think I could do that,' she said. She earned very little and had only recently finished her stint as a decorator's gofer.

'With a little help you might be surprised. Even Tricia Guild had to start at the bottom.'

Pippa sat and thought about it, stunned but excited too. This gorgeous stranger who had swept into her life was putting all sorts of ideas in her head she would never have dared to dream up on her own. She wondered what her mother would say and where she could possibly raise the finance. Her father had left them a long time ago so her mother was a single working parent.

'Think about it and we'll talk again.' He paid the bill and then walked her home. The next night he took her straight to bed where they had the most amazing sex. Cassie's existence had not been mentioned and would not be for a matter of weeks. But Pippa was level-headed enough to assume that there must be a wife in the background. And, at twenty-two, she had far too much ahead even to think about settling down at this stage.

*　　*　　*

The first time Pippa set eyes on Cassie was two years into the affair. The shop was already up and running; Charles had been as good as his word and even come through with a hefty financial loan. It was Friday lunchtime and business was slow so she'd turned the sign on the door to Closed and popped off to Knightsbridge to have her streaks redone. The gorgeous Emilion was, as usual, running late so she sat in the corner and flicked through *Hello!* while he finished perfecting the style of his current client. Having quickly exhausted the vapid magazine, Pippa closed it and watched the proceedings, smiling at her stylist's antics as he skipped around with a mirror to display the back of her head to the woman seated in his chair. She was slim and serene with quite beautiful hair, now softly swept into an elegant pleat which drew attention to her fine-boned face. She nodded and smiled and thanked him profusely and, when she left, tipped him substantially.

'Thanks, Mrs Buchanan. Have a safe journey home. I hope we'll see you again before too long.'

The name attracted Pippa's attention so she watched more curiously as the woman put on her coat. She was tall, about five foot ten, Pippa guessed, with thoughtful eyes and a shyish smile as Emilion rushed ahead and opened the door.

'Who was that?' asked Pippa, with interest, as she took her place in the chair. The face, she thought, seemed faintly familiar. Perhaps she was an actress or something. She certainly had the bone structure and the poise.

'Mrs Charles Buchanan,' said Emilion, running expert fingers through Pippa's hair. 'She lives in Cornwall but comes here to get her roots done. I've been doing her hair for years. Nice lady. Loads of class, if you know what I mean. Her husband's a well-known interior designer. You may have heard the name.'

Small world, thought Pippa, giving nothing away. She was slightly shaken by the encounter and would have to give it some thought. It was one thing to know that her lover was married, another to actually see the wife. Who looked, as Emilion had said, like a lady, classy, well dressed and refined.

She decided not to mention to Charles that she'd inadvertently seen his wife. He might not be happy with the thought that their paths could so easily cross. But her curiosity had been aroused and now she wanted to know a lot more. Charles rarely spoke of his family, seemed to think it was not the done thing, so the knowledge she had was still sketchy in the extreme. She did know Cassie lived mainly in Cornwall, in the house she'd shared with her daughters and previous husband. And came to London less and less, which was how Charles managed to spend so much time with Pippa. In the old days he'd gone home every Thursday but had started to find the driving too much so now he either flew or went less often, breaking his journey on the way. He talked, with obvious pride, of his son and the two step-daughters he also considered his. But of Cassie, his wife for the past nineteen years, he said nothing.

*   *   *

The next time she saw her was two years later when she suddenly walked into the shop. Pippa, in the stockroom at the time, heard the clang of the bell and went rushing out, only to stop in her tracks when she saw who was standing there. Cassie, elegant in well-cut tweed, slightly preoccupied and clutching an envelope.

'Miss Harvey?' she asked and, when Pippa nodded, relaxed into a lovely smile. 'Oh, I'm so glad. My husband sent me. He suggests you're the person to help me with a problem.'

When her heart stopped racing, Pippa started to listen and the tension slowly flowed out of her when she heard what Cassie wanted.

'I am doing up our London pied-à-terre and need some fabrics to go with these.' She proffered samples of wallpaper and paint. 'For the main reception rooms.'

'Right,' said Pippa, limp with relief. She could tell that Cassie suspected nothing. 'If you'd care to come into the stockroom, I am sure we can find you something that will suit.'

As she pulled down rolls and brought out samples, it all came flooding back. An action replay of that very first meeting with Charles. Cassie now was beaming broadly, revealing her striking good looks. Her dove-grey blouse matched her eyes exactly; she was clearly a woman of exquisite taste.

'Bless you, you angel. He said you worked miracles. Another horrible chore I can strike off my list.' She left the shop with laden arms but paused when she reached the door. 'Perhaps you'll come over for cocktails one evening. I would love to show you the revamped flat. I'll get my husband to set something up very soon.'

'Why not?' said Charles with his customary calm, apparently unfazed by his wife's suggestion. 'I'd quite like to show you the flat myself. I think you'll agree she has done a brilliant job.'

There were times when Pippa just didn't get him, he sailed so close to the wind. How could he do this, to either of them? Having talked with Cassie and liked her a lot, she now felt an absolute bitch. But Charles, undeterred, took it all in his stride, flicked through his diary and suggested a day, then pencilled it in and told her he'd check it out.

'Wait till you see how the curtains look,' he said. 'I don't think you'll be disappointed.'

So Pippa found herself, a few weeks later, ringing the bell of the Pont Street flat and being admitted by a smiling maid in black. Having left her coat, she was shown into the drawing room where both the Buchanans were entertaining a group of assorted friends.

'Miss Harvey!' said Cassie, advancing to greet her.

'Please call me Pippa,' Pippa said.

'Pippa,' said Cassie, 'I'm so glad you came. Grab a drink and let me show you around.'

The flat, as Pippa had rather expected, was done in the most impeccable taste, understated like Cassie herself, but with a keen eye for detail. There were bowls of hydrangeas, brought up from Cornwall, which subtly picked out the colours of the newly made drapes. The bedroom was plain, pale wood and white linen, with piles of books on the bedside tables and fluffy white towels in the en suite bathroom, which smelt very faintly of grapefruit.

'I love it,' said Pippa, incredibly moved and increasingly feeling a duplicitous interloper.

'Thank you,' said Cassie. 'Your praise is praise indeed. I feel very guilty that I'm hardly ever here and leave my poor husband too much on his own, having to fend for himself.'

Does she know? thought Pippa but was certain she did not. Cassandra Buchanan was a very nice woman, with thoughts on too high a plane to stoop that low. Pippa felt rather grubby at being here at all and wondered if the burning letter A was evident on her forehead. She lingered behind to freshen up while Cassie returned to her guests, and wondered how long would be appropriate to stay. If she made her exit too soon it might be noticed.

She needn't have worried; on rejoining the group, she found that the focus of attention had swung to the charismatic son, who had only just arrived. Aidan, nineteen, had dropped in on a whim, planning to crash in his parents' flat, unaware that they were entertaining. From the guilty flush on his handsome face, Pippa could see that in some way he'd been caught out. Somewhere, probably in a nearby bar, an innocent girl was doubtless waiting while Aidan checked to see if the coast was clear. Or else he had other plans for the night and hadn't selected the victim yet. He was so much like the old man, it made Pippa smile.

But she was in no position to smirk. She felt totally treacherous at being there at all, so made her farewells as soon as she could and slipped off into the night.

When Charles came home he seemed preoccupied; Pippa put it down to overwork.

'I am sorry, my dear,' he said, after a while. 'But I have to go back to Bristol again. One of my clients there wants a consultation.'

'This weekend?' She'd been hoping to relax: lunch at Hurlingham, a game of tennis, and a video for after the twins were safely in bed.

''Fraid so,' he said. 'It's very short notice but the contract should be worth a great deal of dosh.'

In the old days Pippa would have wanted to go too, might well have proved an asset to him, but the boys had drained all her energy away. She would ask her mother to keep her company and perhaps fit in a couple of early nights.

'When do you think you'll be back?' she asked.

'Sunday morning should do it,' he said. 'They can't expect me to dance to their tune all weekend.'

'I tell you quite frankly,' said Pippa's mother, 'I never thought you'd hang on to him. No disrespect, but he does have a roving eye.'

'Had,' said Pippa, correcting her. 'These days he's got far too much on his plate ever to find the time to play around.'

'Well, I'll hand it to him, he's certainly done you proud.'

They were settled in the sunny breakfast room, the babies playing at their feet. The white-painted walls had been picked out in lemon, which enhanced the sunlight and brightened the whole place up. In its former existence it had been panelled and fusty, part of the scullery and pantry. It was amazing to see what could be achieved with a little imagination and adjustment. Plus, of course, a sufficient injection of cash.

Pippa, looking no more than fifteen in her sprigged cotton robe with her hair unbrushed, was sipping mint tea and leafing through the papers. Her mother, spellbound by the beautiful twins, had transmogrified from a bitter divorcee into an infatuated granny. Tom – or was it Jack, she was never sure – was reaching out with one tiny hand towards the pile of bright building blocks she had brought as her latest gift. He crawled towards them, happily gurgling, then swiftly demolished the precarious structure with one sweeping wave of his hand. Doting granny cried out in delight, then carefully reconstructed the pile and sat back, enchanted, to see if he'd do it again. Wham – a bull's eye. 'You know something,' she said. 'I think perhaps Tom is left-handed.'

'Jack,' said Pippa, barely glancing up, involved with the Sunday papers. Her mother was always noticing things about the twins. But she knew she was lucky to have her around, available at the shortest notice, willing to play and be bored and just love them to bits.

'In which case,' said her mother, rebuilding again, 'they are very probably mirror twins. Genetically identical but a mirror of each other.'

'Really?' said Pippa, still only half listening, deep in the details of the latest football scandal, glad to have someone to share the burden and let her relax for a change.

'Yes,' said her mother, watching them both now, two gorgeous babies with coal-black hair that she now observed swirled softly in opposite directions. 'So is Jack right-handed?'

'Tom,' said Pippa. And then, growing aware of her mother's impatience, 'I can't say I've ever noticed. Does it matter?'

'Of course not, my precious,' crooned her mother to the baby, picking up a struggling Jack who was still fixated on the bricks. She nuzzled her face against his neck but he arched his back and drummed his tiny heels until she was forced to put him back on the rug. She thought, though did not say it aloud, that he seemed not to like too much physical contact, unusual in a baby so young and not at all like his brother.

So she moved to Tom who cooed in delight and held out his arms to be lifted.

'Who's my big boy then,' she said in delight. Wham went the blocks over the floor as Jack demolished them again.

Somewhere offstage a door clicked shut and Charles strode into the room. In his weekend clothes, he looked sporty and fit, the great charmer her daughter had married whom, privately, she still didn't trust at all.

He stood in the doorway, beaming down at them all, then crossed to give his wife a peck.

'What a lovely tranquil domestic scene after the weekend I have had.' It was heading towards the cocktail hour; the sun would soon be over the yardarm. Time for a gin and tonic.

Pippa, laying her paper down, rose and gave him a hug. He smelt of clean linen and cologne and his hair was immaculately cut.

'Have you had breakfast?'

'Two hours ago. I wanted to get back here in time for lunch.'

With her arms round him, she leaned against his chest and her mother was bound to admit that they made a striking couple. His eyes were tender as he looked at his small sons and her secret reservations ebbed away. Perhaps, after all, it would work out. She fervently prayed that it might.

17

The hearing was brief and to the point. 'Francesca Wilde,' said the presiding judge. 'You are hereby accused of the manslaughter of Chad Barnaby.'

Since she had already confessed and taken full blame for starting the fire, the accident that had caused Chad's death was due entirely to her, which she didn't dispute. He, as far as the inquiry went, had been asleep in the hostel.

'Murder,' she muttered in silent frenzy but nobody was listening. The evidence was conclusive; the case was wound up. Since Frankie had just passed her eighteenth birthday, she was sentenced to eight years in jail. The inquest, which she had asked to attend, had been equally succinct. A heavy door in the blazing building had fallen, pinning the victim to the floor. There was no way he could possibly have survived. Commiserations were offered to Frankie after which she was formally arrested.

Her mother had asked to attend the hearing but Frankie insisted it should not be allowed; she still had her civil rights. From this point on, she would be on her own and that was how it would stay. All she could wish for now was an early death.

'Don't be too hard on yourself,' said the judge. 'You have done great wrong but are still little more than a child. Playing with fire does not make you bad. Prison will teach you many lessons from which I hope you will learn.'

'Chad Barnaby's death was entirely my fault,' said Frankie, stubbornly resisting help. 'I neither want nor deserve any kind of reprieve.'

She was sent to a prison on the Isle of Man where she would stay for the whole eight years unless she was granted remission for good behaviour. She no longer cared where she was or for how long; her life was effectively over. She still had Chad's picture in her locket but found it too painful to look at now. But she thought about him all the time, still unable to come to terms with the fact that he was dead.

Before leaving Middlesbrough to start her sentence, she was allowed to visit his grave, a patch of dug earth in the prison yard, with only a wooden marker on it, bearing his ID number but not his name. A pauper's grave for an unwanted foundling. His death ironically mirrored his inauspicious start.

The other prisoners were a varied bunch, some old lags whom she learnt to keep clear of, plus a bunch of misfits, in mainly for drug-related crimes. Sunk as she was in deep desolation, she didn't even look for a kindred spirit but kept herself to herself as much as she could. Word went round that her man had died so they mainly left her alone.

Around that time Frankie first met Magda who was to have such a lasting effect on her life. A social worker with a psychology degree, the older woman was on the prison staff to liaise with and counsel prisoners with emotional problems. Against Frankie's will, Magda arranged sessions in a vain attempt to get her to talk and unburden herself of her grief. Magda had read the case notes and sympathised.

'You must try to come to terms with it. It wasn't your fault, just an accident.' She hadn't even been there when the fire broke out.

'It was my fault,' said Frankie stubbornly. 'I had done it before and told him how. If it weren't for that, he would still be alive. In effect, therefore, I killed him.'

'Only by default,' said Magda. 'You must stop beating up on yourself.'

But Frankie stubbornly closed her ears, turned her face to the wall and wanted to die.

Only weeks into her sentence, Frankie heard of another death. The colonel, her stepfather, out with the guns, had been involved in a fatal shooting. No one had actually witnessed what happened; she was only told he was dead. Her mother was asking for Frankie's release to be at the funeral. The authorities were prepared to allow it but Frankie flatly refused to go.

'You ought to be there to comfort your mother,' said Magda, 'at the very least.'

'I hated him,' said Frankie, 'and am glad he is dead.'

'But he was your mother's husband.'

'I don't care.'

She was clearly more damaged than Magda had thought. She made it her top priority to help to sort her out.

18

Cristina first burst upon a startled fashion world at the tender age of sixteen. Her father, a mixed blood itinerant worker, who had raised eleven children in the Amazon basin, left them all to fend for themselves and she, without any contest, was the one who came out on top of the pile. At thirteen she was living off the streets in a steamy quarter of the Rio slums when a scout for an international model agency spotted her scavenging in rubbish bins and, struck by the child's quite astonishing beauty, signed her up on the spot. Bewildered and not quite comprehending, she went along with what he said and, in only a matter of months, advanced from dire poverty to being the latest fashion find. The agency, World Models, seeing her potential, invested shrewdly by sending her to school. They predicted that, once she was properly trained, her face would become internationally known. Even then they were the front-runners in the field; their judgement was rarely proved wrong.

She had no need of parental approval, had lost all contact with them when they threw her out. In later years she had little recall of how she had managed to survive on her own, only that, occasionally for weeks at a time, she'd had almost nothing to eat. Now, while they groomed her at model school, they stuck her in a hostel with a bunch of other hopefuls, overseen by a draconian older woman who taught them manners and stopped them stepping out of line. It was, Cristina supposed, looking back, her version of being at boarding school. She learnt about hygiene and diet and nutrition, to handle a knife and fork, to improve her posture by standing up straight, and basic yoga. They also gave her makeup lessons and stopped her chewing her cuticles. Despite her wild and exotic beauty, she was still just a child who had grown up rough, whose only preparation for life was what she picked up on the streets. They paid her peanuts but provided all her meals as well as somewhere safe and warm to sleep. After the years of fending for herself, the scratchy sheets and basic amenities seemed to her the utmost luxury.

Once a year there was a fashion show, plus the occasional newspaper ad, for which they taught her to pose and do runway and stand still for endless interminable hours while the photographers did their work. She came out well: magnificent cheekbones, provocative eyes and skin like caramel velvet. Her body, though still skinny and under-developed, already showed promise of what was to come. Apart from that, there was little to do, except for some rudimentary education, so Cristina, boiling with impatience, started to look around. And quickly found, in

120

a tobacco kiosk, the answer to her terminal boredom: an ad for a life-class model, urgently required.

She got the job (well, of course she did) and started spending her Wednesday evenings posing nude for a motley group of lecherous, untalented men. But this exposure was the making of her; she had no problems with stripping off. And the more they ogled, the more she preened, their open-mouthed lust defining the person she was. She told the school she was taking tango lessons and no one thought or cared enough to check. It was all part of her learning curve, flaunting her naked body for easy cash.

One thing rapidly led to another and Cristina grew more ambitious; more ambitious and also much more venal. What she'd achieved by this stage of her development she had done entirely by herself. She was greedy now for all she could grab from life. The art class was one thing but the men were old and the pittance they paid her not worth the strain of having to hold one position for such a long time. She looked around and found another ad, this time for a dancer in a strip club.

The dancing was easy once she'd mastered the rhythm, a slow gyration to a pounding beat without ever moving from the spot. All she wore was a tasselled G-string beneath which men often stuck money bills (though forbidden by law from actually touching her flesh). Cristina revelled in their admiration as she writhed and cavorted beneath a spotlight, and had no shortage of hangers-on, each one jostling for a chance

121

to walk her home. At first she didn't give in to this, since the school locked its doors at eleven p.m., until it dawned that their sole concern was that she should be there in time for early classes. So she took her pick of the drooling punters, and found it a nice little earner on the side.

They weren't all disgusting, mainly out-of-town businessmen, lonely, bored and invariably vapid, simply in search of something to brighten their nights. Cristina, discovering a natural talent, preferred the physical side of things to the tedious hours she spent practising for the catwalk. The men were grateful and often brought her gifts and made her feel like the star she wanted to be. Her savings grew and she bought nicer clothes so that some of them even took her out on the town, where she quickly learnt about menus and fancy food. Bit by bit her confidence grew and with it a streak of pure avarice, destined to stay with her for the rest of her life.

The movie approach came out of this sideline and Cristina was far too flattered to turn it down. A fat man with a large cigar slipped her his card as he left the club, muttering something about a screen test. Not mentioning it to the agency, with which she had signed an exclusive contract, she fixed a date for a free after-noon and turned up, for once on time, at a seedy-looking warehouse. All the windows were boarded up and she found herself in a large bare room with a bed in the middle of a white-painted stage, covered with synthetic fur. A man in an eyeshade, clearly the director, was giving instructions to the camera crew while a handful of others just stood around and watched. The lights were so bright, she could make little out and shielded her eyes as the director called her over and introduced her to the man who would act as her co-star. He was powerfully muscled and wearing just tight jeans; she could hardly keep her eyes from his bulging crotch.

Even her antics in the sleazy club had not prepared her for this. She was asked to strip while they all looked on and then to revolve while they studied her from every angle. Cristina, hearing their murmurs of approval, proudly strutted as though on the catwalk, regarding them haughtily down her imperious nose. Someone handed her a pair of spike-heeled boots and asked her to slip them on, then bestraddle the man who was now on the bed, in the process of peeling off his jeans.

'Action!' called the director and the cameras rolled.

There was neither script nor dialogue; all she did for the next forty minutes was obey the barked-out instructions from the director. Unspeakable things were done to her while the lights blazed down and the crew looked on and the man on the bed, who was hung like a bull, invaded her body with such extreme force that she thought he might split her in half. It was violent and painful yet also exciting and Cristina, panting and slicked with sweat, was disappointed when the director at last called out: 'Cut!'

A movie star, that was what she was going to be. They rinsed her down and touched up her makeup then asked her to go through the whole performance again.

'Good,' said the director, when the cameras finally stopped rolling and the crew began packing up. 'You're an absolute natural. We'll be using you again. Leave a contact number when you go and please close the door behind you.'

They did ask her back and she did it all again, though this time with a couple of extra leading men. A career as a skin-flick actress quite appealed to her, as long as they didn't use her name. And there was no telling where it might all lead; there were Hollywood stars, she had read, who had started from less. But, as it so happened, her luck was on the turn. The agency told her they had found her an opening to model clothes for a mail order catalogue. Not especially well paid at this stage but steady work that would mean wide exposure that could, in the long run, lead to better things. Cristina would have liked to think it through but the catalogue needed a speedy reply. Or so the agency said. So she turned her back on her movie career, moved out of her lodgings and into a hotel in a slightly more salubrious area of town. She had made no friends so had none to leave. Her modelling career was about to take off and she still wasn't quite seventeen.

The work was easy, though hardly inspiring, and Cristina hated the clothes. But she liked the money, which bought independence: the luxury of finally having her own place with a door she could lock behind her when she went out. Or, indeed, when she stayed at home. Something that, other than a cardboard box in a smelly doorway beneath a railway arch, she had never in her life experienced before. The hours were regular, nine till four, but having to stand and keep changing her clothes was far more tiring than she had ever expected. Also she found the arc lights draining; by the time they broke for lunch she was often a wreck. The building had its own canteen but Cristina rarely went up there. Instead she would hang around in the studio, smoking and watching the photographer's assistants rearranging the props. The minute the boss had left the room, illicit bottles would materialise and Cristina would graciously join the boys in a tot, until one day the boss caught them at it and warned her that it would ruin her complexion, her figure, her liver and, unless she was lucky, her life. She pouted and sulked; she answered to no one and would bloody well do as she liked, it was only a job. But when her tantrum made no visible impact and she felt his indifference to her charms, mortified, and secretly piqued, she stopped. But it never ceased to rankle.

The work might be tedious and grindingly dull but when she saw the results, she was staggered. The man was truly a creative genius who could take the most mundane of garments and, with his magic camera, transform them from high street tat to international couture.

'It's all to do with the lighting,' they explained. 'And the love affair he has with the lens. He lives and breathes photography and it shows.'

Jorg Schreiber, a German, was in his mid-thirties and already quite a star of the fashion world. He was here, in Rio, on retainer to *Vogue* and doing a bit of catalogue work on the side. He was so preoccupied with his craft that he could go whole mornings with scarcely a word, just curt instructions for her to alter her pose. The results, however, were more than worth it. With her nostrils flaring like an Arab stallion's and tossing back her great mane of hair, she strutted and posed like the best of them on the catwalk. He wore black leather and a single gold earring and often went days on end without bothering to shave. Cristina, who was still very much a child, had never met anyone like him. She was awestruck right from the moment they met because of his prodigious talent.

He might not be turned on by her but his camera certainly loved her and when he studied the roughs he was obviously pleased. He asked if she'd do a private session to add to his fashion portfolio and Cristina, thrilled, was only too pleased to oblige. She thought that, apart from anything else, it might help to bring them closer together. She was used to men coming on to her, could not understand why Jorg still kept his distance.

'Sweetheart, you don't stand a snowball's chance in hell,' said one of the cheeky (now snotty) assistants, bored with her attitude. 'Can't you see that he bats for the other side?'

But Cristina, having no idea what he meant, simply turned her back.

* * *

Dreams, as Cristina was soon to discover, occasionally do come true. World Models, impressed by his skill and reputation, permitted Jorg to sign her up so that, shortly after, she flew with him to New York. Since he was already retained by *Vogue*, there seemed no shortage of fashion assignments and *Harper's Bazaar* were also keen to get in on the act. 'The face of the future,' the headlines proclaimed so that very soon, wherever she looked, Cristina saw herself on buses and hoardings. She looked phenomenal in the latest fashions, with her dusky skin, her sultry smile, her sinuous figure, which had now developed curves, and the scornful light in her eyes. There was nothing and no one she couldn't now afford. Except, as she was yet to find out, the one thing she truly desired.

Jorg's studio, on the Upper West Side, was part of his penthouse apartment, high up and with sweeping views across Central Park. Cristina assumed she would stay there too, as there was bags of space and he lived alone, but, without attempting an explanation, he booked her into the Sherry-Netherland Hotel. Only a cab-ride away, he told her, unless she felt like stretching her legs. Cristina, mortified, was very angry. New York was even more dangerous than Rio, which at least she knew and where she spoke the language. He had dared uproot her and bring her here, yet remained indifferent to her happiness or comfort, leaving her alone most nights to sulk in her hotel room. Movies and room service were all very well, especially in a luxury hotel, but what she craved was company and somebody to adore her.

Things started to change as her face became known and the world began to beat a path to her door. When the photographs hit the media, she became a celebrity overnight and the invitations started pouring in. From that point on she was rarely alone, nor did her telephone cease to ring. Cristina Calvão, in a matter of weeks, became the star of the fashion world because of the German's fantastic vision, though, of course, she never knew that. She accepted it all and became a star but it did not make her happy. Although she was barely aware of it, there still remained a yawning hole in her heart.

It was Tuesday night and, on West 54th Street, the rain was sluicing down making little difference to the crowd of fans clustered outside the new hot venue where a bunch of heavies were restraining them from breaking through the cordon.

'You and you,' said the man at the door, picking at random the prettiest girls and allowing them into the club, which had only just opened.

A limousine with darkened windows purred to a halt at the kerb and two dusky beauties in shimmering gowns stepped delicately over the swirling gutter while their driver, carrying a huge umbrella, ushered them safely inside.

'Diana Ross!' cried a voice from the crowd. 'And with her Cristina Calvão!' They had just seen Brooke Shields and Michael Jackson, while Truman Capote had also been glimpsed with, it was rumoured, Andy Warhol. They were all in a mega party mood, despite the fact that they were soaked to the skin and stood little chance of gaining admittance to the newest, coolest club in town: Studio 54.

Inside, all was dark and the music deafening as the girls dropped their wraps with the hat-check girl and joined the party of celebrities gathered there on the personal invitation of their host, Steve Rubell, who was waiting at the bar.

'Darling,' said a movie star, as she kissed Cristina. 'I simply adore your dress. Is it Versace and would it fit me?'

'No,' said Cristina, affecting boredom. 'Armani.'

Beneath her studied nonchalance, Cristina was thrilled to be there, part of the in-crowd and on the guest list of every cool function in town. The gown was exquisite and understated, a gleam of pale satin beneath the strobe lights, and round her neck she wore fifty thousand dollars' worth of diamonds from Harry Winston, lent her for the night. It was like Oscars night in L.A. but better. Here, only people hand-picked by the host were welcome. Champagne was passed as the crowd air-kissed and some of them slipped off into corners to indulge in the drugs which were also freely available. By nineteen, Cristina had really grown up and maintained the slightly petulant expression that now summed up her attitude to life. Keen not to show how excited she was, she maintained a mask of weary boredom that quickly became a snarl.

As the crowd undulated and Cristina glanced

around, careful not to lose her indifferent air, she suddenly saw him, there at the bar, deep in conversation with Calvin Klein. The only man in New York who turned her on: Jorg Schreiber, as always in head-to-toe black, the lights gleaming dully off his hair. A jolt of electricity shot right through her and Cristina hurriedly broke away, leaving the movie star standing there in mid-sentence, totally forgotten.

'Jorg,' she said a moment later, having forced her way through the crowd.

'Cristina,' he said, with no sign of emotion. 'I hope you are enjoying yourself.' He introduced her to Calvin Klein, then made his excuses and left.

There was no one in New York she could talk to. In the time she had been there she had made no real friends, but she badly needed to unburden herself about Jorg. She could not understand his continuing indifference when *Women's Wear Daily* and the glossy magazines were calling her the face of the year, one of the most beautiful women in the world. Because of the bitchiness of the business, the thing she lacked most was a confidante; while the men were throwing themselves at her, the women stayed firmly away.

Back in her room, she broke into hysterics and hurled her hairbrush at the bathroom mirror, which broke with a satisfying crash. Well, all to the good; they could charge it to him. It was his tab, anyway, since he'd made the booking, so the more expenses she could run up, the better. She ripped off the dress, which had been a freebie, and wrapped herself in a towelling robe, retaining Harry Winston's gems because of the way they looked against her skin. She might try modelling for De Beers; she would get the agency to fix it.

She pulled out the pins and let her hair cascade, then stood in front of the full-length mirror and asked herself, as she had so often, why she could not make him want her. Over and over she saw the way his eyes caressed her from behind the lens, but as soon as the session was over he seemed to switch off. Yet she had never seen him with anyone else nor heard any gossip about his private life, which, in a bitchy profession like this, was unheard of. She'd done everything possible to get his attention – rages, tantrums, once getting drunk and tearing off her clothes in front of him. It was in the studio when the back-up team had left and she'd stood there, swaying, in the blazing light, wearing nothing but her four-inch heels and a seductive smile.

But the body that most men lusted after and would give all they'd got to possess left the only one she wanted unmoved. He barely looked up from polishing his lenses before laying them reverently into their case.

'Put on your clothes,' was all he said. 'We can't have you catching a chill at this stage.' And then he asked her to stay and lock up because he was running late.

Homesick and bitterly disappointed, Cristina returned to Rio for Carnaval. The contract she'd signed with Jorg was almost up; she doubted he'd want to renew it. In any case, the sunshine beckoned; the New York winter was severe and Cristina's spirit shrivelled in the cold. World Models were thrilled by her huge success and would line her up work wherever she wanted. There was also talk of Los Angeles and a screen test. No one knew about her skin-flick days and she would ensure that they never did. It was part of the childhood she preferred to forget, along with her dicey antecedents.

She left without saying goodbye to Jorg; if he cared, then let the bastard sue. When it came to the crunch, all he did was take snaps whereas she had become an international star, famous throughout the world and now earning millions. The agency sent a stretch limousine to meet her off the flight and had booked her into a five-star hotel right on the beachfront at Ipanema, where she planned to chill out for a while before doing any work. She was more than worth it so the agency could pay. She had entered this city as a starving beggar but returned like a conquering queen.

Back in her homeland, at the height of the season, Cristina's dreams about Jorg quickly faded away. She was now a world-class celebrity and, accordingly, much-feted. Doors that once had been slammed in her face were now thrown open in ardent welcome and there wasn't an A-list occasion to which she was not automatically invited. There was also masses of work when she deigned to do it and her modelling fees had gone right through the roof; she could ask for whatever she wanted. The agency found her a penthouse apartment in a portered block, with a maid. They supplied a P.A. as well as a driver whom she kept on call night and day. It was an easy life, being flattered and spoilt, though the new Cristina failed to see it that way.

And then, one morning, as she walked along the beach, she came face to face with a blue-eyed stranger and suddenly understood what was wrong with Jorg.

19

Magda Kaplinsky, at twenty-nine, was ten years older than Frankie. Having trained originally as a clinical psychologist, she had later entered the prison service where her chief responsibility lay in trying to fathom the underlying causes of crime. In Frankie she found a strong-willed young woman, highly intelligent though hard to control, whose battle against authority stemmed from a deep-seated sense of inner grievance. Exactly what that grievance was, she stubbornly refused to discuss. At the age of fifteen, from an affluent background, she had burnt her parents' home to the ground and, when questioned about her motivation, had persistently clammed up. The later tragedy of her boyfriend's death, which had destroyed her will to live, was more easily understood. She had helped set the fire for altruistic reasons, to enable him to escape from the institution. It had taken Magda months to break through, though lately Frankie had been showing signs of gradually opening up.

In their regular sessions Magda just listened, allowing the girl to talk or not as she chose. Sometimes

Frankie just sat and stared, twisting a tissue between nervous fingers of which the nails had been chewed right down to the quick. At other times, when her mood was more buoyant, they would chat about ordinary things. Magda attempted to draw her out, keen to discover what made her tick; inevitably, the conversation always returned to Chad. She believed she was responsible for his death; by telling him how to set a fire, she had effectively murdered him. She felt her sentence was, if anything, too short.

'You couldn't have known what would happen. It wasn't your fault.'

'I knew enough to have tried to stop him. He used the paraffin though I warned him not to. He was just so frantic to get out.' Her face had crumpled; there were tears in her eyes. Whenever she spoke of Chad she visibly shook.

Magda repeated: 'It wasn't your fault.' She reached across and touched the girl's hand. 'You must learn not to blame yourself and come to terms with what happened.'

When Frankie had been in prison a year, her mother applied for a visitor's pass but Frankie refused to see her, though wouldn't say why. Her hands tensed up and her mouth was tight; her eyes were like chips of ice. Yet her mother had recently lost her husband; surely the time had come, Magda said, for them to be making their peace. Whatever had happened in the past was over now that the colonel was dead. And she'd still need somewhere to live when they let her out.

'No,' said Frankie, implacably. 'I never intend to see her again. She blew it when she married that man and turned a blind eye to what was going on.' Which was as far as she'd ever go, no matter how hard Magda pressed her. The past was closed, she would not discuss it. Magda couldn't get her to say any more.

When she spoke of Chad, as she frequently did, Frankie's ravaged features instantly softened. And, between the bouts of anguished weeping, she built up a picture of the boy she still loved, without whom she felt she could not have any future. He was tall and handsome, funny and bright, and had always acted as her protector. She opened the locket she constantly wore and shyly showed Magda his picture. An intelligent face with a cocky grin stared from the silver frame and Magda's heart went out to the grieving girl.

'He looks a great guy,' was all she could say, a lame response to a person so patently suffering. But when she reached over and touched Frankie's hand, it was not immediately withdrawn.

'Sexy, too,' she said, with a rare smile. 'He said that he couldn't live without me. He talked about marriage and settling down. He badly wanted children.'

He had killed a boy quite unprovoked and later burnt the hostel down. Hardly the actions of a sensitive soul but it wasn't for Magda to point that out. She hoped that, in time, Frankie's suffering would cease and that she would one day forget him.

20

Charles surprised Cassie early on by saying how much he longed for a son. He loved her daughters, both of them, and pandered to them right from the start but she felt in her heart he was still too young to think about babies of his own. She, on the other hand, was ten years older; if she left it too long she would find it much harder to conceive. So when, within the first year of their marriage, she found herself pregnant, both were thrilled.

'Now our union is truly complete,' said Charles, embracing her tenderly.

Cassie beamed; she had never been happier. After the sadness of losing Edwin and the guilt she had felt at remarrying so soon, at last she felt absolved. Her daughters had acquired a loving stepfather, and they greeted the news of the baby with genuine joy.

'I hope it's a boy,' said Daisy to Charles as they groomed the horses in the stable yard. Since coming to live on the Hawksmoor estate, Charles had become an accomplished rider and exercised Edwin's big hunter daily, with a little tuition from the girls.

'Either would make me equally happy,' said Charles with his usual diplomacy, though in his heart he fervently hoped for a son.

'Better than a nasty snivelling little girl,' said Rose, at sixteen as acerbic as Aunt Sybil, taking after the Hawksmoor side more than her mother's.

'By the time she reaches the snivelling stage, you'll be away at college,' said Charles. Rose was bright and planned to train as a lawyer.

'But I'll be here to look after her,' said Daisy, who still liked playing with dolls. A baby sister would be nice, more interesting than a puppy or a kitten. She loved the new family setup they had with her handsome stepfather who treated them like pals and on whom she had something of a secret crush, though she'd die if he ever found out.

'Whatever,' said Charles, as he finished his grooming and slapped the horse lightly on the rump. 'You two will still be my precious girls. You know I will love you however it turns out. This baby won't come between us. I promise you that.'

Sybil still had her own rooms in the house, though since the marriage she visited less often. Cassie put it down to natural tact, something she didn't associate with Sybil. Perhaps her sister-in-law was mellowing with age.

'You know you're always welcome,' she said. 'This house is as much yours as ours.'

Sybil, frenetically pulling up weeds, paused and regarded her levelly for a second. 'Thanks,' she said, continuing her work without any further comment.

She hadn't yet made up her mind about Charles; the jury was still out. Although he was always impeccably civil and greeted her as a much-valued friend, she could not entirely understand why he'd fallen for Cassie. The obvious answer was money and cachet; the Hawksmoor estate was worth a great deal and Cassie was socially well connected not least, if Sybil were honest with herself, because of her own not negligible fame. Yet, to be fair, he appeared to adore her, followed her with his eyes wherever she went. And both the girls were crazy about him, talked about little else. To their teenage perception, he was rock-star glamorous, lights years away from the elderly father who had always been slightly remote, however well meaning.

'What do you think?' Sybil asked Tremayne as they sat together in the local pub, over a neighbourly beer. They had few secrets, this misogamic pair, who had known each other for many decades and shared a brotherly kind of taciturn friendship. The farm manager stared silently into his glass while rehearsing his own reservations.

'I don't think I trust him,' he finally said, unable to explain quite why.

'Could it be because of his charm? Slightly too good to be true, would you say?' Sybil, the sculptor, with her sharp eye for character, was usually well on the mark. Yet she liked the man, could not deny that, found his congenial presence life-affirming. It was good to have youth and exuberance around after the stagnant years.

'Could be. Don't know. We will just have to watch him.' He secretly nurtured warm feelings for Cassie himself.

'But he makes her happy.'

'Apparently so.' The pair sat on in comfortable silence, pursuing their separate trains of thought.

Aidan Christopher Buchanan was born on the night of a full moon. The light lay silvery on the grass as the midwife cut the umbilical cord and handed the tiny bundle to his father. Charles, delighted, took him in his arms and rocked him gently to stop his crying.

'My son,' he said proudly while Cassie lay and watched. 'Don't you think he looks exactly like me?'

He most certainly did, with the same blue eyes and, later, the same lustrous curls. 'Peas in a pod,' the guests all agreed when they met together at the Hawksmoor house to welcome him formally into the world, a much-wanted baby who would always be very well loved.

His half-sisters hovered beside his cot, jealously guarding their precious new toy, taking it in turns to cuddle and wind him, perfect little mothers in the making.

'It has all worked out so well,' Cassie whispered. 'Who would have thought it, a year ago?'

'The instant I saw you, I knew it was destined,' Charles murmured softly as he kissed her.

The Elwes family was there in force, keen to get to know Charles better and to welcome aboard his son. These days Richard was running the estate, his father having retired, so the two new landowners had much in common. As well as the bond of relationship in law, their land abutted so they often met. Henry, the brother who lived in the States, was keen to know what Richard thought.

'He's a nice enough chap, though a tad on the brash side. Doing his best to learn the ropes and keep our Cassie happy.'

'He always seems to be smiling,' said Henry, distrusting Charles on sight. 'What do we know about his background?'

'Not a lot so far,' said Richard. 'Try asking him yourself.'

Charles responded with charm and grace and took Henry's probing in good part. He gave the same answers: he'd been raised in India and later sent home to public school. His parents, sadly no longer alive, had spent most of their marriage abroad.

'Have you no siblings?'

'Alas, no,' he said. 'Becoming a part of the Elwes clan has helped me fulfil a cherished dream.'

'I think he's cute,' declared Henry's wife, and there the matter rested.

Life in Cornwall resumed its even tenor, with Charles as nominal head of the house. While Cassie continued her daily routine – cooking, gardening, walking the dogs, dropping in on her mother for coffee – Charles boned up on managing the estate and did his best to stay on top of things. His brother-in-law was extremely helpful and he also relied a lot on Tremayne, who had started off guarded and openly resentful but now appeared to be coming round. Most of their meetings took place in the village pub.

'I think he's starting to like me,' said Charles. 'Perhaps because I treat him as a mate.'

Now he felt confident on a horse, he also started to ride to hounds and looked very dashing in his hunting kit, which he wore whenever he had the chance.

'A bit of a showman but none the worse for that.' Even Sybil was starting to come round.

The house, since Cassie refurbished it, was back to its earlier splendour. Charles, with his specialist knowledge of art, persuaded her to shift to the attic some of the darker family portraits and insipid Victorian landscapes. In their place he hung some vibrant new paintings which he brought back from one of his London trips and displayed in salient positions throughout the house.

'Where did you get them?' asked Cassie, delighted. They certainly made a difference.

'They're on loan,' said Charles, 'for as long as it takes for us to decide if we want to buy them. It's up to you but I don't think we can go far wrong.'

It made good sense. She had plenty of money and now it was his home too. As he pointed out, she was simply looking to the future. The artists he had carefully chosen would, in due course, appreciate. She spoke to her broker, then told Charles to proceed. It was quite an investment but, apparently, a sound one and this way they could enjoy the spoils.

Aidan, from an early age, displayed his father's restless spirit as well as his sharp intelligence. Gazing down at him in his cot, Cassie, overflowing with love, was occasionally disconcerted by the look in his knowing blue eyes. At moments she almost expected to hear the familiar worldly chuckle, with its innuendoes of a misspent youth and slightly risqué humour. How alike they were, father and son; one a clone of the other.

'Why, there's an old soul if ever I saw one,' was Tremayne's instant comment on first meeting Aidan. He had dropped by with papers for Cassie to sign and was bound to admit, though reluctantly, that this odd new marriage appeared to be suiting her well. He had rarely seen her more radiant; she looked a good ten years younger. Post pregnancy she had put on weight which suited her height and her sculptured bones. Her skin was as clear and unflawed as her daughters'; her eyes shone with happiness. She had taken to twisting her heavy hair into a careless knot, which became her. As she stood in the doorway, waving him off, her son clasped protectively in her arms, a shaft of envy punctured Tremayne's wintry heart. He wished her only the best out of life but sometimes found it hard that she seemed to love this cocky new husband even more than the first one. If only he'd had the courage to speak out in those first lonely days of her widowhood. But Tremayne had never been a man of impulse, which was why he was still on his own.

It gave him pleasure to watch Aidan grow and take his first staggering steps. The child, it seemed, was entirely fearless so that, from the moment he could walk unaided, his endless curiosity led him into all kinds of scrapes. Sometimes, in order to help Cassie out, Tremayne would take him off her hands and drive around with him in the truck as he went about his business. All the workers on the estate would stop what they were doing to greet him and Aidan, right from the start, became a favourite with them all.

'You'd better watch out that he doesn't get spoilt.' Charles seemed doubtful about the friendship though Cassie suspected that he was simply jealous. She had known Tremayne for most of her life and it touched her to see him with her son, gravely explaining country matters in words he could understand. He'd have made a wonderful father, she thought; perhaps it was still not too late. Aidan came home from these expeditions carrying trophies that they had found: a kestrel's feather, a plover's egg, a tiny quivering field mouse.

'In the spring we are going to grow baby frogs,' he told his parents importantly.

'Well, mind you don't fall in,' said Cassie, though she did oblige with a suitable net, left over from when the girls had gone through this phase.

In time a jam jar of frogspawn appeared which Cassie put on the windowsill so that Aidan could watch it slowly hatch into tadpoles.

'Do we really need this muck near our food?' Charles was less than impressed.

'It's educational,' Cassie explained. 'He will learn a lot about nature just from watching.'

Charles, it appeared, was growing fidgety. He no longer found running the Hawksmoor estate enough to satisfy his agile brain. With Rose at Oxford and Daisy working, the house seemed suddenly empty and, although still fascinated by his young son, he felt the need of a larger challenge in his life. They enjoyed a limited social round, within the boundaries of a tight little circle. The neighbouring properties were huge and rambling; Charles began to show a marked interest in their contents.

'Did you see what was hanging over the fireplace?' he said one night as they drove home.

'That flat-looking painting of sailing boats?' Over the years, she had seen it many times yet never really looked at it, assuming it to be an amateur work.

'It's a genuine Alfred Wallis,' said Charles. 'Circa 1930, I'd guess. My God, these houses are loaded with stuff that people don't even know they've got.'

'Worth a lot? It doesn't look it.' As always, she was impressed by his expert eye.

'Could go as high as a hundred thousand bucks. He's in the Tate and the Museum of Modern Art. An interesting primitive painter from these parts. Started off as a fisherman.'

'Well, whatever you do,' said Cassie, amused, 'please don't go offering to buy it. We certainly don't have money like that for picking up every picture you like. Besides, in these parts things like that just aren't done.'

'But it oughtn't to stay where it is,' said Charles. 'The fire is drying it out. Wallis painted on pieces of driftwood. Take a closer look next time we're there.'

'How come you know so much?' asked Cassie, never failing to be surprised. At times Charles came over as a bit of a bullshitter, yet he did seem to know his stuff. She sometimes wondered where he had got his knowledge.

'I don't really know. Just picked it up. I told you I used to deal in pictures.'

He started slipping up to London more often, returning, after a few days, seemingly revitalised and full of new energy. She knew he found the estate confining and started to worry in case he wandered off.

'I often wonder,' she confided to Daisy, 'if he misses the wheeler-dealing of the art world.'

More and more, as they visited neighbours, Charles unearthed hidden treasures. He saw Cassie's point about not being pushy, yet used his charm to winkle out if the owners properly understood what they had. More often than not they had no idea and were grateful to him when he told them. The owner of the Alfred Wallis agreed to allow him to get it valued and was very pleasantly surprised when he found a buyer.

'You're wasted here in the sticks,' said the man. 'You should be up there, in the smoke, doing what you do best.'

*　　*　　*

They settled into a new routine, congenial to them both. Charles spent most of the week away, either in London, making contacts, or travelling around the countryside, seeking out art. He soon had a lucrative power base of clients who used him specifically to track down paintings they wished to acquire for their private collections. He loved the work, found it energising, and was soon staying away for much longer periods, only coming home on alternate weekends.

'I miss you, of course I do,' said Cassie. 'But I am thrilled your career is taking off. I hated to think you were stagnating down here.'

The management of the estate was now back in the capable hands of Tremayne, which meant that all concerned had got what they wanted. Cassie had her work cut out just looking after her boisterous son and helping Daisy, recently married, furnish her new house. At the end of the weeks when Charles was due home, she would put her mind to looking her best and cooking his favourite dishes in order to spoil him. Daisy would often take Aidan in order to give them some time to themselves and, as a result, their sex life improved immeasurably. Daisy, hoping for a family herself, was devoted to her younger brother so, in the end, it all worked out to everyone's satisfaction.

'You know,' said Cassie as they lay together. 'You ought not to have to live in a hotel. You work so hard, it just isn't fair on you. It would probably work out cheaper in the end if we bought our own place in London.'

Charles, who had already worked it out, silently

exulted. There were times when having a richer wife got him down.

'Do you think we can spare the capital?' he asked, running his fingers over her breasts and smiling as she arched her back in response. Foreplay was something he had always excelled at. He had certainly had enough practice.

'It depends where it is and how big,' she said, her eyes still closed and her mind unfocused. 'I hear that Battersea's coming up. The kids could use it when they go to London. And even I, on my shopping excursions, would prefer it to that hotel.'

They smiled at the long-standing private joke, but having a place of their own made sense. Charles was now earning substantial commissions; it would pay to have somewhere where he could entertain.

'Battersea's great but a little far out. I was thinking of somewhere more central.' Like Knightsbridge or Chelsea; in the end he'd get his way. The trick was to keep her believing she'd thought of it first.

It was late afternoon and Cassie was weeding; Charles would shortly be home. Supper was slowly cooking in the Aga and Aidan was quietly engrossed by the pond, fishing net in hand.

'Don't get too close,' Cassie called to him. He'd been told many times to stay away from the water but, with Aidan, she could never be certain. And he'd been unusually quiet for so long; in a moment she'd go and see what he was up to. Charles had wanted the pond filled in but it made a lovely wildlife feature; deer and foxes drank from it and the herons came down to try to catch the fishes.

Aidan was trying to find his frogs. A few weeks earlier, he and Tremayne had ceremoniously emptied the tadpoles into their natural environment. Aidan had cried when the last disappeared; he wanted to keep one as a pet. But Tremayne, backed by Cassie, had quietly explained that, as frogs, they'd be happier in the pond.

'It is nature's way of doing things,' he said. 'They'll be here whenever you want them.'

At the time Aidan seemed to have understood, though Cassie suspected he was moping. Without any siblings close to his age and too many fawning adults around, plus the fact that his father was often absent, he showed signs of turning into a little monster. Now he was sitting quietly on the lawn, playing with something in the grass. Cassie, relieved, went back to what she was doing.

From somewhere close came the sound of mowing; the gardener was working overtime because the lord of the manor would soon be home. She smiled and reflected how much she loved them, her husband and their maverick child. Who would have thought eight years ago that things could have turned out so well.

'Aidan,' she called, as the mower drew closer. It was one of those great big industrial things, lent by Tremayne from the main estate to keep the garden in good shape. She turned to check that her son was safe but he was still deeply engrossed with something in the grass.

'Move,' she said, 'or the mower will get you.' And, although he took no notice of her, he did roll out of the way.

'What the fuck!' suddenly screamed the gardener, grinding to a precipitate halt, and when Cassie ran over to see what was wrong, his face and shirt were splattered all over with blood.

'Frogs,' said the man, when he'd wiped himself down and inspected the carnage in the grass. 'I swear I never even saw them.'

21

It was due to Magda that Frankie got to work in the vegetable garden. She needed taking out of herself and the fresh air would be good for her. She spent too much of her time alone, brooding in her cell, refusing to mix with the other prisoners, and the daily circuit of the prison yard was, at its best, entirely soul-destroying. The strenuous effort of digging the soil was bound to prove beneficial and might help take her mind off her endless grieving. It would also provide a valuable lesson in basic survival skills. One day she would have to fend for herself so the more she learnt now, the better. Frankie was reluctant but could not refuse. When the prison officials approved the plan, she was set to work on a regular basis, under the supervision of the head gardener.

'Now don't go getting ideas,' said Magda, remembering Chad's ill-fated plan, but Frankie's spirit was far too crushed ever to contemplate anything like that. She seemed resentful of this change of routine, would rather have been left alone in her cell to rot.

'Well, I guess it beats sewing mailbags,' said Magda but failed to raise a smile.

Slowly, however, as time passed by, Frankie grew less morose. The physical effort was having an effect and not only did she start looking better but her appetite and her mood improved until she was almost civil again and no longer snapped at Magda. She stopped referring to Chad quite so much and occasionally talked about other things. Magda hoped that she might, in time, even come to terms with his death.

Once she had finished preparing the ground, uprooting weeds and tilling the soil, the next stage of the operation was far less concentrated work. Under the watchful eye of the gardener, Frankie was allowed to do much of the planting herself. She recalled a lot from her country childhood and settled contentedly back on her heels to make regular holes in the newly mulched soil with her dibber. Once the boss had approved what she had done, then came the more interesting matter of the seeds. She opened the packets and dribbled them in, in meticulously straight rows.

'I think you may have cracked it,' said the governor, watching from her office window. 'If so, you have done an excellent job, my dear.'

Magda was pleased; she hoped so but wasn't expecting miracles. These things took time. The girl was very damaged and pain like hers could not just be driven away. But it was a start. She would build on that and pray there would be no backsliding.

* * *

As Frankie grew fitter, she got prettier too and Magda started to see how she once must have looked: tall and graceful with glossy dark hair and classic features that came alive when she smiled, which she still seldom did. They must have made a striking pair, she thought, recalling the photograph, and once again her heart was stirred by the terrible sadness of it all. Whatever Frankie might be guilty of, she did not deserve to have lost her great love in such horrific circumstances. No wonder she couldn't stop blaming herself; the terrible image of his death was enough to drive anyone crazy. Magda resolved to do what she could to improve the quality of Frankie's life and help to lead her back to a more normal existence.

Since Frankie had taken so well to gardening, enjoyed the outdoor life and the back-breaking work, a plan was evolving in Magda's head which she'd keep to herself till a more appropriate time. Now that she had disowned her mother, Frankie had nobody left in the world to whom she could go when they finally let her out. Even if she had to serve the whole sentence, without remission for good behaviour, she'd be only twenty-six when she was released. Far too young to fend for herself when she'd been locked up since her middle teens and had no experience whatever of life outside.

Magda's plan, which she didn't divulge, was to stick around until Frankie got out then do whatever she could to help her adjust. It wasn't part of her job description; her official duties would end at that time. But, over the years, she'd grown fond of the girl and now couldn't bear the prospect of letting her go. She thought of discussing her thoughts with the governor but knew she would probably not approve. Instead she decided to wait to see how things eventually worked out.

22

Clive was the most considerate of lovers, making every meeting a special event, with flowers, chocolates or a bottle of vintage champagne. It was weeks before he made a move, by which time Jenny was starting to lose her cool. She had flipped for him from the very start, knew it would break her heart if he went away. She couldn't face up to another disappointment, truly believed he had feelings for her if only he would let them show and not keep her constantly guessing. Then one starlit night, as they stood by the brook having a final drink before bed, he placed both their glasses on a nearby table, drew her to him and kissed her. Jenny practically fainted on the spot, overwhelmed with relief.

'I've been wanting to do that since the first time we met,' he murmured as they stood entwined, her head against his chest, eyes closed, all of a sudden in heaven. 'I was careful not to move too fast for fear of scaring you off.'

That night they went upstairs together, to her private quarters and not his rented room, and from then on he stayed in the pub as her guest. He tried to arrive before opening time and drag her upstairs for a personal moment before showering and coming downstairs to the bar. This routine suited both of them; he made an excellent host. She asked if he'd ever done bar work before and he laughed and said for a while in his youth while he was still sorting out who he was and making up his mind about his future. Where had he worked? she asked and he told her Mayfair. In those days he'd been a bit of a lad. I'll bet, said Jenny, but couldn't fault him. He knew how to mix almost any cocktail and could flip a glass high from behind his back and catch it in front in one hand. That was the trick that kept Toby amused. He made Clive do it again and again until he pleaded exhaustion and begged to stop. He'd been driving all day, he reminded them both, and was not as young as he had been.

'He's really great with the kid,' said Vanessa, who judged men on that kind of thing. Skill with a child came high on her list; he was certainly earning brownie points with her. 'And you say he doesn't have kids of his own?'

'No,' said Jenny. 'Which does seem a waste. Since he is such a natural.'

Toby adored him and would not go to sleep until Clive had been up and read to him, then stayed to tuck him in and switch off the light.

'What's his family background?' asked Vanessa. 'Does he have brothers and sisters with kids?'

'Don't know,' said Jenny. 'I don't think so.' The truth

156

was she knew very little about him. Their meetings, only every second week, were so high-octane on the sexual front there was little time left for anything else, least of all conversation.

After two years under Jenny's rule, the pub was starting to flourish. It had always been popular with the locals but now was drawing in tourists as well, a younger and more adventurous crowd than before. The village was two miles from the centre of Bath and attractive because of its river location. The waterwheel was now working again and, on sunny evenings and weekday lunchtimes, the crowd would carry their drinks outside and sit at the wooden tables by the brook, watching the waterbirds. On wintry nights, they'd squash into the bar and warm themselves by the blazing fire which Jenny kept going throughout the year, except at the height of summer. Logs were delivered from a timberyard but she still had to lug them in every day, heavy work that damaged her hands.

Joyce was still valiantly running the kitchen but Jenny was taken with Clive's idea that she should be offering more upmarket food. As it was, the workload was as much as she could cope with, what with having to look after Toby, but the longer she stayed there, the more she saw the Coot and Hern's ultimate potential. Jenny had always been highly ambitious; walking out of her job was just an unfortunate blip. She was still only in her early thirties, and her expectations were high; she liked the idea of a gastropub that could, if she really worked at it, eventually perhaps become nationally known. Clive worked out a rudimentary business plan which, at night, they both pored over, juggling with numbers which were, to Jenny, alarmingly high yet seemed not to worry him at all.

'In a setup like this you cannot lose. Bath, according to all the guide books, is still the hottest tourist spot in the country.'

Since he spent so much time on the road, he knew a fair bit about such things and had a definite taste for indulgent living. He also spent much of his time in London and was well boned up on the restaurant front. Gastropubs were a fairly recent concept, only now coming into their own. The Coot and Hern had all the essentials to turn it into a top-notch venue, provided she did as he said and invested more money.

'It's spending money to make even more. You know it makes sense,' he said.

The stumbling block would be the finance. She had no savings left of her own, having sunk all she'd got into the down payment, and still had a massive overdraft. There was no point in talking to her parents; what savings they had were carefully invested against the time when her dad would no longer be working. Also she felt he still disapproved of his daughter's being a publican, would rather she'd taken the old-fashioned route and gone for conventional marriage. Which was out of the question, at least for now, though somewhere deep down she was cautiously starting to hope.

Clive solved the financial problem by saying he'd help her raise the funds.

'Are you sure?' asked Jenny, overwhelmed. 'Do you

really think you should risk it? They say opening a restaurant is the fastest way to go broke.'

'Don't worry,' he said. 'It won't be my money. These things can be arranged. Besides, I have absolute faith you will make it work.'

'What does he do when he's not in Bath?' Vanessa wanted to know. Handsome, urbane and obviously caring, Clive seemed almost too good to be true. Single, too; given half a chance, she'd have snapped him up herself. She had been with her current boyfriend too long; he wouldn't marry her and was starting to get on her nerves.

'He works in the wallpaper business,' said Jenny, 'for a highly prestigious London firm. His territory covers the whole of the southwest, which is why he is always on the road.' Except for the time he spent in London; he hadn't said much about that.

'Where is he based?'

'I'm not quite sure.' She realised it sounded pathetic. She imagined some kind of anonymous digs though he'd never actually said that. When he was here and she lay in his arms, or watched him keeping the punters happy, all she could think was how happy she was and how well things had turned out. She rarely thought about Douglas these days, except to compare him to Clive and be glad she'd moved on.

'He must have some sort of family,' said Vanessa. 'An adoring mum or an aged nanny. Nobody travels through life entirely alone.'

Clive had even met Jenny's parents, who had come

to vet him as soon as they could. She could see her father was hugely impressed though he tried hard not to show it. A man of few words, he was always suspicious of anyone he could describe as posh.

'I'll tell you something,' he said when Clive had gone. 'He won't be coming to visit us in Neath.'

Her mother, glad to see Jenny so happy, was already hearing wedding bells. He might be older but seemed besotted. And the way he played with Toby was really lovely.

'Now,' she said before they left. 'Don't you go driving him off with your independence.'

Apart from building a much larger kitchen, according to EU regulations, the place would require some general sprucing up for the sort of clientele they hoped to attract. Clive planned to do it all himself. He was, after all, an expert in this area, advising people what colours to choose, sometimes helping them rethink their whole décor.

'We won't be needing wallpaper, will we?' Most of the pub was wood and stone, apart from the bedrooms which had been recently done. Vanessa had overseen all that and every detail was perfect. She had even provided teddy bears to make the visitors feel at home, and magazines on the bedside tables in place of the Gideon Bibles.

'Wallpaper's only a part of what I do.' He had, he explained, a select group of clients to whom he offered a comprehensive service. These customers gave him a free hand to redesign their interiors within an agreed ballpark figure. As they talked, Jenny realised how little she knew about the rest of his life but, unlike Douglas, he seemed to be totally open.

'So where do you do all the office work?' she asked. 'You must have a permanent base.'

'In my car or at the clients' houses. It's a business I'm gradually building up while still on the road for the firm. A natural adjunct to what I'm paid for.' He grinned. 'The only office I need is my trusty laptop from which I am seldom parted.'

Which explained where he was when he wasn't with her. Driving for miles on the motorway or holed up in a service station, catching up on his paperwork. It didn't sound much of a life for him. How lucky for both of them that their paths had crossed.

'Why not suggest he moves in with you? He's handy to have around.' Vanessa changed partners on a whim; the chief priorities of her life were her children, her pets and her home.

'I can't,' said Jenny. 'It's much too soon.' Though she'd hung around all those years for Douglas and look what had happened there. She was determined never to raise the subject. It had to come from him.

Now and again he didn't show but, on those occasions, he always phoned. A business appointment, some unexpected meeting; occasionally a consultation with a client who could only manage weekends. He seemed to spend most of his time on the job which, as he was quick to point out, was also true of her. A disadvantage of living over the shop was that she could never be totally off duty. Something or other would always come up that only she could deal with. But he was still a paid employee; it seemed unfair when he worked such punishing hours.

'What does he do at Christmas?' asked Vanessa but Jenny didn't know. She fantasised about having him there, playing Santa in front of the fire, but when she raised the courage to ask, he said he usually went away.

'Skiing in Austria. I do it most years. With a bunch of my old army cronies. It's become a sort of sacred tradition. I couldn't let them down.'

His only other regular break was two weeks in August when he went on cricket tour. He had played with the team all his adult life; they were like a band of brothers.

'He certainly is a man's man,' said Vanessa. 'I wouldn't have had him down as that.'

Behind the bar he was in his element, very much the genial host. The women jostled for his attention and he treated them all with his dazzling charm but, mainly, it was the men with whom he clicked. They considered him a jolly good bloke and accepted him as Jenny's partner, despite the fact that he was hardly ever there.

'Tell him that you have needs too,' said Vanessa, who didn't entirely approve. She expected men to be in constant attendance.

'I don't want to crowd him,' Jenny explained. She had learnt that lesson the hard way, from Douglas. Even though she had always known about the wife, her life had been on perpetual hold because he always cancelled at the last minute. She had usually spent her birthday alone, as well as every Christmas. If only for that reason, she intended never to become dependent on Clive.

'In many ways it works perfectly,' she told Vanessa over lunch. 'Because we are so much apart, we don't get bored with each other. And he only gets to see me at my best.'

'What will you say if he pops the question?' Vanessa was pretty sure she knew. She had seen Jenny through the Douglas affair and prayed things would work out this time.

Jenny had no need to answer. It was written all over her face.

To avoid the expense of hiring a chef, Jenny decided to do all the cooking herself. In recent years she'd had lots of practice and would rather work in the kitchen than in the bar.

'What we are really after,' she explained, 'is elevated domestic cooking.' Precisely what she'd been doing all these years for her friends. 'None of that overrated fancy stuff. The pub is where people feel most at home. They come here to relax and eat comfort food.'

'You'll still have to show your face now and then so they don't forget who is boss.' Clive, who'd been reading up on the subject, was starting to sound like an expert.

'I'll stick my head round the door now and then, wearing my tall chef's hat.' She liked the idea of becoming a chef, the fulfilment of her long-held dream. If everything worked out, she could get her diploma, when she could find the time.

Joyce was content to become sous-chef, making sauces and keeping the dishwasher stacked. Since orders for food would be taken at the bar, all they needed now was some part-time help to serve the meals and clear away the plates. Then Clive came up with the backing and they were away.

'Smells divine. What is it?' he asked, planting a kiss on Jenny's neck as she slaved away at the stove.

'Beef and mushroom pie,' she said, passing him a forkful of filling. 'It's the Worcestershire sauce that gives it that extra kick.'

She turned to greet him; her face was red and shiny from the heat and her hair was tucked beneath her white gauze hat.

'How's my girl?'

'I'm great,' she said. It was four weeks since they'd last been together, though they'd talked almost every day. Something last minute had happened in his life that had caused him to cancel his last planned visit but Jenny had been so rushed off her feet, she'd scarcely had time to miss him.

'Pour yourself a whisky,' she said, 'and a glass of red wine, please, for me.' She needed to roll the pastry out and cut neat lids for the rows of pie dishes that Joyce would later place in the oven in batches.

'I don't suppose you have time for a quickie?'

'No chance,' she said, with an eye on the clock.

Twenty minutes to opening time and she still had to change her clothes. 'But you might stand in for me at the bar, then pop upstairs and read to Toby.' At times they felt like man and wife, a feeling she very much liked.

They made an effective team, though she hated it when he had to cancel without, it seemed, a very convincing story. She knew there were other pressures on his time but he could have made that extra effort, particularly as he now had a stake in the place. Still, here he was and he did look good. Whereas she was all sweaty from the stove, he was his usual immaculate self, casually leaning against the counter, sipping Glenmorangie. With his silvering hair and those bright blue eyes he looked more like an actor than a salesman.

'What else is on the menu tonight?' At least he showed interest in the food.

'Braised rabbit with cider, rosemary and cream. John Dory with anchovies and capers. Oh, and a wonderful new dessert. Wait until you taste it. Geranium-scented panna cotta, trimmed with red gooseberries.'

She varied the menu as much as she could, while also including the staple favourites, and was experimenting with a lot of new dishes. She gave him a spoon and made him taste it, was pleased when he rolled his eyes.

'You're a genius,' he said, embracing her. 'Meanwhile, it's practically zero hour so scoot.'

*   *   *

The investment money, he told her later, came from a private source who was also a friend. Someone he knew socially, with whom he played the odd game of golf.

'I did up his place in Somerset,' he said. 'He was so delighted with the result, he now trusts my judgement implicitly and is willing to take a punt.' Not so much money that Jenny need worry but enough, for now, to cover the planned improvements.

'Surely he wants to see for himself.' A chance, perhaps, to meet one of his friends.

'He's not really bothered. Some time in the future. Right now he's got a lot of stuff on his plate.'

The first thing they did was extend the kitchen, with a brand new cooker, twice the size of the old one, which involved some fairly major structural alterations, as well as a lot of noise and mess. While this was happening, Jenny worked out menus that involved as little cooking as possible; when necessary she could use the oven upstairs.

'It's a little like camping,' she told Vanessa, 'but should all be worth it in the end.'

Meanwhile, they ripped out the jukebox in the bar and hung some wooden-framed paintings to brighten the walls. Vanessa, who had an eye for these things, trawled the junk shops for copper jugs and horse brasses, which they also hung on the walls. They planted huge terracotta pots with trailing ivy and cyclamen and placed them around the bar and dining room. It was fun and Jenny enjoyed herself, watching her dream come alive. One day she'd invite her old team to come down and write it up for the magazine but not until she felt she had got it perfect.

Much of her time, outside opening hours, Jenny spent sourcing ingredients and forging links with small food producers who could match the quality she was after. Here the years spent writing her column really did pay off. Her name was known as an expert in the field so the butchers, cheesemakers and other local vendors were only too pleased to oblige her and went out of their way to help.

'I must say,' said Vanessa one day, as they lounged outside by the waterwheel. 'I wasn't convinced you would pull it off. But you've certainly done so in spades.'

By far the highlight of Jenny's life was the moment, on every second Thursday, when Clive arrived around opening time and joined her behind the bar. She would stay no longer than twenty minutes, enough to greet the early drinkers, then withdraw to the kitchen and take on her role as chef. Joyce would have been there a couple of hours, preparing vegetables and making sauces, contentedly doing the basics for Jenny to work with. As a team, they fitted very well together and the bar staff were excellent too. But the nights Clive was there, Jenny really came to life. By now the regulars were used to him and most of them knew him by name. With his jacket off and his sleeves rolled up, he epitomised the genial host and drew them to him with his lethal charm and irrepressible good humour. Now and again he'd pop down to the kitchen or up to the nursery to settle Toby. Everyone felt much happier with him around.

Only Vanessa still had reservations but she'd long been Jenny's best friend. 'You must work awfully hard,' she said, cautiously trying to find out more, still not convinced that this charming man was one hundred per cent bona fide.

'I do,' said Clive. 'As it happens. For my sins.'

'It's a shame you can't be around a little more.' Vanessa rarely pulled her punches. 'It is tough for Jenny too, you know. Running this place on her own.'

'I do know,' said Clive, 'and am really glad that she has such a good friend as you.'

Later that night, when the pub was closed and the last of the drinkers had finally gone, Clive poured two glasses of vintage brandy and they went outside to drink it under the stars.

'To us,' he said, raising a toast to them both. 'May it last for ever. I know it can't be easy at times but what we have is better than marriage. I am here because I love you. I think you know that.'

Jenny's eyes were shiny with tears. 'I love you too,' she said.

23

Life grew fractionally easier to bear, though a day never passed when Frankie didn't think about Chad. She found tending her vegetables quietly sustaining, liked the calm repetitiveness of it all. Slowly she made peace with herself, as far as she was able, and found the constant activity kept her from brooding. She even made a couple of friends which meant she was less cut off. They would sit and chat in the social hour, play cards together and sometimes darts and, bit by bit, exchange their personal stories. The other two, Bella and Sadie, were older, one a time-hardened prostitute, the other a failed con artist. But Frankie found them both entertaining, once she had dropped her defences a bit, and they, in turn, were surprised to find that beneath the morose exterior she did have a sense of humour.

'What's a kid like you doing in 'ere?' Bella, the prostitute, wanted to know and, when Frankie recounted her story, shook her head in disbelief. 'They oughtn't of locked you up for that,' she said. 'You was only defending your man.'

'And had surely been punished enough,' added Sadie. 'If they'd had any heart, they'd have let you go, if only for reasons of compassion.'

'Life isn't like that,' said Frankie calmly. 'Besides, it no longer matters. At the time I was so shattered by his death, I couldn't even think straight. And I needed somewhere to live, after all. At least they have given me bed and board.' And stopped her learning to fend for herself or think about a career.

She took up yoga, then meditation from which she learnt to face her own death, which made what happened to Chad that much easier to bear. Having been raised with no religion she wasn't expecting to meet him again, but if she did, there were questions to which she wanted answers.

Magda, observing, was pleased with her progress and slow emergence from her morbid trance. She made an appointment to see the governor. Frankie had now served five years of her sentence and would soon be up for parole.

Frankie was summoned to the governor's office. Her mother was asking to see her. 'No,' she said, without thinking twice. 'I won't see that woman again.'

'Not just a woman. Your mother,' said the governor. 'It isn't natural to turn your back. She really needs you, you are all she has left. Give her a chance and hear what she has to say.'

'No,' said Frankie flatly, refusing to budge.

But the next day Magda took her aside and explained it would be to her own advantage to do as the governor said. 'Soon you'll be due for parole,' she pointed out. 'Don't let pig-headedness stand in the way of your getting out early for good behaviour. If that happens, the colonel will have won.'

She offered to be there when her mother arrived but Frankie preferred to see her alone.

'Don't worry,' she said. 'I can handle this. Though don't expect the meeting to last very long.' All the sparkle had gone from her eyes. She looked as she had six years ago, bitter and deeply disturbed.

Her mother, when Frankie was ushered in, was seated nervously beyond the grille and seemed to have aged a lot since Frankie last saw her. She had lost some weight and it didn't become her. Her once pretty face, with its laughing eyes, was now haggard and pale. Her hair, which she'd always kept freshly tinted, was grey where it straggled from under her hat. She was dressed in beige and looked nervous and uneasy. For a nanosecond Frankie almost weakened. She took her seat and they stared at each other in silence.

'You look well, dear,' said her mother. 'Surprisingly so.'

'Hard labour,' said Frankie. 'They have got me hewing rocks. Well, as somebody pointed out, it beats sewing mailbags.'

An uncertain smile flickered on her mother's face. She had never been able to tell when Frankie was joking. 'I hope they're not treating you badly, dear,' she said in a loud stage whisper. She was wearing a dusting of pale blue eyeshadow which, on a woman

171

her age, looked grotesque. She had always been a girlie woman, the characteristic that had first attracted the colonel.

'What do you think?' asked Frankie baldly, staring at her with hostile eyes.

For a nervous few seconds her mother fluttered and rummaged in her bag for a tissue. 'I have missed you, dear,' she said falteringly. 'I would like to think we might one day be close again.'

'Close!' snorted Frankie. 'You have to be joking. You don't know the meaning of the word. All you ever did was fuss over that man, yet you never saw what was going on under your nose.'

'I don't know what you mean,' said her mother, dabbing at her eyes. 'I tried to be a good mother to you. I can't think where I went wrong.'

'Warder!' said Frankie, rising to her feet. 'I want to return to my cell.'

As she turned to go without saying goodbye, her mother attempted one final bid. 'Won't you come home when they let you out and see if we can't make a go of it? The house, without either of you, seems so empty.'

'Tough,' said Frankie, 'you should have thought of that before.' And left.

'How did it go?' asked Magda later.

'Badly,' said Frankie abruptly. All the old anger had boiled up again and the more relaxed Frankie they were getting to know had disappeared entirely. Instead of responding to Magda's concern, she stared blankly at the wall.

'The news from the governor is good,' said Magda, deftly changing the subject. 'All going well, within a few weeks you may get an early release.'

'So what?' Frankie shrugged, no longer caring. 'I have nowhere else to go.'

'As it happens,' said Magda, playing her trump card, 'I think you may find you are wrong.'

Her plan, which she'd worked on for several years, had been approved by the governor. After thirteen years in the prison service, she felt she had done all she usefully could and now was planning a major change in her life.

'I am joining a group of women in Belgium, in a spiritual commune. They live together and are self-supporting from working mainly with their hands. There are potters, weavers, all kinds, producing work which they later sell to support the commune.' She glanced at Frankie, who hadn't spoken. 'I was rather hoping you might join us. The community spirit is very uplifting and it isn't nearly as worthy as it sounds.'

Frankie was silent for several minutes. Then, just as Magda was losing hope, she turned and said shyly: 'Okay.'

'Terrific!' said Magda, embracing her tightly. 'I promise you won't regret it.'

24

'Come along, slowcoach, what's wrong with you today? At this rate, you'll never get fit.' Dino, tall and impossibly handsome, was bouncing backwards on the balls of his feet while Pippa put on an extra spurt and tried hard to catch him up.

'It isn't fair,' she panted, 'your legs are much longer.'

'Shouldn't make any difference,' he said, grabbing her wrist to check the watch that monitored her heart rate. 'Move!' he said. 'You're not giving it your best. What were you up to last night?'

'Taking care of my husband and children,' said Pippa, suddenly defensive. The truth was, the nanny had been with the twins while she and Charles were out on the town, trying out yet another trendy new restaurant.

Being a full-time wife and mother as well as running a business on her own was starting to take its toll on Pippa who, these days, seemed to be permanently tired. And yet her husband retained all his original bounce. Charles could sail through a heavy workday and still put back a whisky or two as well as a bottle or more of expensive wine. She had no idea where the stamina came from. By his age he ought to be slowing down.

Now that the twins were at the toddling stage, life had become that much harder. No longer could Pippa just dump them in the playpen and get on with the business of running the shop. These days they demanded too much of her attention; somewhat against her natural instincts, she'd been forced to place them both in nursery school.

'I feel so guilty,' she confessed to her mother.

'Don't,' said her mother. 'These are modern times.' Meaning, though without spelling it out, that she didn't want her grandsons left with her. Besides, she reasoned, the nursery was better, providing company and mental stimulus to two such intelligent, hyper-active boys. They were far too much of a handful for the nanny, who was only part-time in any case, as Pippa wouldn't have anyone living in. 'You are lucky to have a husband who's so rich.' Her mother had radically changed her tune since the relationship began.

'But he works for it. Hard,' Pippa reminded her. He had so many irons in so many fires, he sometimes didn't come home for nights on end.

She had moved her workouts to the early morning in order to fit them in before starting work. The nanny would give the children their breakfast while, twice a week, come hail or shine, Pippa would put on her tracksuit and trainers and pound round Barnes Common with Dino. The route he'd worked out took precisely one hour and he'd drop her back at her own front door in time to shower and change her clothes, then deposit the twins at the nursery school on her way to the Fulham Road. The days of her driving in with Charles were gone since his hours had become so erratic.

'I hardly get to see him these days,' she frequently moaned to Dino.

Still, she couldn't complain: it was what she had wanted and, at one time, thought she might never have. An attentive husband and two gorgeous babies – and all before she had reached the age of thirty.

Occasionally, when Charles was away and the nanny could be coerced into staying, Pippa took the evening off and went on the razzle with her friends. They met in a wine bar in the Fulham Road or across the river in Putney. They were mainly female, about her age, and all had jobs that they liked a lot. Only, unlike her, they were single and unattached.

'Don't you miss your freedom,' they asked, 'now that you're half of a couple?'

And Pippa admitted that, yes, she did. She missed the laughter and female chat, the vulgar jokes and sexual confidences; the general camaraderie they all shared.

'How are the twins?' they asked politely, making it clear that they couldn't care less, that their single lives were too engrossing for them to envy her.

Of course she put a good face on it: the twins were lovely, her husband a dear. Life was perfect, he spoiled her rotten and now, good heavens, she'd have to fly because the nanny would be fretting. She was pretty certain that, once she'd gone, the rest of them would sigh and relax and raise a glass to their single state before moving on to a club.

The nanny was waiting, a little distraught. Jack, she told Pippa, had been playing up. Not just in his usual naughty way: he'd been having what seemed like a fit. Pippa was up the stairs in a flash, rebellious thoughts entirely forgotten, and down on her knees by the lower bunk bed to see what was going on.

'Jack?' she whispered, stroking his hair, and he turned and stared at her with the eyes of a stranger.

'I think you are overreacting,' said Charles. 'The poor little blighter is only eighteen months old.' He had arrived home late from a very long drive, dreaming only of a good night's sleep, to find the house in a state of hysterical uproar. The doctor was there and so was Pippa's mother, all of them fussing around the child who was seated, unmoving, in the centre of the rug, staring blankly into space. Pippa was crouched beside him, rubbing his hands.

'He doesn't seem to know me,' she wailed, raising a tear-stained face to Charles. She was now consumed with guilt at having been out.

The nanny, pale-faced and shaken by it all, had not quite known what to do for the best and so had called Pippa's mother.

'You should have tried my mobile,' scolded Pippa

but the girl hadn't thought of that. She had badly needed some reassurance and the older woman was fortunately at home and had arrived in a cab within twenty minutes. Not sure what to do, they had gone ahead and summoned the doctor who had roused himself, grudgingly, from his fireside and come.

'I don't think it's anything serious,' he said, relieved that the head of the house was now home. 'I have checked his temperature and looked at his eyes and the wee lad seems perfectly sound.'

'Jack,' said Charles but the child didn't blink, just continued to stare into space.

'I think what he needs is a good night's sleep,' said Pippa's mother, taking over, calmer now that the doctor had checked Jack out. 'You know what they can be like at this age, running fevers without any warning. You were constantly giving me frights when you were a baby.'

Pippa gathered the child in her arms and took him upstairs to the nursery while Charles picked up his car keys again to drive the nanny home. 'It was good of you to come,' he told the doctor, melting the dour old Scot's ill humour with a blast of his lethal charm. 'It's a gross imposition to have called you out. I thank you most sincerely.'

'My pleasure,' said the doctor, mollified. 'It is always better to be safe than sorry where babies are concerned.'

'I'll wait till Charles gets back,' said Pippa's mother, flopping down on the couch, exhausted, when Pippa came downstairs and went immediately to the fridge for a bottle of wine.

'What do you really think?' she asked, still worried and guilty at having been out. 'Is that sort of thing really normal at this age?'

'Of course it is, darling. He is only a baby. It is probably just a phase he's going through.'

But later, in the privacy of the cab on the short journey home to Richmond, she faced up to a private fear she had had since the twins had started to crawl and she'd first become aware of Jack's behaviour. She silently prayed that her hunch was wrong. If not, her daughter – and that meant her, too – was in for considerable heartache.

'Just occasionally,' said Pippa to Dino, as they practised Pilates on the breakfast room floor, 'my husband makes me feel an incompetent fool.'

'How so?' asked the trainer, as she worked on her abs. He took great interest in Pippa's marriage which he still hadn't quite figured out. Charles Buchanan, though still in peak form, was, in Dino's private opinion, too old for his spirited wife. Charming, yes, and generous too. But there was something about him he didn't quite trust. Not that he knew him well at all; they only met in passing.

Pippa related the incident with Jack and Dino listened intently. Twice he had witnessed the child having tantrums when he hadn't been able to get his own way. But that was quite normal with kids that age; what he really needed was a slap. He kept that to himself, however, since Pippa was not in the mood for jokes. She blamed herself for having left him with the nanny, felt it was somehow her fault.

'You've got to have some sort of life of your own. You can't fuss over them all the time.'

'But it's my responsibility,' she said. For falling pregnant in the first place.

She still felt guilt about the break-up of his marriage, the more so since Cassie had taken it so well. The twice they had met she had seemed such a lady, calm and gracious and slightly withdrawn, with fine grey eyes and a thoughtful air as though her mind were set on higher things. Yet Pippa had ruthlessly snatched her husband at a time when her own youngest child was just leaving home. She couldn't believe she had been so restrained, had let Charles go without a murmur.

Cassie was hardly ever mentioned these days, except when Aidan came by. Pippa got a buzz out of seeing him with the twins, the likeness between them was so striking. She hoped her boys would grow up just like him, as tall and good-looking as their father with the same irrepressible laugh and magnetic blue eyes. When you saw the Buchanans all together, there was no mistaking the dominant gene. It made her mother laugh, it was so nearly absurd.

'There is not a trace of Cassie in Aidan, nor of me in the twins,' Pippa said. She wondered fleetingly if there'd be another wife, then quickly suppressed the thought as downright unhealthy. But Dino, who understood her well, had picked up her train of thought.

'Does he have any other families tucked away?' He would not put it past the crafty old bugger, who seemed to have been less and less home since the babies were born. But he kept his tone deliberately light, was far too fond of his client to want to upset her.

'Are you kidding?' said Pippa, with a slightly forced smile. 'Don't you think two is enough?'

Hakkasan was pulsating with life; Pippa couldn't catch what Charles was saying as the suave black waiter led them to their table. It was the newest hot restaurant to open in London and everyone who was anyone was there. Starlets and B-listers out in force; it took him back to his earlier life, before he had been encumbered.

'What?' yelled Pippa, as Charles mimed a question then, getting the gist, yelled: 'White wine.'

'Won't you have something more exotic?' But since she still couldn't hear, he let it go. He was getting too old for this type of trendy joint, yet couldn't bear not to keep up. He raised a finger and summoned the waiter and ordered a bottle of Cristal.

'What's this in aid of?' asked Pippa suspiciously.

'Aren't I allowed to spoil the girl of my dreams?'

Pippa smiled; she could hear him now. That was Charles all over. Whenever he sensed she was slightly fed up, in he came with this sort of grand gesture which always won her over. He certainly knew which buttons to press. She remembered the diamond brooch he had bought her, which she hardly ever wore. It was still too old and formal for her but either she would grow into it or she would pass it on to the wife of one of her sons. Or perhaps they would still have a daughter of their own; she hadn't entirely ruled that out. She was just too tired with the shop and the twins to contemplate it now.

The food was delicious, she handed them that, and, once she grew used to the volume of sound, she relaxed and began to enjoy herself. The champagne certainly helped.

'You are looking especially pretty tonight.' Charles leaned forward and kissed her hand and, just for a second, she wondered what he was after.

'You don't look so bad yourself,' she said, proud as ever to be seen with him, grateful that they had stayed together even after she'd thought she couldn't win. She just wished he wasn't away so much. These days he seemed to be travelling most of the time. She knew it was because of his career but wished that sometimes he'd just stay home and spend more time with her and the boys before they were too much older. He was missing their childhood and that was a shame. Before he knew it, they'd be off to school and only home for the holidays, if Charles had the final word, as he usually did.

'Do you still love me?' she found herself asking before she could bite back the words. How grotesque; she was acting like a loser after he'd spent all this money to bring her here.

'Of course I love you and I always will.' His grip on her fingers grew tighter. His eyes, of that eerie electric blue, locked into hers and left her limp. 'Whatever else happens, remember this. I won't ever let you down.'

Part Two

25

'Calm down,' said Magda, when Frankie called, incoherently gabbling. 'You know it can't have been him. You saw him die.'

'It was him,' said Frankie. 'Though God knows how. I am telling you the evidence of my eyes. He was only feet away from me, though I don't believe he saw me.' If only she'd managed to yank the window down.

'It isn't possible,' said Magda firmly. 'Please calm down and get a grip on yourself.' She had long feared something like this could happen, that Frankie might suffer a total breakdown after all the years spent bottling up her grief. It was one of the reasons she'd invited her to Lier; she hadn't thought Frankie strong enough then to be able to cope on her own. But nearly thirty years had passed and she hardly mentioned his name any more. Perhaps she'd been wrong about the vegetable market but she had thought the responsibility would do her good. These monthly excursions into the real world had been designed to take Frankie out of herself. If only the fan-belt on the truck hadn't broken so she'd had to start taking the train.

'Come home,' she said, 'and we'll talk it through.' What she needed was a course of intensive treatment. Magda had been wrong to imagine she could sort her out without professional backup.

'I have to find him.' She was practically screaming and clearly not listening at all. 'I have checked the trains. He was headed for Bruges. There's another due in just a few minutes. If I don't get home tonight, don't worry. I'll call and let you know what's going on.'

She was starting to sound completely off her head, like a teenager high on speed.

'Wait,' said Magda. 'Don't ring off. At least let me go there with you.' Too late, for Frankie had ended the call. And when Magda attempted to reconnect, she found she had switched off her phone.

There was nothing she could do except wait for Frankie to call again. Perhaps, after all, it was no bad thing; might help her finally get him out of her system. If only she could exorcise Chad's ghost, she might at last be able to move on.

26

The puppy had been a gift from Claude, in the days when he pandered to her every whim and Cristina complained that he left her too much on her own. A cream chihuahua with great soulful eyes, Fifi arrived in a scarlet hatbox, wearing a diamond bracelet round her throat. Cristina had fallen upon her with glee, transferred the collar to the safety of her wrist, then spent a few weeks, until she grew bored, smothering the animal with love. She bought her all sorts of unnecessary things: a mink-trimmed coat, a sheepskin bed and a travelling case disguised as a handbag in which to carry her around. The Paris restaurants were lenient about dogs so Fifi accompanied her everywhere, except when she dined alone with Claude, who simply wouldn't allow it. On the occasions Fifi was left at home, it fell to Yvette to take care of her, to walk her twice round the garden daily and ensure that she did her business only outside. Even so, Fifi had become so spoilt that she frequently piddled on the marble floors, causing Yvette to scream in rage and threaten to wring her scrawny neck.

Except when Cristina was in the mood, Fifi lived in the servants' quarters where she grew adept at begging for food and nimbly avoiding the gardener's vicious boot.

'I can't imagine why she wanted her.' Yvette could never find much to praise in her self-indulgent mistress. 'She treats her like an unwanted toy. It's a shame. She should really be put down.'

'The dog or Cristina?' Serge asked languidly, lighting another cigarette.

His question didn't merit an answer but Yvette flashed him a conspiratorial grin. Though the pair were often at loggerheads, on the subject of Cristina they always agreed. Monsieur was a gentleman through and through whereas she was just mixed blood trash.

But when Cristina went out on the town, the dog became an accessory, with a great satin bow attached to her collar to tone with whatever her mistress was wearing. The servants might continue to sneer, yet it did seem that they were stuck with Cristina unless, of course, Monsieur should get wind of her much discussed marriage plans. Considering she owed her lifestyle to him, she was wildly indiscreet in the house, a clear indication of her contempt for the staff. She screamed at them and pushed them around, yet never apparently stopped to think that they might tell tales out of school if she wasn't careful.

'You owe it to him to let him know,' said Serge, who was strongly on the master's side, but Yvette didn't dare to interfere and risk possibly losing her job. Let things take their own course, she said. Though the arrogant cow had certainly got it coming.

There was still no word from Rocco and Cristina was frantic. Perhaps he had mislaid his phone. She had no other means of contacting him, since he constantly moved around. And to make matters worse, today was Monday and Claude would return from the country later, expecting her to be looking her best and to entertain him tonight. She sat and scowled in the beauty parlour, the dog on her lap and her phone in her hand, making endless unnecessary calls while the pedicurist silently worked on her feet. Every few minutes she barked out an order: she needed a tissue, a magazine, another *tasse du thé*. And a bowl of water for her panting dog who looked bedraggled, her ribbon drooping, as though in need of a beauty treatment herself.

Several more times she tried Rocco's number but his phone still appeared not to be switched on. So, once again, she called the house to check with Yvette if he'd left her a message.

'No, madame,' said Yvette again, biting back her irritation at these constant, meaningless interruptions which kept her from doing her job.

'If he does, please give him my mobile number and tell him I need to talk to him. I'll be home by one, so tell him that too, and warn Monsieur, if he gets home first, that I'm not feeling terribly well today and would like an early night.'

Yvette rolled her eyes despairingly at Serge, still

lolling around in the kitchen, watching her iron. 'Madame is a nasty piece of work,' she said. 'Monsieur deserves a lot better.'

'I wouldn't mind taking her off his hands, provided I didn't have to listen to her moan. It seems all she ever does is complain. Yet look how pampered she is.'

'She should try changing places with me,' said Yvette. 'Then she would find out what hardship really is.'

The pedicurist had finished her job and was now applying a final coat before standing back to admire her work, which had taken the best part of an hour. Her next appointment was already waiting; Cristina's constant demands slowed everyone down.

'Voilà!' she said as Cristina stopped talking, indicating with her hand the immaculate job she had done.

Cristina, with a pointed lack of enthusiasm, paused before making another call, and studied her toes for a long and critical moment.

'No,' she pronounced. 'I don't like the colour. Take it off and start all over again.'

After Cal had left and she'd screamed and cried, drunk too much and bent the ear of every passing acquaintance she had in Rio, Cristina, with the help of the magic white powder, had managed to reconstruct herself and crawl back into the semblance of a career. Her reputation went before her: unreliable, the fashion houses said. Also no longer quite the beauty she had been. Her life's excesses had taken their toll so that, by her late twenties, by the stretch of no one's imagination could she be styled this year's face or even the year before's. As her life went into a downward spiral and the important bookings started drying up, her friend, the adventuress, Marie-Hélène, belatedly came to her aid.

'Chérie,' she said, rapidly scribbling down a number. 'Call this woman and mention my name.'

'Why?' asked Cristina.

'Never mind,' said her friend. 'Let's just say that I owe you.'

Madame Zarco was a slim, discreet widow of indeterminate age, with jet-black hair drawn back sleekly into a knot and lips of a glossy ruby red, the only clue to her hidden sexuality. Her role in Brazilian society was simple: she organised dinners and villa parties in order to introduce beautiful women to out of town visitors, passing through. Her fees were steep but the women didn't pay; the entire financial burden was borne by the men.

'I suppose it might fill in an evening or two.' Cristina was doubtful but growing short of cash, since these days her habit cost more than she could afford. And, whatever her shortcomings on the catwalk, she was still a sensationally beautiful woman who turned heads wherever she went. Madame Zarco was delighted to add her name to her list and introduce her to a shady social world consisting mainly of C-list footballers and starlets on the make. The villa parties turned out to be fun and gave Cristina a chance to display her still voluptuous charms. She was putting on weight but it suited her style and the men couldn't get enough of her. At almost every function, she was the star prize.

Over the years one thing led to another which was how Cristina found herself in Paris, courtesy of Madame Zarco's social list. It was early spring and the fashion shows were on. Each day she took her place in the front row, idly flicking through the glossy brochures while the cameras clicked around her. The designers lent her clothes for each occasion, as Cristina's face was still widely known, and her days were crammed with parties and receptions at which she was well received. A lot of the time she was bored and ungrateful yet her socialising did fulfil a function of sorts by introducing her to a much wider circle. And it was better than rotting at home in Rio where the phone rang less and less.

Claude Daumier styled himself an entrepreneur though Cristina was never entirely sure what that implied. It seemed to mean he had loads of money as well as an aristocratic background and a town-house close to the Bois de Boulogne, though his main abode, where his wife resided, was his château outside Neuilly. They met at one of the endless receptions that filled Cristina's aimless days, and his invitation to lunch lit a spark in her addled brain that told her that at last her luck might be changing. Cristina, by then, was thirty-four and Claude at least thirty years older but he kept himself in excellent shape, dressed in a chic though conservative style and possessed a kind of insouciance that she found immensely attractive. A

Parisian to his fingertips, he moved in the social circles she admired and had long aspired to be part of. Also, somewhat to her surprise, he was competent in bed.

They fell into a relationship that admirably suited them both. He persuaded her to remain in Paris and set up home in his elegant house, whilst also making it clear that they'd never marry. His wife and children were sacred to him, in a different compartment of his life. As long as Cristina behaved herself, the arrangement worked for her very well, took care of her pressing financial needs and gave her a coveted role among the elite. She liked the city, which she found more inspiring than the endless beachscapes of Rio de Janeiro, which had finally started to pall. She was growing up.

For a while she enjoyed this new bourgeois life, presiding over Claude's dinner parties, firing orders at the staff and throwing her weight around. He paid all her bills without a murmur, liked her to be expensively dressed, even found her tantrums amusing since they usually climaxed in bed. For a man of his age, he remained very fit. There was little that she could justifiably complain of.

At first she resented his weekends with his wife but soon came to see them as the benefit they were; she had the run of his house and driver and slowly started to build a life of her own. Love had never been mentioned between them; what they had was a business alliance that amply suited them both. And since love was something she had almost never known, it was not a commodity she missed.

* * *

After twelve years, though, of being Claude's mistress, Cristina was feeling distinctly jaded and yearning for something she couldn't quite specify. Security she had in abundance, as well as social recognition of sorts, since Paris was very worldly about such things. But that, she now felt, was no longer enough. At forty-six, she craved something more, was beginning to feel that this static life was making her listless and staid. And so, on the pretext of homesickness, she returned to Rio for Carnaval and a chance to soak in some sunshine and see a few friends.

Marie-Hélène was long since gone, married now to a minor prince and living in Salzburg, so they said, in fading rococo splendour. The rest of the pack had also dispersed, to wherever such party girls end up, and Cristina found herself even more lonely than in Paris. In the end, she called Madame Zarco who expressed herself pleased to hear from her and invited her round for a soirée the following night. It was better than hanging around in bars and she owed the woman a favour or two so Cristina dolled herself up and went on the razzle.

And, like Cinderella's, her life changed at midnight when Rocco Pereira and a bunch of drunk cronies belatedly burst into the room.

And now she was faced with a life-threatening dilemma. To marry Rocco she would have to tell Claude, which would put her immediately in the wrong and meant that Claude, if he chose to, could evict her. She had few illusions about his affection;

there had been a time when he doted upon her but that was ten years ago. She had watched his admiration wane with every temper tantrum she threw and, in her saner moments, she knew that her days in this house might be numbered. Which was, if she were honest with herself, the greater part of Rocco's attraction. Not only was he sexy and younger but he earned a fortune as a racing driver and could, if she played her cards skilfully enough, take her away from all this.

Which was where the main complication arose. Without the house and the façade of Claude's wealth, she was realistic enough to know that she lacked the wherewithal to catch and hold him. Such knowledge had only come slowly to her, after a lot of hard knocks. She no longer considered herself a world-class beauty. Hence the dilemma which she had to face up to: she couldn't afford to lose him. And there was the rub.

On cue, the door was gently pushed open and Fifi, on delicate paws, pranced in. She shivered and grovelled till Cristina swept her up and smothered her muzzle with lipsticky kisses, glad for a few mindless seconds to have something to love.

'What do you think I should do, chérie?' she whispered in the dog's bat-like ear but Fifi merely whimpered and licked her nose. With a heartfelt sigh, Cristina acknowledged that this latest mess was of her own making and that she had some urgent decisions to make.

When she married Cal, they had both been high and Cristina had only faint memories of the occasion. She recalled the heat and her shimmering dress and walking barefoot across baking sand, with her arms full of flowers he had recklessly bought at the roadside. She also remembered how handsome he looked, with his golden tan and his sparkling blue eyes, dressed entirely in white, including his shoes. He always had been a bit of a ham, with one eye cocked for the paparazzi who seemed to be drawn to his presence whatever he did. She remembered also the ring he had bought her, platinum studded with five carat diamonds, which she'd hurled through the window during one of their spats and never found again. What she couldn't recall, though, was who else had been there; if anyone traceable had witnessed the event.

She realised now she had one simple choice, either to try to locate the paperwork or else to let sleeping dogs lie. For twenty-three years, since Cal walked out, she hadn't given the subject a thought, not even when she first hooked up with Claude. Her marriage had been and gone in a blur and no longer seemed relevant to her life. Until she met Rocco, the thought had never struck her that she might want to marry again. If she chose to do nothing, as was her inclination, the odds were that no one would ever find out. After two decades, and on another continent, the chance of a witness turning up seemed laughably remote. She had no idea where Cal was now, nor even if he were still alive, though she felt her heart would have somehow known if he weren't. He was only three years older than her which, even though she lied about her age, made him no more than forty-seven now.

Had there been photos? She couldn't remember, had certainly never seen any since, did not possess a treasured wedding album. Yet the paparazzi had been out in force, tipped off by somebody in the know, most probably Cal himself. Since she was, at that point, the queen of the catwalk, both of them A-list celebrities, it was hard to believe they had not hit the tabloids at least. After the wedding, they'd driven slowly through Rio, she standing up in their open car, throwing handfuls of flowers to the cheering crowds. Cristina smiled; it was all coming back. She remembered how happy she had been. The start of an idyll she had thought was for ever, though the truth was it lasted for less than eighteen months. And if she remembered, then others might too. It was too much of a gamble to take the risk.

But then she considered the ramifications and was once more struck by colossal doubt. If marrying Rocco meant losing Claude's patronage, she risked messing up the rest of her life should it ever emerge, at some future date, that she hadn't been legally free. More than anything else in the world, Cristina valued her independence. Since the days of scavenging and sleeping rough, she had done much of which she wasn't proud but her main achievement was to have survived and, by anyone's standards, remarkably well, considering. She glanced around her luxurious bedroom, with its walk-in closets and chandeliers, and knew that she dared not risk mucking things up and losing this lifestyle on one simple roll of the dice.

She had to protect what assets she had, so she picked up the phone and put in a call to her lawyer.

27

By the time Frankie got off the train in Bruges the weather had worsened to driving sleet, so dense she could hardly see anything at all. Magda's mitts were completely sodden so she'd peeled them off and stuffed them in her backpack, and her chilblains throbbed within her inadequate boots. She splurged on a cab to the centre of town and had it drop her at the tourist office, which seemed the logical place to start her quest. The woman there, though, had no knowledge of Chad and even less interest in helping her. The tourist invasion had not yet begun and the town, unusually, was more or less deserted. So it shouldn't be hard to track him down; it was all much smaller than Frankie had thought and he couldn't have just been passing through, since Bruges was the end of the line.

In a state of considerable agitation, she decided to follow the tourist route and stop off at likely places to ask if they either knew Chad by name or had seen someone answering his description. In her temporary state of dementia, it never occurred that his striking looks might have gone unnoticed. From the fleeting glimpse she'd had of him, it appeared he had not aged in any way. As the sleet grew heavier, she skidded on the cobbles as she ducked in and out of every café and bar, asking – pleading – if they knew where he was, the man she knew must be somewhere near, whom she desperately needed to find. But the people, though kindly, looked at her askance, discomfited by her sodden state and the madness in her eyes.

'If I were you, I'd go home, my dear, before you catch your death of cold.' The weather was growing dramatically worse. They were mostly closing early.

Frankie, having drawn a blank, wandered aimlessly along the canals, too distraught to absorb the beauty of the unspoilt medieval town. She was soaked right through and frozen to the bone, on top of which it was now growing dark and she had almost no money. She couldn't afford to stay overnight or even buy anything to eat. As it was, she would have to walk back to the station, if only she could remember where it was.

'Come home,' said Magda when Frankie called, still sounding quite demented. 'Let me know once you're on the train and I'll pick you up in Antwerp.'

Her heart went out to her fragile friend who had surely suffered enough without this, though from long experience she knew not to try to stand in her way. When Frankie set her mind on something, she listened to neither reason nor logic and this weird hallucination had clearly unhinged her.

'Come home, dearest,' said Magda, more gently, 'and we'll talk things over together.'

'I have to find him. I know what I saw. Please don't keep saying I dreamed it all up.' Wrapped in a blanket beside the fire, with a mug of hot chocolate clasped in both hands, Frankie was slowly thawing out and her teeth had at last stopped chattering. From the kitchen came wonderful cooking smells. They were preparing a pheasant casserole as a treat and had all discreetly left her alone with Magda.

'It's time to give up, love. You know it wasn't him. Don't be so hard on yourself. Chad has been dead for thirty years. After all, you were at the inquest. It isn't healthy to torture yourself in this way.'

But Frankie stubbornly shook her head. In this sort of mood, she refused to listen. Magda could only keep quiet and hope that, after she'd had a good night's sleep, she would get things back into perspective.

28

The flat, Charles argued, was a snip at the price and, when Cassie came to see it, she had to agree. Queen Anne style in ornate red brick, built in the 1880s, 'Pont Street Dutch' as Osbert Lancaster dubbed it. The owners, a diplomat and his wife, were moving permanently to Hong Kong and keen to make a swift sale. It was roomy and comfortable, though their décor was drab and would need some sprucing up. But Cassie liked the size of the reception rooms which would mean that Charles could entertain in style; also the fact that, with four bedrooms, each of the children would have claim to their own space. Not that Daisy and Tim would ever use it, but it might make a nice London pad for Rose, now articled to a solicitor in Penzance.

For years Charles had angled for a base in town but, since it was Cassie's money they were spending, she naturally got to have the final say. Aidan, at eight, was becoming a handful but would shortly be going to prep school in Knightsbridge so the Pont Street flat would be just the thing since Cassie considered him far too young to be boarding. The Elwes males always went to Eton so his name had been down for Sussex House before he could even crawl.

It would mean a bit of a sacrifice for her, having to forsake her beloved Cornwall for eight weeks at a stretch, three times a year. The grandchildren occupied much of her time but now it was natural for her son to take precedence. She would put her energies into the flat and act as a full-time wife for once. She felt guilty at having neglected Charles so much.

'At last we can do some proper entertaining. I look forward to meeting your London friends.' For the past few years Charles had travelled so much, he only ever got home at weekends and even then on a very sporadic basis. When not off visiting wealthy clients, he stayed in a hotel. He liked his work as a private dealer, which now took up most of his energy. Life as a country squire was all right but wheeling and dealing more his style. The light of challenge shone bright in his eyes whenever he felt he had pulled off a coup; he certainly seemed to have found his natural niche. Cassie often wondered where he had got his flair and taste.

Much of it, of course, he'd absorbed from her, though Cassie would never acknowledge that. Moderation in all things was her creed; the Cornish house and, later, the flat were models of studied understatement.

Daisy's children, Willow and Sam, were miniatures of their mother. With their huge brown eyes and angelic smiles they were good enough to eat, Cassie said. She could not have too much of them, was always content to babysit and get to play the role of doting granny. Since they lived only five minutes away, Daisy often dropped them at her mother's house where Willow kept her Shetland pony. Charles was teaching her to ride.

'He looks good in the saddle. I'll grant him that.' Sybil still viewed him with slight mistrust, though she liked the way he dealt with her brother's grandchildren. She and Tremayne were leaning on the gate, watching Charles, sleek in breeches and boots, putting Edwin's hunter through its paces. Whatever his antecedents might be, he had taken to riding like a real pro. Willow, enraptured, clapped her hands and begged to be hoisted up into the saddle and Charles, with his usual good humour, cheerfully obliged. Sam, the baby, gurgled with joy and stretched out his arms towards the horse. In a couple of years he'd be up in that saddle himself.

'We still don't know where he came from,' said Sybil. 'His past continues to be a closed book which he seems reluctant to open.'

Tremayne, still harbouring a grudge against Charles, viewed him through deeply cynical eyes. 'Superficially he's just too perfect.' He was jealous of the man's charisma. It seemed he had every woman in his hand. Even Sybil now, which really unnerved him.

'I'd like to know what he's up to,' he said, 'in all the time he is not at home, leaving poor Cassie here on her own. It isn't right.'

'Hardly on her own,' said Sybil, 'with so much family around her.' She shot him a shrewd incisive glance. 'I hope you're not suggesting he plays away.'

Not that it hadn't occurred to her too. He was ten years younger than his wife and oozed sex appeal. He would have to be pretty much of a saint not to give in to temptation at times and saintliness wasn't something that sat well with Charles.

'What precisely do we know about him? He must have some sort of a past.' He'd been twenty-four when he'd married Cassie. What had he done with his life before that? It certainly seemed, to Tremayne's jaundiced eye, that a lot had never been explained.

'I'm not exactly sure,' said Sybil. 'I believe his parents lived abroad. They were always travelling, according to Cassie, and the poor boy was sent home to boarding school at far too early an age.' One reason Aidan was going to a day school, so that his mother was there when he came home. She would be on hand to help with his prep and generally make a fuss of him. Both her daughters were now off her hands; in her heart she hated the thought of losing Aidan too.

'He is going to have to board at Eton.'

'But by then he will be thirteen.'

'Still too young, if you want my opinion.' Tremayne had never left this part of Cornwall, except for his two years' National Service, and still showed no signs of restlessness or any desire to move on.

'Cassie's father and brothers all went there. It's an Elwes family tradition.' Her own brother, Edwin, had been privately tutored because of his dicky heart, which had clouded his life.

'So what was Charles doing,' Tremayne persisted, 'in the years between school and marriage? Did he go to varsity – he seems the type who would?' But even that they had to take on trust.

Sybil admitted she didn't know. She had tried asking Cassie who was equally vague. They had met not long after Edwin's death and fallen for each other on the spot. It was something Cassie rarely mentioned, at least to her former husband's sister, though there was no disguising the light in her eye whenever Charles entered a room. Without doubt it had been a genuine love match; Sybil had no problem with that. The only emotion she secretly felt was envy.

But what *was* known about the man? Tremayne continued to chew on that as he went about his daily duties, running the Hawksmoor estate. Charles Buchanan was a very smooth talker whose appealing smile and extreme good looks had an effect on everyone who met him. Not only the women, the men as well, which was what most troubled Tremayne. He had watched Richard Elwes, Cassie's brother, usually very much down to earth, pay serious attention to what Charles was saying, as if he had any knowledge at all of running a country estate. You really don't like him, he had to admit, confronting himself in the shaving mirror. But he also acknowledged that whatever it was went deeper than simple jealousy. His main concern was Edwin's legacy and safeguarding the family's interests.

* * *

Pont Street would be ready for occupation a month before the start of the autumn term, which put Cassie under considerable pressure to get things shipshape before they could move in. Charles, as always, was whirling around, buying pictures and delivering them to clients. Since he spent so much of his time on the road, he had lately invested in a fancy car, a Bentley convertible with ample room to stack paintings in the boot. Also it made the right impression on his clients. He had turned a hobby into a prosperous sideline and now found artworks for private collectors whose specialist interests he knew. The galleries well acquainted with him allowed him to have the pictures on loan and then cold call on appropriate clients, where he usually pulled off deals. He was endlessly popping over to Jersey where some of the biggest collectors were based and, as his social circles increased, so did his reputation. These days what he principally did were total renovations.

'By rights,' chuckled Cassie, as she showed him cloth samples, 'it's you who ought to be doing up the flat.'

'I don't have the time,' said Charles disarmingly. 'Besides, you couldn't afford me.'

The first thing she did, once the diplomat left, was have the living room walls repainted a lovely luminous antique white in place of the dowdy dark green. That, with diaphanous ivory curtains, totally transformed the room and made it seem a lot larger. Next on the list was Aidan's bedroom which she decorated to his specifications and turned into a cave-like schoolboy den. With his football pennants and personal computer, it was soon the image of the one at home, with a spare bunk bed so a schoolfriend could sleep over.

Although Cassie missed the Cornish routine and the daily visits of Daisy's children, for all sorts of reasons she'd felt it important that Aidan get right away. Though normally equably tempered, like his father, there were times when his behaviour had begun to alarm her. At first his nose had been put out of joint by the arrival, in quick succession, of Daisy's children, just eighteen months apart. When Willow was born he'd shown no curiosity but acted as though she were just a toy that failed to hold his attention very long. Once, though, Cassie had caught him by her crib, pulling the covers up over her head then down again in order to shout in her face. He was playing peek-a-boo, he explained, but Cassie suspected him of darker motives. She never mentioned the episode to Daisy or left him alone with either baby again.

Aidan was six then; now he was eight and Daisy had caught him undressing Willow in order, he said when she screamed at him, just to look. Cassie had defended him: he was just a growing boy displaying a healthy interest in living things. But, from then on, she kept them apart and was relieved when they took him at Sussex House. She still shuddered to remember the incident of the frogs.

*　　*　　*

With new connections through the school and the growing momentum of her husband's career, life developed a frantic pace to which Cassie was not accustomed. Her Cornish existence was very sedate, especially now that both girls had left home and Charles spent most of his time away. Her idea of a perfect night in was kitchen leftovers from the fridge, and perhaps a concert on Radio 3 while she read by the fire. She had lost the habit of trivial small talk, not that she'd ever excelled at it, and privately felt that the other mothers, all considerably younger than her, were uniformly lightweight. During term-time the invitations flowed in and she couldn't use Aidan as an excuse, since all the other parents were in the same boat. Most had nannies or else didn't work and all had space for a child to sleep over which here, in fashionable Knightsbridge, was much encouraged. Cassie's feeble protests about doing his homework fell upon deaf ears. The boys were bright, their futures assured, so let them play and make social contacts before they had to knuckle down for the tough stuff.

Charles was as bad as the other parents. 'He's only a kid,' he said. 'Wait until he moves on to Eton. That's when he'll really have to sharpen his act.'

It was at the opera house one night that they ran into Millicent Ferneyhough. An insipid-looking woman in, perhaps, her mid-thirties, she stood alone in a corner of the Crush Bar, nervously sipping a lemonade and looking uncomfortable and lost. Her mousy hair was pulled tightly back and anchored with an Alice band, a style too young for a woman her age that didn't do anything for her. Cassie became aware of her first, feeling herself being watched, and glanced around to see whose eyes were on her. Not on her, it turned out, but on Charles; the woman looked as if she were seeing a ghost. The wife of an out-of-town client, no doubt, though she lacked any visible style.

'It seems as if that woman knows you,' she said, nudging Charles, who was casing the room. 'Perhaps you should go over and say hello.' Though leave me out of it, she nearly added. She saw so little of Charles, as it was, the last thing they needed tonight was a hanger-on.

Charles glanced over then grimaced and shrugged. 'Never seen her before in my life,' he said.

He carried their glasses back to the bar, leaving Cassie alone and undefended, still uncomfortably aware of the woman's stare. When she looked again, the stranger was advancing with a very determined look.

'Excuse me,' said the woman, 'but the man you are with. Do you mind if I ask who he is?'

'My husband,' said Cassie with a sinking heart. Exactly what she dreaded was happening again. This insignificant country mouse was about to attach herself to them when company was the last thing they needed. She wished people would learn to leave him alone. Especially on a rare evening like this when, for once, she had him to herself.

'And his name . . . ?'

'Why do you want to know?' Cassie was suddenly

on her guard. Drawing herself up to her full five foot ten, she locked eyes with the smaller woman.

At that moment Charles returned, bearing two more flutes of champagne, whereupon the stranger switched her attention to him.

'It's Millie,' she squeaked, almost spilling his drink as she frenziedly grabbed at his sleeve. Handing both glasses to Cassie to hold, he carefully blotted the moisture.

'Charles Buchanan,' he said, offering his hand, 'and this is my wife, Cassandra. I don't believe I have had the pleasure . . .' Already his attention had drifted off; he was looking around again.

'But,' said the woman, clearly confused, 'you look so much like him. I thought . . .'

'Excuse me,' said Charles, relieving Cassie of his glass, 'but there's someone over there I need to talk to.'

He vanished back into the tightly pressed crowd, leaving Cassie alone with the stricken woman, who now seemed extremely distressed. Her hand shook and her face was pale, with two bright spots of colour on her cheeks.

'Are you all right?' asked Cassie, concerned, offering a steadying hand. 'Let's sit down and I'll fetch you some water. It's pretty stifling in here.'

Millie feverishly flapped her hands and shook her head in embarrassment. She had made a mistake and now felt a fool; words appeared to have failed her. It was rude of Charles to have been so abrupt and Cassie was far too kind to abandon her too. She spotted an empty table in the corner to which she carefully propelled her. The least she could do was stay and chat until the woman was less distressed. But never again, she silently vowed, would she let Charles get away with such gross behaviour.

The five minute bell rang and Charles was no longer in sight. He was out there somewhere, working the room, and would, presumably, come back to claim her in time for the final bell. Millie's high colour was slowly subsiding as she sank back into her mouse-like state, in her drab brown silk and old-fashioned tippet and, Cassie now noticed, truly dreadful shoes.

'Who, might I ask, did you think he was?' she began, but at that moment a man hurried up, muttering something about the impossible traffic. He nodded to Cassie and took Millie's arm; she was clearly more cherished than it had at first seemed. This portly man with the florid complexion appeared to be very possessive.

'I have to know,' repeated Cassie before they walked away. 'Who was it that you thought he was?'

Millie turned and smiled at her, safe now and almost coquettish. 'Oh, no one special. Just someone from my past.' Cassie could swear that she almost smirked. 'Cosmo Banbury, my first husband. Haven't seen him in yonks.'

'Right,' said Cassie, once they were home and Charles was pouring himself a whisky. 'Who was that woman and where does she fit in? It was obvious that she knew you.'

'She's the Countess of Rochester and that was her

husband.' He dropped an ice cube into the glass before slumping into his favourite chair.

'So you did know her after all,' said Cassie sharply.

Charles merely grinned and slowly savoured his drink. 'You are looking very fetching tonight,' he said. 'Once I've knocked this back, let's get off to bed. I have to make an early start in the morning.'

'Enough!' said Cassie, suddenly furious, 'Kindly stick to the point. Why did she think that you might have been her husband? And who is Cosmo whatever-it-was? I've never heard him mentioned before. What was she on about?'

He shrugged then flashed her that roguish grin that worked every time with the ladies. 'Who knows?' he said. 'She was clearly deluded. I met her once at a debutante ball the night she came out, simply aeons ago.'

'And?'

'And nothing. As I recall, we had a brief fling and then ran away. And, yes, since you ask, we may have got hitched but only as part of a drunken lark and under other names. Her daddy made certain that things went no further, you can bet your life on that. The fellow was loaded.'

Cassie's anger had turned to suspicion. 'And are you still married?' she asked.

'To her? Don't be daft. You're the only wife I've got and, furthermore, the only one I want.' He blew her a kiss, which she disregarded, and hauled himself to his feet. 'I'll tell you the rest in the morning,' he said. 'Right now I'm bushed and really must turn in.'

*   *   *

On the whole, though, Charles was a satisfactory husband. Cassie had few complaints. He was fun, he was sexy and, when he was around, still treated her like a princess. He might, on occasion, be careless with the truth and she'd learnt to take what he said with a strong pinch of salt. She had had one husband who was honest to the core but Charles, she had to admit, was a lot more fun.

She settled into the new regime, the week during term-time in the Pont Street flat, driving to Cornwall every Friday, returning Sunday night. It meant a great deal of driving for her but it was important that Aidan should have his mother around. She put much of her energy into doing up the flat and was more than pleased with the result. Instead of her solitary walks with the dogs, now being exercised by Tremayne, she bustled around the backwaters of Chelsea, picking up bargains like a magpie. Charles, who erred on the flamboyant side, was impressed by how little she spent.

'If every client was as thrifty as you, I'd go out of business,' he said.

When Aidan was eleven and apparently doing well, Charles and Cassie were summoned to the school to discuss, the headmaster said, a serious matter. His face was grave when he greeted them and he instantly came to the point. The boy stood accused of petty bullying; two sets of parents had complained. His behaviour in general was getting out of hand. He was becoming a subversive influence and needed to be controlled.

'What absolute tosh,' said Charles, quick to rise. 'The kid is only eleven. He is simply being high-spirited. At his age, I was the same.'

'He's been threatening them and stealing their sweets. On one occasion, he blacked a boy's eye. A younger boy, I might add.'

'Playground scrapping is par for the course. Self-defence is a necessary skill in order to survive.'

Cassie placed a restraining hand on his arm, but Charles impatiently shrugged it off. His volatile temper was quickly aroused when his son was criticised.

'I don't think you quite understand,' said the head, his manner increasingly frosty. 'Unless Aidan learns to behave, he will be suspended.'

'Keep your fucking school,' cried Charles, leaping to his feet. 'I'll be damned if I let him grow up a sissy. I'm removing him forthwith.'

'Now what will we do?' asked Cassie as the three drove home in muted silence. She saw her son's outrageous behaviour reflected in his father.

'No problem,' said Charles, his good humour restored. He always thrived on a fight. 'All we need now is to get him into a crammer.'

29

There seemed no point in returning to Bruges while the weather was still this bad. Magda suggested that Frankie try surfing the net.

'What exactly am I looking for?' asked Frankie, who had zero computer skills. It might help occupy her mind, thought Magda, and stop her falling apart.

'Anything at all remotely connected. You'll be surprised at what you find. It's simply a question of working out how to locate things. Start with Google.'

Under Magda's direction, Frankie typed in Chad's name then waited apprehensively to see what, if anything, emerged. And when, within seconds, his name popped up, she gasped in disbelief. There were several references, from two separate sources – the *Middlesbrough Evening Gazette* and the *Daily Mail*. With trembling fingers, she brought up each one in turn.

The *Gazette*'s report was from 1975 with details of the fatal fire. It included a grainy picture of Chad from the centre's personnel files. The headline was 'Death by Misadventure' and Frankie's name wasn't mentioned at all. The *Daily Mail* had covered the inquest and, later, Frankie's arrest and trial. Overwhelmed, she began to sob and Magda put her arm around her.

'Are you sure you want to continue?' she asked, alarmed at how fragile Frankie was.

'Yes,' said Frankie, 'I have to know.' There could be no turning back.

There was an earlier item from the *Daily Mail*, about Chad's knifing of the bully, for which he had been sent down.

'That's what he was in for,' said Frankie. 'Murder.' He had looked angelic but was ruthless underneath; after all these years, she acknowledged that, though it hadn't stopped her loving him at the time. It was not his fault. He'd had a tough beginning, with no one to give him unconditional love. Even his temporary foster parents had turned their backs at the first sign of trouble and returned him to the institution to rot. Small wonder he'd later gone on to kill. He had never really stood a chance.

'He certainly led an eventful life,' said Magda, 'in such a short space of time. I wonder how he'd have turned out had he survived.'

'He did survive. I know that now.' Frankie practically bit off her head. 'It was him on that train; I am certain of it. Or, if not him,' she added defiantly, 'someone who looked just like him.'

Magda attempted to hug her again but Frankie shook her off. Instead of consoling, she wanted a result. They had come this far on the internet, there might be other stuff there if they dug around.

'Could it have been a close relative, a brother or cousin, something like that? Shall we look up other Barnabys?' There must be a logical explanation or else Frankie was going bonkers.

'The name wasn't real; they made it up. The gardener's boy discovered him so the vicar named him for the boy and the church. They do that with foundlings.'

'But everyone comes from somewhere,' said Magda. 'He must have had parents once. Think.' Though she disapproved of this crazy obsession, she could never resist a puzzle.

For most of the morning they tossed it around instead of doing their scheduled chores. It was far too wet for working outside but Magda had the accounts to get through and Frankie was hogging the computer.

'Make a list,' Magda said to her, 'of anyone ever close to him. There must have been someone before you came on the scene.'

Frankie stared blankly then shook her head. 'Nobody I know of,' she said. 'At the time I met him, he hadn't a friend in the world.'

'Barnaby, the gardener's boy? What do we know about him? Put him on the list as well as the vicar. Have we any idea where St Chad's church was? Yorkshire, I think you said.'

'That's all I know. I'm not good at this. We simply never discussed that sort of thing.' She remembered most the passionate sex but refrained from mentioning that. There were certain areas still out of bounds between them.

Magda made a pot of coffee to help them focus their minds. 'After they found him, where was he sent?'

'Barnardo's.' She did remember that. Though not which branch of the home it was, presumably the one nearest to the church. With a sudden surge of renewed energy, Frankie put that on the list.

'And then what happened? At what point was he fostered?'

'Round about seven, I think he said. By a well-heeled family with a fancy name. One of those poncey ones that sounds made up.'

Magda waited, her pencil poised, but Frankie's memory failed her. 'I know they were pretty mean to him. With luck, it will come to me later.' She added it to the list and went on thinking. The tears had gone and her eyes now shone. Magda certainly seemed to know her stuff.

'In what way were they mean to him?' she asked, as she poured more coffee.

'They sent him off to public school. Then, when he stepped slightly out of line, took him away and returned him to the home.'

'Do you know when?'

'I could work it out.'

'And which was the school?'

'I think Repton.'

Frankie's cheeks had begun to glow as her optimism came flooding back. At last she felt they were starting to get somewhere.

'What was the terrible thing he did,' asked Magda, 'to deserve such a drastic punishment?' The way people behaved sometimes made her feel sick. To send a child to a privileged school, then turn their backs on him for bad behaviour. It was like returning a rescue puppy because it messed on the rug.

'Smoking in the playground,' said Frankie, remembering Chad had made a joke of it.

'That's all?'

'It was dope.'

Which did make a difference. 'And after that?' Magda asked.

'Borstal,' said Frankie. After he'd killed that boy.

Not exactly a saint, thought Magda, but who could blame him, with a background like that? If a child went wrong at an early age, it was often hard to go straight.

'Can you think of anything else?' she asked.

Frankie shook her head. 'That brings us up to when we met. From that point on we spent our time together.'

Magda woke in the middle of the night with Frankie shaking her pillow.

'Tewson-Finch! It just came to me. I told you it was a poncey name. Chad always used to laugh about it, reckoned he was lucky they didn't adopt him.'

'Stick that on the list,' said Magda, only partly awake. That should be enough, at least, to make a start.

30

Life for Jenny could not have been better. The Coot and Hern was doing really well and she dearly loved her new role as chef, though found it sapped her energy, the more so because she was also still acting as manager. She had never worked harder in her life which, after Condé Nast, was saying something, but this work was more on the physical side, leaving her healthily tired and able to sleep. Even Toby had quietened down and rarely interrupted her nights any more. Her daily routine was orchestrated to move as precisely as clockwork. Up at 6.30 to feed the child, then a brisk hour's run in the neighbouring fields while Hamish, the resident barman, acted as nanny. Back by 8.30 to be ready for the drayman and then to walk Toby to his school nearby before returning to the pub to make order out of chaos. Mrs Jones, the cleaner, was in every morning but Jenny took charge of the grate; swept out the ashes from the night before and carried in logs from the outhouse. The fire was a pivotal point of the bar; it had to be properly tended. Hamish was there to lend a hand but most of his mornings were spent with his books. With Jenny's encouragement, he was working part-time for a catering diploma.

'I never thought I could be this happy,' said Jenny to Vanessa as they made tomato chutney. 'I seem to have everything on my plate: my son, the pub and now Clive.'

Vanessa, who was slim and fair, smiled as she scalded preserving jars. 'Where is he, by the way?' she asked. 'I don't think I've seen him in weeks.'

'Working extra long hours, poor love. Sales conference followed by recruitment drive. They really make them slave at Osborne and Cole.'

'But he still enjoys it?'

'Loves it,' she said. 'And he's building his own consultancy on the side.'

'Which means?'

'He couldn't be happier either,' said Jenny, with new-found confidence.

'Has he got plans to quit?' asked Vanessa, whose expertise was interior design and who lived, these days, entirely off freelance work. She had finally given up on marriage, though she always kept a boyfriend around to share the bills, which made sense.

'I think so,' said Jenny. 'Though I'm not entirely sure. These days there's never enough time to talk.' What they mainly discussed, when they did get together, were farmers' markets and seasonal dishes and the past month's profits. They had taken a gamble but one that paid off. By carefully sticking to a limited menu, they were making their stamp on the local community, as well as pulling in diners from further afield. Joyce was still content with her role of sous-chef, preparing vegetables, making sauces and keeping a simmering stockpot on the go. The team was effective: two in the kitchen, Hamish and Simon behind the bar and two girls from the village who came in part-time to lend a hand. On alternate Thursdays, when Clive was there too, acting host from behind the bar, they now had the highest turnout of the week.

'I miss him a lot when he's not around. I wish he had fewer commitments.' Even after two years together, Jenny was still starry-eyed about Clive and Toby lived for the alternate Thursdays when he swept back into their lives.

But she couldn't grumble. It beat churning out articles and meant doing something she really enjoyed, while living a healthy and productive life. As well as making money. The kitchen door stayed open on all but the very coldest of days, and the fragrant smells of the verdant garden mingled with those of the cooking. Whenever she felt like taking a break she would stroll across to the waterwheel, lean on the railing and watch the brook chattering below.

'Do you ever think about Douglas these days?' Vanessa, who remembered the worst of all that, occasionally checked it out.

'Not any more.' Jenny shook her head. She was prettier, lither, somehow younger too and her brown eyes sparkled with vigour. Despite the amount of cooking she did, forever tasting and adjusting flavours and trying out recipes on family and staff, she still didn't gain any weight. She was proud of the fact she was still a size eight, though she did run five miles every day. 'That part of my life seems so long ago. To think, I wasted six years on him.' And his son, who had never even met him, would soon be five.

'It's odd he doesn't seem to want to see the baby.' Vanessa, whose children came first, above everything, had never been able to understand that. Though she'd never liked Douglas.

'That was the deal. The baby or him. He made that clear when I told him about it, though I never believed he would carry things through to this extent.' It was just as well he had, however. If he'd stayed in touch, it would have complicated things. Though she hadn't known that in those months of bleak despair.

'Does Toby ever ask about him?'

'He doesn't even know he exists.' Clive was the father figure in her son's life, which added to Jenny's quiet contentment. Two years of his unfailing support had made a huge difference to her morale. Never in her life had she felt more secure.

Most of her energies went into the pub. Their reputation was growing fast so that practically every night they had a full house. The brewery was pleased and her debt much reduced. If things kept up at this rate and they were careful with their spending, she hoped soon to be able to pay it off in full.

It was Clive's idea to have matchbooks printed, giving details of the pub and where it was, which he promised to hand out to his business contacts.

'Advertising never hurts,' he said. 'If you leave a supply of them on the bar, it will help spread the word and increase your clientele.'

She occasionally asked him about the sleeping partner, the golfing acquaintance who'd provided the loan. He had never been over to look at the place nor, as far as she was aware, even asked to see the accounts, which seemed unusual.

'Isn't he, at the very least, curious to see it?' she asked. In a way, she felt slightly snubbed. She had worked so hard to get things right. She couldn't believe he was so detached, unless he was very rich indeed, which was not something Clive had implied.

'Don't worry about it. He's just very busy. Has loads of other irons in the fire. I am sure he will come by when he's good and ready.' Clive was always so re-assuring and, after all, the man was his friend. She knew he was right: there was no point in fretting when apparently nothing was wrong.

'I don't even know his name,' she said. 'I'd like the chance to thank him.' Without the loan, she couldn't have done it. The least she owed him was a meal some time or even a Christmas card.

'It's not important. I really mean that. You have more urgent things to occupy your mind.' He firmly shooed her back to the kitchen while he popped upstairs to settle Toby and check that the television wasn't still on. It was only much later, after Clive had left, that Jenny remembered he still hadn't told her the name of her mysterious benefactor.

*   *   *

On Mondays she drove round the local suppliers, sourcing produce for the week ahead and planning her menus according to what was in season. They were a nice community, the smallholders around Bath, doing something they really believed in and trying to stay afloat in a tightening economy. On every level Jenny sided with them: the food was fresher and tasted much better than the big suppliers' and she sympathised with their aims. The supermarkets were killing them off; they needed solidarity to win through. She tasted cheeses and home-cured hams, watched them bottling pickles and lemon curd and bought jars of fresh honey for cooking and the overnight guests. Much of what she bought was organically grown, except in cases where she suspected too much hype and went instead for the outward appearance of the vegetables.

Each morning she spoke to her suppliers and put in orders for the day, a lot of her choices depending on the weather. If the seas were choppy, the fish wasn't fresh, and when the weather was hot people's appetites changed. It all became obvious once she had worked it out.

'How come you know so much?' asked the bar staff.

'Just natural talent,' said Jenny cheerfully, not bothering to tell them that, for all those years, she'd had her own culinary column in a major magazine. Then she had started to find it a drag; now everything she had learnt was emerging and serving a useful purpose. Nothing in life is ever wasted after all.

She liked the community and, as she got to know them, more of them came crowding into the bar. One of them, Alistair, dropped in most nights, still in waxed jacket and muddy boots, bringing her samples of leeks and beets and the wonderful cabbages he grew. Originally he had been an accountant but had packed it all in when his marriage fell apart. Now he tended a couple of acres and was building a whole new life for himself with an optimism that equalled Jenny's own.

'He's nice, that fellow,' said Joyce with approval. 'He lives in that lovely stone cottage down Newbridge way. I knew his mother from the WI until she passed on, poor soul. Now I believe he lives there all on his own.'

'Now, now, Joyce,' called Vanessa from the pantry, where she was checking stock and making lists. She loved the activity at the Coot and Hern and was down there, helping out, whenever she could. 'Don't start trying to matchmake, please. You know it never works.' Though privately she agreed with Joyce. Alistair Grey was a lovely guy, funny, nice-looking and obviously bright, and about the right age for Jenny. She knew enough from experience, though, not to start trying to sell him to Jenny. She never really listened to advice: where men were concerned, she was oddly naïve and resolutely blinkered.

The other locals were a colourful crowd, some of them straight out of central casting. A group of old men who played darts every night and sat and grumbled about the weather; four elderly ladies who gossiped in a corner, and a mixture of the local youth. Even the vicar was a regular patron who liked his gin and tonic at opening time. It helped him to do the

Lord's work, he explained, before he started his evening rounds. He often came back for a second when he was through.

Since the Coot and Hern had been serving food, the clientele had upgraded. People came now who had never been regulars, drawn by the ratings and word of mouth, and found the cooking so good that they came again. And, more to the point, brought their London friends. Jenny's celebrity was growing fast. Practically every night they were fully booked. Something was certainly going right; Clive's matchbooks were proving effective.

'We don't want too many or the standards will drop,' she occasionally told Vanessa.

That was the beauty of the place, not so large it could fit in a crowd but with sufficient covers to make a good profit. Sophisticated in an understated way, it retained a lot of its original charm with the beams, the woodsmoke, the crooked doors that had been that way for centuries. When people went upstairs, you could hear the boards creak.

Sex with Clive remained thrilling and intense. The gaps between their reunions kept it hot. With Douglas it had to be done on the sly for, somewhere in the background, a wife was watching. With Clive, though, things were entirely different. He was there as often as he possibly could be and the sheer anticipation was worth the wait. And, in between, he was always on the phone. They spoke, on average, several times a day which meant the excitement of it never wore off.

'I feel like seventeen again,' Jenny reported to Vanessa. 'What with the regular leg-wax, pedicure, the lot.'

Vanessa laughed. 'I envy you,' she said. After a while, even in the steadiest relationship, romance was inclined to pall. Jenny was looking her absolute best which, considering her strenuous workload, was a real achievement. 'Clive is obviously good for you. Has he said anything yet about settling down?'

'No,' said Jenny, 'though I must confess I would quite like another child. Toby will soon be five. He could do with a sibling.' At thirty-six, she was starting to cut things fine. Clive, who was considerably older, still showed no signs of committing himself. Vanessa was puzzled; it didn't entirely add up. When he was there, he appeared besotted; all the pub's regulars could vouch for that. His charm and devotion were frequently remarked on. 'Make an honest man of him,' they all said.

'Just how old is he?' asked Vanessa. Whatever the answer, he looked pretty good. Surely he must be having similar thoughts.

'I don't know for certain,' Jenny confessed. 'It isn't something we've ever had reason to discuss.' After the trauma she had been through with Douglas, she was frankly scared of putting pressure on Clive. Was content with the status quo without rocking the boat. Though his absences were becoming more frequent, a fact that secretly worried Vanessa. There came a point when the music stopped and the seesaw went either up or down. She couldn't bear to see Jenny hurt again.

'Why not throw a surprise party for him? When's his birthday?' she asked. It could do no harm to make some sort of statement, help him to make up his mind. All he needed, if Jenny was right, was an appropriate nudge. Otherwise Jenny might just as well call it a day.

Jenny, however, remained unconvinced. What could she lose? Vanessa asked. The answer was: the lot, if she got it wrong.

Alistair Grey, who was in most nights, eventually raised the courage to ask her out. The Young Farmers were having their annual June bash, to tie in with the summer solstice, and he wondered if Jenny would like to come as his date.

'Sorry,' she said, without even checking. 'But my boyfriend is usually here at weekends. Perhaps we could fit something else in during the week.'

Fool, thought Vanessa, swapping glances with Joyce, but neither presumed to make any comment. Jenny knew her own mind and resented interference. It didn't stop them conferring, however, once she was safely out of earshot.

'I worry about her at times,' said Joyce. 'She spends too much time on her own, just working. At her time of life, she ought to be having more fun.'

'I couldn't agree with you more,' said Vanessa, relieved to know she had an ally. 'Clive's okay but he isn't here enough. She is letting her youth pass her by.'

Joyce was very much of the same mind and still

favoured Alistair Grey. Having known his mother and seen where he lived, she felt he would make a perfect partner for Jenny, who ought to snap him up before she missed the boat.

The weekend of the Young Farmers' Ball approached and Clive called, late on the Wednesday night, to say he wouldn't be there that weekend; he had to be somewhere else on a business call.

'Where?' asked Jenny, suddenly annoyed. Other things lately always took precedence over her.

'I am sorry, my darling. I hate to let you down but our global president will be in town and wants to meet all the salesmen on Saturday night.'

Saturday was the night of the ball; it was too late now to let Alistair know. She tried not to let him hear her irritation. 'And you can't get out of it?' It reminded her of Douglas; she knew what he would say before he spoke.

'Absolutely not, my sweet. More than my job is worth. I will try to call if I get the chance. I'm as disappointed as you are.'

'So I'll have to wait another whole week,' she said, blinking back sudden angry tears. 'I was hoping to spend some quality time with you.'

She knew immediately, from his silence, that she wasn't going to like what was coming next. She heard him flick through the pages of his diary and hesitate before he broke the news. 'Next week I'm on my cricket tour. This year we've been invited to Corfu. Surely I told you that?'

'You didn't, no.' She was suddenly mad. He had

started to take her too much for granted. In the early days he'd been here without fail, every other Thursday night, on his way through to visit his West Country clients. Apart from anything else, it wasn't fair on Toby, who had learnt to look forward to his regular visits almost as eagerly as she did. But, rather than having it out with him, which was what she knew she ought to do, she simply muttered something abrupt and rang off.

They knew her well enough now to sense her moods, the loyal regulars in the bar, who were used to her greeting them with a smile on her face.

'What's up with you, girl? Cat got your tongue?' Mrs Dawkings, a lunchtime regular, never pulled her punches. She said whatever was in her mind, usually with an expression of stone, though Jenny had learnt that her bark was far worse than her bite. She sat in the corner with three of her friends, all widows who'd lived there most of their lives and liked to discuss the goings-on in the village.

'Sorry,' said Jenny, handing them menus, though they knew the contents off by heart. 'I'm a bit rushed off my feet today. There's a crisis in the kitchen.'

'What's happened to that man of yours?' There was no fooling Mrs Dawkings. 'I haven't seen him for a week or more. I hope there hasn't been a falling out.'

'No,' said Jenny, managing a smile though inside she felt like snarling. 'He's off playing cricket with his friends. It's a regular fixture every year. This time they've gone to Corfu for a week, lucky sods.'

'Corfu without you? That's disgraceful,' they said, the four of them shaking their heads. 'You should have gone too and spent some time in the sun. You work far too hard as it is.'

'I couldn't leave the pub,' said Jenny. 'Someone has to do the cooking and at this time of year, as you know, we are always busy.' The bar was filling up with tourists; it was still only just after twelve. By one she would have people waiting to be seated.

'Still, it's a shame,' said Mrs Dawkings. 'A pretty girl like you. Serve him right if you found someone else while he's gone.'

'Though he's awfully charming,' she heard them say as she hurried back to the kitchen. They all adored Clive; he had them eating from his hand. They just couldn't understand why he didn't pop the question.

And neither could she. She banished the thought and turned up the heat to sear the scallops. Joyce had already made the pea purée to go with them. Working this hard was sometimes a bind. Without her full-time commitment to the place, Clive might, indeed, have invited her to go too. But then, of course, she couldn't leave Toby. It was all so complicated. There were times, like this, when she longed to quit and settle down to have another baby.

The telephone rang; it was almost two.

'Get that,' she said as she sliced the duck breasts and poured on the rhubarb sauce. A party of six had arrived unannounced but they'd manage to squeeze them in. Trade was roaring, so she couldn't complain, and it did help to keep her mind off Clive in Corfu.

'It's Vanessa,' said Joyce. 'Shall I tell her to call back?'

'Please,' said Jenny, preoccupied. This last bit was the trickiest part. She had to get it just right.

'She needs to talk to you right away,' said Joyce. 'She says to tell you it's urgent.'

'Blast!' said Jenny. 'She'll just have to wait. Tell her I'll be there in a tick.'

When at last she got to the phone, Vanessa sounded terribly hyped up. 'Are you watching the tennis?' she wanted to know and when Jenny said no: 'Switch it on.'

'Why?' asked Jenny, exasperated. Not in the middle of lunch, for heaven's sake. But it wasn't like Vanessa to interrupt without a very good reason.

'It's Wimbledon. I've just seen Clive. He's sitting front row, Centre Court.'

Jenny, abandoning Joyce to finish up, fled to the bar and switched on the set, regardless of the few drinkers still sitting there. She watched and waited and raked the crowd but none of the close-ups revealed his face so, in frustration, she switched the thing off and hurried back to the phone.

'You must be mistaken. He's in Corfu, playing cricket with the boys.'

'It was him. I swear it. They showed him up close. Relaxed and smiling like he always is, looking un-usually spruced up.'

Jenny went silent. Then: 'Who was he with?' She couldn't believe this was happening.

Vanessa paused. This was hard to say but she knew it was important that she didn't chicken out at this stage. 'A woman,' she said. 'Much younger than him. Pretty and blonde and well dressed.' Looking quite radiant, she could have added, though she didn't out of deference to Jenny's feelings. She had thought very hard about phoning at all but felt she had the right to know. Since he'd said he was off playing cricket with the boys, he deserved to be caught out. On prime-time television, too, for the whole of the world to see.

Jenny's head was reeling; she couldn't take it in. Could she have got the dates wrong? Had the cricket tour not started yet? Pride came to her rescue.

'It'll be a business thing,' she said casually. 'The global president was over last week; Clive's probably entertaining a visiting VIP.' Though she knew from Vanessa's voice that it wasn't the case.

'There is one thing more you ought to know,' she said in a gentler voice. 'Neither was paying much attention to the tennis. They were far too absorbed in each other.'

They hadn't heard of him, of course, when she telephoned Osborne and Cole. No one of that name had ever worked there. Also, there was no global president. The company had always been solidly British, still owned and run by its two original founders.

'What are you going to do?' asked Vanessa, who'd come speeding over when she heard the news, appalled to have been the cause of so much grief.

'I haven't a clue,' said Jenny in despair. 'All I have is his mobile number. The awful truth is, I don't even know where he lives.'

31

Frankie was frustrated. They were getting nowhere. She decided to go back to Bruges. At last the fan-belt had been repaired so she'd fit it in when she went to the market and take a detour from Mechelen on the way home. The weather was slightly better now, no longer driving sleet, but none the less she put on several layers. She didn't want to tell Magda for fear she might want to come too. And this was something she had to do on her own.

'I might be late back,' was all she said. 'I'll let you know if I'm delayed.'

'Drive carefully,' said Magda calmly. She hadn't known Frankie all these years without figuring out how she ticked.

She shifted the vegetables very fast and drove on to Bruges with an empty truck, arriving early in the afternoon and parking close to the ring road. It wasn't raining but the sky was dark; it might start again at any minute. She headed first for the tourist office because it was so central. This time, however, she didn't intend to go in. She more or less retraced her steps, and when the downpour started, ducked inside a cosy-looking bar she didn't remember seeing before. It was warm and panelled, with a wood-burning stove, and she suddenly realised how hungry she was. She looked around for someone to serve her but the place appeared deserted. Yet the door was open and the lights were on; the clock stood at twenty to three. She decided to wait so pulled up a chair as close to the stove as she could get, then unwound her very long scarf and peeled off her mitts. Moules would be good, she thought, studying the menu, perhaps with some frites on the side. She was feeling flush from the vegetable sale and, although the money was not strictly hers, she knew the others would say she had earned a meal.

Footsteps entered the room from behind her and when she turned, there he stood. A tall, fit man with glossy black hair and the most arresting blue eyes. The one she had glimpsed from the train; there was no mistaking. The shock of seeing him face to face made her positively dizzy; for one awful moment she thought she was going to faint. She closed her eyes and clutched the table but the pounding blood in her ears made her deaf so that when he gently touched her shoulder, she jumped.

'Are you all right? You look ghastly,' he said, going behind the bar to fetch her some water. When he returned, she was shaking so hard she very nearly dropped the glass on the floor.

The voice was his, there could be no doubt, though he showed no sign of recognition. He was like a ghost, unaltered by time, yet his hand, when he'd touched her shoulder, had been flesh and blood.

'Is there anything else you need?' he asked, sincere concern on his face. 'Did you come in here for something to eat?'

Frankie, still stunned and unable to speak, simply gawped at him and nodded. Moules and frites, she tried to say but her voice seemed frozen in her throat so all she could do was point at the bar and a bottle of the house red wine.

'A glass of wine?' Perhaps he thought her mute, but took it all in his stride. He carefully filled a heavy goblet, wiped its stem and brought it across, then asked again if she wanted anything to eat.

This time she managed to croak out the words and watched him react when he realised she was English. From the way she was dressed, in old workman's clothes and boots so worn they were falling apart, he must have taken her for a Flemish peasant. These days she wore no makeup and her hands, without the mitts, were swollen and cracked. She looked a total wreck, she could see it in his eyes, but all vanity had deserted her years before. Yet now she was suddenly face to face with him, self-consciousness swept over her, filling her with unaccountable shame. He hadn't altered, not in any way, but she was totally changed. Worn out and defeated; unmistakably old. In sudden panic, she looked around, seeking somewhere to hide.

'Moules and frites coming up,' he said, wiping her table with his cloth before placing before her a great steaming bowl of mussels. It was years since she'd eaten as much as that, and had now lost all trace of appetite, but she made a valiant effort to pick in order not to offend him. 'More wine?' he asked, proffering the bottle again and she silently allowed him to top up her glass. She very rarely drank at all and it went straight to her head.

'Nasty weather,' he said conversationally, resuming his place behind the bar and polishing a row of newly washed glasses.

'Who are you?' asked Frankie, still deeply in shock, wondering if she was going mad or, at least, in the early stages of dementia.

She saw from the way he looked at her that he'd no idea why she'd asked the question. His gaze was direct and guileless; he didn't know her.

'Me?' he said, taken by surprise. 'My name is Aidan Buchanan.'

All afternoon Frankie sat in that bar in a stupor of mindless shock. Now and again Aidan wandered over, to wipe the table or freshen her drink, and each time stayed on to chat. The bar was empty, he had nothing to do and something about her intrigued him.

'And the name Chad Barnaby rings no bells?' She just couldn't leave it alone.

'Sorry.' Aidan shook his head. She could see from his eyes that he thought her crazed; either that or drunker than she appeared. Yet something about her attracted him. After thirty years of working outdoors, a vestige of her former beauty still lingered. She must have been more than twice his age, pushing fifty would be his guess, yet he found her presence slightly unnerving. His sexual curiosity was aroused. Whatever it was that was driving her lent her a kind of pathos that got to him. Now that her hair was almost dry, it framed her face like a raven's wings, and beneath the shapeless mannish clothes her body was firm and well honed.

'Who are you, Aidan,' she asked again, 'and where are you from? I need to know.'

'Originally Cornwall,' he replied. 'Though my parents now have a place in London.'

'And they are?'

'Charles and Cassandra Buchanan.' His eyes were wary. He was suddenly on his guard. She was asking too many questions for a drunk. So he didn't add that they were divorced or that his father had recently married again.

The bar was slowly beginning to fill as time moved on and the workers came in to escape the relentless rain. Aidan's shift would shortly end so he brought her a final glass of wine and refused to give her a bill. He looked at her as she sat there, slumped, no longer watching, just blankly staring, lost in some desolate hidden despair of her own. A strange, gaunt woman with a secret sorrow. He longed to ask her questions but didn't dare.

'I'm leaving now.' He touched her shoulder, rousing her from her reverie. 'I think it's probably time that you left too.'

243

Frankie considered then meekly rose and followed him out of the bar.

The night with Aidan was electrifying and released in Frankie a torrent of raw emotion. Despite the quantity of wine she had drunk, she was totally sober and in the grip of an overwhelming passion. When she slowly removed her clothes, he was staggered by her beauty. All the years of punishing work, combined with a very frugal diet, had kept her body in perfect shape with no superfluous fat. Also, she knew what she was about even though she had been celibate for so long. Aidan had never known anything like it, had stepped aboard a rollercoaster that propelled him along at incredible speed and left him gasping for more.

'To hell with who I am,' he panted at last. 'Who in God's name are you?'

She didn't answer; she wanted him again. Their bodies fitted together so well that the next time she hit a high she screamed out, 'Chad!'

'Enough,' said Aidan, mortified at being called by another man's name. He rolled away and lit a cigarette.

'I'm sorry,' said Frankie, leaping from the bed. 'It has all been a terrible mistake.' She rapidly dressed, splashed water on her face, picked up her backpack and moved towards the door. She'd been out of her mind. She was forty-seven while Aidan was still just a kid.

'I'm sorry,' she repeated. 'It was all a mistake. I took you for someone else. I hope you'll forgive me.'

'Wait,' he said, not wanting her to leave. 'You can't just walk out on me like that.' His eyes looked bruised, and he was fighting obvious emotion. Something extremely powerful had happened. And yet she was leaving, without a backward glance. Aidan had never been treated that way. He found he didn't like it.

Frankie turned and looked at him, then smoothed his hair beneath her hands and kissed him full on the mouth.

'Who is this Chad?' He looked ready to fight. She thought a moment then made a decision: she pulled out her locket and showed him the picture inside.

'Christ,' said Aidan, turning pale. 'Where on earth did you get this?' It was like a mirror; he couldn't believe it. He turned to Frankie for an explanation but all she did was shrug.

'The love of my life. He died long ago. I am sorry I had to involve you. But now I think I have managed to lay his ghost.'

'You can't just leave.'

'I have to,' she said. 'I live in a closed commune outside Antwerp and it isn't possible to see you again. I only hope you will find a way to forgive me.'

'Hang on a sec,' he said, thinking fast. 'In case you should ever change your mind.' He scrabbled around in the various pockets of his clothes, still strewn across the floor, then scrawled on the back of a half-used matchbook the number of his mobile.

He stood at the window and watched her leave, tall and gaunt with a kind of dignity; she didn't even turn to wave. He waited until she was out of sight then found his phone and dialled an overseas number.

32

Pippa was not at her optimistic best. She was fretting again about Jack. The nursery school had dropped quite a hint that his behaviour there was not all it should be. There had been a couple of screaming fits which upset the other children. Tom, however, remained quiet and placid; though identical to his brother, a model child.

'Well, they certainly didn't get their temperaments from us. Neither of them,' said Pippa's mother. 'You were always such a happy little girl, though you also knew your own mind. Jack seems to have some demon in him and, as for Tom, I am not quite sure. Sometimes he seems to be on another planet.'

They were still quite ravishingly beautiful, though, attracting attention wherever they went. Strangers stopped Pippa in the street to get a closer look.

'You should sign them up with a model agency,' was something she grew tired of hearing.

'No thank you,' was her stock reply. 'They are vain enough as it is.'

Part of her malaise was due to the fact that Charles

was travelling more and more and these days, it seemed, was scarcely ever home. It was hard enough raising a couple of small boys, especially when one of them was hyperactive, but having to do it virtually on her own was beginning to take its toll. She had entered this marriage with such high hopes and, although she still adored her husband, she did feel a little let down on the family front. She was lucky to have her mother around to help out when she was needed. Now that she was semi-retired, she had more time on her hands.

Pippa was working shorter hours and worried about the effect on trade. The girls were great, and reliable workers, but it wasn't the same as being there full time herself.

'Where is Charles now?' her mother often asked and the truth was Pippa didn't always know. When he gave up Cornwall, having split from Cassie, she had fondly imagined he'd be home at weekends to help her out and be a proper father.

Even Aidan had defected now, off doing bar work before settling down. Pippa was quite surprised at how much she missed him. From being a thrusting young businesswoman, these days she felt dull and out of date. It was months since she'd last had a girls' night out or any real fun at all.

When he did come home, Charles was still her dashing lover and it gave her a lift just hearing his key in the door.

'Daddy's home,' she trilled to the boys. 'Let's get you bathed and ready for bed and then he will come upstairs and read you a story.' Then she slapped on some makeup and tripped down the stairs, giving a show of being a dutiful wife.

'How are you, my darling?' He crushed her in his arms and she breathed in the welcome scent of expensive cologne. Once Charles was there, things were always better; there was nothing he couldn't sort out. Her loneliness and slight claustrophobia, her grievance at having to cope on her own. The latest alarm from the nursery school about Jack's increasingly aberrant behaviour. If only he'd take the time to listen, which he did less and less.

While she checked the casserole in the oven, Charles poured them both a drink, then came to watch her make the salad and whip up his favourite dressing.

'More balsamic,' he said, licking his finger. 'And a tad more lemon, I would suggest.'

'How do you come to know so much?' she teased him as she did his bidding and had to concede, when she tasted it, that he was right.

'I get around. It's a bit of a bore but with all this travelling even I occasionally eat.'

'Like where?' she asked. She really wanted to know but his answers, as usual, were annoyingly vague. A lot of his business was still in the West Country where, since the divorce, she had not expected him to go. He mentioned a place called the Coot and Hern where the food was especially good.

'The where?' she said.

'The Coot and Hern.'

'What sort of a name is that?'

'Tennyson, actually,' said Charles rather smugly, liking to feel superior.

'And when did you start reading poetry?'

'I am more romantic than you think.'

Once he'd changed his clothes and tucked in the boys, they settled down to a cosy meal and Charles sniffed with appreciation when she lifted the casserole lid.

'Smells wonderful. What is it?' he asked and she told him beef cooked in beer. One of Delia's reliable perennial classics.

Charles tasted it and seemed suitably impressed. He half closed his eyes as he savoured the first mouthful and gave it his full concentration. 'More garlic,' he said, 'and a handful of wild mushrooms would make this a dish truly fit for the gods. Bravo! You have done it again, my dear.' He leaned across and kissed her.

Pippa, enraged, though she wasn't sure why, suddenly went for his jugular.

'What do you mean, *bravo*?' she screeched. 'What in fuck's name have *you* ever known about cooking?' He came and went, took it all for granted, left her to run the house and take care of his sons, when all the time her own business was losing ground because she wasn't there and couldn't give it the attention it deserved. *That* was her baby, which she'd started from scratch, and not these demanding twins she had never really wanted. A voice in her head told her that was not true, that she'd been willing to be a single mother, but now was no time for rational thought so she ignored it. Charles, transfixed, watched her sudden rage then told her quietly to calm down. Whereupon she went off like a roman candle, an accident all too ready to happen the minute he crossed the line and the time was right.

Women. She saw the look in his eyes as she bit back her tears and gulped down some wine, too fast to enjoy the fragrance of the bouquet. She shakily picked up her knife and fork and tried to enjoy the meal she had cooked while Charles implacably watched her with distant eyes.

'Hard day?' he asked, with a hint of the cool sarcasm she'd finally learnt not to rise to.

'Normal,' she said as she picked at her food. He was right; it could have done with more garlic, which didn't improve her mood.

They ate in silence while Charles cleared his plate then graciously allowed her to give him some more.

'What gets into you, babe?' he asked later, when they were in bed. 'I have tried to give you whatever you wanted, the house, the children, even marriage.'

'Don't start on that again. What a wonderful wife Cassie was.' What bugged her more than anything else was the condescension in his voice, as if it was her fault alone that she had got pregnant.

Charles simply gave a theatrical sigh and switched off his reading lamp. 'If that's the way you want it,' he said. 'Let's talk when you're in a better mood. I have had a really tiring day. I've been driving all afternoon.'

Cassie, that was the secret, thought Pippa; he had never really got over her. She saw that very clearly now it was too late. The mother of his oldest son whose place the twins could never usurp; a woman with charm, integrity and class, not to mention money. Pippa had never been able to understand why Cassie had let him go just like that after the twenty-two years they had been together. She was ten years older than him and perhaps had had enough. Maybe had simply run out of steam. She had certainly preferred the remoteness of Cornwall to whooping it up on the London scene the way, until the twins arrived, they had done almost every night.

As Charles nodded off, Pippa lay in the darkness, wide awake and thinking about her life. She was not yet thirty, only half Cassie's age, yet the former wife, she was certain now, still retained a hold upon her husband. What, she wondered, was Cassie's secret except that, by letting him go, she had somehow won. She had liked what little she had seen of her and respected her decision to walk away. She wondered if, at some future time, she would ever have the guts to do the same.

'Where is Cassie these days?' asked Pippa, serving an extra special breakfast to compensate for last night's hissy fit.

Charles looked up vaguely from the paper. 'Venice, I think,' he said. 'Why do you ask?'

'Just wondered,' said Pippa as she stirred his eggs

to just the consistency he liked. 'Do you ever hear from her?'

'Very rarely and then only about Aidan. She worries about him travelling abroad on his own.'

As well she might; despite the charm, Pippa would never trust that boy, would not want to leave him alone with the twins. There was something about him that had started to alarm her.

'I'm surprised she can bear to be away from Cornwall.'

'Nothing to do with me,' said Charles, returning to the day's news.

Charles, however, turned out to be wrong. Cassie was back in London. Pippa ran into her several days later by chance. She was having her hair washed when Cassie walked in and crossed the salon to greet her.

'Pippa?' she said. 'What a lovely surprise. How are your beautiful twins?'

'Holy terrors and wrecking the place. About to hit the Terrible Twos.'

Cassie laughed. 'I sympathise. I remember Aidan at that age. All you can do is run for cover. I promise you that it gets better.' Though not for some time.

'But when?' Pippa laughed. 'That's what worries me. I am not at all sure I can stand it for very much longer.'

Emilion was waiting with scissors ready so she made her excuses and shuffled away, but she kept an eye on Cassie in the mirror, impressed by how well she looked. Divorce appeared to be suiting her. She'd lost years since the last time they'd met. Trimmer, happier, far more stylish, she had even finally cut her hair, which complemented her classic bone structure and magnificent eyes. I'd guess she has a lover, thought Pippa, inexplicably jealous.

She was at the desk, paying her bill, when Cassie approached her again. Even in a gown, with her head swathed in a towel, she still contrived to look chic. 'I hope you don't mind my asking you this but I'd love to see them one day,' she said. 'Aidan says they look just like him and I must confess I find that thought beguiling.' She was smiling warmly and quite sincere. Pippa was touched and grateful. Not many women in Cassie's position could bear to hold out the hand of friendship to the person who had actively wrecked her marriage.

'Any time you care to,' said Pippa. 'Come over for tea or whatever. Charles is away so much these days, we'd all be glad of the company. The boys are always delighted to be admired.'

Cassie already had the number and promised to call very soon. Since Charles was off on his travels again, Pippa never got round to telling him.

'How is Aidan?' They were drinking tea and the twins were playing with the toys that Cassie had brought. Cassie was dressed in something soft and draped that suited her tall and willowy figure, with pearls that must have cost an arm and a leg. Pippa, who hadn't had time to change, was wearing a raspberry pink velour tracksuit that could have done with a wash.

'Aidan's fine,' said Cassie brightly. 'Though I'm not

entirely sure where he is.' The poor little soul looks worn out, she thought, and I'm not at all surprised. The twins had started to squabble loudly and Pippa went over and picked one up. She brought him back to sit between them, trying in vain to calm him down.

'May I?' asked Cassie, holding out her arms, and when Pippa, defeated, handed him over, he almost immediately stopped his bawling and instead started sucking his thumb. 'Now which one are you?' asked Cassie gently, stroking the coal-black curls that were so like her son's. 'I am sorry,' she apologised to Pippa, 'but I still can't tell them apart.'

'Tom,' said Pippa. 'Normally the quiet one. Lately he's been acting as disruptively as Jack.'

That figures, thought Cassie, who'd researched the subject since Aidan had started reporting back. It very much seemed, from what she had heard, that Jack might have some sort of behavioural problem and, since identical twins are just that, sooner or later what was wrong with Jack was likely to show up in Tom. Poor Pippa. Cassie didn't envy her one bit.

The child, who had spotted Cassie's pearls, removed the thumb and reached out for them, flashing his radiant smile in pure delight. Cassie deftly kept them out of harm's way and cuddled him till he relaxed.

'Now how on earth did you manage that?' asked Pippa, greatly impressed.

'Practice,' said Cassie. 'Don't forget that I have been through it all too.' Though Pippa, poor thing, had a double dose and the sooner she sought professional help, the better. She cast around for a lighter topic to avoid getting on to trickier ground. 'Aidan tells me that Jack is a genius at art.'

Pippa's careworn face lit up. 'They say at the school that his drawing skills are exceptional for a child his age. The only time he settles is when he is drawing.'

'It's a wonderful gift,' said Cassie. 'You must help bring it out. I think he must have inherited it from his dad.' Charles, who had spent his adult life relying mainly on charm and fast thinking, also possessed that unerring eye for spotting a really good painting. Such a talent must have come from somewhere; it wasn't something you just picked up. If only he'd be more open about his background.

'Well he definitely didn't get it from me,' said Pippa, pouring more tea. 'I couldn't draw anything to save my life and neither could my mother.'

Having Cassie here had brightened her up; she liked the woman a lot. Being able to discuss the twins with someone who listened and empathised was a tremendous relief, especially now that Charles was so seldom around.

'I really ought to be going,' said Cassie. 'But thank you for letting me come here. Your boys are gorgeous, a lot like Aidan at that age.'

'Well, I hope they grow up to be like him,' said Pippa, pleased with the praise. 'They couldn't hope for a nicer older brother.'

'Yes,' said Cassie, avoiding further comment. There were things about Aidan that Pippa didn't know and Cassie hoped she would never find out.

* * *

Cassie's stories about life in Venice filled Pippa with wistful envy. She made it sound so colourful and romantic. She had taken to dropping in fairly often, bringing small presents for the twins and sometimes even pushing them out in their stroller.

'I am sure you could do with a break,' she said, with her gentle and tentative smile. 'I know how overwhelmed I often felt when my own children were this age.'

Pippa was grateful for Cassie's concern and glad of a break from the mind-numbing tedium. It gave her a chance to catch up on correspondence and get up to date with her various suppliers, something she found hard to do with the twins always under her feet.

'Are you sure you can trust her?' her mother had asked, jealous of another woman encroaching on her turf.

'Absolutely,' said Pippa with scorn. 'What do you think she's going to do? Take them back to Italy with her or push them under a bus?'

'You never know,' said her mother darkly. 'She certainly owes you no favours.'

'She's a warm and generous-hearted woman, which you'd know if you'd ever bothered to meet her, and, after all, Aidan is half-brother to the twins.' Also, in London Cassie seemed a bit lost. She was staying alone at the Basil Street Hotel even though Charles had magnanimously suggested that she use the Pont Street flat. It had, after all, once belonged to her, bought with her former husband's money. If anyone really owned it, it was Cassie.

'Why is she here?' he was curious to know, slightly suspicious of his former wife's motives. It irked him that she had become so self-sufficient.

'She is renovating a Venetian palazzo and doing research in the British Museum in order to get the period details right. But most of her time she's in Cornwall with the family. She misses Aidan very much.'

'Hmm,' said Charles, still a little concerned, not at all certain that he liked the idea of his two wives palling up.

Pippa, every weekday morning, dropped off the twins at the nursery school, then drove on into Fulham to open the shop. In the old days, when she was unencumbered, she'd stay there at night until seven or eight. Now she had to leave mid-afternoon to pick up the boys, except on those days when her mother would do it for her. She found it frustrating since, on the whole, the more serious buyers came in later and she wasn't there to greet them with her sales spiel. The girls were good but not in her league. When Pippa was there it was rare that anyone left the shop empty-handed. There was nothing, however, that she could do except patiently wait for the twins to grow up. At least when they were four they could move to a proper school.

On this particular afternoon she was talking to a rich American when the phone in the stockroom started to ring and one of the salesgirls answered it.

'It's for you,' she said, thereby breaking the rule that a customer must never be interrupted. And this particular one, skilfully played, might well turn out to be a winner. She had bought a house in Virginia Water and was planning to refurbish it right through.

'Not now, please,' said Pippa tersely. The girl knew better than that. 'Tell whoever it is that I'll call them back.'

The girl went back to talk to the caller then hovered anxiously in the doorway, clearly undecided what to do next.

'What now?' said Pippa, overly impatient. The girl should be able to handle something comparatively simple like that. When she was that age and temping at Liberty's she could juggle three customers all at once, with a bright and friendly smile for each one, and not keep them waiting too long. She'd maintained those standards throughout her career which was why the shop was doing so well; her name had become a byword for efficient reliability.

'I'm sorry,' said the girl, 'but it sounds rather urgent. It's somebody calling from the school.'

'Please excuse me,' said Pippa, turning pale. 'Alison here will take care of you while I am gone.'

'Don't worry,' said the American lady. 'I know what it's like with kids. Mine are all grown up by now, thank the Lord!'

A teaching assistant was on the line, telling Pippa not to be alarmed but that they thought she probably ought to come.

'What's happened?' asked Pippa, instantly panicking, convinced the woman was about to tell her something catastrophic.

'It's Jack, I'm afraid,' said the motherly woman, in a voice designed to soothe. 'He is having one of his little turns and we can't seem to calm him down. He's been screaming now for fifteen minutes and nothing we say or do has any effect.'

'I'll be there as fast as I can,' said Pippa, all thoughts of the affluent customer wiped from her mind. 'Sooner or later he will scream himself out but tell him that Mummy is on her way.' As if he was likely to listen, poor little beggar.

She reached the car in a matter of seconds and set off into the early rush hour, her heart pounding in her mouth. These little seizures were becoming more frequent and no one knew what was causing them. The word epilepsy had even been used, though not, so far, by a doctor, and each time Pippa thought about that, she broke out in a cold sweat. The traffic in the Fulham Road was even heavier than usual. There must be either an accident ahead or else some afternoon function going on at the hospital or the football ground.

'Come on,' she muttered impatiently, wondering whether she ought to call Charles or wait until she knew just how serious things were. He was off again, she had no idea where, but would presumably answer his phone, though she hated to appear to be checking on him. When the traffic still refused to move, she broke another of her rules, only to find that his mobile was switched off. So, agitated and close to tears, she called her mother instead.

*　　*　　*

They had moved the child to the first-aid room and his tantrum had more or less passed. The teaching assistant, looking somewhat tense, greeted Pippa at the school's front door, apologetic at having disturbed her at work.

'He is a lot calmer,' she assured her, 'but we felt it best that you should come.'

Pippa strode past her with barely a word and into the small clean room that was pointed out.

Holy smoke. She stopped in her tracks and one hand flew to her mouth in disbelief. For the small tear-stained figure tucked up tightly in the bed wasn't Jack at all but his brother, Tom.

33

Frankie couldn't get Aidan out of her head. Whatever had happened between them had shaken her up. He might be younger but was very much a man; the memory of their frenzied lovemaking had left her fractious and dissatisfied. Something deep inside her had stirred and now refused to go back to sleep. She slumped into a deep depression and turned her back on the world. Magda, with her built-in radar, sensed there was something seriously wrong and waited for Frankie to open up, which she didn't. Whatever had happened the night she stayed away appeared to have cut very deep.

Fate, however, then intervened. Within the week a letter arrived informing Frankie that her mother's estate had now been settled, leaving everything to her. Not enough money to make her rich but sufficient to give her some independence, should she choose to take it. Magda feared she might leave the commune but, as Frankie had often observed, where else had she to go?

Except, she now realised, to England in search of

Chad. With Aidan she seemed to have drawn a blank yet she couldn't let the matter rest. She had the list she'd drawn up with Magda; now she could afford to take the next step. If she systematically traced Chad's roots, she might discover where Aidan fitted in. She regretted now leaving him so hastily, but also knew it would have been wrong to stay. She would go to England and track down his parents. She knew their names were Charles and Cassandra and that they lived in London. Not a lot to go on but a start.

Rather to her surprise, the other women were in favour of her plan. She had never been to London before but now could afford the fare.

'Take Eurostar,' said Sister Agnes. 'It's the fastest and most efficient way.'

'And go first class. Why not treat yourself?' They all knew she hadn't had much of a life and richly deserved a bit of spoiling.

'You can act as our emissary,' Magda suggested. 'Make yourself useful while you're there.' It would help give some purpose to the trip; she couldn't bear to think of Frankie tilting at windmills. She also worried what she might do when she saw there was life beyond Antwerp. This way she'd have a reason to come back.

'An excellent plan,' said Sister Agnes, whose pottery lately had been winning awards and who very much hoped to find a market for it. 'We will put together a portfolio to demonstrate what we're doing here. Who knows, this could be our major breakthrough, put us all on the map.'

They got together in the barn to draw up a plan of action. Between them they were impressively productive. Magda's lace was quite exquisite; they all agreed that it needed a proper showcase. She worked in the old traditional way, which had hardly changed since the fourteenth century when Flanders had been a world centre for lace.

'Take some samples as well as pictures and show them around the specialist shops. They might be persuaded to order in bulk.'

'Not too much bulk,' protested Magda, though it was obvious that she liked the idea.

'How on earth do I start?' asked Frankie, scared at what she was taking on. Bruges was the furthest she had ever travelled. London suddenly seemed a daunting prospect.

'Common sense,' said Magda briskly. 'You'll know what to do when you get there. Be glad, at least, that you speak the language. And get your passport renewed.'

Armed with a slim portfolio, her backpack and a single bag, Frankie embarked on her daring expedition. Magda, who dropped her at Antwerp station, hugged her with controlled emotion. 'Take care,' she said, 'and keep in touch. And don't stay away too long.'

'Just as long as it takes,' said Frankie, her fighting spirit restored. She was nervous about the actual journey, at having to go through the Channel tunnel, but suddenly keen to get on with it and see what she could unearth. It had crossed her mind to contact

Aidan but she had mislaid his mobile number, which was the only personal data she had. Doubtless it was all for the best; she shouldn't have done what she did with him, felt ashamed because he was still so young. His parents, though, were another matter. If she could find them, she might get a clue as to where he had got his astonishing looks. Chad remained her lasting obsession; she would not rest until she had traced his roots.

"Bye,' she said, kissing Magda briefly. 'Thanks for everything you've done.'

'Take care,' said Magda again, suppressing all emotion. 'Bon voyage and good luck.'

34

Luise Barras was taken aback when he got Cristina's call. It had been a good ten years since she'd been in touch. The husky, petulant voice hadn't changed though; he could well imagine the discontent on her face.

'Luise, cheri, how are you?' she said and then, without pausing for his reply, launched straight into her request. Less a request, more of an order. She clearly hadn't improved much in patience or manners. She was planning to marry again, she explained, which would require written evidence of the divorce. A tiresome matter, to do with French law, but she needed it right away.

'Divorce?' said Luise, for a moment confused. Ten years was a very long time.

'My divorce from Cal Barnard,' she said. 'We married in '77.' Or thereabouts; she was typically vague. Could obviously not remember the details herself. Not surprising, the way she'd lived then, perpetually fuelled by drink and drugs. He hadn't even known she was now in Paris.

'My dear,' he said, 'you have caught me on the hop. I will need a little time to look up the papers.' He had no recollection of a divorce but wasn't going to say so until he was certain. Cristina had always had an ugly temper, would fly off the handle at the least excuse. The difference was, she was no longer a big star; Barras, along with the rest of the world, no longer jumped at her bidding.

'Well, make it snappy,' Cristina said, ending the call without a word of thanks or even a goodbye.

Damn, she thought, even more depressed, having heard the hesitation in the lawyer's voice. It looked horribly as if her premonition might be valid. In which event, what should she do next? Unless she managed to pin him down, Rocco was not a man to hang around. As it was, she couldn't be more aware of the age gap.

Barras rang back in a couple of hours to report he had turned up her personal file but there was nothing to indicate a divorce. 'Are you sure it took place in Rio?' he asked. 'As far as I recall, he was not Brazilian.'

'He was English, I think.' The truth was, she'd never known much about Cal apart from the fact that he turned her on. In those days they'd lived for the moment and little beyond.

'So what should I do now?' she wailed, gripped by sudden panic.

'The only person to answer that is the man himself,' replied Barras.

'Whom I haven't heard from, or of, since the day

he walked out. I don't even know if he's still alive.'
Things would be much simpler if he were not.

'After he left you, where did he go?' She was every
bit the flake she always had been.

'I have no idea. We parted badly. Please, Luise, you
have got to help me. It's a matter of life and death.'

At least it had served to improve her manners.
The Brazilian moved heavily in his chair and
checked the pages of his appointments book. 'By
chance, it so happens I shall be in London at the
end of next week. Leave it with me and I'll see what
I can find out. But I'll need a copy of the marriage
certificate. Perhaps you could fax it to me before I
leave.'

'The marriage certificate? Do I have that?' Cristina
was back in a state of panic. She had no idea where
to look for such a thing, assuming she'd ever even
had it.

'Where do you keep your birth certificate?' Barras
was losing his patience. He was bored with the endless
fecklessness of this child/woman.

'In my jewellery box, I think.'

'Well, that's where I would look first.'

He was certainly going to make her pay through
the nose for this, but he had been her on and off lover
for years and he'd never forget what a knockout she
had once been. He would put a London associate on
the case who could sift through papers at Somerset
House or wherever it was the Brits kept such records
these days.

'Don't hold your breath, though,' he warned as he

rang off. Even for such a sensational beauty, there was only a limited distance he would go.

The Public Records Office revealed very little, not even a copy of the marriage licence. Barras's man, who went there in person, could not even find a birth certificate for Cal.

'You are certain that was his name?' asked Barras, bored with the situation already and regretting ever having taken Cristina's call. She had always been trouble.

'Of course,' she screamed. 'I married him, didn't I?' Though the truth was she didn't even know what Cal was short for. Calvin, maybe, or Caliban; even Calamity Jane.

'It doesn't sound very English to me. Are you sure he wasn't American?' asked Barras.

'Not sure, no.' She was quieter now, recalling the doubts she had always had and the strong suspicion that he'd never been straight with her. 'There must be something you can do,' she wailed. 'Where else can you look?' At any moment, Rocco might show up. She dreaded to think what he'd say when he heard this latest news. He'd be off again at the slightest hitch. She had sensed all along that he wasn't wholehearted about it.

'Leave it with me,' said Barras, softening. 'I promise to let you know as soon as I can.'

Cristina ran through what knowledge she had of the dashing youth she had married and realised it amounted to not very much. She had been so dazzled at that first erotic meeting that nothing else had mattered at all, so that, after he'd dumped her and then returned, they had whirled into wedlock with barely a second's pause. She had always assumed that there'd been a divorce, though it hadn't much mattered till now. All she had wanted, when the music stopped, was to be shot of him once and for all; it drove her crazy just having him hanging around. In those days, still at the height of her fame, she had had no shortage of would-be suitors, could take her pick of the crème de la crème of Brazil.

Now she racked her brains for any small detail that might help throw light upon where he had gone. Having claimed to be a traveller of the world he could be almost anywhere at all. She vaguely remembered having had the impression, though now she couldn't remember why, that he'd already been through a quickie first marriage, despite the fact that, when they wed, he was still only twenty-two. It might explain his reluctance to commit as well as the undisclosed source of his wealth. At no time had he ever claimed to have come from an affluent background.

All of this she passed on to Barras, who dutifully noted it down. It was a measure of her desperation that this time she remembered to thank him, though made no suggestion that he should send her a bill.

The lawyer's associate in London, however, was made of sterner stuff and had all sorts of contacts in different strata, some only inches above the gutter, which was exactly what seemed to be called for in this case.

'He sounds to me like your typical chancer,' said a tabloid journalist in the pub. 'If I were you, I would flick through the headlines and the court reports for that year and the one before.'

The newspaper headlines for 1977 revealed nothing at all that seemed to match up with the very few facts he had. But when he moved on to the court reports, something caught his eye that immediately clicked: an account from 1976 of a society divorce where the bride had eloped from her coming-out ball and fled to Paris without her parents' consent. The father, a heavyweight property man, had pursued the couple across the Channel and paid off the youthful bride-groom on the spot, provided he got out of town. Once the settlement had been agreed, the marriage was quietly annulled. The bride was a certain Miss Millicent Hoare; the bridegroom, one Cosmo Banbury, whose profession was given in the report as barman.

Same initials, C.B., thought our sleuth, mentally striking his forehead. A very long shot but, what the hell, it might just be worth looking into.

'Go for it, boy,' said Barras, amused. He was starting to be intrigued by the story himself.

When Rocco Pereira burst into her life, the world rocked on its axis. It was years since she'd found a man so intensely exciting. Though he was drunk and boorish in his behaviour, Cristina was thrilled by his brutish allure so that, without further ado, they had fallen into bed. Twelve years behind her made him thirty-three, with a lean hard body running slightly to flab because of the decadent lifestyle he led. Still feted as a racing driver, although no longer top of the league, he spent his time moving from track to track and taking part in the international rallies. He had girls in many ports, but Cristina had reached a stage in her life when she found it expedient to turn a blind eye on all that. What she didn't know, she need not grieve over. She had learnt her lesson with a series of sharp knocks since falling from the top of the modelling tree.

The subject of marriage had come up quite casually, during a night of sensational sex that had left them both sated and reeling. He was drunk, of course, and Cristina was coked; together they made the most exquisite music and the light that shone in their slightly glazed eyes was pure love. He also assumed, since she lived in Paris and had once been queen of the international catwalk, that she was a lot better off than was actually the case. Pereira had expensive tastes, not all of them admissible to the taxman. Motor racing was very well paid but only as long as you continued to win and thirty-three was cutting things rather fine. He was slightly over the hill already and looking for a haven in which to drop anchor. Cristina Calvão was an enviable trophy until he could luck out with somebody younger. At which point, as was his wont, he would move on.

None of this did Cristina suss out; she thought she had stumbled upon the real thing. Though at an age when she ought to know better, emotionally she was still adolescent and hadn't felt like this since she'd met Cal. The torch she had carried for him all those years ago was now rekindled for Rocco Pereira. Insane, maybe, but she'd go to any lengths to satisfy her urgent carnal needs. She carried on with her wedding plans, without telling Claude, assuming that somehow, in her usual way, she would manage to muddle through.

The Countess of Rochester received him in the kitchen where she was trying to bath a dog. She stood there in her dowdy clothes, water all over the linoleum floor, nervously drying her hands on her apron before extending one to him.

'Yes?' she said, in a slightly squeaky voice, but her pallid cheeks turned to brightest red when the young man mentioned the name of Cosmo Banbury. 'Yes,' she repeated when her heart had stopped fluttering. 'He was, indeed, my husband once, though not for very long.'

The nice young man seemed harmless enough so she made them both a pot of tea and they sat side by side at the scrubbed pine table to drink it. Her straight brown hair was pinned tightly back and her face could have done with a lick of paint. Other than that, apart from the clothes, she was not unappealing, he thought. And, now that she had regained her composure, keenly engaged in what he had come here about.

The story he'd read in the papers was true. She made no protest; in fact, seemed shyly proud. The romance had been sudden and very short-lived. By the time they had reached the Paris hotel, her father was hot on their heels like the wrath of God.

'He was most unsuitable but, oh, if you had seen him.' The light in her eyes enhanced her face, making her almost pretty. 'The handsomest man I have ever known and, for one glorious month, he made me very happy.' She challenged him now but was back in control. 'You probably think me silly,' she said, 'but may you one day find such happiness yourself.'

She quickly regrouped and returned to reality. What was it he wanted to know? Time was passing; the family would be home. Though grown up now, they still expected to be fed.

'Where is he now? Have you any idea? It's urgent that I find him.'

'I don't know,' she said and he saw she told the truth. Her father, cold-bloodedly though probably right, had paid him off like the cad he undoubtedly was, on condition that he went abroad and stayed away for a specified time, until the marriage had been annulled and he could do no more harm to Millie. Towards which end, the money agreed on was paid over in instalments. Into a nominated foreign account.

'In Rio,' she said without his having to ask.

After some thought and a glass of dry sherry, she made the decision to tell him more. 'As a matter of fact,' she virtually whispered, 'I saw him again some years ago. He appeared not to recognise me but I knew him.'

Still handsome, still charming, still the centre of

things. Still working the room with a gleam in his eye. Her heart had almost stopped in her chest when she'd glimpsed him across the crowded bar that night at the opera house. Then she remembered the wife and her face lost its glow.

'He was with a woman, his wife he said. She was tall and elegantly dressed. When I called him Cosmo he didn't even flicker. Said I was mistaken and walked away.'

The sleuth was perched on the edge of his chair; this was better than anything he'd hoped for.

'Do you know what name he goes under these days?'

'Yes,' she said, with quiet satisfaction. 'I wrote it down in case I ever forgot.'

No chance of that, it was etched into her heart, the name of the man she had worshipped at seventeen, who had wooed and won her then tossed her aside like a foolish and frumpish rag doll.

'These days he styles himself Charles Buchanan. Charles and Cassandra, he said.'

At this point Luise Barras took over, now that things appeared to be hotting up. He had not hoped for such a speedy result. Charles Buchanan was easily found, with business premises in Walton Street and a residential address in nearby Pont Street. The man had clearly done well for himself, despite the fact that he seemed always to be on the move. The person who answered the office phone said Mr Buchanan was currently travelling and could she take a message? The lawyer said no. Instead he tried the private number.

The phone was answered by a man. He was, he said, Charles Buchanan's son and what was this about?

'It's a slightly delicate matter,' said Barras. 'I wonder if we might meet. I won't take up too much of your time, I promise.'

'Come here,' said Aidan. 'My father's away.' And his mother was safely in Venice. Something sounded intriguing here, and he was curious to know more.

'I'll be there at six,' said Barras, his mission achieved.

When Aidan saw the marriage licence a sudden chill shot through him. Although it was written in Portuguese, he saw immediately what it was though neither of the names was familiar to him. 'What's this to do with my dad?' he asked. 'Who is this Cal Barnard?'

'Who indeed,' said the silky lawyer. 'I was rather hoping that he might tell me that.'

The bride, he explained, at the time of the marriage had been a world class model. The groom had since mysteriously vanished, though his bank in Rio had now confirmed that the money he'd kept in his savings account had been transferred to a London branch. In the name of Charles Buchanan.

'I suspect you see what I'm driving at,' said Barras, a highly civilised man.

Just at that moment his mobile rang and, with an apologetic shrug, he turned his back and walked out of the room, to take the call in private. With lightning speed, Aidan grabbed the marriage licence, attached to a letter with a Paris address, and scribbled down the sender's details before the lawyer returned.

'Great,' he said, with his dazzling smile. 'I am sure

my dad will be riveted. I am not sure where he is right now but I'll certainly leave him a message to contact you.'

That night Aidan went to say goodbye to the twins. He had to go away again, he said.

'But you're only just back,' protested Pippa. 'Couldn't you wait at least till your father gets home?'

'Sorry,' said Aidan. 'There is something I must do. Just tell him from me, if you will, to watch his back.'

'Sounds intriguing. Won't you please fill me in?'

'Can't,' said Aidan. 'It is strictly between me and him.'

He played with the boys until one of them screamed and Pippa hurried over and gathered him up. He was tired, she said, it was time they were in bed. She tried to get Aidan to read to them but he said he hadn't got time.

'At least stay and have a drink with me. Your father will never forgive me if you don't.'

Aidan flashed his bewitching smile, so reminiscent of Charles. 'I'd like that more than anything,' he said. 'But I have to get going or else I'll miss my train.'

More than that he would not divulge, not even where he was going. But he hugged the twins tightly before he left and told them both to be good to their mother.

'You never know what may happen next,' he said.

Cristina was puzzled by Barras's call; puzzled and very frustrated. He had found out what she wanted to know: that there hadn't been any divorce. Cal was alive and living in London, under the name of Charles Buchanan, and had at least one other living wife, Cassandra. It was up to Cristina what she chose to do, confront him or turn a blind eye. His own advice, more as friend than lawyer, was to take the latter course.

'I can't see what you'd achieve,' he said, 'by blowing the whistle on the man. From all accounts, he is very successful and carries considerable clout. If it came to the crunch in a court of law, it could be a lengthy and painful business, initially based, without documentation, on nothing more than your word against his.' And he knew which side he would back, though didn't say it.

'You are saying I'm still his legal wife?'

'I'm afraid so, chérie,' he said.

She had no idea who to turn to now; Barras was reluctant and too far away and she also sensed he was washing his hands of the case. But she had to act fast before Rocco showed up. She had seen enough of his violent temper not to want to tell him the painful truth. She almost considered appealing to Claude, who was good at sorting her problems out, but even she could see that was going too far. She fleetingly thought about contacting Cal, had a strong desire to see him again, but the time had come to be realistic; he had dumped her at the height of her fame, and now had another wife.

So, in the end, she chose to do nothing and take the chance that things would never come out. If she moved to Brazil once she'd married Rocco, she'd be safe. It meant turning her back on all she had now but that was, in any case, likely to happen once Claude found out about the approaching wedding. He had taken his wife on a luxury cruise to celebrate their ruby wedding. It might, she thought, mean a total reconciliation.

'Yvette,' she screamed, 'come and run my bath. And tell the chauffeur that I'll need the car.' At a time like this only one thing could calm her. Cristina was going shopping.

35

The surging crowds at Waterloo station were almost enough to turn Frankie round and send her straight back to Antwerp. Brussels had been bad enough but there she had only been passing through; here she had to confront an intimidating city. She grabbed her bags and followed the flow towards the taxi rank outside. She had heard about the underground but had no desire to try it. She had booked a room in a Chelsea hotel where her mother had stayed when she came down to shop. It was also handy for Walton Street, where, she'd found out from directory enquiries, interior designer Charles Buchanan had his offices and showroom. Beyond that, she wasn't sure how to proceed. For the first time ever in her life, she found herself having to cope on her own and wasn't sure that she liked it.

She arrived quite late so called it a day. Once she'd checked in and unpacked her bag and had a drink in the small friendly bar, she found herself too pent up to want to eat. So she went back upstairs, took an early night and willed herself to sleep, which wasn't easy. She tossed and turned, disturbed by traffic and the voices of people passing in the street. She was here, in one of the world's great cities, for the first time in her life but was too intimidated to venture outside. In the morning, though, she would give it a go. Her determination to track down Chad remained undiminished.

Over breakfast she studied the map and worked out how to get to Walton Street. She was almost on the King's Road, said the waitress, but Frankie had no desire to look at the shops. She sat there, in her austere grey suit, with her short straight hair and sensible shoes and not a trace of makeup on her face. All she cared about was this mission; the faster she could get on with it, the better.

She found the showroom easily enough, then walked up and down the street several times before she had the nerve to go inside. It was somehow smarter than she'd expected; Aidan, for all his dazzling looks, had struck her as unassuming. But this place was the epitome of chic; when at last she found the courage to enter, a smart young woman looked up from her desk and asked if she could help.

Frankie got a grip on herself. 'I'd like to speak to Mr Buchanan.' She had no idea what she'd say to him, though had brought the portfolio as a calling card.

'Mr Buchanan isn't here.' She hadn't expected that. 'May I ask what it's about?' asked the girl politely.

Frankie stared blankly back at her, uncertain how to proceed. The plan that had seemed so simple in Antwerp had already come unstuck. 'I have some samples I want to show him.' She remembered Magda's contingency plan. 'I represent a small Beguinage in Belgium.'

The girl clearly didn't know what that meant. 'We don't deal with the trade,' she said. They were, she explained, a small design group, working solely for private clients, and got everything they needed from their own suppliers. Seeing Frankie's obvious disappointment, she politely offered to take a look. There might be someone, she said, she could pass her on to. She was clearly taken by what she saw, especially Magda's lace.

'I know just the person you should show it to.' She scribbled down an address. 'It isn't far, just along the Fulham Road.' Then took her to the door and showed her the way.

Pippa was alone in the shop when the doorbell clanged and a stranger walked in, tall and dark and looking slightly forbidding.

'Hi!' said Pippa with a welcoming smile. The twins had lately been behaving better which meant she'd been able to get a little more sleep. 'What can I do for you?'

She was blonde and pretty and slightly overweight; Frankie warmed to her instantly and felt far more at her ease. 'I've brought these samples,' she said rather gauchely. 'Someone suggested that I should show them to you.'

Pippa watched as Frankie opened the case and gasped when she saw the lace. 'Exquisite,' she said, really meaning it. 'And yes, I am definitely interested.'

They spent very nearly an hour together while Pippa ordered several lengths of lace, dependent on how much Magda could make and how quickly. Workmanship of this calibre was well worth the wait, she said. She already had several buyers in mind, was pretty certain she could easily shift it.

'I'm glad you found me,' she said, hugely pleased. 'Now is there anything else you need help with?'

Frankie showed her pictures of Agnes's pottery and the filigree silver that Sylvia produced. Pippa looked at it all and was very impressed. 'What a talented bunch you are,' she said. Then she suggested that since it was almost lunchtime, Frankie should stick around.

'My husband will be here any minute. Wait and I'll introduce you. It's very possible he'll be able to help you with contacts.'

Frankie hesitated then said no; she was anxious to be off. She had done her bit and got orders for the lace; now it was time to get on with her quest. Out there somewhere Chad's ghost beckoned. She had left it long enough.

'Do stay in touch,' said Pippa, when she left. 'I am sure we can do more business.' Strange woman, she thought, and rather sad. I'd love to know what her story is.

Three minutes later Charles arrived and whisked her away to lunch.

36

Ten days in Venice, facing a blank future, empowered Cassie in unexpected ways by opening her eyes to things she'd not thought about before. Here she was, on the brink of turning sixty, having never had to fend for herself or worry about the harsher realities of life. An adoring father, two husbands and two brothers; men had always looked after her and played a supervisory role. Even Tremayne had done his bit in helping to shield her from the daily grind by running the estate so efficiently on his own. Her childhood had been comfortable and Edwin very well off. Even Charles, with some help from her, had built a healthily flourishing business which meant that neither now had financial worries. She had graciously allowed him full use of the flat while she went to ground in Cornwall to think things through. Daisy was there, with her teenage children, and Rose, now an established solicitor, often turned up at weekends. Aidan was at Oxford, and hardly likely to want to live at home again. She had managed, by putting up no resistance, to keep the marital break-up civilised. In the eyes of the world, whatever else they thought, she was truly a dignified loser. What she felt inside was much more complex. She had not yet come to terms with that at all.

After the first annihilating blow, she had reeled for a while like a headless chicken. Despite her astuteness, she had not seen it coming, had turned a blind eye to her husband's obvious faults. In the twenty-two years they had been together, she had only been mildly aware of the fact that his devotion to her was imperceptibly cooling. His absences had grown longer and more frequent but she had put that down to the boom in his new career. Each fresh client took up more of his time so that Cassie no longer expected him home every weekend without fail. It was part of the price they were paying for success and made their reunions that much sweeter. One thing she'd never even wondered about; she had always known she possessed his heart and that he was totally faithful.

She was weeding the edges of the croquet lawn when she heard the purr of his fancy car at a quarter past four, three hours before he was due. She rose to her feet and wiped her hands, then pushed back her heavy hair in delight. His visits home were all too infrequent; it was like an unexpected birthday treat. He parked outside the front door and she watched him swing his long legs from the car and reach in the back for his briefcase. Time sat very lightly on Charles; from this distance he was still the dashing young buck who had wooed and won her in that hotel all those years ago.

She ran to greet him with a radiant smile, untying the apron she wore to collect the weeds.

'What a lovely surprise!' They'd have tea together, out on the lawn within earshot of the waves. All three dogs had appeared from nowhere, wagging their tails and wriggling in ecstatic welcome. When the master of the house came home, all attention was switched to him. Somewhere back in the kitchen the maid would be boiling the kettle and laying a tray with a laundered cloth especially for the occasion.

'Cassie, my darling.' He took her in his arms but his swift embrace was peremptory. She was aware he wasn't kissing her which spoke volumes.

'What's wrong?' she asked, picking up the vibes as she saw the sudden evasion in his eyes.

'Nothing, my dearest, but we do need to talk. I cancelled the afternoon and came straight home.'

He strode ahead of her into the house, tossed his briefcase on to a chair, then hurried upstairs to change his clothes and escape her incisive probing. All too soon it would have to come out; throughout the week he had dreaded this confrontation. The more he could do to delay it, the better for him. But not for her; she was there already, wringing her hands as she supervised the tray, trying to keep her breathing steady and not give too much away. Freshly baked scones and homemade preserves. The maid had done it all perfectly. She rinsed her hands and tidied her hair, then went back into the garden to wait. Whatever it was, she wasn't going to like it.

*   *   *

A younger woman; she should have guessed. Cassie covered her eyes for a second, then sat up straighter and carefully poured the tea.

'Do I know her?' she asked and he silently nodded, but when she heard it was Pippa Harvey, she froze.

'Pregnant, you say?'

'With twins,' he said.

'How long?'

'Three months.'

'No, not the pregnancy. The relationship, I meant.' She took deep breaths and tried hard to keep calm but the saucer rattled when she handed him his tea. 'Well?' she said, a shade more sharply, watching him visibly squirm.

'Five years,' he said.

'You louse,' she cried as, all of a sudden, things started to fall into place. His absences, his slight abstraction; the guilt, she saw it now clearly, on the girl's face. She had taken it then for appealing shyness but all the trollop had actually been doing was casing the joint and eyeing the lie of the land.

For a while they sat in uncomfortable silence, neither wanting to say the unthinkable words.

'You must marry her,' said Cassie calmly, with sudden resolution. 'Those babies will need a legitimate father and I'm far too old for you anyway.'

With quiet dignity, she rose and left him and walked down the lawn to the rocks at the edge of the sea. The sharp salt breeze swept the tears from her eyes and she stood there, facing the restless surf, knowing that life, as she'd known it till now, was ended. She had loved him completely but had feared this day might come. In a way, she was almost relieved that the waiting was over.

Venice had been an impromptu decision once the papers were signed and she knew there was no going back. She had to get away from home, could not bear to watch her marriage dissolve and all she had worked so hard for fall to pieces. She thought about Pippa, whom she'd rather liked, was disappointed that it had to be a person she knew. But if not Pippa, it would have been someone. She realised now how blinkered she had been. She remembered the incident with the Countess of Rochester and how, even after that, she'd suspected nothing. He had shrugged it off and she'd totally dismissed it; the woman was clearly demented, he'd said, and she, the older sophisticate, had believed him. She wondered now about other women. He was away so often these days she couldn't tell. Enough; such thoughts were purely erosive. There was absolutely no going back and the years were running out fast. On an impulse, she rang the reception desk and extended her stay for a few more weeks. She had nothing to hurry home for now so would make the most of the trip.

Venice became Cassie's new obsession, reminder of happier times and an earlier life. From that point on, when she could get away from the pressures of family and the Hawksmoor estate, she travelled back and forth at least once a year. She found the Danieli too imposing for her needs so moved instead to a family-run hotel with a quiet courtyard, shaded by massive trees, where she could sit and read between her excursions. Sometimes she took the vaporetto and travelled the length of the Grand Canal, absorbing the breathtaking scenery that had remained unchanged since medieval times, soaked in art and history and intrigue. Time had stood still here for centuries and little had altered in the thirty-eight years since that first idyllic honeymoon trip with Edwin. She recalled the earnest girl she had been, fresh out of school and with few expectations except to grow old with a man she had always revered. When she thought about him and compared him with Charles, words could not begin to describe the difference. But though Edwin had always been staunch and fair, as reliable as the stable clock, she still would not have missed a moment of her turbulent second marriage. She had known when they married about Edwin's heart; he had suffered with it mildly throughout his life. Though his passing had been sudden, it was not unexpected, and she'd never thought she would ever find love again. Nor, at the time, even wanted to. At thirty-three, she'd believed that all that was over.

She spotted the palazzo entirely by chance, a decaying ruin, crumbling into the canal, its painted façade like the face of a whore who had been out too long in the rain. Beautifully sited close to the Ca' Dario, the Palazzo Dandolo was elegant, though worn, and listing slightly to one side, which made it look tipsy. Several times she passed it, up and down, until its fading charms began to ensnare her. Without help and extensive capital investment, it looked too fragile to survive much longer, even though it had stood there for almost six hundred years. She wasn't rich, not to that extent, but she suddenly knew what she wanted to do; she had to have it. She made up her mind on the spot. This was the dream she'd been searching for, a beautiful ruin in dire need of rescue, a project to take the place of her shattered marriage.

'I have to have it,' she said to the agent, once she had tracked her down. No messing about with fake business finesse; when Cassie went after something, she was relentless. From the look of the place, it had been empty for years, a neglected ruin that nobody wanted despite its prime position on the Grand Canal. She'd worked wonders in Cornwall and also in Pont Street, had honed her talents to a very fine edge and was now prepared to take on the challenge of a life-time. No more marriages, she was through with all that; from this point on, a woman on her own, she would do as she damned well pleased. And finance herself.

'I'll give you whatever you ask,' she said. 'As long as it falls within my budget and providing you don't renege. You have just five days to talk to the owner or else my offer will be withdrawn.' Greener pastures was her implication though, privately, her heart beat fit to burst.

The Italian agent, jaded and weary, looked at Cassie with renewed respect, liking this sort of fighting talk, which she hadn't expected at all. The woman she'd taken for a dowdy widow was now revealing nerves of steel and virtually flashing her chequebook as she spoke.

'Three days,' she promised, suppressing a smile. There was no fool like an old one but business was business.

'He will meet you there,' she reported next morning. 'The owner won't consider selling until he has talked to the buyer.'

'That's fine with me,' said Cassie, slightly daunted, having not expected her crazy whim to draw such an instant response. What she would do about money, she didn't yet know. All she did know, without hesitation, was that she had to have the place and do all she could to restore it to its glory.

'Ten o'clock outside,' said the agent. 'I would come myself, but . . .'

'No need,' said Cassie. The last thing she wanted at this delicate stage was this woman messing things up. 'All I need to know is his name. The rest I can handle myself.'

'Why, the Count Dandolo,' said the woman, surprised. 'I thought you understood it was still in the family.'

'Great,' said Cassie, her spirits sinking. Just what she needed right now, the Count himself. But, having started, she was not turning back. For only the second time in her life, Cassie was doing her own thing.

It was drizzling slightly, as it does in Venice, a fine cool rain that was more of a mist, which swept in from the lagoon and shrouded the sun. Cassie, nervous but simulating calm, arrived at the palazzo at the appointed hour, cautiously looking around for this formidable man. Knowing Italians, he would doubtless keep her waiting; she resigned herself to a wasted morning and started to wander about. Viewed from all angles, the property was daunting, four storeys high with a water entrance and obvious subsidence into the canal that needed fixing fast. The only other person not hurrying past was a silver-haired man quietly studying the façade. That's him, she thought, and strode purposefully over before she could lose her nerve and scuttle away.

'Scusi,' she said to his motionless back. 'Would you, by chance, be the Signor Contino?'

'You've been listening to too much Mozart,' he said, turning to her with an affable smile. 'Mario Dandolo, at your service. I prefer Professor to Count.'

The hair was silver but the face was not old, with inquisitive eyes behind rimless lenses that looked at her with appreciation as she offered him her hand. Younger than her but older than Charles; to Cassie an excellent omen. And the softly modulated accent was pure mid-Atlantic.

'Professor of what?' she asked as he juggled with the keys.

'Architecture mainly,' he said. 'Here in Venice.' But also at Harvard where he spent the main part of the year.

Which was why, with reluctance, he'd decided to sell. The palazzo, his family's home since the

Renaissance, was more than he could afford to maintain any more. He had sunk what inherited money he'd had into the basic structure, renewing the piles and shoring up the walls to prevent its total collapse from sheer neglect. The interior, though vast, was cavernous and gutted. It would take many years of devoted work to restore.

'Though it breaks my heart, it has got to go,' he said. 'But only to a suitable buyer. One who will cherish it as much as I have and give it a new lease of life.' He looked at Cassie appraisingly and seemed to like what he saw. His children, he explained over coffee, were now all grown and had gone their separate ways, while his wife, an American, preferred her own country. Would not consider forsaking New England to live in a mosquito-ridden swamp, which was how she liked to describe the Venetian lagoon.

'How sad,' said Cassie, thinking of Cornwall. Though now she knew that the die was cast and her fate about to be sealed. Provided, of course, she could find some way of raising the requisite capital fast. It might be a ruin but didn't come cheap; it encapsulated six centuries and was an important part of Venetian history. She would be hard-pressed to find the money but was resolved that nothing should stand in her way.

It's only money. She had often heard him say that, but when Cassie confronted Charles his jaw visibly sagged.

'You want to *what*? Let me try to get this straight.' For a second, he placed his hand on his forehead, then looked at her again with incredulous eyes. He had aged, she reflected; it was doubtless those twins. The glimpse or two she had had of them had kept her awake at night. But they, thank goodness, were not her problem. Pippa had brought this all on herself and would have to deal with it. She had, after all, been the catalyst of the break-up.

'I want to sell the flat,' she repeated. 'I need the money for something else.' He had, after all, his Walton Street showroom as well as the villa in Barnes. And the flat had been paid for by Edwin's estate, was actually nothing to do with Charles though Cassie was far too well-bred to mention that. She'd already discussed it with the family and they'd leapt at the idea. A Venetian palazzo, how very romantic. The ideal setting for Cassie, they felt, and a project to stretch her innumerable talents which they, if not her husband, fully acknowledged. She was every bit as gifted as Charles, though no one had dared to say so before, and had mouldered too long in the country in semi-retirement. Rose was prepared to risk her career and come out and help for as long as it took, while Sybil's eyes gleamed as she quietly considered what might be in it for her. A summer school for aspiring sculptors; something she'd always wanted to do. From the surveyor's plans, which Cassie brought home, there was more space than she could ever dream of using.

'I definitely think you should do it,' she said. 'Edwin, I know, would approve.' The studious child he'd so lovingly nurtured was finally finding her wings at last. Not before it was time, after all she'd been through.

Charles was wholly incensed with fury, his customary suavity totally gone. Never, in all these years, had she seen him like this.

'You don't even speak the lingo,' he said, his blue eyes blazing, his mouth in a snarl, his fists, she noticed, clenched as though he might strike her.

'As a matter of fact, I do,' she said calmly, resisting the urge to argue. There were things about her he still didn't know. His own career had always come first and she had done what she could to encourage it. Now she saw she had nurtured an egotist, and took full blame for that, but was reluctant to provoke an uglier mood. The money she wanted belonged to her, though he was acting now as though she were trying to rob him.

'You don't need the flat any more,' she said firmly. 'Your house is plenty big enough for your needs.'

'That's not the point.' He was shouting now. 'I need it to entertain business contacts. I can't expect them to trek all the way out to Barnes.'

Cassie couldn't help smiling at this; he looked so like Aidan in one of his snits. Though normally equable, the boy had a tendency to fly through the roof at the slightest cause even when he knew he was in the wrong. But Aidan was only just out of school; his father was almost fifty and should know better.

'Why are you laughing? It isn't funny.'

'Indeed,' she said. 'I only want what is mine.' She'd behaved impeccably over the divorce, removing all

295

obstacles from his way in order that it could go through fast and legitimise his twins. She had kept the house, which had always been hers, but allowed him sole use of the Pont Street flat and asked for nothing at all from his burgeoning business. Over the years he had borrowed large sums, to plough into the business, he'd said, but so far she hadn't seen a penny's return. Had she turned nasty, which was never the intention, she might well have gone for fifty per cent. As it was, she had walked away with nothing of his. But now she needed to sell the flat in order to buy the palazzo. And if he attempted to stand in her way, she would bring in lawyers without hesitation. She had been a loyal and forbearing wife long enough.

As his anger grew, he began to shake and Cassie was instantly sickened, for she recognised in his contorted features the face of the son they shared. She had started to wonder if Aidan might be unbalanced; there were certain things she had never told Charles. His year away, spent travelling in Europe, had come as a secret relief to her. She had seen his behaviour echoed in the twins and knew that Pippa had a problem on her hands. But never before, in their twenty-two years, had she ever seen Charles quite like this.

'Pull yourself together,' she said coldly and left.

He was waiting for her at an outside table close to the Rialto bridge when Cassie arrived to sign the final papers. She had raised the money, completed the deeds; now all that was left was her signature and a final handshake to solemnise the deal. It was a clear bright morning in early spring and the chill had gone from the air. The sky was a deep cerulean blue, straight from a Renaissance painting, and the sunlight sparkled on the waters of the canal. Mario, as he had asked her to call him, wore jeans and an open-necked shirt and was staring wistfully at the palazzo that any minute would cease to be his, always assuming he wasn't about to rescind. This was the moment she had lived for for months, too superstitious to enter the date in her diary.

'Cassandra,' he said, taking both her hands and looking as though he was about to kiss her. 'These past few months have meant much to me, spending so much time with you, even though it means having to forfeit my birthright.'

Cassie blushed like a bashful maiden and lowered her eyes from his gaze.

'Mario,' she said. 'I give you my word that I'll do everything in my power to honour your trust.'

The architectural details he would handle himself on his occasional visits back from the States. They'd already spent many evenings together, poring over his intricate drawings, discussing the future of the palazzo as if it were to be a home they shared. Cassie had promised he would always be welcome; she would keep a suite of rooms for his sole use.

'And you,' he said. 'How will you manage here alone? In summer it will be hot and the streets over-crowded.'

'I'll manage,' said Cassie. 'My daughter is coming.

And my sister-in-law, an eminent sculptor, has plans to visit us too.'

'But not your husband?' The question was loaded. They'd steered clear till now of discussing their private lives.

'I have no husband,' said Cassie simply, seeing the wakening interest in his eyes. 'He moved on,' she explained, 'to a younger wife. And now has a whole other life.' I am redundant, she reflected silently. Even my son is no longer around.

'Cassandra,' he said, 'you're a beautiful woman who should not be living alone. If it weren't for Harvard, I would stay here like a shot and hope to get to know you better.' He raised her hands to his mouth and kissed them and the look in his eyes sent a shiver down her spine. She was not too old to feel something, after all. 'I'll be back,' he promised, 'after the next semester. I will give you what help I can in restoring my home.'

'But your wife . . . .'

'My wife doesn't care,' he said. 'She prefers to play tennis and meet her friends. The reason I moved to the States was because of her.'

He said little more but she felt she understood him; he still had the Dandolo blood in his veins and Venice was the home for which he pined.

'I'll be back,' he repeated. 'Just as soon as I can.' And she knew that this was a man whose word she could trust.

37

The place to start would be Middlesbrough where they met, which was also the town where he'd died. She fingered the locket she never took off though she could no longer bear to look at his picture. She felt what had happened with Aidan had defiled it; felt bad about betraying the love of her life.

She bought a road map and rented a car; though not accustomed to driving on the left, she thought it simpler than the train, and once she hit the north she'd be more at home. She would bypass the Wirral; there was nothing for her there. Even her earliest memories had been spoilt. So she'd head for the detention centre where she'd gone straight after the fire. It was an unbelievable twenty-eight years since she was there.

She enjoyed the drive, found the motorway easy. She was used to driving a heavy truck so the rented Toyota just skimmed along and put her into a more relaxed holiday mood. The legacy had freed her to enjoy herself a bit; she even stopped for lunch and a cigarette. She remembered the sulky child she had been, fifteen years old and full of hate for the man who had done her so much damage. Chad's intervention had been very timely; if it weren't for him, she might not even have survived.

She arrived in Middlesbrough mid-afternoon and went in search of the old detention centre. The town had grown vastly bigger since those days and she couldn't identify any landmarks but did eventually, aided by the map, track down the right location. The building still stood but its windows were broken and coils of barbed wire were there to repel intruders. She stopped outside and lit up again. The shock of being back moved her profoundly.

She got out of the car and rattled the gates but no one came; the place was obviously deserted. A sharp breeze blew some old rubbish around; it was nothing more than a desolate wasteland. Eventually Frankie was forced to give up, return to the car and think about what to do next.

The social services, once she found them, were pleasant and willing to co-operate, though, faced with them, she wasn't quite sure what she was after. Anything they could tell her about Chad before he was sent to this horrible place; Borstal she already knew about and, before that, Barnardo's. The woman provided the relevant details and wished her success with her quest. It would mean another long drive to Yorkshire but at least she was on her way.

Barnardo's were not at all proud of Chad. His name was not on their roll of honour. At first they seemed reluctant to talk to her at all. Frankie's persistence, though, finally paid off. The man checked the records and gave her chapter and verse. Chad had spent two spells with them, from his birth in 1955 until 1962 when he had been fostered. The foster parents had sent him to Repton, whence he had been expelled at fifteen, after which they had washed their hands of him and sent him back to the orphanage.

'Shocking behaviour, I know,' said the man. 'People like that have a lot to answer for. No community spirit or conscience. They should not have been allowed to foster at all.'

'And after that they'd deserted him?'

'Well, he knifed a lad. Some argument in the play-ground. He always had a volatile temper. He ended up in Borstal.'

'Do you have the address of his foster parents?' She knew she was fighting against the odds. But Frankie, inspired, could also be very persuasive.

'This is most irregular,' said the man. 'I'd be much obliged if you wouldn't mention my name.'

Frankie knew, from his complicit smile, that privately he approved of what she was doing. She didn't explain her connection to Chad, just that he was a distant family member. The Tewson-Finches lived in Derbyshire which was why, presumably, they'd sent him to that school. What a waste of effort and money, they must have felt.

She loathed Yolande Tewson-Finch on sight, from the moment she opened the door. Nouveau· from her bouffant hair and the spastic smile on her lifted face, she was X-ray thin and wearing expensive cashmere. Frankie hadn't bothered to phone; thought she might find out more if she simply turned up.

'Yes?' said Yolande, expecting a delivery. She must be at least in her early eighties but was very well preserved.

Frankie smiled and charmed her way in. 'I'm here to talk about Chad,' she said and watched the sudden wariness in her eyes.

'Chad? He's been dead for thirty years. What about him?' the woman said. Cold, just as Frankie had assumed she would be; a woman without a heart.

Frankie looked round the opulent house, with its fake antiques and rococo mirrors, and reflected that, on the whole, Chad had turned out well. What polish he'd got must have come from the school. He certainly hadn't got it here. And this vile old woman could well have destroyed him by turning her back at the time he had needed her most.

'Why did you get rid of him? I know the story,' said Frankie.

'He was out of control,' Yolande snapped. 'Threw back in our faces all we'd done for him by getting expelled from the school.'

'For smoking?' said Frankie. 'He was only fifteen.' She had been that age herself when she set the fire.

'Precisely,' said Yolande, through tightened lips.

'So why take him on in the first place?' she asked. If you weren't prepared to be a proper mother and offer unconditional love.

Yolande considered and her fish-eyes softened. 'He was the cutest child I had ever seen. At seven years old, with those great blue eyes, he looked like a little angel.'

'And yet you dumped him just like that,' Frankie virtually spat.

'It turned out he was a natural delinquent and that we were well shot of him. He later killed someone. Tainted blood. There was nothing else we could do.'

Except to love him and back him up. Frankie was suddenly feeling sick. The sooner she got out of this house, the better.

38

'Calm down,' said Clive, 'or you'll make yourself ill. I still don't understand why you're so upset. What do I have to do to convince you that it wasn't me at the Centre Court? Apart from the fact that I rarely watch tennis, I was in Corfu with the lads who can vouch for that.'

'But Vanessa saw you . . .'

'She was mistaken. Tell her to go and get an eye test before making any more false accusations. She meddles too much, as it is.'

'She only wants what is best for me,' said Jenny, still not entirely convinced though he hadn't turned a hair when she'd brought it up. Just laughed and asked if she was having him watched. She had yet to tell him about Osborne and Cole, did not want him thinking she was turning into a snoop. But that was the thing that baffled her most, the fact that they'd claimed not to know who he was. There had to be some sort of logical explanation; maybe she'd simply misdialled. She felt ashamed of doubting his word. She would talk to him later when both were less stressed; right now, she didn't want to rattle his cage. So instead she asked about the cricket tour and he filled her in on scores and things, although she had never really seen much point in the game. In the Welsh valleys where she had grown up, rugby football was a second religion and, since childhood, she had screamed from the stands along with her father and his friends. She still tried never to miss an international.

Now Clive was back, looking tanned and relaxed, he reclaimed his place behind the bar. The locals all told him how much he'd been missed. Thursday nights were not the same without his benevolent presence. He laughed and offered free drinks all round. He wasn't the landlord but knew that Jenny would approve. He had always emphasised the importance of goodwill; she might never have got off to such a good start without his intervention.

'You spend too much of your time away,' said Mrs Dawkings darkly. 'A girl like that needs a man around. It doesn't do to leave her too much on her own.'

'And there are plenty here who would take your place.' Mrs Bailey, one of the clique, was in total agreement. She glanced significantly along the bar to where Alistair Grey stood drinking alone, a thoughtful man in boots and a waterproof jacket.

'Ladies,' said Clive, at his most beguiling, 'I can't disagree with what you say. If it weren't for the fact that I have a living to make, I assure you I'd be here all the time. Please don't hold against me my need to work.'

He left them and moved along the bar, twisting down glasses and flicking them in the air before concocting his exotic cocktails, an innovative feature he had introduced.

'Well,' said Mrs Bailey, with a heartfelt sigh. 'He certainly knows how to chat up the ladies. I don't mind admitting, I wouldn't turn him down.'

'All mouth and trousers,' growled Mrs Dawkings, though she couldn't disguise the glint in her eye as she watched him strutting his stuff.

'It was him,' said Vanessa. 'Without a shadow of doubt. How many men have that rakish charm and those luminous cobalt eyes?' Though not enamoured of him herself, she could quite see where the attraction lay, was secretly glad that her heart was otherwise taken.

'He says not,' said Jenny tiredly. 'And that your eyes need testing.'

'Me and forty million other television viewers? I don't think so,' said Vanessa, incensed. She had never completely trusted the man and now he had started playing games.

'I'm afraid I have to believe him,' said Jenny. 'He has given me his word that he wasn't there.'

'And what does he say about the job? Did he manage to wriggle out of that one too?'

'I haven't got round to asking him yet,' said Jenny, unsure of what he'd say. She wanted, more than anything else, to trust him.

The memory of Douglas's evasiveness still made her slightly sick. Clive was an altogether nicer man who always treated her extremely well and had shown his solid devotion right from the start. Take the way he behaved in the bar: he made no secret of their attachment so that all the regulars knew that he was her man. He would not risk putting his neck on the line if he were not totally straight. Yet Vanessa was a loyal friend who would never risk hurting her in any way unless she was pretty sure of what she'd seen.

'I'll talk to him later, after closing time, and find out the truth about Osborne and Cole.' Which was something she didn't look forward to in the least.

'Look, my darling,' he said to her later. 'We have to talk about these jealousy fits. It isn't like you, you are usually so well balanced. What is it – your time of the month or something like that?'

'No,' said Jenny, profoundly annoyed. 'What I asked was a perfectly reasonable question. I called your office and they claimed not to know who you were. Can you blame me for being confused? For the past four years, since we very first met, you have told me about your strenuous job.' Principally to explain his regular absences.

At first he looked deeply put out. He picked up his drink and paced the room, then stepped out into the cool night air and the sound of the babbling brook.

Cripes, thought Jenny. Now I've really done it. She had gone one step too far this time and ran the risk of driving him away.

But when he returned, he was smiling again; he took her in his arms and held her close. 'I'm afraid you're a little too smart for me,' he said, once he'd smothered her with kisses. She was right about the job, he confessed; it wasn't quite what he'd said. He hated himself for not being straight with her but his hands, at least for the present, were tied; he wasn't entirely his own man. The story about Osborne and Cole had been only a front.

'But they do exist?'

'You spoke to them. And I've had dealings with them in the past, even if they don't remember me now.' They made a convenient front for him while he got on with his real work, the nature of which he wasn't allowed to divulge. At least, for now.

'You mean you are undercover?' she asked, slightly incredulous yet intrigued. This man was far deeper than she had ever suspected.

'Something like that,' said Clive, relieved, since she seemed to be taking it all so well. 'It's the reason, my darling, that I travel so much and haven't been able to give you a fixed address. Soon, I hope, it will all be in the open and you, I promise, will be the first to know.'

'I think he's a spy,' she reported to Vanessa. With all that charm, she should have known he was more than just a travelling salesman. Parts of that story had simply not added up.

Pull the other one, said Vanessa, but only to herself.

Meanwhile, Jenny was cooking up a storm, growing in confidence every day and constantly adding to her repertoire. She stuck to the staples, like cottage pie, but boldly advanced on the gourmet side until she began to get write-ups in the papers. Not just the papers local to Bath but the *Sunday Times* and the major glossies. A couple of her old colleagues even came down. She entertained them in her private snug and they caught her up on the London gossip. Douglas, they told her, though cautiously, had now embarked on a new affair and appeared to be treating the girl in the same casual way.

'Anyone I know?' asked Jenny, willing it not to hurt.

'No, she's only been there a matter of months.'

She was younger, they said; in her middle twenties. Exactly my age at the time, she thought, but kept her mouth firmly shut and said not a word. So he hadn't changed; in a way she was glad. It would have hurt her considerably more if he'd finally left his wife.

And how was she? they wanted to know. Was there anyone new on the scene? Yes, she said and told them about Clive, though not the bit about what he did for a living. They seemed impressed by the meal she laid on and promised her, off the record, an excellent write-up. She was making quite a name for herself which was why they had bothered to come at all. She felt optimistic as she showed them out. Things at last appeared to be really working.

Clive was off on his travels again but now she knew not to ask where to or when to expect him back. Since he had told her his need for caution, she tried not to talk about him much at all except, of course, to Vanessa, who already knew.

'So what does he claim to be?' she asked, the disbelief quite clear in her voice. 'A plain-clothes cop or a customs man? Insurance investigator? What?'

'I am not allowed to know,' said Jenny, 'but it certainly must pay well.' He never seemed short of a bob or two and his car was a Bentley convertible which she'd always thought rather plush for a travelling salesman. That, and his mastery of perfect martinis, elevated him to James Bond status. Which made the spy theory plausible; she adored him all the more.

'What has he said about the mystery financier?' Vanessa was still very much on his case. She knew the damage that Douglas had wrought, was determined Jenny should not go through that again. She had never really been sure of Clive; he was much too good-looking to be kosher.

'Not a word,' said Jenny blithely. 'But now I realise it doesn't matter. Whoever it is has obvious faith in what we are doing here at the Coot and Hern.'

Alistair Grey asked her out again but Jenny was reluctant to go in case Clive suddenly returned without notice. It was two whole weeks since he'd last been here; he hadn't even called.

'You're crazy.' Vanessa and Joyce agreed. 'When did he ever consider you? He comes and goes but only as it suits him. And doesn't show much remorse if he suddenly cancels.'

'Are you sure he isn't married?' asked Joyce, her innocent tone belied by her searching look.

'Of course I am,' said Jenny impatiently, wishing

they'd let the subject drop. Lately she had the feeling they were ganging up.

'Why?' asked Vanessa, leaping straight in. 'Has he actually spelled it out?'

'Of course not,' said Jenny. 'He knows I trust him. That kind of interrogation isn't for us. We're already much closer than that which is really what matters.'

A significant glance, not lost on her, passed silently between the other two before they let the subject drop. Are you thinking what I am, it said quite clearly.

'Leave it alone and get on with your work. In less than an hour we'll be opening up.' Joyce still had the sauces to prepare and Vanessa should really get home to her kids. She was good to give them so much of her time but, right at that moment, Jenny would rather she left. She was starting to grate on her. Clive was right when he said she interfered.

The secret backer was on Vanessa's mind; she still thought it awfully strange. Who would invest such a sizeable sum yet show no interest in the profits? Jenny told her sharply to shut up.

'You are always interfering,' she said. 'Clive's right. It's none of your business.'

'Have it your own way,' said Vanessa, now cross. 'But don't come crying to me when it all goes pear-shaped.' She drove off home in a bit of a huff, leaving Jenny feeling miserable and contrite. She gave her time to reach her house, then phoned and apologised.

'I don't know what's got into me,' she said. 'I must be over-working.'

Or worrying about things unspecified. Vanessa had a shrewd idea but wisely made no comment.

Jenny tried asking Clive again but only made him angry. 'What is it with all the questions?' he asked. 'It's that bloody Vanessa sticking her nose in. Tell her to stay out of our lives. She only gets in the way.'

Jenny, of course, didn't pass this on; Vanessa was her dearest friend. But she also didn't want Clive upset. She tried cooling the friendship but that didn't work. Vanessa was no fool and knew exactly what was going on.

'Listen, my sweet,' she said to Jenny. 'If you don't want me around, I'll shove off. But I'll always be here if things go wrong. Don't let that bastard wreck your life just because he can't be honest with you.'

Undercover work, my eye. Far more likely to be another woman.

Toby was growing fast and was now almost seven, an intelligent child with a questioning mind to whom Clive was a father figure, the only adult male he had ever been close to. While Clive was away, he longed for his return and greeted him with a barrage of questions the moment he walked through the door. Clive would sweep him into his arms and swing him up high above his head and the child would cry out with joy and feverish excitement. On these occasions Jenny's heart lit up and she wondered whether the time had come to suggest giving Toby a brother or sister. She was almost forty and cutting things fine, yet didn't want to upset the applecart.

'Did you never want children of your own?' she cautiously questioned Clive. 'You seem to be a natural, certainly with Toby.'

'It's really a matter of timing,' he said. 'Yes, some time I would like a family, especially if they turned out like this little lad. But I need a more stable lifestyle before committing to that extent. It simply wouldn't be fair, the way things are now.' He looked at her with his bright blue eyes as if appealing for understanding. She moved silently over, with a brimming heart, and enclosed them both in a hug.

'I really think he is coming round,' she confided to Joyce as they cooked. 'Toby certainly regards him as his dad.'

'Well, he'd better get a move on,' said Joyce, pessimistic as always. 'That is, if it's you he's planning to have them with. You may look good for your age but you're no spring chicken.'

'Thanks,' said Jenny, by no means offended, swiping at her with a cloth. 'You sure know how to make a girl feel good.'

Clive was here for a long weekend; nothing could spoil her mood right now and, since he was starting to share his secrets, almost anything could still happen. She badly needed to talk to Vanessa but hesitated about ringing her. They weren't on the best of terms any more since their slight contretemps over Clive. If only he would get on and pop the question, she would do what she could to restore the friendship.

Providing, of course, that the two of them promised not to fight.

The following Saturday, when Clive wasn't there, Alistair Grey turned up in the bar with a woman. They stood at one end and he ordered gin and tonics while the bar staff craned to get a proper look.

'Don't tell Jenny,' said Hamish to Simon. 'I've a hunch she might not like it.'

She was in the kitchen, preparing the meal, when Joyce popped down to bring the bad tidings; always the albatross of doom, she just couldn't help herself. 'I think you should check the bar,' she said, trying to keep the glee from her voice. 'There is someone there I think you should know about.'

Jenny, preparing the venison salad, scarcely gave it a thought. 'Not Clive?' she said, but when Joyce said no, she kept her mind on the task in hand and showed no further interest. Clive would be gone at least another week; her mind was exclusively on the job. Whatever was disconcerting the staff left her unconcerned.

'Just go upstairs and take a peek,' said Joyce. 'I'll finish that for you.' She practically elbowed Jenny from her place, made her remove her chef's whites, comb her hair and stick on some lipstick.

'Why?' asked Jenny, mystified, but Joyce could be as annoying as Vanessa.

'Take a break and go up to the bar. Have yourself a glass of wine. They need to see you from time to time; you work much too hard as it is.'

'Hi,' said Alistair, when she appeared, and introduced her to his date. A big-boned woman, taller than him, with ruddy cheeks and a lusty laugh, dressed in the countrywoman's uniform of boots and a sage-green Barbour.

'Hi,' said Jenny, extending her hand. 'Welcome to the Coot and Hern. I don't believe I have seen you before. Are you from these parts?'

'I hope I shall be soon,' said the woman, fairly obviously gloating.

'Well?' said Joyce, when Jenny returned.

'Seems nice,' replied Jenny vaguely. 'It's probably time he settled down. Now where did you put the langoustines and have you finished the garlic mayonnaise?'

'It's useless,' said Joyce when she bumped into Vanessa. 'Nothing we say does any good. She is stuck on the fellow even though he treats her like dirt.'

He seemed to be away a lot but that was the season, he pointed out. In the summer months what it was he did was always extraordinarily busy. Jenny didn't really care. The tourist trade was in full swing and she had enough on her hands as it was without also having to worry about Clive. She was working flat out all her waking hours and the place was fully booked, with a waiting list that extended for weeks in advance. She had to bring in extra help yet still had no time to relax. Toby was dispatched to Neath, where her parents could make a fuss of him and he could connect with another adult male. Perhaps he would pick up a smattering of Welsh and learn about rugby from his gramps. Jenny knew he'd be spoilt to death which, at that age especially, was important.

'I miss him, of course I do,' she said. But she couldn't object to the amount of trade they were doing. Almost more than Toby, though, she found she missed Vanessa. But still hadn't quite the courage to give her a call.

Joyce frequently met Vanessa in town, often by arrangement. Vanessa worried about Jenny a lot and didn't want to lose touch. She could always call her but that wasn't the point. She knew she was not a favourite with Clive who resented the closeness of the two long-time friends.

'It's almost as though he is jealous,' she said. 'Which is crazy when you think of it. We go back almost twenty years, have always been there for each other.'

'He begrudges anyone close to her, even me at times.' Joyce had watched Clive following Jenny around, disliking how friendly she was in the bar, breaking up any conversation he deemed to have lasted too long. It was an odd conundrum; he neglected her yet, when he was there, appeared to want to possess her. 'It's a matter of dogs and mangers,' she added. 'Doesn't want her enough himself but is keen no one else should have her.' Like Alistair Grey who still looked wistful when his Amazonian girlfriend wasn't there. 'If I were Jenny, I'd snap him up and not waste any more time on that sweet-talking rogue.'

Vanessa wholeheartedly agreed with her. One of

these days, she sincerely hoped, they would finally catch the bastard out red-handed.

When Clive came back after three weeks away, he seemed unusually tired. He had lost a lot of his natural bounce, was less keen to serve in the bar but spent more time at the back with Toby, newly returned from South Wales. As Toby got older, the pair grew closer. It warmed Jenny's heart to watch them talking like a couple of ancient buddies.

'He's great with kids,' she remarked again. If only she could persuade him to have some of his own.

'When are you going to settle down?' she asked one night as she sat on his knee, her arms round his neck.

'When my life is more stable,' he said, carefully extricating himself and going to the bar to get them both drinks. It seemed to suit him, this peripatetic existence, belonging nowhere, constantly moving around. Whatever it was that absorbed his life, she knew she was only a part of it. Occasionally, in her darker moments, she wondered what awful secret he might be concealing. The girls had asked how she knew he wasn't married and she'd almost bitten their heads off. The truth was, she knew nothing of the kind, feared to find out from some neutral source that the dream of happy-ever-after she clung to was no more than pie in the sky. Provided that she never found out, she could continue to dream. It was a pathetic way to live, a throwback to the Douglas years, but while she was working this hard, she had no other choice. Maybe, once the season was over, she would pluck up the courage to confront him. But then, on the other hand, she might not. She was scared of what she feared was the truth, that he'd never loved her at all.

39

From Derbyshire Frankie drove on to Yorkshire, in search of the church where Chad had been found. She was fired up now with a new incentive; her encounter with that hateful woman had made her doubly keen to track him down. St Chad's was somewhere in the Hull environs. She bought a map of the neighbourhood and tried to find it without asking. In a tree-lined enclave in a tiny village she finally located the Norman church, square and rough-hewn with a vaulted roof, unchanged throughout the centuries it had stood there. The morning was bright, and there was no one about. She locked the car and strolled across the grass, still fresh with early dew.

She stood in the porch and looked around. It was here the baby had been abandoned. She imagined him swathed against the night air and wondered how long he had lain there. The door was ajar so she stepped inside, inhaling the musty aroma of beeswax and wood. The flowers at the altar were freshly done; the church appeared to be still in regular use. She wandered in search of some tangible sign that the boy she had loved and lost had once been here. If she closed her eyes and focused her mind, perhaps she might even make contact with his spirit. It had been so long, she was parched by her desire.

'Can I help you?' She hadn't heard his approach; he seemed to have sprung out of nowhere. Surprised, Frankie turned to face a smiling verger.

'I was looking for the parish records. I wondered if you kept them here in the church.'

'Only those for recent years. The rest are kept under lock and key. If you tell me what it is you want, perhaps I can help you look.'

The man was small and quite affable, too young, she thought, to have known about Chad who had never even lived in this village at all. But his offer of help appeared genuine and he seemed not to be in a hurry. So she explained her reason for being there and said she'd like to see the documentation. When asked about her motivation, she lied and said she was an archivist. Someone had asked her to trace his family roots.

'The best thing I can suggest,' said the verger, 'is that you stop by at the vicarage and ask if you may look at the relevant records. The vicar's hobby is genealogy. I am certain he will be only too pleased to assist you.'

He pointed her in the right direction, towards an attractive, ivy-clad house with gables and a beautiful flower-filled garden. Frankie thanked him and did as he suggested. It was just before ten; the vicar would still be at home. Her pulse was working overtime. She was apprehensive about the next connection.

She was greeted by the vicar's wife who was outside, pruning the roses. Yes, she said; her husband was home. She wiped her hands, put down her secateurs and went to call him through the open window.

The vicar's interest was immediately caught; he invited Frankie inside. His wife obligingly made them coffee and they all settled down in the panelled study where Frankie explained in more detail why she had come.

'Fifty years is a very long time. There are few people hereabouts that go back that far. The name, you say, was Chad Barnaby? I don't believe that's a local name. Do you have any more information to narrow the field?'

Frankie told him all she knew. The baby had been abandoned in the porch and found by the gardener's boy, who heard him crying.

'Ah,' said the vicar, recognition dawning. 'I think I do remember the case. Barnaby was the gardener's boy so they named the baby after him.'

'Right!' said Frankie, exhilarated. Things were proving easier than she had hoped. The vicar unlocked a huge wall cupboard in which some leather-bound tomes were stored and very easily turned up the relevant year. 'Nineteen fifty-five,' he said. 'Almost half a century ago. Have you any idea of the time of year?'

'June,' said Frankie. 'And also full moon. He was found around the summer solstice.' It all came back, what Chad had said, and how he had been named for the church and the boy.

The vicar found it very quickly, the handwritten entry for 23 June in which the baby's name was recorded as of 'unknown parentage'.

'And there's nothing more?'

'I'm afraid not,' he said. 'This book is simply a record of births, marriages and deaths.'

But then his wife piped up and said: 'There's a resident in the village almshouse called Barnaby Corbett. Perhaps he's the one.'

Barnaby Corbett was gnarled and frail with bad arthritis and obvious cataracts that made him look much older than he was. Frankie feared that he might not understand her. She sat beside him in his sunny room and explained what she was after and a jolt of excitement shot through her when he smiled.

'The baby,' he said, his expression softening. ''Twere me that found him, that's the truth. A right little cracker he were and no mistake. Someone had dumped him in the porch and I heard him crying when I was tidying up.'

'Can you tell me anything about him?' asked Frankie, on the edge of her chair with anticipation. All this was helping to bring Chad closer to her.

'Just that he was right bonny,' said Corbett. 'With the bluest, brightest, most knowing eyes. He looked to me like an ancient soul who had been around a number of times already.'

'And his mother never turned up, is that right? Nor even left a note to explain?'

'He was certainly never claimed,' said Corbett. 'In the end he had to go to Barnardo's, even though the vicar asked questions from the pulpit for several Sundays in a row. But there was a note, which the vicar kept to himself.'

'I don't suppose you remember what it said?' She could hardly bear the suspense. The mother must have been at her wits' end to take such a drastic and final step. Frankie couldn't help but pity her.

Corbett fell silent and stroked his chin, looking back into the past. He hadn't remembered that baby in years but now, despite his sightless eyes, he could see it as clearly as if it were here in this room. Raven black curls and those brilliant eyes that seemed to conceal some inner knowledge. Devil's spawn; he remembered the poor girl's note.

40

Things were looking serious. The doctors were wary of making a firm pronouncement. They had taken Tom in – both twins, in fact – and were giving them extensive tests before they could decide what should be done. Cassie, who'd come at Pippa's request, sat with her in the visitors' room, holding her hand and trying her utmost to calm her.

'It will be all right,' she said constantly, treating her just like one of her own. It was hard to believe, a shattering truth, but Rose and Daisy were older than Pippa by very nearly a decade. And yet this was her ex's child-bride and the hand she held so firmly in her own had done unimaginable things with her own former husband. It made the mind boggle; she tried not to consider it until the door swung forcefully open and Pippa's mother stood on the threshold, looking as vengeful as the wrath of God.

'What's she doing here?' she practically barked, the once peroxided hair now muted to a more becoming shade of tarnished brass. She was something in PR, Cassie thought, though only worked part-time these days. If it weren't for the scowl, she'd look very much like her daughter. Slimmer, though, and better dressed but, then, poor Pippa was going through very bad times.

'She's here because I asked her,' said Pippa, defiantly clinging to Cassie's hand and daring her mother to make any sort of scene. The mother, whose name Cassie couldn't remember, hovered before them with a face of doom until Pippa, wailing, begged her to try to calm down.

'It isn't the end of the world,' she said. 'But I need Cassie here because she is Aidan's mother.'

Cassie, ever the diplomat, invited the woman to join them, letting go of Pippa's hand as she did so. 'We are all in this together,' she said. Well, you two are; I am not. 'And since our boys all share the same blood, it makes absolute sense that we all pull together until we know the best thing to do for them all.' It wasn't any kind of joke; far from it. She'd been through it all herself. But, from what she had seen of those babies, they did require help. And she was here to do what she could. She was, after all, only human.

The mother glared but took it in; she sank on to an adjacent chair like a deflating balloon. The stress was getting to all of them; no wonder, considering the implications. Cassie would either stay or go, whichever seemed for the best. A nurse came in and offered them tea and told them the wait would soon be over.

'Don't worry,' she said, with an optimistic smile. 'I am sure things aren't nearly as bad as you probably think. This is always the worst time, the waiting part.'

They were calming down and making light comments about the weather and how the evenings were growing shorter, when the door to the room crashed open again and Charles Buchanan strode in.

'What's *she* doing here?' he asked apoplectically, pointing at Cassie with a shaking finger and looking as though he might expire on the spot.

As Pippa went through it all again, Cassie rose gracefully to her feet, held out her hand to her former husband and invited him to sit down. It was time, in any case, that she went, she quietly explained to Pippa. Her presence was clearly not welcome here after all.

'But I want you here.' Pippa was growing desperate, scared of what the prognosis might be. Cassie said she had things to do and asked her to be in touch when she knew the results.

'I am sure the nurse is right,' she said, her magnificent eyes full of genuine concern. 'But it's better to be safe than sorry at this stage. Don't you agree?' This last remark was addressed to Charles who looked as though he would gladly throttle her.

'Get the hell out of it,' he snarled. 'You don't belong here at all.'

'Charles!' said Pippa, deeply shocked. 'That's no way to talk to your former wife. Especially as she is only here because I begged her to come.'

'Don't worry,' said Cassie, stooping to kiss her. 'I have to be going in any case. I have a meeting at four with my accountant.'

Pippa's mother conceded defeat; Cassie had class to the nth degree and had handled the situation with consummate grace. 'I hope we'll meet again,' she said, rising to her feet and offering her hand. 'I know you have been a huge support to my daughter.'

'Anything I can do,' said Cassie, acknowledging with charm the other's climb-down. 'While I'm in London, which won't be for very much longer.'

'You must come to the house before you leave.' Pippa was also now on her feet, reaching out to the woman she had grown to admire. 'Perhaps for tea with my mother one day?'

'Over my dead body!' hissed her husband.

The medical report, when it finally came through, could possibly have been worse. Yes, they were almost certainly autistic but had been caught at a young enough age to allow for something to be done, with careful handling.

'Both of them?' said Pippa, stunned.

'Identical twins,' said the doctor gently, 'which means their genetic imprint is the same.'

'But Jack . . .'

'Has a very developed talent. His drawing skills are extremely advanced.'

'And Tom?'

'Still lacks the manual skills but will learn to compensate.'

'And how do we cope?' Pippa's mother stepped in, having pulled herself together now Cassie had gone. Charles was pacing and muttering to himself. He showed great signs of agitation but didn't seem able to listen constructively. Something Cassie had done had driven him wild. Pippa had neither the time nor the inclination to find out exactly what, at least for now. The twins were what mattered, not their aberrant father. From the expression on the doctor's face, they were yet to hear the worst.

'Diet and discipline are mainly what counts, though tantrums are unavoidable. The children must be forced to observe a regular routine.' No running around with food, he explained. They must not be allowed to leave the table until they had finished eating.

'Mainly it is old-fashioned common sense.' He looked to Charles as an older man. 'The way we were obliged to behave by our parents.'

'But how did it all come about?' asked Pippa's mother. 'It isn't something I've ever encountered before.'

'It's largely genetic,' the doctor said. 'The genes are found on an area of the sixth chromosome, known as human leucocyte antigens. The tendency is inherited from the father.'

They all looked at Charles who appeared not to hear. He was still in a white hot rage about something else.

Something was clearly rattling Charles though he didn't say what it was. He seemed to have serious matters on his mind. Not just the health of his infant sons; some of their symptoms he had seen in Aidan who had turned into a fine and engaging young man. These days Pippa found Charles hard to talk to; he appeared to be drifting away from her, which only succeeded in adding to her general gloom.

'Just when I need his support,' she complained, 'he

seems to be off on some tangent of his own.' Despite his frequent absences, till now he had always been at her side, loving and supportive when she was down. She wondered if he had business worries; if so, he had never said a word, but these days he rarely discussed such matters with her.

Her mother, as always, sympathised, aware that Charles was now moody and detached, no longer the charming seducer he had once been. His thunderous mood had to do with his first wife who had jerked the rug from beneath his feet by going ahead with the sale of the Pont Street flat.

'Not that I blame her,' said Pippa's mother, won over by Cassie's charm. 'She had a basinful when he dumped her, yet did nothing to stand in the way of a speedy divorce.' A lady, that was what Cassie was, with old-style morals and standards. In her position, she'd have taken him to the cleaners, though she judged it inappropriate to mention that.

Cassie needed the money to finance a project, entirely reasonably since it was hers, left to her in trust by her prosperous first husband. Besides, Charles still had the house in Barnes as well as his plushy Walton Street showrooms. Neither she nor Pippa could understand his sudden rage, which seemed to stem from Cassie's new-found independence.

'I think he still loves her,' said Pippa despondently. 'I was only ever meant to be a fling.'

'Where is Aidan these days? Do you know?' Despite his sometimes erratic behaviour, Pippa missed her stepson's high-spirited company. She loved to watch him playing with the twins, the three of them all so much alike with their glossy curls and luminous eyes and irrepressible laughter. She found his presence a constant tonic, remembered the comment her mother had made about how she should have chosen the younger model. The way his father was acting now, her mother might well have been right, though she wouldn't admit it.

'I assume still on his travels,' said Cassie, who had dropped in for tea and to say goodbye. She was off to Venice at the crack of dawn, having raised the necessary cash. 'He hardly ever contacts me now. Has always been closer to his father.'

It was true the pair were as thick as thieves on the rare occasions they got together yet Charles hadn't mentioned Aidan for quite a while. If they were still in regular contact, he never bothered to tell her. She sometimes wondered if he might be jealous; Aidan was just that bit too close to her own age. Not that Charles seemed to care either way; lately his mind was fixed on other things.

'Do you think he'll visit you in Venice?' asked Pippa, wishing that she could be going there too. She was sick of Barnes and the daily grind and her constant worrying over the twins. She longed to be like Cassie, fancy free.

'I shouldn't be at all surprised,' said Cassie, drawing on her gloves. 'The last I heard he was heading for Paris on some urgent mission for Charles. I am sure, as soon as his money runs out, he'll be back to Mama like a shot.' She smiled and said she really must go. She still had a lot to do before she left.

'Well, if you do see him, please give him our love. And tell him he's always welcome here. We could even put him up, now the flat has been sold.'

Cassie paused and regarded her shrewdly. 'That's kind of you,' she said, 'though don't make a fuss. He's a grown man now and can stand on his own feet. The more we pander, the less he will do towards knuckling down to a proper job and thinking about a career.'

Dino was thoughtful as they pounded round the park. He hated to see Pippa's spirits at such a low ebb.

'So what's with this Aidan?' he wanted to know. He featured a lot in the conversation though he was just the son of the elderly guy she had married. Dino had never really understood why she'd settled for Charles in the first place. She was sparky, vivacious and as smart as they come, or had been till she had fallen pregnant. Her reputation as an entrepreneur still dazzled his other clients. In the gossipy circles in which he moved, few people's private lives were safe. The upwardly mobile and super-rich mingled anecdotally through their trainer.

'Aidan is Charles's oldest son. Half-brother to the twins,' she said. 'He used to drop by on a regular basis. Now we've not heard from him in months.'

'So?' asked the trainer, still not understanding. She ought to be glad not to be encumbered. From the stories he heard from his other clients, the children from an earlier marriage were to be avoided at all cost.

'It's just that he's good with the boys,' sighed Pippa, not fooling him for an instant. 'If I knew where he was I would beg him to come home but even his father says he hasn't been in touch. Which is fairly unusual because they have always been close.'

'And you fancy him like mad,' said Dino. 'Don't even try to deny it.'

Pippa, with glowing cheeks, confessed that she did.

'So what do you plan to do about it?'

'There is nothing I can do,' she said. The marriage, she saw now, had been a mistake. She had been content with just the affair and Dino had counselled her then not to get more involved. Him and her mother; she should have listened. Before she had even hit thirty her life was screwed up.

'Have you talked to your husband?'

'What is there to say?'

'The truth, maybe. That you made a mistake and would now like to call it a day.'

'And be left on my own with the Terrible Twins? I don't think so,' said Pippa in horror. She found these sessions an immense relief, therapy as much as exercise, and regarded Dino as one of her most trusted friends. While he kept his eye on her rising heart rate, she poured out her daily troubles to him and usually felt a lot better when they were through.

'The gym is cheaper,' Charles had said but Pippa would not be fobbed off with that. Though she'd sacrificed many of her little extravagances, it would take a lot to persuade her to part with Dino.

'So what's the story?'

'I still don't know. I just wish he would come home and help out with the twins.' And let me know where he spends his time; in the face of an emergency, I'd be lost.

Pippa's friends weren't a lot of help either when she summoned them, on a whim, for Saturday lunch. Her mother had valiantly taken the twins and would entertain them till she got the signal. Pippa was grateful but her mother didn't need to be thanked. They were in this together was the way she saw it; she still felt guilt at not having intervened before Pippa committed herself. If only Pippa's father had still been around, but she'd seen him off when Pippa was small; it must run in the family, this wayward streak. Pippa offered the nanny too but her mother assured her that she could cope. Keep them active and tire them out. It had worked like a dream with Pippa.

Charles was away for a couple of days and had seemed rather vague when cross-examined. Business combined with a country sojourn might be all very cosy for him but left his wife feeling boring and neglected. So she bought in some salads and a case of good wine and told the girls to convene at half past twelve.

They ooh-ed and aah-ed about the house; most hadn't seen it since it was finished, and none seemed to care very much that the twins weren't there. They were seven in all, and of the group only Pippa was married, though a couple of the others had live-in partners. The dining table was covered in dishes and a floral arrangement sent by Charles, who had seemed relieved that Pippa would not be alone. When he'd rung to wish her a good weekend and she'd asked exactly where he was, the line had gone suddenly crackly so he'd ended the call. There had been a time when she wouldn't have cared, would have put it down to the luck of the draw, would have shouted her love and gone back to preparing the lunch. Not any more. She gritted her teeth and wondered whether she should reveal that her marriage was up the spout.

As it happened, there wasn't enough time for that; everyone was talking at once, each of them keen to put across her own viewpoint on matters germane to them all. When Pippa went to fetch more wine, she smiled to hear the unbroken babble and realised how much she'd been missing her female friends. They were all in fairly prominent jobs, one a rising young politician, two of the others journalists, had a lot to say that was interesting and shouted to get it across. By the end of the afternoon, when they left, Pippa found herself quite worn out. It would almost be a welcome break to go and collect the twins.

'The grass,' pointed out her mother wisely, 'is nearly always greener. It's a lesson in life that few of us ever learn.'

When Charles eventually came home, he still seemed out of sorts. He'd been doing a lot of driving, he said, and hadn't the energy to talk. Pippa, who had bought them a ready-made meal which she planned to heat in the microwave and then pass off as her own, poured him a whisky. Sooner or later, his mood would improve, and then she would try to find out where exactly he'd been. He kept on saying that business was booming, so he had no excuse to be quite so grumpy when he staggered in after all those days on the road.

The twins, on the whole, were being reasonably behaved, quietly bickering in the corner but not yet declaring war. The afternoon with their granny had proved effective.

'How've they been?' he asked at last, pointing at them with his glass.

'All right,' she said, 'all things considered. Though my mum took them off my hands for most of today.' She skirted round the subject of the lunch; did not want him to think she'd been having fun. Once she'd have told him every detail and he might even have listened. Those days, though, were long since over. He picked up the evening paper and started to read.

Somehow Aidan had to be the key, if only she knew how to find him. Pippa brooded as she microwaved the meal and wondered what on earth to do next for the best. If Cassie were still around, she'd have called her. She felt that they now had a real connection, based, to some extent, on the plight of their sons. But Cassie had left no contact number and was back in Venice, getting on with her life. Suddenly Pippa saw how ironic it was.

'Why are you laughing?' He raised his head as she carried in their steaming plates and indicated that he should open the wine.

'At nothing, I'm afraid,' she said, 'that you'd ever understand.' Then she pulled up her chair and silently started to eat.

'Do you happen to know where Aidan is?' she asked him next morning at breakfast.

'No,' he said, suddenly alert. 'Not exactly. Why do you want to know?'

'No particular reason,' said Pippa. 'It's just that we haven't seen him in a while and it's nice for the boys to have an older brother.'

Charles looked at her long and hard before returning to the paper. Conversation between them these days had reduced itself to a minimum. After breakfast she caught him talking on his mobile but he clicked it off the moment she entered the room. Something was going on, though she didn't know what.

Later she found him burrowing through the bureau, hurling stuff to left and right, apparently in a frantic search for something. He barely looked up when Pippa entered but continued to yank out drawers and make a mess.

'What are you looking for?' she asked him idly, by now indifferent to his varying moods. He often acted as though she wasn't there.

'My passport,' he said. 'I may have to go away. Something has suddenly come up in France. A client with a private collection, keen for me to try to locate a Stubbs.'

'I have never seen your passport,' she said. Since their marriage they'd barely been anywhere together because of his constant travelling and the twins. 'But you might look upstairs in the chest of drawers. That's where I always keep valuables. The bureau is far too obvious to a burglar.'

He checked the time. 'I have to be off. I've a meeting in Walton Street in twenty minutes.'

'Do you want me to have a look for it?'

'Don't bother,' he said. 'I'll be back by noon. But you might lay out a couple of ironed shirts.'

He treats me like a skivvy, she thought, as she cleared the dishes and dumped them in the sink. The cleaner would be in today which meant one less chore for Pippa. No wonder Cassie had let Charles go so meekly.

She went upstairs to shower and dress, though she left the bed for the cleaner. She hated to give her such menial tasks but Pippa's own time was so overcrowded that she hardly ever got to the shop these days. Remembering the shirts, she opened the drawer and flicked through a pile that had just come back from the laundry. She loved the smell of freshly starched linen; Charles had never stinted himself and every-thing he owned was top-notch quality. Beneath the shirts her hand brushed against something small and compact in an envelope. She pulled it out; perhaps she'd unearthed his passport.

Eureka! At least she could do something right. She

opened the envelope to check and found not one but three matching passports tucked in a rubber band. Pippa examined each one of them, staring in baffled confusion.

41

The sky was dimming; it was growing late. She had reached the end of her list. She had thought about going to visit the school, which would have involved another wide detour, but the odds were against there being anyone there who had been around in Chad's day.

She got back on to the motorway and stopped at a service station. She was tired, dispirited and suddenly hungry, with a terrible urge to cry. The unloved child she had always been took over, her agony unresolved. She should never have come in the first place; it was madness. All of a sudden, she longed for the only place where she now belonged, with Magda and the Antwerp sisters who had charitably taken her in.

She sat within a circle of light, alone at a grimy Formica-topped table, a defeated woman, past her best, who had lost all traces of beauty. Her mission had failed; she could only go home. She thought fleetingly of nice Pippa Harvey and regretted that she had been so abrupt. If she'd stuck around and met the husband he might have produced some more business contacts but she'd gone off on a wild goose chase of her own.

London was still several hours away and Frankie was daunted by the volume of traffic, the more so since it was now almost dark and the motorway lights had come on. After the byways of rural Belgium, she wasn't accustomed to traffic like this; also she hated having to drive on the left. Over a meal of burger and chips, she got out the atlas and studied the route, working out how she could drive only on minor roads. She had nothing at all to hurry back for; London continued to scare her stiff.

She groped around for a cigarette and then found, to her mild irritation, that she'd lost her lighter. It was only a cheap one but she couldn't be bothered to join the queue and ask for a box of matches at the till. Instead she dug deeper into her backpack to see if she had another and found a half-used matchbook she hadn't known was there. After she'd lit up, she saw that it was the one on which Aidan had scribbled his number. In her state of confusion at the time, she must have stuffed it away and then forgotten it. She stared, transfixed, at the row of figures and wondered whether to give him a call. It was weeks now since that ill-fated encounter but she hadn't been able to get him out of her mind. She had used him badly, which he hadn't deserved; the least she could do was apologise. With luck, he would still be in Bruges.

Anxiously she punched out the number and was

almost relieved to find the line was dead. She fingered the matchbook thoughtfully and pondered what to do next, then slowly focused on the advertisement on its printed cover. The Coot and Hern, on the outskirts of Bath, was precisely what she felt like: an anonymous haven in a country backwater where she could go to ground. The idea of Bath had appealed to her since her childhood addiction to Georgette Heyer. She had the car and unlimited funds and nothing to hurry back for. Without further delay, she called the number and booked herself in for the night.

42

The great carved doors of the house stood wide open as a bunch of workmen and domestic staff unloaded spindly-legged gilded furniture and relayed each piece inside. The butler, Gérard, stood anxiously watching, ready to pounce should anything go wrong. A scratch on the woodwork, a mark on the marble; this house, in the sixteenth arrondissement, was not accustomed to such barbaric treatment. It was most irregular, this sudden invasion, at a time when the master was off on a cruise, beyond even satellite reach. The Slut, however, would not listen to reason, was hell-bent on doing this sacrilegious thing of marrying a stranger in the master's own home, presumably without his knowledge or consent.

'Shut up, Gérard,' Cristina said rudely, whenever he attempted to have his say. It was her house now and he mustn't forget that, not if he wanted to keep his job. She made all the decisions here; there was nothing more to be said. There was not a lot that the butler could do, though the rest of the staff were all on his side. It was true the Slut had presided here for

342

the past twelve horrible years. But she wasn't the wife, had no formal standing, though Madame Daumier must certainly know. Why else had she not set foot here in all this time?

The Daumier marriage was typically Parisian; they had an understanding. And the country château, where Gérard spent half his time, was sufficiently luxurious to keep her contentedly at home. Monsieur spent three days of each week with her there and four back here, with the Slut. Gérard, though respecting his energy at an age when most men were beginning to fail, nevertheless could not condone his taste. The only good thing was, once he knew about the marriage, Monsieur would undoubtedly throw the bitch out which was something everyone in the household awaited. Meanwhile the travesty continued right under his nose.

'You are sure you can't get him by email?' asked Serge, enjoying every second of the sleazy charade, even though it would mean a probable end to his hours of voyeurism up the convenient ladder.

'Non. He is on a private yacht and does not wish to be disturbed. His wife's decision; she wants him all to herself.'

The gardener sniggered and the butler smiled. The two men knew each other well enough not to need to spell out too much detail. They had put up with so much abuse from this woman that the only reason both were still here was solidarity with the master, whom they liked as well as respected. Admittedly, there was a certain amount of private amusement. And now she'd transcended her own worst excesses by planning this vulgar wedding.

'What is she wearing?'

'We have yet to find out.'

Yvette, their normal source of gossip, had been unusually silent on the subject. 'You will simply have to wait and see,' she said, with a twinkle in her eye, relishing what they would say when the secret was unveiled. One thing Yvette was pleased about: she had not given in to her wish to resign but had hung around to witness the dénouement. And, if everything went to plan, it should certainly prove well worth the wait. She didn't want to spoil the spectacle for them.

'And what of the bridegroom?' Serge asked Gérard, once the chairs and tables were all safely stowed and the vanload of shabby workmen had driven away. 'It seems he hasn't been heard from yet. He is surely cutting things rather fine. What time is the ceremony scheduled to take place?'

'Seven o'clock tomorrow,' said Gérard. 'The string quartet is booked to be here at six.'

The two men strolled to the rear of the house where a swarm of gardeners were trimming dead flowers and manicuring the lawn. 'Shouldn't you be out there helping?' asked Gérard.

'I have only the hanging baskets to arrange,' said Serge with a nonchalant shrug.

It was all the most colossal upheaval, principally suffered by Yvette, who was, of course, always first in the firing line. The shouting, the swearing, the hurling of abuse; occasionally also of plates. Cristina was at her foulest worst. No one would ever have suspected that, in fact, she would shortly be a bride. She stomped around with her phone glued to her ear, gabbling in Portuguese or imperfect French. Part of the sluttishness of her behaviour was that, in her long sojourn in Paris, she had never bothered to learn the language properly. She screamed at everyone she could think of, the manicurist, the hairdresser, the maid, the caterer, the party planner, the butler. Most of all she screamed at the airlines because they couldn't tell her when her bridegroom was due.

'I think maybe he's not coming at all.' Despite the abuse and the extra work, there was very much merriment downstairs in the kitchen. The bridegroom was now a full five days late and, as far as anyone knew, Cristina still had not heard a word from him.

'She is out of her mind. She should just give up and go back to where she came from.' Though Serge would still be prepared to take her on, but only at a knockdown price as very damaged goods.

The gown that Yvette was so secretive about was a frothy meringue of sugar pink satin, trimmed with strawberry lace. The neckline was tastefully slashed to the navel and similarly down the back, while the sleeves were more of the same pink candyfloss. She looks like a female impersonator, thought Yvette, as she struggled to zip it up.

'*Merde*,' shrieked Cristina, 'you clumsy cow. You pinched my flesh. Watch out!'

Only because she had put on weight; the bodice bulged beneath her bust and, should she happen to sneeze, she would burst right out.

'Perhaps Madame should go without breakfast,' Yvette said diplomatically, itching to get her hands on the seams which should be let out by half an inch at least.

'No,' screamed Cristina. 'I need a tighter bustier. Go through my closets and find one, you fool.'

She flounced, half dressed, across the room and scowled at herself in the full-length mirror. Downstairs the hairstylist patiently waited to get his hands on that unkempt mane which the bride, in her middle forties, refused to have cut. There were hours to go before the deadline but a huge amount still to do. The alterations to the gown which would, for certain, have to be made once the termagant shrieking into her phone could be persuaded to agree. The hair and makeup, which often took hours; the selection of the jewellery. All these details had been left till now while Cristina paced and worried and cursed, waiting for any word at all from the man she was planning to marry.

One of the maids was walking the dog, after which it would fall to Yvette (who else?) to groom and gussy it up. For this occasion, the pathetic mutt would be decked out with a huge pink bow of the same material as the bridal gown. And, in place of a bouquet, the bride intended to carry it in her arms.

'I only hope she remembers,' said Serge, 'to hurl it into the crowd.'

*   *   *

Behind her bluster and extreme bad temper, Cristina was in a secret panic, scared of losing not only face but everything else as well. She was still appalled at not being divorced but, since this was something she dared not admit, could not discuss it with anyone else and thus took it out on the staff. Part of her longed to see Cal again but when she called the number in London that Barras had told her belonged to him, the phone was answered by a letting agent who told her the flat had just been sold. She seemed to be up against brick walls all round; no Rocco and now no Cal. There would, however, soon be a Claude; his cruise was to end in a couple of days. With her customary carelessness, she had cut it fine but now it looked as though everything might backfire. The thought of Claude's arriving home before she had managed to tie the knot filled even fearless Cristina with something like dread. She could charm her way out of most situations but Claude's sense of humour regarding her had been on the wane for some time. If only that blasted Rocco would call and put her out of her misery. If this was how married life would be, perhaps she should back out right now.

She called everyone she could think of in Rio but nobody seemed very sure where he was. One of his pals, a habitual drunk, vaguely thought he might be in France but seemed unaware that he was about to marry.

'Who's the lucky girl?' he slurred; Cristina banged down the phone without saying goodbye.

She swallowed her pride and called Madame Zarco,

mortified to have to admit that she didn't know where Rocco was. Somehow their wires had got crossed, she said, and now she appeared to have lost his itinerary. Of course, he would soon be arriving in Paris for the wedding.

'A wedding, chérie? How exciting for you. I wasn't aware that Daumier had become free.'

'Not Daumier, Rocco. I assumed that you knew.' He obviously hadn't broadcast the news, which magnified the dread in her heart about a hundredfold.

'Chérie! How delightful. No, I hadn't heard. I haven't even received my invitation. It must have got lost in the mail.'

Cristina mumbled a feeble excuse: they were keeping it small, it was very low-key. They loved each other too much to be able to wait. The only thing was . . .

'You don't know where he is.' There was no disguising the note of pure malice in Madame Zarco's voice.

So, instead, she took out her anger and frustration on any poor innocent who stood in her way. The whole house, metaphorically, shook with Cristina Calvão's black mood.

The party planner had now arrived and was supervising the floral arrangements that were being carried in from another van. The marble foyer had a vast creation, to match the colours of the bridal gown, and silver bowls of sugared almonds were being distributed. The grand piano in the main salon had been unveiled by the string quartet and would be used to herald the bride's triumphant arrival down the stairs. Balloons and ribbons festooned the stairway down which the glamorous figure would glide to Handel's 'Arrival of the Queen of Sheba'.

'*Tiens!*' said the butler, with distaste. 'They are turning the whole performance into a circus.'

After the ceremony was over, dancing was planned outside on the lawn so paper lanterns had been hung in the trees and the sound engineers were annoying the gardeners by stretching their cables across the lawns that had just been so carefully mowed. From somewhere in the background came a crash; a table of glasses had been pushed over so now they were out with their brushes and brooms, clearing it up before Cristina appeared.

The couturier had been persuaded to come and artfully loosen a few of the seams and now Yvette, with her nimble fingers, was sitting upstairs in Cristina's room, carefully redoing the delicate stitches.

Downstairs, in the kitchen, the caterer's staff were getting under the housekeeper's feet while a couple of waiters were sampling the wine and becoming noticeably tipsy.

Five o'clock and still no sign of Rocco. Gérard, by now, was ringing the airlines. No more flights were due in from Brazil, certainly not in time for the wedding; unless he was coming from somewhere else, it didn't look as though he could possibly make it.

'Ought we to tell her?' They took a secret vote and

the consensus was to let things proceed. By now they were all having too much fun to care.

'Who's going to get to pay for all this?' Serge was curious to know.

The butler shrugged. He had no idea. The way the Slut always ran her affairs, the bills would undoubtedly stay unpaid until she was taken to court. Or until the master stepped in, as he usually had to. Not this time, though; she had properly blown it. Unless Rocco arrived in the nick of time, made her his bride and bore her off, Cristina was well and truly stuffed. To put it at its mildest.

'Madame,' said Yvette, rubbing her eyes, 'the alterations are finished.' She lifted the gown with reverent care and laid it across the untidy bed. Despite the basic contempt she felt, the spirit of the occasion was getting to her. Cristina, lying on crumpled sheets, was still in an ugly, belligerent mood. She had had her bath and was taking a rest before she allowed the stylist in to sweep her hair up into a fancy concoction.

'Aren't you going to try it on?'

'No point,' said Cristina sullenly. 'If it doesn't fit now, it never will. There isn't time for any more adjustment.' As usual, as though it were Yvette's fault. The maid said nothing as she bustled around, tidying up her sewing things, but mentally she looked at Cristina and spat.

The stylist came in, with his sidekick in tow, and Cristina settled before the glass to allow them to do their best. The makeup girl was waiting outside until it was her turn to work her magic and turn this overblown former beauty into a semblance of what she once had been.

'Rather her than me,' said Yvette, when she popped down to the kitchen to get her more tea.

Quarter to six and he still hadn't come. By now the bride was fully dressed and her hair was finally being tweaked into shape. Her caramel skin was glowing with health and her eyes were great globes of enticing fire. Her waist was compressed, the seams were still holding and the petulant scowl upon her face was starting to fade as she looked at herself with delight and appreciation.

'Pop downstairs and check with Gérard in case there is any news,' she said and Yvette, who hadn't relaxed all day, wearily did her bidding. As if he wouldn't have let her know; the whole thing hinged on the groom's being there. Gérard, who had also been ceaselessly working, was standing now in the main salon, surveying its finished splendour. The house was looking its glamorous best; inside he swelled with proprietorial pride. He almost wished the master might see it now. These fine old houses dressed up very well, the perfect setting for such an occasion, if only the bride were not a slut and the groom apparently missing.

'Of course there's no news,' he said to Yvette, his eyes glued to the rococo clock. 'And I'd wager a thousand euros he isn't coming.'

The string quartet were tuning up; they were due to start playing in fifteen minutes, or such had been their instructions from the bride. Soon the guests would start to arrive, the handful of B-list celebrities Cristina had managed to rustle up among her soi-disant friends. The champagne corks had begun to pop and the first few glasses were being poured. Downstairs the staff were taking a break and prematurely toasting the happy couple. They had worked hard and were feeling no pain. Whatever else might happen tonight, this certainly was one wedding they'd never forget.

When she'd married Cal, it had been so simple. They had walked barefoot along a beach, Cristina with her arms full of freshly picked flowers. She'd been beautiful then, only just nineteen and the toast of the international catwalk. How far she had tumbled since those halcyon days that she'd lived through in a coke-fuelled haze and only barely remembered. When she'd married Cal, it had been for life yet had lasted less than two years. This time she meant to make it work, provided the bastard showed up in time. The scowl returned to her botoxed face and she jerked away from the stylist's hands in sudden irritation.

'Get me a glass of champagne,' she snapped and the man went scurrying to do her bidding. She would force herself into a party mood and wait for the doorbell to ring.

Which it did, right on cue: a resounding trill that instantly halted the sound of music from below.

'Wait!' she yelled. 'Don't open the door! Leave it for me. I am coming.'

She took one last twirl in front of the mirror then, satisfied with what she saw, picked up the skirts of her voluminous dress and headed for the staircase. Down she tripped in her satin slippers, dyed to precisely the right shade of pink, and across the marble hallway, strewn with petals. Gérard was waiting but she gestured him aside.

'Go!' she said. 'And allow me to greet him alone.' She turned and waved the musicians away, and the waiters lounging with their laden trays. When she greeted her bridegroom, finally arrived, she wanted to be on her own.

The bell rang again, more peremptory now, as if the caller were growing impatient. If she didn't hurry he might go away and then where would she be? Cristina studied herself in the glass and tweaked one strand of her burnished hair, artfully tousled by the fashion industry's finest. Her lips were glossy and pneumatically plumped. She looked the image of innocent love, eagerly awaiting her future husband.

'Coming!' she cried, sounding almost coquettish as she crossed the last few paces to the door and fumbled with the intricate locks she'd rarely ever had to deal with before.

Upstairs in the boudoir, straightening the bed, Yvette heard the sound of the heavy door opening, followed by total silence and then a gasp.

'Cal?' she heard her mistress say on a rising note

that rapidly turned into a terrified scream that brought them all running.

The front of her dress was soaked with blood and the knife that had punctured her heart was still in there, quivering.

43

The Coot and Hern, when she finally found it, was even more delightful than Frankie had hoped. Ivy-clad and built of grey stone, it stood by the side of a boisterous brook, with a waterwheel that had been restored and now was working again. It was almost eight and the place was packed; the car park was jammed solid. A steady buzz issued from behind the doors and the bottle-glass windows twinkled in friendly welcome. A picture from a Christmas card; for the first time since she had left the commune, Frankie felt at home.

The main door led into a narrow hall, oak-panelled and furnished with real antiques and an opulent Turkish rug in glowing colours. The beams were low and the genuine thing; the whole place smelt of cooking and woodsmoke, reminding her faintly of the barn in Lier. She tapped the polished brass visitors' bell and looked around with appreciation. Now this had certainly been worth that nightmarish drive.

A door at the end of the corridor opened, emitting

steam and a strong whiff of garlic, and a flustered woman, done up in chef's whites, peered out.

'Can I help you?' she asked though she obviously had her hands full.

'The name is Wilde. I booked a room. I am sorry to have arrived so late but I've just driven down from Middlesbrough,' she said. By a wildly circuitous route.

'Oh yes. I'm sorry, we are understaffed. If you don't mind waiting another two ticks, someone will be out to check you in. Let me order you a drink from the bar and you might like to look at the menu. As it's Thursday night, we are pretty full up but I've kept a table for you. You were lucky to get a room at all but we had a last-minute cancellation. By the way, I'm Jenny Matthias.'

Nice, thought Frankie, flopping into a chair and picking up a copy of *Country Life*. Five minutes later someone else appeared, a dowdy woman in sensible shoes, who checked Frankie in, then led her upstairs to a pretty room with a dormer window and a teddy bear on the bed. 'The bathroom's through there. We'll expect you down by nine. If you've had a chance to look at the menu, I can take your order now.'

Everything on it looked simple and scrumptious. Frankie, nostalgically, settled for pheasant then stretched out on the bed for a ten minute nap. The trip, so far, had been disappointing. Now, perhaps, things might start looking up.

She had brought few clothes so didn't change, just washed her face and combed her hair, then went downstairs with some trepidation, to confront the crowded bar. The dowdy woman came hurrying over, with a glass of red wine and nuts in a bowl, and steered Frankie to a corner table, close to the blazing fire.

'We'll let you know when your meal is ready. The dining room is through those doors. We always used to eat in here but have recently expanded.'

'Thanks,' said Frankie, stretching her legs, relieved to be out of the car. She settled down to enjoy her wine and watch the general activity at the bar. She was so unaccustomed to social life, to her it was like living theatre.

Most of the drinkers were young and trendy, though a group of stalwart older women sat at a table across the room from her. They were clearly regulars, in their down-to-earth clothes: ancient Barbours with wellington boots, contrasted with single-strand pearls and shapeless tweeds. One of them even wore a hat, a battered felt that had seen better days. It was clear from the rhythm of their conversation that they all knew each other very well. And, from the glances they shot at her, they recognised Frankie as somebody new, presumably just passing through. A group of old men played darts in a corner; what was most attractive about this pub was the natural interaction of new and traditional. A bunch of younger women, loud and brash, obviously on a girls' night out, were clustered around an older man with a shock of silvering hair. From the way they screamed and jostled for position, he was clearly a magnet to the ladies. Born to the job, that was obvious, as he skilfully mixed them cocktails and kept them laughing. Mein host, she thought, though the chef was a woman. She wondered where he fitted in.

It was decades since Frankie had been in a pub, not since her teens on the Wirral. She thought back to her stepfather, the colonel, who sometimes, when they'd been out with the guns, treated her to a half of shandy, on condition she didn't tell her mother. They had been conspirators in those days; he had thought of her as the son he'd never had, with the dogs and her pony and that glorious open air life. She wondered now how things might have been if she hadn't burnt his house down. But he'd had it coming after what he'd done, which she'd never been able to tell her mother, nor even Magda or anyone else, come to that. His unexplained death in a shooting accident still seemed like divine retribution, though, despite her years in a spiritual commune, she had never believed in stuff like that.

There was a small commotion by the open door as a fair-haired boy, around six or seven, ran in and clasped the landlord round the knees. Laughing and full of bonhomie, he swept the child up into his arms and swung him high in the air till he squealed with delight. The women all cooed and petted the child, a wholesome scene that Frankie envied. Perhaps she too might have had a normal life if she hadn't fallen so obsessively in love. And if he had survived.

A waitress summoned her to her meal so she left

the heart-warming family scene and moved to a table in the adjoining room.

The meal was superlative, out of this world; certainly worth the drive and the wait. Frankie had never eaten so well in her life. After the pheasant and honeyed parsnips, she had raspberry crème brûlée and some local cheese.

'My compliments to the chef,' she said when the waitress came round to clear the plates and ask if she'd mind moving back to the bar for her coffee. Through the long, drab years she had lived in Belgium her diet had been adequate but sparse. The vegetables she had diligently tended had helped keep her healthy and underweight but the spartan regime had long ago started to pall. Home cooking was better than prison fare, but that was the most she could say. The commune's ideals were on a higher plane; they ate in order to stay alive and never even thought about fleshly pleasures.

What with the wine and the warmth from the fire, combined with the hours she had spent on the road, Frankie, lulled by the excellent meal, found herself dozing off. She would certainly sleep well tonight and might stay on for a few more days, if they could fit her in and her room was still free.

'Would you care for a nightcap?' The landlord was hovering as he went around picking up glasses. It was late; the place was emptying fast. Soon he'd be calling for final orders though she, as a resident, was under no pressure to leave. She was half asleep but comfortable so ordered one more glass of the excellent wine. He smiled down at her then walked away, a handsome man with twinkling eyes that dimly reminded her of someone else.

Aidan's eyes, she realised. That same compelling blue.

'Chad?' she said, jerking wide awake, but the man was no longer in the room.

44

The first thing Cassie did, as soon as she could, was move out of the hotel and into the palazzo even though, at first, it meant having to camp. She was used to old buildings with cavernous rooms; had spent so much time on her own in Tintagel that even the echoing silence failed to alarm her. She missed the dogs and the sound of the sea which had always helped her to sleep at night, but the constant busyness of the canal more than made up for that. Whenever she paused to take a break, she would stand at one of the tall arched windows and never grew tired of the moving pageant below. It was almost like having gone back in time; the restless scene could have changed very little in all the years the palazzo had been standing.

The ground floor storerooms were no longer in use but the first floor *piano nobile* was still partially furnished. Vast old cabinets, with faded paintwork, loomed inside each of the family rooms and some of the ancient mosaic floors were still in remarkably good nick. Mario, over the years, had done much to protect the structure from the weather, so at least she didn't have problems with leaking roofs. Most of the walls were flaking and cracked and the floors that weren't tiled were very creaky. To do the work properly would mean huge investment. Cassie determined to do what she could by herself.

She bought a bedroll, a hurricane lamp, and a primus stove which she hoped not to use, then set herself up in one of the smaller rooms. In order to keep the draughts at bay and give herself some privacy, she hung a baize curtain over the entry arch. She indulged herself with a battery radio and a pile of books she had brought from home. Then she found an old trestle table and unrolled her plans. The years with Edwin were paying off; she knew more about Renaissance architecture than she had even remembered. During the mornings she simply wandered, enjoying the city and seeking inspiration from the many and varied buildings all around her. She also looked for local craftsmen to help her with the heavier work. Mario had been generous with introductions; just the mention of his name instantly opened doors. At night she would eat a simple meal, then settle down by her hurricane lamp to swot up on the relevant details before she embarked on the actual renovation. The weather was warm, so she needed no heating, was glad to come in from the mugginess outside in order to cool off. She wore cut-off jeans and cotton shirts and her skin acquired a becoming glow, though she shaded her face beneath a wide-brimmed straw hat.

'Aren't you lonely?' asked Daisy, when she phoned, alarmed to think of her mother there all on her own.

'Not in the slightest,' said Cassie cheerfully. 'I have far too much on my plate to think about that.'

Once they knew that she wasn't a tourist, the Venetians were very friendly. Her fluent Italian and natural charm won them over immediately and soon she knew a handful of locals by name. She bought her food in the nearby shops and picnicked, perched on a wide window ledge, though at night, since she couldn't be bothered to cook, she nearly always ate out. She had her mobile, which she seldom used, calling the family instead every week from the land-line in a nearby neighbourhood bar. The family had that number too in case they should suddenly need her. Cassie found it all hugely exciting; by marrying young she had missed out on college yet here she was, at almost sixty, living the life of a student.

'In England I'd soon be drawing my pension,' she marvelled to herself. But she hadn't felt this youthful and fit in years.

She missed her daughters and they missed her, but they promised to visit as soon as they could, though she warned them the place was still just a ruin, not even remotely habitable. She tried to get them to understand that that was all part of the massive chal-lenge. 'It's like being a Guide all over again,' she said.

Rose was hoping to come out and join her and didn't mind roughing it in the least. She was sick to death of her stolid legal life and fancied a change of scenery. If she liked it enough, she might even quit the job and risk finding casual work in Venice. If her mother could turn bohemian, so could she. She was taking Italian lessons at night as well as studying her father's art books. He had left his children a rich and compelling heritage. Rose was a lot like her father's sister, with the same gaunt features and forthright manner. She lacked Aunt Sybil's artistic flair but shared her sharp tongue and fertile brain.

Daisy was still being comfortably domestic and Sam and Willow were now in their teens. Roughing it on a building site was not their idea of a family holiday; the kids would prefer to go somewhere where they could surf.

'I can't see why they need a holiday at all,' grumbled Daisy, who was always chasing after them. 'All they ever do as it is is spend their lives loafing about.' With a husband who played golf when he wasn't working, she did rather get the rough end of the deal. Besides, she still had to walk the dogs and keep an eye on her mother's house. Tremayne was constantly in and out but plants needed watering, rooms kept aired and the weekly cleaning supervised. It was interesting how Daisy had turned into a hausfrau. Nothing genetic on either side explained that.

'We will come,' she promised, 'when it's up and running and we don't have to live in a slum.'

'Which won't be for many years,' said Cassie, 'the way the place is looking now.' She promised to keep a photographic record of the step-by-step progress she made.

From Aidan lately there had been not a word. None of them knew where he was.

'He'll turn up. He usually does.' Though secretly Cassie was starting to worry. He had not been in touch with her for several weeks.

In May, at the end of the spring semester, Mario Dandolo returned. He maintained an apartment in Santa Croce and strolled across to the palazzo within minutes of getting in from the airport and dropping off his bags. He discovered Cassie in workman's overalls, industriously scraping down a wall.

'*Bene*,' he said with admiring approval. 'I hadn't understood you'd be so hands on.'

'It is harder than I had thought,' admitted Cassie, pushing back the hair from her sweating forehead. 'But at least it's a start before the workmen move in.'

Mario strolled around in deep thought, savouring the timeless atmosphere of the place that had been his family's home for the past six hundred years. It was obviously a moving moment and Cassie had the tact to leave him alone. It must be like parting with the Cornish house, only worse.

'I think,' he said eventually, when he wandered back to join her, 'that I made a very wise move selling out to you. I feel it is now in the proper hands. My ancestors would approve.'

'Thank you,' said Cassie, touched and pleased. It meant a great deal to her to have his blessing. 'I feel it's the challenge I have waited for most of my life.'

To celebrate, he asked her out for dinner locally

that night. Cassie, sick of her own company, accepted with delight. She found him enormously *sympathique* and wanted to get to know him better; it seemed a shame that he now lived so far away. The problem was what to wear. She had brought few clothes, and the primitive way she was living at present was not conducive to looking her best, though the manual work she engaged in daily had firmed her figure and brought a new colour to her cheeks. Feeling positively decadent, she took a shopping trip to San Marco and finished up with a hair appointment at a fashionable salon in that area. It was years since she'd had a proper date and she felt as excited as a debutante, though she knew that, of course, all he wanted to do was talk. They had quite a lot in common, she sensed; it was a real treat to be with such a cultured man.

'My dear, you look enchanting,' he said when he called for her at the palazzo. The dress was chic and understated, its simple cut belying the extortionate price. She had teamed it with fashionable strappy gold sandals which emphasised her long tanned legs, but what he most admired was the up-to-date hairdo. 'You have cut your hair! I like it,' he said. 'If you will permit me, it takes ten years off your age.'

'It's the first time I've had it cut since my teens,' confessed Cassie, suddenly bashful. 'Both my husbands preferred the old-fashioned look.' Also her son, though she didn't mention him. She had been, she realised, for far too long under the yoke of meeting male approval.

'Both husbands! We have a lot to discuss,' said Mario, taking her arm.

The meal was perfect and they sat outside, an echo of that lonely night when Cassie had first arrived in Venice after Charles exploded his bombshell. Then she'd been timid and quite at a loss, not knowing what she would do with herself or how she could possibly face the future without him. Now, three years later, she had come into her own, had adjusted to being a woman alone and not just somebody's wife or somebody else's mother. She was independent, healthy and well off, with a brand new start in the city of her dreams, and only on the brink of her seventh decade.

'Tell me about all these husbands,' said Mario, quietly refilling her glass. He seemed to be genuinely captivated by her.

'There's not a lot to say,' she said, warmed by his obvious admiration. 'At the time they seemed all important, now less so.'

It wasn't that she hadn't loved them; she had, both times, with all her heart. With Edwin she'd been the receptive pupil; with Charles, the indulgent mother figure, once the initial exuberance of sex had worn off. She had turned a blind eye to his numerous faults though saw them quite clearly now in his son. Which was why she had started to feel she had somehow failed.

At last, however, she had found her match. She looked across at her dinner companion and saw recognition mirrored in his eyes.

*   *   *

No matter how happy she was in Venice, Cassie still had commitments at home so hoped to get back there at least every two or three months. For a start, it wasn't fair on Tremayne to expect him to run the estate single-handed, even though he'd been doing just that since Edwin's death. She sometimes wondered why he stuck around, then remembered he had been born in those parts. In some ways it meant as much to him as the palazzo did to Mario, even though his forebears had never actually owned it. Land and property were very important; Cassie now understood why Charles had objected so strongly to losing the Pont Street flat.

But Charles and Pippa had a life of their own that no longer impinged on hers. Since the property row Charles had kept away though Cassie couldn't resist making contact with Pippa.

'How are the twins?' she wanted to know and Pippa, touched that she still seemed to care, was keen to pour her heart out. Not so good, though she hesitated to say that.

'Can we meet?' she asked and Cassie said yes and invited her for lunch at Harvey Nichols.

'I daren't risk asking you to the house. He hates the fact that we get along and still can't forgive you for getting rid of the flat.'

'Too bad,' said Cassie, unconcerned. What a spoilt little boy he had turned out to be. Perhaps her fault, but he'd always been such a charmer.

Pippa was looking pale and drawn, a shadow of her former self. She had lost some weight but her eyes were dull and her hair quite lustreless. She no longer resembled in any way the foxy minx who had snared and run off with Cassie's husband. But how were the twins? Cassie truly cared, especially so since there'd still been no word from Aidan.

'Good days, bad days. Things are much the same. Jack is still excelling at drawing while Tom, on the whole, is sweeter-natured except when he's having one of his bad turns.'

'What do the doctors have to say?' Cassie had read up everything she could but, nevertheless, still wanted to know. Whatever it was was hard to put a name to.

'They say if they catch them early enough, they can take them from being under-performers to mainstream students at school.'

Aidan had had no problems with learning. He had sailed through Eton and, later, Oxford. His character flaws had been mainly behavioural. She remembered the tantrums and later the fights. More than once he had been on detention for bullying but had never, ever displayed the slightest remorse.

'What does their father have to say?' He had always taken Aidan's side and seemed to find his boorish behaviour amusing.

'He doesn't appear to be worried at all. In fact, to tell the truth, I don't think he cares.'

They kissed and parted; Pippa had to get back and Cassie promised to call before she left. She would love to take those children in hand and give them the bene-fits of country air and space enough to be able to work off their demons. She couldn't ask but felt fairly sure that the marriage had taken a turn for the worse. A less nice person might have gloated but Cassie was genuinely concerned.

Sybil, though now in her early eighties, had lost none of her sharpness or bite. She still had plans for the sculpture school and had had some good feedback from the city of Venice. Mario had offered to lend it his patronage.

'Who is this count?' she asked, intrigued and not a little suspicious.

'Oh, just the man,' said Cassie vaguely, 'from whom I bought the palazzo. He is hardly ever there these days, spends most of his time in the States.'

Her casual air did not fool Sybil, who had known her too well for so long. Cassie looked positively radiant these days, with her stylish clothes and becoming hairdo. A glow like that did not come just from working one's fingers to the bone. But she knew enough not to interfere. Cassie would tell her in time. And if it meant a new man, then good luck to her. The way that bastard had treated her, she deserved all the happiness she could get. She had been an exemplary wife to Edwin and that was what counted with Sybil.

But Cassie's concern was for Sybil's future. She felt she should no longer live on her own. She was still very strong and could wield her chisel but the St Ives studio was up steep steps and worryingly remote for a woman her age. Suppose she should have a fall or something; she wouldn't be able to let the neighbours know. But try telling that to Sybil Hawksmoor. She was every bit as stubborn as Rose. Still, it was worth a try.

'Why don't you move in here full time? You'd be company for Tremayne. We could build you a workshop in the grounds and you'd be a good guardian for the house. You could even help Daisy walk the dogs if you ran out of things to do.' Cassie stopped; she must not overdo it. They were all entitled to their independence. And far be it from her, a new recruit, to tell an old campaigner how to live her life.

Sybil looked at her, long and hard. 'I'll think about it,' she said.

This time, now she was a resident of Venice, Cassie eschewed the motor launch and came in instead, as the natives did, by train. The experience was worth it for the aesthetic pleasure alone. The scene that greeted her, as she issued from the station, was enough to stop anyone in their tracks. She stood and gloated at the panoply before her, more like a painted stage set than a living city. Then she briskly wheeled her single bag down to the vaporetto, to take the boat eight stops along the Grand Canal.

She was coming home. Her heart was light as she dragged the bag from the landing stage and along the narrow path to her own front door. Shopkeepers shouted and waved to her and she couldn't wait to get inside and back to work on her mammoth project, now the focus of her life. She had done her duty and checked up on her girls, had seen that everything was in good hands and that life still continued serenely without her there. Tim was a bore but Daisy was fine and the children, in their separate ways, delightful. Rose was the prickly character she'd always shown signs of becoming, close in looks and attitude to her aunt. Once she'd made her choice and taken that daring leap, there was nothing to stop her achieving whatever she wanted. There would always be room for all of them here as well as in Cassie's heart.

Pippa, who wasn't in any way hers, yet still preoccupied her thoughts, had a long and difficult journey yet to travel. Cassie wished her only well and would always be there for her. She planned to keep in touch on a regular basis.

She let herself through the palazzo's street door with the gigantic iron key and stood in the sun-streaked atrium, imbibing the place's echoes. It smelt of dust and mould and time, spiced up by drying plaster. She was back in the place she wanted to be, where she hoped to remain for however many more years she had left. A huge task lay ahead of her but Cassie wasn't afraid. She stood and let the place wrap itself around her.

One small niggle, though, teased her mind as she lugged her bag up the mighty staircase and into the small cosy nest she had made for herself. The girls were okay; the grandchildren too. But what, in heaven's name, had become of Aidan?

45

'Where is he?' asked Frankie, almost crazed with agitation. 'The man who was here before, I presume the landlord?'

A woman she recognised as the chef had taken his place behind the bar, small and trim with bright dark eyes and a most infectious smile. She wasn't smiling now, however; her expression clouded the moment Frankie appeared.

'He's gone,' she said, 'and is not coming back. I don't know why but he suddenly said he had something urgent to do.'

'What?' asked Frankie, disbelieving. 'We only spoke a few minutes ago.'

'That's how long it took,' said Jenny, undisguisedly hostile now. 'And, by the way, he is not the landlord. That's me.'

'Sorry,' said Frankie. 'Only I assumed . . .'

'Perhaps you assumed too much.'

Frankie had no idea what to do. She had to catch up with him fast and find out for herself. It was like the moment she'd seen Aidan on the train. Only this time she had a gut reaction that told her it really had been Chad.

She tried, more humbly, to win Jenny over. She'd been perfectly affable earlier on, when Frankie had arrived.

'Might I ask what name he goes under these days?' The age was right, she just hadn't been thinking straight. And she couldn't have mistaken those eyes. 'I think I knew him many years ago. Before you would have come on the scene.' Perhaps before she was even born, though she wouldn't go into that.

'He's called Clive Barclay,' said Jenny, less fiercely. 'And he's my live-in partner. We have been together five years.'

'And the child?'

'Not his, if that's what you're wondering. Though Toby looks upon him as his father.'

Desperate now, Frankie thought very fast. The nightmare was happening all over again, only this time she was determined not to lose him. She thought of telling the whole story to Jenny but caution warned her not to. It was late and if he had really gone, there wasn't a lot she could do tonight. In any case, she'd had too much wine to drive.

'Could I stay on for a couple more days?'

'No,' said Jenny, 'we are fully booked up.' She showed no sign of wanting to talk so Frankie went meekly to her room.

All night she smoked and paced the floor, trying to figure things out. This strange encounter had not been accidental but engineered by Aidan. If he hadn't given her the matchbook in the first place, she wouldn't have known where to look. But why would he do it; she could see no point, though it did prove there must be a connection. Someone was playing games with her but now she'd make sure that they stopped. She had wasted her whole life on Chad, mourning a man she'd believed to be dead and now found was very much alive. A man in his prime, with a family setup as well as a thriving business. When she thought of all she had sacrificed for him, she very nearly choked.

First thing in the morning she settled her bill then went straight out to the car. She was through with dreaming; it was time for action. No more meandering along leafy lanes, admiring the English countryside, but straight back on to the motorway and to Middlesbrough by the fastest route.

And this time she had only one port of call: the police.

46

The first thing Jenny did after Frankie left was get on the phone to Vanessa.

'I'm sorry,' she started, 'it was all my fault.'

'Bollocks!' said Vanessa. 'I'll be right over. As long as you guarantee that that man isn't there.'

'He's not. He's gone. I don't know where or even if he'll ever be back.' She felt as though she'd been punched in the head, could not believe this had happened. The man she'd thought she could trust with her life had suddenly bowled her a googly. When Vanessa's car drove into the yard, Jenny was out there waiting for her and the pair embraced like the soulmates they'd never stopped being.

'You look ghastly,' said Vanessa bluntly. 'What you need, I feel, is a drink.'

'At ten a.m.?' But she didn't resist and allowed Vanessa to make them both Bloody Marys. They sat outside by the weeping willows. It was Friday morning; she should be cooking but, hell, could not have cared less. Piece by piece she narrated the story of how this strange woman had turned up and the shock she'd glimpsed on Clive's face the instant he saw her.

'Who was she?'

'I still don't know,' said Jenny. 'She booked in under F. Wilde. Tall and sort of ravaged-looking, wild by name and by nature. A throwback from his past, she said, no one he's ever mentioned to me, though he certainly didn't greet her with any warmth. Acted, in fact, as if they were strangers though I could see, as the evening progressed, that he practically never took his eyes off her.' She'd been moving, as usual, between kitchen and dining room, so had only seen a little of what went on.

'In what sort of way did she look at him?'

'Hardly at all, which was also strange. She seemed to be totally self-absorbed and only spoke to him briefly, to order drinks.'

The bastard was up to his tricks again; Vanessa was secretly pleased, though she hated to see her best mate suffer and Jenny had clearly not slept at all. Her hair was matted and her eyes were like pits in her normally cheerful face.

'So why did he go?'

'I don't know,' said Jenny. 'He just upped and left while she was still in the bar. Muttered something about things he had to do, then vanished into the night.'

'Will he be coming back?' asked Vanessa, hoping the answer was no.

'I really don't know,' said Jenny, eyes brimming. 'Oh, why,' she asked, grabbing Vanessa's hand, 'do I always get it so wrong?'

'You don't,' said Vanessa. 'It isn't your fault. All you

have been is unlucky. Let me make a couple of quick calls and I'll stay here all day and help out.'

There were strangers in the bar at lunchtime, among the regular crowd. Nothing unusual in that, though they caught Jenny's eye. A man and a woman, inconspicuously dressed, they stood close together and spoke in low voices as though unwilling to be overheard. So why don't they go outside? she thought. There were plenty of empty tables there. There was simply no accounting for people's stupidity.

'Keep an eye on those two,' she muttered as she pushed past Vanessa, who was manning the bar. 'I feel there is something slightly fishy about them.'

'Are they regulars here?'

'I've not seen them before. And I don't believe they have made a booking for lunch.'

The pair edged their way to a corner table and proceeded to order a number of drinks, presumably expecting others to join them.

'Will there be more of you?' asked Vanessa. 'I can try to clear you a larger table.'

'No thank you,' said the man. 'It's just us two.'

'And will you be wanting lunch?' she asked. 'The kitchen is fairly busy right now so I suggest you put in your orders soon or else you may not get served.'

'Thanks,' he said. 'We're just passing through. But I would, if I may, like to take a look at the menu.'

Vanessa brought it, along with their drinks: four glasses of wine, two white, two red, as well as a dry martini, American style. Odd, she thought, for a couple like that, who she would have guessed might have been teetotal. The woman, in particular, seemed very uptight. And the wines were all different, which also seemed strange. Well, each to their own, she thought as she bustled away.

'On reflection,' said the man when they left, 'we would like to book a table for tonight. I hope we haven't left it too late. You are obviously very busy.'

'Let me check it out,' said Vanessa. 'I need to talk to the boss.'

Jenny, harassed and over-heated, was searing scallops with one eye on the clock. By this time of day she was working at fever pitch.

'I don't believe we can fit them in unless we get a cancellation. Tell them that if they care to chance it, they can go on the waiting list.' It was the best she could do but not her fault that they hadn't bothered to book. There had been no word from Clive and her heart was breaking.

'Are you okay?' asked Vanessa quietly.

'Not really but I'll cope,' said Jenny. 'Be a pal and call Toby down for his lunch?'

Clive returned in the early evening, just as Jenny was opening up, as suave and relaxed as he usually was, exactly like the night he had first walked in.

'Hello, my sweet. Sorry I'm late. I would have called but I hadn't got my mobile.' He kissed her as if there was nothing wrong, though she felt him tense when Vanessa appeared, ready to start on the evening shift and stand in for Clive behind the bar.

'What's she doing here?' he asked Jenny sharply, almost losing his cool.

'Helping out,' she told him firmly. 'After you left me in the lurch.'

In the circumstances, there was little he could say so he greeted Vanessa with a degree of warmth which didn't fool her one bit; she knew he detested her. But the early drinkers were drifting in so they both knuckled down to the job in hand, while endeavouring to stay as far apart as they could.

'Who was that woman?'

'What woman?' he asked, as he took off his jacket and rolled up his sleeves in readiness for battle to commence.

'The one who was here last night,' said Jenny. 'Who had booked a room and stayed down here till we closed.' The one with the crazy staring eyes and the tragic look of a drama queen. Who had behaved as though she had seen a ghost and needed urgent sedation.

He paused and shrugged. 'I have no idea. You can't expect me to remember them all.' Then he whipped down some glasses and gave them a rub, ready to mix his famous cocktails.

Jenny, feeling decidedly brighter, popped upstairs and spruced herself up, then returned to the bar her usual smiling self. For a while she lingered on in there, chatting with the regulars, something she always liked to do to make them feel really at home. Joyce was valiantly manning the kitchen, ready to step aside when Jenny came down.

The bar was full, with a few new faces, which usually happened on Friday night when strangers from out of town swelled the regular crowd. She spotted the couple who had asked for a table and had their names on the waiting list. They appeared quite content as they chatted together in a corner. They must have liked what they saw at lunchtime or else they would not have come back so soon. There were also two men who had just come in, formally dressed for a weekend night, who ordered halves of beer and stood looking around. Jenny was feeling cheerful again. Her man was back; there was nothing wrong. As usual, she had just overreacted and jumped to a false conclusion. The place was buzzing; they were fully booked. She felt enormously proud of the Coot and Hern.

She was just about to return to the kitchen, when the door swung open and the Wilde woman stalked back in. Entirely different from how she'd been last night, with flashing eyes and a flush to her cheeks, she pushed her way through the crowd to the bar and confronted Clive head on.

'Hi, Chad,' she said. 'Remember me?' She fumbled at her throat and pulled out a locket. 'See, I still have your picture round my neck.'

There was a sudden hush as everyone listened. Something dramatic was going on and they had ring-side seats. Clive, in the process of pouring a beer, glanced up briefly without recognition then handed the glass, with a smile, to the waiting punter.

'Don't pretend you don't know me,' she said. 'You

tried that last night and it didn't work, though I must admit you very nearly got me. You are going to tell me next that you don't know Aidan.'

The crowd pulled back to allow her space and she stood there, openly challenging him, an imposing woman with mixed emotions in her eyes. In a flash her sad, wan look had gone; overnight her ancient beauty had revived. Jenny, watching quietly from the doorway, experienced a frisson of fear. Whoever she was, she wouldn't be going quietly.

'I'm afraid you're mistaken,' said Clive, without a flicker. 'I don't believe we have met before. Apart, of course, from last night,' he added. 'When I have to say you were somewhat the worse for drink.'

'Don't give me that,' said Frankie, snarling. Jenny stepped forward to intervene but Frankie impatiently shrugged her off, looking as though she would like to break his neck.

'I've already told you,' Jenny explained, 'that this is Clive Barclay whom I've known for years. We all have, isn't that right?' she said and everybody nodded.

Frankie never even glanced at her, acted as though she hadn't heard; just continued to stare at Clive with impassioned eyes.

'His name is Chad Barnaby,' she said. 'Something I can prove. Or will do once he has taken the necessary tests.'

The two of them continued to lock eyes; she certainly had his attention now. Vanessa, watching from a corner of the room, could swear that he turned perceptibly paler. Blimey, she thought, for once he has run out of words.

'See,' said Frankie, in a quieter voice, removing the locket and passing it round. 'That's how he used to look when I last saw him. Younger, yes, and a great deal fitter. But if you look closely, you will see it is indisputably the same man. He was on remand,' she added. 'We both were. Me for arson and him on a murder charge.'

Total silence. Nobody spoke. Now everyone's eyes were on Clive.

'Well,' he said, his composure restored. 'The very least I can do, I suppose, is offer you a drink on the house.'

'How much of this is true?' demanded Jenny, once she had shunted the three of them out of the bar and into the privacy of the snug where they wouldn't be overheard. Vanessa had wanted to be there too, feeling that Jenny needed backup, but someone had to run the bar. On Fridays they brought in extra help.

'Call me if you need me,' she said, aware of the smouldering hostility. There was no doubt now in anyone's mind that what Frankie had said was the truth. Even Clive didn't try to deny it. He had stopped protesting, had gone unusually quiet. All the more reason to watch him, thought Vanessa. She had never trusted him in the first place and now was being proved right.

'All of it,' admitted Clive. 'I won't deny that I used to be Chad. But, heavens, that was so long ago I can't believe it still matters. All we were was a couple of kids having a bit of a lark.'

'I loved you,' said Frankie, 'and you let me down.' There was no disguising the tremor in her voice. 'I helped you escape and then waited for you. You never came so I turned myself in and later confessed to your murder.'

'Well, more fool you,' he said, slightly sneering, having recovered his savoir faire. 'I owe you nothing. You should have run when I did.' He had brought a bottle of malt whisky through and was now topping up his glass.

'Tell me the truth, did you ever love me?' Frankie almost pleaded. The look between them was enough to cut glass but he didn't so much as waver.

'I've told you,' he said. 'We were simply kids. What did we know about life or love? I'll tell you, the best thing you did for me was help me get out of that place and I'm grateful. I guess I still owe you one.'

'But I went to jail for your murder,' she said. And have spent the rest of my life in mourning for you.

'Well, thanks. What more can I say?' he asked, raising his glass in a mock toast.

Back in the bar, Vanessa was coping though she longed to know what was going on. Joyce, alone in the kitchen, was holding her own. She had popped in there a couple of times, to check that things were under control, to find Joyce positively cheerful and quite unfazed.

'Are you all right?'

'I am better than that.' The homely woman in the sensible shoes appeared to be having a ball as she cooked the whole meal. For years she'd stood back and watched Jenny do it, yet her culinary skills were just as great as Jenny's. All she had lacked was confidence and the guts to go it alone.

'So dinner is served as usual?'

'It is.' Joyce relished the thought of being, for once, in control. There were a couple out there who were taking more than the usual interest in how the place was run; she had watched them closely as she'd scurried through with assorted hors d'oeuvres. Joyce might be frumpy but she wasn't a fool and had been in this business for most of her life, never a star but the eyes and ears of the place. She knew what she thought, and she wouldn't divulge it. She was just extremely glad that it was tonight of all nights that she, at last, would get the chance to demonstrate what she could do. Thank you, Clive, she said to herself. She had never remotely trusted the man, but at least he had helped to brighten things up. And, in all fairness, had always been lovely to her.

They were still in deadlock with hackles raised, like a couple of cats set to fight to the death. Jenny, alarmed, was scared of what might happen.

'Who is Aidan?' Frankie spat at him, stopping him in his tracks.

'What do you know about Aidan?' he asked.

'Just that he's some sort of sociopath. Without whose intervention I'd never have found you.'

'Leave Aidan out of this,' said Clive, with a new grim note in his voice. He rose to his feet and moved towards the door.

'So tell me who he is,' she said. 'He looks exactly like you.'

'He's my son,' said Clive, shocking Jenny to the core. 'And I won't have him getting involved.'

'Too late, he's involved already,' said Frankie. 'More or less up to his neck. And, by the way, I know what you did. You killed a gypsy and dumped him in the fire, so that everyone thought the body was yours. Ingenious, I will give you that. It even fooled the police.'

'How did you find out, then?' he asked, intrigued and slightly admiring.

'At first I didn't. I mourned your loss and sacrificed my whole life for you but then I met Aidan and the pieces started to fit.'

Clive, suddenly silenced, did not say anything, and nor did Jenny who'd been listening, stricken, throughout.

'I have just been back to Middlesbrough,' said Frankie, 'to talk to the police. With the help of the local newspaper, we finally figured out the truth. A gypsy boy was reported missing at the time.'

'Really,' said Clive, with a sudden sneer. 'You girls are certainly full of it.' He picked up his bottle and started to leave but Frankie stopped him with one last question.

'I have to know. Did you ever love me?'

Jenny was waiting for his answer too.

He turned and stared at both of them with no compassion in his ice-blue eyes. 'I never learnt the meaning of love,' he said.

'I'm off,' he said, a few seconds later, taking his jacket from behind the door and nodding to Vanessa as if they were friends.

'One moment, sir,' said a man in a suit, who'd been quietly drinking a half at the bar. 'I wonder, before you go, if we might have a word?'

47

All Frankie desperately wanted now was to get out of England as fast as she could and turn her back on the whole unsavoury business. Had she been able, she'd have gone straight to Waterloo station, dropped off the car and caught a train to Brussels that night, without even stopping in London. But the trains didn't run after nine p.m. and she still had a two-hour drive. So she'd check back into the Draycott Hotel and hope to get on Eurostar in the morning.

It was raining on the motorway, just as it always did at home, which made her nostalgic for Magda and her friends. She was through with sex and perfidious males; in future she planned to spend her time only with women. She should never have come here in the first place, stirring up trouble best left undisturbed, but the trip, at least, had knocked on the head any unfulfilled dreams she might still have. She hadn't completely taken it all in, except that Chad was alive after all and appeared to be having a whale of a time within his different personas. Someone had died but it wasn't her fault. The gypsy boy's body had been in the hostel before the fire was even set. Chad had gambled on her witless devotion to make her do just what he wanted her to and never to question the outcome.

Now she saw clearly that he'd never loved her, had only ever used her as a pawn. All his life he had been a killer, which now explained her own stepfather's death. The colonel had been a sexual pervert but hadn't deserved to die in that way, shot by his own gun in front of his dogs. Chad killed casually, without compunction or any thought of the repercussions. She'd trusted him yet he'd slipped away, leaving her to carry the can and serve a sentence for something she hadn't done. In all the years she had suffered and grieved, he had been out in the real world, living off other women, it seemed, without a thought for the one he had betrayed.

She was grateful to the Middlesbrough police for listening courteously to her story and not dismissing it out of hand as the loony ravings of a sad old spinster. Instead, they had shown her the newspaper archives and helped her search through the relevant files until they'd unearthed the brief paragraph which mentioned the missing traveller. The rest was up to the forensic squad; they still had the boy's remains in the unmarked grave. And, more to the point, they now also had Chad, in custody without bail.

First thing in the morning, she spoke to Magda and said she would get on the next available train. But, being Saturday, it wouldn't be easy. Weekend breaks were top premium with Eurostar. Magda told her not to worry if she couldn't get a seat, there really wasn't any need to hurry back. She had come so far and spent so much, it seemed a waste not to stay on a while and, at least, see a little of the London she'd never known. She worked so hard throughout the year, she was long overdue some sort of break and Magda sensed that she needed to sort out her head.

'We are thrilled with what you have done for us.' The orders for lace alone made the trip worthwhile. She knew, without asking, that something was wrong, that Frankie was far from being herself, but she would wait until she felt like opening up. She offered to meet her in Brussels with the truck but Frankie told her that she could manage. She knew she had bridges to mend with Magda, was aware she'd been brusque and withdrawn. All that would keep, however, till she was home. They had the rest of their lives together to come to an understanding. From this point on, she would open up and try her hardest to love again. It would take some doing and a lot of pain but she still had a great deal to give.

She wished she'd been able to get to know Jenny whom, in other circumstances, she felt she would have liked. She had obviously worked wonders with the pub, while also raising a child on her own. She deserved a genuine happy ending instead of the shit she'd had flung in her face. When, some weeks later, news filtered through about Jenny's winning a Michelin star, the note that Frankie sent her was warm and sincere.

*   *   *

Frankie took Magda at her word and picked up some leaflets at the desk about tourist attractions in London. First, however, there was one more thing she felt she would like to do. The sisters had been so good to her in encouraging her to take this trip, the least she felt she should do in return was try to drum up some more business. Pippa Harvey had been very helpful and given her much of her precious time. After she'd finished a leisurely breakfast, she would stroll back along the Fulham Road in the hope that she might be up for ordering more lace. This time she might even meet the husband; she felt guilty at not having stayed around before.

Pippa, however, was not in the shop. A nice young woman stood in for her and said she would not be back that day, owing to a family crisis. She asked if she could help but Frankie said no.

'I only wanted to say goodbye. I am leaving this afternoon on Eurostar. Perhaps you'd tell her that I'll definitely be in touch.' A pity, she thought as she walked away. That was somebody else she'd have liked to know better.

48

The news was totally devastating; Pippa still hadn't fully taken it in. Charles had been arrested on undisclosed charges.

'I don't even know where he is,' she wailed. 'Or why they can't let him out on bail. They won't even let me see him. They say I'm not really his wife.'

Dino was seated at her kitchen table, patiently listening as she poured out her woes. He normally didn't approve of coffee but was willing, on this occasion, to turn a blind eye. She was clearly distraught; he would do all he could to help get her over the trauma. He had grown enormously fond of her in the years she had been his client.

'Tell me again what happened,' he said, reaching across and taking her hand. In all the years she'd worked out with him, he had never known her this tense.

It started with finding the duplicate passports after Charles had asked her to lay out his shirts. 'He was going away on a sudden trip but didn't say where to. Only that it involved a client and a Stubbs.' She blotted her eyes; her nose was running but she seemed quite unaware of that. In her dirty tracksuit, with unwashed hair, she looked the picture of desolation. What would do her most good was a run round the park but Dino was wise enough not to mention that. Her spirit was more important than her body; right now she could use all the comforting she could get.

'And the passports were all in different names?'

She nodded and finally blew her nose. 'All CBs, that immediately struck me. His own name, Clive Barclay and Cal Barnard. I had no idea what was going on but assumed he'd explain when he came to fetch them.'

'But he didn't come?'

'He called instead. To say there had been a change of plan and he had to go back to the West Country for a meeting.'

'And you didn't ask him about the passports?' It didn't surprise the trainer one bit that the man had turned out to be a crook. He hadn't much liked him, the few times they'd met. He was too good-looking and far too cocky, besides being much too old for Pippa; talk about cradle-snatching. He agreed with what her mother had said, that she should have held out for the son. From all accounts, he was simply a younger version.

'And then what happened?'

'The police arrived. To say they were holding him pending inquiries. He is wanted in connection with several incidents which is why they won't let him out on bail. It sounds pretty serious, don't you think?'

It did indeed, no question of that, but Dino was paid to counsel and not to alarm. He looked at Pippa's tear-stained face and wasn't sure what advice to give, except that she get herself a first-rate lawyer. Which, having considered, he kept to himself. She was quite upset enough as it was without his adding to her grief.

She didn't tell her mother about it, could not face having her on her case. When Dino left, she went upstairs to try to make order out of chaos. The next workout session they had together would be in another two days. Because he hadn't remembered his diary, he had promised to call ahead of time to check that the hour they had fixed was still all right. The twins, meanwhile, were at nursery school. She had until four to pick them up, by which time she hoped to have got a grip on herself. How could he have done this to her, she asked herself tragically in the mirror as she brushed the tangles out of her hair and plastered on some warpaint.

Pippa had been a star in the making when she'd completed her Courtauld course; had remained that way till she'd got enmeshed in the life of Charles Buchanan. And, even then, she had made it work, had milked him for contacts and all he could give; had been content, at that stage of her life, with being his bit on the side. Few of her friends had understood. They had urged her to make the break while she could and find somebody who was nearer her age and could offer her a future. But at that time Pippa's prime concern had been to make her shop a success.

Charles had given her loads of support; even now, she wouldn't deny that. And, without the unplanned pregnancy, she'd have been content to leave things as they were. At twenty-seven, with the world at her feet, marriage had been the last thing on her mind, until the pregnancy was confirmed and she'd felt she had no other choice. She had ended up as Charles's wife and, incidentally, mother to autistic twins. End of story as far as Pippa was concerned and she still hadn't yet turned thirty.

The thought only made her cry again so she stepped into the shower instead and then had to start the makeover process from scratch. The person she longed to talk to most, certainly more than her own mother, was Cassie, in Venice embarking on a new life.

There was no word from Cassie or Aidan but the police were back in a couple of days, keen that Pippa should answer more of their questions. They remained non-committal, were still 'making inquiries', but Pippa sensed, from their brusqueness of manner, that she herself was by no means out of the frame. They cross-examined her for several hours about intimate details of her marriage and how she had first met up with Charles. Whom, disconcertingly, they called Mr Barnaby: not a name she had ever heard before.

She answered their questions as far as she could, trying hard not to lose her cool. It might only make things worse for Charles if she did.

Was she aware he'd been married before?

'Yes,' said Pippa; she knew Cassie well. They'd

become good friends because they had children in common.

So did she know where Cassie was now? Or Mrs Hawksmoor, as they styled her.

'In Venice,' said Pippa, not understanding why Charles hadn't told them that.

He was not being very co-operative, they said. They were here to check out certain facts. They mentioned an 'incident' in Paris and asked if she knew the name Cristina Calväo.

'No,' said Pippa, thoroughly puzzled, asking what it was all about. They refused to give away any answers, simply took copious notes.

In the end, when she was about to explode, they closed their notebooks and called it a day. They would be in touch, they told her politely, and asked her not to leave town.

There were business matters to be arranged so, since Pippa was still the boss's wife, she drove to the Walton Street showrooms to sort things out. No need to let them know what had happened; the press would get wind of it soon enough. The main thing was keeping the business up and running. Pippa, wearing her largest dark glasses, told them that Charles had been called away – family matters she vaguely implied – and asked if there was anything she should do. Nothing, they said, all was under control; he had trained a highly capable staff, which was how he had managed to move around so freely. They asked if she knew when he would be back and, when she said no, didn't seem concerned. Things were ticking over as usual; business was still very brisk.

'I'll let you know as soon as I hear.' She couldn't wait to get out of there. It was almost beyond her capabilities to put a good face on things. Part of her wanted to kick and scream; how could he have landed her in this mess? And, furthermore, how was it possibly true that she wasn't his legal wife? That was the part that puzzled her most, once she'd calmed down enough to think it through. Cassie had agreed to a quickie divorce to ensure that the twins were legitimate. Her marriage, she knew, had been rock solid. So what was this they were saying now? None of it added up.

Even more reason to talk to Cassie, but she hadn't left Pippa a contact number. She was back in Venice, in her famed palazzo, which had brought new happiness into her life and made Pippa frankly jealous. The only person who knew how to reach her was Charles, who was now incommunicado. If only Aidan were still around. This family mess was his as much as hers.

On the way back to Barnes, she dropped into her shop and they gave her Frankie's message. They had missed each other by half an hour but Pippa barely took that in. 'She wanted to say goodbye,' said her staff. 'She leaves this afternoon on Eurostar.' The last thing on Pippa's mind right then was Frankie, whom she barely remembered meeting.

She was slowly beginning to feel less stressed, telling herself there had been some mistake, when the doorbell rang again; she instantly stiffened. She was scared to death the police were back; the thought of going through all that again appalled her. They had made her feel like a criminal when, in fact, she was the injured party. As soon as Charles was home, she would file a complaint. She stood in the hallway, uncertain what to do, until the bell stopped ringing and somebody peered through the letter box.

'Pippa, it's me. Please open up. I know you're in there. I saw your car.'

Aidan! She couldn't believe her ears. 'Wait!' she shouted and rushed to open the door. 'Where on earth have you been?' she cried, falling into his arms with relief. The person in the world she most wanted to see.

'Abroad,' he told her, smoothing her hair. 'What on earth has been going on here? I've never seen you like this.'

'It's your dad,' she said. 'They've arrested him. And they won't even tell me why. Just that they've taken him in for questioning. Some confusion over his passport.'

She wasn't sure she should tell him the rest; he was, after all, Charles's son. Then she realised that he was fully adult, scarcely younger than her, in fact.

'Come on through and I'll fill you in,' she said.

First he checked that the twins weren't there, then poured her a massive drink. He looked fit and tanned and more mature, with those compelling eyes, as blue as his dad's.

'They wanted to speak to your mother, too, but I don't have a contact number.'

'Here,' said Aidan, scribbling it down. 'Though I can't understand why they didn't just ask my dad.'

'They said he wouldn't co-operate. Which is why they won't let him out on bail.'

'It all sounds rather extreme to me. Proper Gestapo tactics.'

'They mentioned the name Cristina Calvão but it rang no bells with me,' she said.

Aidan's sudden change of mood surprised her. 'And did they mention Frankie too?' He ceased his restless pacing.

'No,' said Pippa, taken aback. 'But, oddly enough, someone else just did. She came into the shop just now and left a message for me.'

'Frankie's in London?' He seemed surprised. He grabbed Pippa roughly by the shoulders. 'Where is she? I need to know,' he said. 'It's vital I catch up with her. We have unfinished business.'

'I believe they said she was leaving today.' She shrugged him off and checked the note on the pad. 'On Eurostar this afternoon. I think there is only one. But how on earth does she fit in? I only met her once, peddling homemade lace.'

The phone rang. He told her not to answer but Pippa had picked it up. It was only Dino, confirming their workout. Pippa told him she couldn't talk.

'Tell me more about the police,' said Aidan, obviously rattled now. 'What exactly did they say about Cristina?'

'You know her?'

'Maybe.'

'They told me nothing. Just mentioned her name,' said Pippa.

Aidan's mood had perceptibly darkened; he looked just like his father on a bad day. Pippa hated these temper tantrums, so reminiscent of the twins.

'So what did they want?' he almost shouted. His eyes were turning red.

'Only something to do with his passport,' she said, hoping to placate him.

'Are you sure you're not holding anything back?' He moved towards her menacingly and, as she tried to back away, grabbed hold of her by the throat.

Someone banged sharply on the kitchen door and Pippa struggled to break away but Aidan's fingers were like a vice. 'Keep quiet,' he hissed in her ear.

'Help!' she screamed as she fought like mad and heard the door crash inwards.

'In here!' she yelled as her legs gave way and Dino came bursting in.

'Go after him!' she begged, but Aidan had gone.

49

Lulled by the rhythm of the wheels, Frankie nodded off. Eurostar had been virtually empty and the leisurely lunch had helped to ease her tension. At Brussels she had switched to the Amsterdam train, to a first class carriage from a bygone age where, at least until Antwerp, she could be fairly sure of remaining undisturbed. If her mother's legacy had bought anything, it was privacy. She waved away the refreshments trolley; there was nothing further she needed. Soon she'd be home and back to her spartan regime.

She was deep in a dream that featured Chad when the sliding open of the compartment door awakened her abruptly. The man who stood there, blocking the light, was tall and she couldn't see his face. Instinctively Frankie fumbled for her ticket.

'Hello,' he said. 'Remember me?' unconsciously echoing her own fateful words. He remained there, swaying, as she stared in shock: Chad – at his best from those far off days – the embodiment of her dream.

'Aidan?' she whispered as her senses cleared. God, but he had scared her. She had not expected to see him again, even though their first encounter had been on a train. Too much had happened in the past few days for her to be able to face him now. The sharp emotion she felt was predominantly guilt.

'The same,' he said, with that dazzling smile. 'You've been leading me quite a merry dance. For a while, I confess, I thought I had lost you in London.' In one hand he carried a styrofoam beaker from which he now started to sip. 'Mind if I join you? It has been one hell of a day.'

He seated himself across from her, his long legs pressing against her knees, and when the trolley returned on its rounds he nonchalantly waved it past. They had forty-five minutes, approximately, until the first stop which was Antwerp. Frankie, awake now, was fully alert. She saw, from the gleam in his restless eyes, that he hadn't just come here to talk.

'I am sorry—' she started but he cut her short.

'As well you might be, bitch,' he said, a visible twitch in his lower lid, his face no longer smiling. He was just like Chad, with the same stunning looks. But now she saw, with a frisson of fear, that Aidan was totally out of his mind. As she must have been on that wild night of their first meeting.

'I am sorry,' she repeated, 'for what I did.' He was half her age, she should have shown more restraint. 'I realise now I must have hurt you. My only excuse is that I was under great stress.'

Tentatively she touched his knee but he smacked away her hand. Don't mess with me, the cold eyes said, and now she saw he trembled with bottled fury.

He finished his coffee and crumpled the cup, grinding it under his heel. All trace of affability had fled; she was face to face, she knew, with a seasoned killer.

'What is it you want from me?' she asked, as calmly as she could. She was tall and fit from a lifetime of hard toil but he was taller and younger.

'To shut you up once and for all,' he said, searching inside his inner pocket. 'And stop you doing something really stupid and spilling the beans on my dad.'

His dad. Of course. It was obvious now and should have been so from the start. But then she hadn't known that Chad was alive.

'Who,' she asked quietly, in order to gain time, 'is your mother?' Certainly not Jenny, who had been as shocked as she was when they'd both heard the news.

'My mother, Cassandra, is a very fine lady, too good to mix with the likes of you or that slut at the pub who was carrying on behind her back.' Now he drew out what she thought was a pen then realised, with a jolt, was a spring-blade knife. His face was a solid mask of hatred; there was little doubt what he had in mind. She tried to slither along the seat but he blocked her with his knees.

'Not so fast,' he said, brandishing the knife. 'You are not getting out of it this time. When I called him to tell him you were on his track, he asked me to keep an eye out for you and said he'd fix things when he had the time.'

'He loved me.'

'Oh yes?' He was gloating now and the dazzling smile returned. 'You mean like all the others who tried to trap him? It all began with you,' he spat. 'If you'd never come snooping, we'd all of us still have been happy.'

'Dad,' he'd said, when he'd made the call. 'What have you been up to?' And later, when he'd met the Brazilian lawyer, he'd known he had to act. No one must know about the other marriage, which was why he'd had to kill the Brazilian bitch.

Frankie listened as he rambled on; there was no doubt now that he was mad. It was twenty-five minutes until they reached Antwerp; if she kept him talking, she might still hold him off.

'I don't understand,' she told him calmly, 'what difference that can have made to you.'

'It makes me a bastard,' he virtually screamed. 'Along with those fucking twins.'

She had to do something. This wasn't going to work and Frankie was damned if she'd sit there and let him slit her throat. After all she had suffered because of Chad, things weren't going to end like this. She tensed herself then sprang at him, sticking two fingers into his eyes and knocking away the knife.

The corridor, when she wrenched open the door, was disconcertingly empty. The downside, she realised grimly, of travelling first class. She sprinted towards the dividing door that led into the adjoining carriage, but as she tried to open it he grabbed her round the neck. She could feel the knife-blade under her ear but managed to turn and grab at his crotch then stepped across the dividing gap to the safety of second class.

'Damn you!' he hissed as he doubled with pain and she heard the clatter as he dropped the knife. She was ready for him when he leapt at her and she socked him sharply on the jaw, then recoiled as he lost his footing and slipped through the gap.

The train was travelling at maximum speed and would soon be arriving in Antwerp. By the time they found his body, she ought to be home.

Magda was waiting beside the truck, solid and dependable, just as she always had been.

'Good journey?' she asked as the pair embraced.

'Uneventful,' said Frankie.

HOME FROM HOME

Carol Smith

Oppressed by the aftermath of September 11th, New York novelist, Anna Kovac, answers an ad and exchanges her elegant townhouse for a villa in Tuscany. With two friends from England, Genevieve and Candy, she moves there for the summer to finish her book.

Life in their rural paradise is bliss and all three women rapidly adapt to Italian life. Until mysterious things start to happen over which Anna has no control. Her credit card inexplicably exceeds its limit; text vanishes from her computer screen. When her New York architect and friend, Larry, falls from scaffolding to his death, she panics and rushes home, only to find that the locks have been changed and she cannot get into her house. Someone appears to have stolen her identity, emptied her bank account, sold her possessions – even abducted her beloved father.

Who is the stranger whose advertisement she took entirely on trust? The situation takes a darker twist with a second violent death . . .

HIDDEN AGENDA

Carol Smith

Devasted by the shocking news that an old schoolfriend, Suzy Palmer, faces execution in Louisiana for the murder of her children, London rabbi, Deborah Hirsch, enlists the aid of her former classmates in an attempt to get her off. The Suzy they've known and loved all these years could never hurt a fly; she can't be anything but innocent.

As Death Row draws steadily closer, the friends slowly piece together what has happened. Aided by Miss Holbrook, Suzy's feisty former art teacher, and Markus, a jazz musician who's following the case in New Orleans, they recall their thirty-year friendship – and realise that even more shocking than Suzy's plight is the knowledge that one of their number has betrayed her.

UNFINISHED BUSINESS

Carol Smith

The brutal murder of golden girl, Jinx McLennan, early one Sunday in her exclusive Kensington house, shocks the neighbours and triggers a police inquiry that delves deeply into her colourful past. Single, childless, Jinx nevertheless had it all – brains, popularity, her own successful business, plus a wide-ranging network of lovers and friends. Closest of all were her own small design team, the surrogate family who've been with her from the start: devoted, long-suffering Dottie and her artist husband, Sam; gentle, reliable Ambrose, the team's backbone; Wayne, the zany trainee with the outrageous lifestyle; and Serafina, hot on the fast track, who wants everything Jinx had, but now. Plus millionaire genius, Damien Rudge, the goose who lays their golden eggs. The trail goes cold until, in a shock revelation, it turns out to be a case of mistaken identity. The wrong person has been murdered. Out there somewhere is still a crazed killer with unfinished business who will have to kill again.

FAMILY REUNION

Carol Smith

As her eightieth birthday approaches, Odile Annesley, who has been living alone in France for forty years, contacts her scattered grandchildren to give them details of her will. The five granddaughters see it as the perfect opportunity for a family get-together abroad. Solid Clemency, the perfect wife and mother; London property dealer, Madeleine; Paris dress designer, Elodie; academic Canadian, Isabelle; poor, deprived Cherie, the misfit. And Harry, the golden boy. Each has grown up in their own world but, like all families, the shared characteristics are there. Then the killing starts, the secrets spill and it is clear that one of them is very different indeed . . .

Other bestselling Time Warner titles available by mail:

The prices shown above are correct at time of going to press. However, the publishers reserve the right to increase prices on covers from those previously advertised, without prior notice.

TIME WARNER
BOOKS

TIME WARNER BOOKS

Cash Sales Department, P.O. Box 11, Falmouth, Cornwall, TR10 9EN
Tel: +44 (0) 1326 569777, Fax: +44 (0) 1326 569555
Email: books@barni.avel.co.uk

POST AND PACKING:

Payments can be made as follows: cheque, postal order (payable to Time Warner Books) or by credit cards. Do not send cash or currency.

All UK Orders	**FREE OF CHARGE**
E.E.C. & Overseas	25% of order value

Name (Block Letters) _____

Address _____

_____

Post/zip code: _____

☐ Please keep me in touch with future Time Warner publications

☐ I enclose my remittance £_____

☐ I wish to pay Visa/Access/Mastercard/Eurocard

Card Expiry Date

_____